C46023804$
KT-175-810

AFTER THE BOMBING

1942. Fifteen-year-old Alma Braithwaite and her fellow boarders at Goldwyn's School huddle in an air-raid shelter as bombs rain down on Exeter. Twenty-one years on, Alma teaches music at her old school. She's moderately content, until the death of the long-serving headmistress brings a new broom in the form of steely modernizing Miss Yates. A new student starts too – the daughter of a man Alma hasn't seen since 1942, when he played a pivotal role in her life. Suddenly, Alma is taken back to the summer that followed the raids, a summer of numbing loss yet also of youthful exuberance, friendship and dancing.

AFTER THE BOMBING

AFTER THE BOMBING

by

Clare Morrall

Magna Large Print Books
Long Preston, North Yorkshire,
BD23 4ND, England.

British Library Cataloguing in Publication Data.

Morrall, Clare
After the bombing.

A catalogue record of this book is
available from the British Library

ISBN 978-0-7505-4016-2

First published in Great Britain in 2014 by Sceptre
An imprint of Hodder & Stoughton

Published in Large Print 2015 by arrangement with
Hodder & Stoughton Ltd.

Magna Large Print is an imprint of Library Magna Books Ltd.

Printed and bound in Great Britain by
T.J. (International) Ltd., Cornwall, PL28 8RW

All characters in this publication are fictitious
and any resemblance to real persons,
living or dead, is purely coincidental.

For all Maynard girls, past and present,
especially Celia (Cecil), Alison and Maggy.

Prologue

28 March 1942

A full moon. Lübeck, a Hanseatic city on the shores of the Baltic Sea, is in the grip of a hoar frost. Clear cold air drifts into the streets, forming white ice crystals as it touches colder surfaces. Feathers spread their delicate tendrils on window panes; trees become white-haired, wise and dignified, as snow-like deposits coat their branches; telegraph wires are streaked with silver, dipping under the icy burden; a translucent sheen blankets the pavements. The hand of cold squeezes and everything compresses, huddles together for comfort. The sky is deep and black, with a limitless vista of space. The moon, a vast, shining orb, with edges as sharp and defined as if it has been drawn with a draughtsman's precision, is reflected in the still waters of the canals.

A distant murmur grows into a drone, a rumble, an ever-increasing wall of sound. At eighteen minutes past eleven, the first of the 234 Wellington and Stirling bombers descend out of the blackness of the sky to two thousand feet and drop their bombs. They are like swarming locusts, intent on devouring everything in their path, expecting to leave bare bones in their wake.

Heavy bombs break open the brick and copper roofs of the medieval buildings and incendiary bombs set them on fire. Timber-frame houses burn easily. The RAF leaves a corridor of destruction three hundred metres wide. Hundreds die; thousands lose their homes. The city is transformed into a skeleton.

Nobody believes Lübeck or Rostock (bombed at the same time) are important strategic cities, but at the heart of the decision to bomb is the discovery that what people care about most is losing their homes. Demoralisation is as devastating as bombing. The authorities have studied the effect of the blanket bombing of Coventry.

Hitler's secret weapon of retaliation is a tourist guide that fits comfortably into the hand. It has a clean, sophisticated design and is bound in red, with embossed horizontal lines across the front. Baedeker's *Great Britain.* It's good at its job, highlighting the most beautiful and historic cities of England. Hitler chooses Exeter, Bath, Norwich, York and Canterbury.

Part One

i

4 May 1942

Alma Braithwaite is dreaming of her brother, Duncan. His face is just below her own. He's picked her up in his strong, safe hands and is whizzing her through the air as if she's still only three years old. He's looking up at her, his eyes narrowed against the brightness of the sky, his teeth white and pointed in his open, laughing mouth. She can hear her own giggles, rippling through the calm of the summer garden.

Duncan's hands tighten on her waist. Urgency seems to be creeping into the situation.

'Alma! Alma!' It isn't the giggles that are making her shake, it's someone leaning over her, rocking her backwards and forwards. What's going on? Duncan isn't usually so violent. 'Wake up!'

A thin, harsh wail finally penetrates the dream, dragging her back into the present as it intensifies into an ear-splitting shriek. The air-raid siren! Curls – Jane Curley (whose hair is so straight you could darn stockings with a single strand) – is almost on top of her, pulling at her shoulder. 'Wake up! They're coming! The enemy's at the gate!'

'All right, I can hear you,' she says, sitting up and pushing Curls away. 'Get off!'

'They're going to hit us!' screams a voice from the other end of the room.

'Don't be stupid!' shouts someone else. 'They're not interested in us. Why would anyone want to bomb a girls' school on the edge of Exeter?'

'It's obvious,' says Curls, who's now leaning over the end of her bed, rummaging in the pile of her possessions on the floor. 'They've always known about our existence. Goldwyn's girls and Goldwyn's brains are a major threat to their future plans.'

A switch clicks on and light floods the room, dazzling Alma. A high-pitched, reedy voice calls from near the door, 'Hurry, girls! Hurry!' It's Olive Oyl, Miss Rupin, the housemistress, all tight and flustered. A long plait hangs down her back over her dressing-gown.

After the first serious bombing raid ten days ago, all the beds in Merrivale, the boarding house, were brought downstairs to the large hallway, close to the front door, so the girls would be ready for a quick exit. There are nineteen of them, and they've been squeezed in, side by side, the headboards backing up against the walls. You can do somersaults over the beds, from one end to the other, without touching the floor. The girls thought it great fun at first – there were bets on for the fastest round – but as the days have dragged on, and they've had to remake their beds every night, struggling to tuck in the sheets, finding shoe polish on their pillows, they've started to guard their individual spaces more jealously.

Still half blind from the sudden light, Alma crawls to the end of her bed, aware of urgent movements around her as everyone jerks into confused action. There should be a pile of sweaters, shoes and gas masks at the end of every bed, ready for emergencies, but not everyone has been conscientious about checking them regularly.

As the wail of the siren fades it's replaced by the sound of engines. The approaching aircraft are low in the sky – they must have come in beneath the radar, which explains why the siren was so late – a low grey mumble that increases steadily, expanding into the dark spaces of the night, reverberating through Alma's bones.

'They're going to pass right over us.' Miss Daniels, the matron, appears behind Miss Rupin, wearing a black Burberry coat over her pyjamas and tartan slippers. 'Follow me, girls. Quickly!'

Alma crams her bare feet into her outdoor shoes and shoves her head into her sweater. She can't find the sleeves. Where's the hole for her head? Where should her arms go? Nothing is in the right place. She can't co-ordinate her movements. She's in darkness again. She can't find the way out. Her stomach, her breathing, the air around her are vibrating with terror.

'We're running out of time, girls!' shouts Miss Rupin. 'Just grab anything you can!'

Alma's head finally emerges and she forces herself to breathe normally. She twists the sweater round and slides her arms into the sleeves.

Miss Rupin has her hand on the front-door handle, turning it–

'No!' shrieks Miss Daniels. 'The light.'

'I nearly forgot!' Miss Rupin's voice is cracked with panic. She switches off the main light, plunging them all into darkness again, and opens the door. Everyone scrambles for the exit, falling over each other in the confusion, tumbling out in a disorganised mass.

Alma's friends, Curls, Giraffe (more conventionally known as Marjorie) and Natalie, are waiting for her. They make a dash for the door, the last to leave, but Natalie suddenly stops, her eyes round in the white of her face, her red hair, black in the darkness, standing up as if she has had an electric shock. 'My gas mask!'

'Leave it,' snaps Miss Rupin.

But Curls, who never obeys rules on principle, darts away. 'I'll get it!'

'No!' screams Miss Rupin. She's too late. Curls has gone.

'We can't wait,' calls Miss Daniels. 'You'll have to catch us up.' She leads the other girls down the steps to the garden. Alma, Giraffe and Natalie hover uncertainly by the door, not sure whether to obey Miss Daniels or wait for Curls. Alma puts her hands over her ears and shuts her eyes, visualising the bombs falling through the darkness above her, but then changes her mind and removes her hands, afraid that she will miss the whistle of their downward flight and not know where they're falling.

The air around them is thick with the sound of Luftwaffe engines and Luftwaffe propellers, hiding the sound of the Luftwaffe bomb-bay doors opening.

She can hear cries of terror from the girls ahead of them, cut off abruptly as if someone is afraid the noise will betray their position. As if the Germans above them have some kind of radar that can pick up human voices.

'I've got it,' yells Curls, a few seconds later, and she's there beside them in the dark.

'You foolish girl,' snaps Miss Rupin, who has waited for them.

Alma can feel Curls at her side, her head close, fizzing with suppressed excitement.

'Olive's scared,' shouts Curls into Alma's ear.

So am I, thinks Alma, thinking of her mother and father, probably at home, sleeping an exhausted sleep before setting off very early in the morning for the hospital. Will they wake up and hear the sirens? Will they make it to their shelter?

ii

They run. The four girls, with Miss Rupin close behind, throw themselves down the steps and through the garden, following the cries of the girls in front of them. Giraffe takes the lead, her long legs easily negotiating obstacles, stopping every few seconds to allow the others to catch up. There's a moon, but Alma's had her eyes closed and they haven't adjusted to the darkness. She looks down at her feet but can't see anything, and she's running blind, her hands in front of her, not knowing exactly where she is. There must be hundreds of machines up there, thousands, millions, miles deep, an unstoppable wave of predators, wider than the whole of Exeter. The thunder of the engines, like the roar of a shapeless, nameless monster, booms over and around the school, making it impossible to think clearly.

Alma thinks she might be whimpering. She's aware of her throat quivering, her mouth falling open, but she can't hear anything. However hard she tries to control her voice, it's linked to the inside of her head and has a mind of its own.

'Move in single file and follow me,' shouts Miss Rupin, who has somehow managed to get ahead of them.

'It's too dark,' cries Alma. 'I can't see.' She loses her footing and stumbles into the sharp branches of a shrub. The rose garden! She pulls away, but finds herself hopelessly entangled.

'It's all right,' she whispers to herself. 'You can do this.'

But hysteria is making her hands shake so she can't manipulate them and she's struggling to think clearly. She has to run. She can't run: she's stuck.

She pulls viciously and thinks she hears a rip, but still can't break away. She starts to claw at the branches, aware that she's tearing the skin on her hands, but unable to feel anything. 'Help!' she cries. 'Help me!'

'Stand still,' says a voice by her ear.

It's Curls. Immediately Alma stops moving, almost crying with relief now that someone else is telling her what to do. She can feel Curls's hands running rapidly round her sweater, searching for the place where it's attached. One at a time, Curls eases the wool from the thorns, bending the branches round and hooking them back into each other so they won't swing round and reattach themselves.

There's a series of shrieks ahead.

'Don't worry,' yells Curls. 'They've probably bumped into the corner of the science lab.'

Or each other, or more rose bushes.

'You're free,' says Curls. 'Are you OK?'

Alma nods, then shouts, 'Yes!' as she realises that Curls can't see her.

'Come on,' says Curls. 'Run like the wind.'

Miss Rupin's thin, penetrating voice reaches them from ahead: 'Hold hands with the girl in front of you and the girl behind you.'

And then, unexpectedly, they can see. Flares are dropping from the sky on miniature parachutes and the whole of the area is bathed in a brilliant, artificial, greenish daylight. The aircraft, the birds of prey, are becoming visible and separating into individuals, their wings filling the sky. Nazi strangers are up there, thinks Alma, placing Goldwyn's School in their sights, moving the levers that open the bomb bays, laughing to each other as they send the bombs on their way, having fun–

There's a loud thud from somewhere very close.

'Run!' scream Miss Rupin and Miss Daniels, at the same time.

The newly completed air-raid shelter in Top Meadow is ahead, the gaping hole of the entrance unfamiliar but inviting. The boarders throw themselves down the ramp with relief, tumbling in on top of each other. Miss Daniels slams the door behind them.

iii

There's a surreal pause, as if they've fallen through the ground into a black, bottomless pit where time is suspended and the world has stopped. It feels as if everyone is holding their breath.

The building of the shelter was only completed two days ago and this is the first time they've used it. On previous raids, the girls were led by Miss Rupin and Miss Daniels along the darkened road to the nearest street shelter where they sat for hours, their feet in water that was leaking from a damaged mains pipe. They would never have made it there tonight. This bombing is different from anything they've experienced before.

It starts again, more terrifying in the shelter than outside because the sound is magnified, booming across the roof, echoing in all directions. Every bomb seems to be exploding directly above them or just outside the door, threatening to split them open and burn them up. Alma curls herself into a tight ball and stuffs her fists into her ears, but nothing can stop the reverberations. She tries to think about the people out there, those whose homes are going up in flames, the ones who didn't get to a shelter on time, but her thoughts keep returning to her parents. Are they in a safe place?

'Don't think about it,' she says to herself. 'There's nothing you can do.'

A wavering light cuts through the darkness and one or two of the girls give a ragged cheer. Miss Rupin has found a torch.

'It was in my dressing-gown pocket,' she says between the explosions, as if amazed by her efficiency. The pool of light spreads outwards, like the beam of a lighthouse, friendly and reassuring, wavering at the edges as Miss Rupin's hands shake. Everything outside the light diminishes into uncertainty.

The new shelter is surprisingly spacious, with plenty of room for the nineteen girls, Miss Rupin and Miss Daniels. It's built from concrete blocks, with wooden benches round the edges, and the ground is covered with duckboards to protect their feet from the bare soil. Alma, Curls, Natalie and Giraffe find a place on a bench and huddle together.

There's a lull in the bombing, and in the unexpected silence, they can hear breathless sobbing from someone outside the range of the torch.

'My dear,' says Miss Rupin, 'you mustn't worry. We're all safe here.'

It's Miss Daniels, who is trying to hide her distress, muffling the sound with her hands. 'Bubble and Squeak,' she gasps between sobs.

'Oh, no!' cries one of the younger girls.

The girls stare at the hidden shape of Miss Daniels in the darkness. They all know her two black-and-white cats. Bubble has a patch of white on the right front paw; Squeak has a patch on the left.

'They weren't in my room when the siren started. I would have gone to look for them, but there was no time. I couldn't jeopardise the safety of the girls.'

Alma thinks about the cats out in the darkness, interrupted in their search for mice, paralysed by fear, their black heads pressed to their paws, their eyes huge with terror. There's no provision for pets. It's not right.

Miss Rupin moves the torch into her left hand, letting the beam move erratically upwards towards the roof of the shelter. She fumbles in her pocket and produces a piece of paper, neatly folded into four. Everyone watches as she opens it and spreads it out, shining the torch down so she can read it. 'I need to take the register,' she says. 'We must make sure we haven't lost anyone.'

There's another violent thump, a rush of falling stones or bricks outside. Alma grabs Natalie and Curls at either side of her.

Miss Rupin waits for a few seconds until the shaking subsides and the wailing grows calmer, then starts to call out names: 'Rosemary Atkinson.'

'Present, Miss Rupin.'

'Joy Dickson.'

'Present, Miss Rupin.'

The routine is comforting, as mundane as if they're back in the lower-fifth room with their form mistress, Miss Davies. She sits in the high wooden chair behind her desk, on a flowery cushion that she made herself with material left over from her bedroom curtains, and always recites the names as if they're morsels of food rolling around her mouth, some sweet, some sour. She peers over her half-moon glasses to check that the right girls are answering as they wait for the first bell, the signal to walk in an orderly fashion to the hall for Assembly. As they go down the stairs, the girls peep through the windows at the men from Exeter prison in the gardens, digging and planting potatoes in the desecrated flowerbeds.

But now Miss Rupin is shouting. Now she's shining her torch round to identify the girls who are too terrified to speak. And every time there's another detonation outside, she has to wait for the echoes to die down before she can hear anything.

Someone starts to giggle loudly.

Miss Rupin stops. 'Is it entirely appropriate to be laughing?' she says.

'I'd rather go to my grave laughing than crying,' says a loud voice.

It's Curls, of course. Nothing will silence her. She'll be laughing at the end of the world, egging everyone on to destruction and mayhem.

A chill spreads through the shelter. 'That wasn't the right thing to say,' says Rosalind from the upper sixth, her voice prim and self-righteous.

'Nobody's going to die,' says Miss Daniels.

A younger child starts to snivel. Mary, probably, from the upper third. She's been driving everyone mad by crying every night since she arrived last September. She's homesick; she wets the bed (Matron takes care of that, but someone has to get up to go and fetch her); her friend's house in Plymouth has been bombed; her father is in a submarine patrolling the Channel; her mother hasn't written for a whole week.

A prolonged series of ear-splitting explosions

drowns her wailing and brings an end to the register.

'Do you think we should light the storm lanterns?' says Miss Daniels, in a brief lull.

'Yes, yes, of course,' says Miss Rupin.

'She forgot,' says Curls, in Alma's ear. 'Olive Oyl's slipping out of control.'

Using the torch, Miss Rupin distributes boxes of matches to the three sixth-formers. The older girls, who were given instructions a few days ago while the shelter was being built, take it in turns to light each lantern. Rosalind goes first. Her hands are shaking as she struggles to ignite the match, scraping it across the rough edge of the box too cautiously at first. But once it's alight, she places the flickering flame by the wick of the hurricane lamp and holds it until it has almost burned down to her fingers. The oil from the base creeps up and takes hold, settling into a steady flame. Rosalind screws the glass back on and hangs the lantern on a hook screwed into the centre of the roof. The space fills with a soft, intimate glow. The other two girls repeat the procedure.

'There,' says Miss Rupin. 'It's almost cosy.' Some of the whimpering subsides.

'What's behind there?' asks a girl, examining a curtain that has been set up at the far end of the shelter.

'It's an Elsan closet,' says Miss Daniels.

There's a pause. 'What's an Elsan closet?' asks Natalie.

'It's a lavatory,' says Curls, and everyone giggles.

'They're full of tar,' says Giraffe. 'They put them in bombers. My uncle is an observer in a Lancaster and he says you can't use them. The splashes make you all black.'

'Well,' says Alma, with a shudder, 'there's no way you'd get me on that.'

'You may not have a choice,' says Curls. 'Needs must.'

'If Giraffe's uncle is anything like as tall as Giraffe,' says Elizabeth, from the Upper Fifth, 'it's no wonder he has trouble with the tar.'

'He's taller,' says Giraffe. 'I'm only a girl.'

Alma's thoughts return to Miss Daniels's cats. She's trying desperately to banish a vision of Squeak. He's lying on his back, his white paw stained with blood, crushed by a piece of fallen masonry, his eyes wide and glazed, his handsome whiskers torn off in the blast.

'This shouldn't be happening,' says Natalie. 'I'm an evacuee. I came to Exeter to be safe.' She was sent away from the London Blitz. 'I want to go home – it can't possibly be any worse there than it is here.'

'Buck up, Nat,' says Giraffe, who has never been known to show fear. She's so used to pounding down the hockey pitch towards girls half her size that she believes she's invincible. 'It could be worse. We could be dead.'

'Someone needs to tell Hitler,' says Curls. 'Stop the war immediately. Natalie wants to go home.' A nervous giggle spreads among the girls.

iv

Alma squeezes closer to Curls, Giraffe and Natalie in the corner by the door. They should have brought blankets. They're shivering with cold and fear. 'You were so fast asleep when the air-raid warning went off,' Curls says to her, 'I nearly couldn't wake you.'

Alma tries to smile. 'I was dreaming,' she said. 'I thought the noise was just me laughing.'

'Laughing? Was it entirely appropriate at a time like that?' says Curls.

It's impossible to know which sounds are bombs and which are anti-aircraft fire, as though the guns have been set up on Top Meadow, directly above the shelter. Lines of detonations crack over their heads, as if someone is running over the grass. A machine gun? Are the Huns flying so low that they can fire at any sign of life on the ground?

An engine shrieks. A plane is diving towards them – it's going to crash, right on top of them – Alma hunches her shoulders, bracing for the moment of impact, shrivelling into herself. A huge blast shakes the shelter. Another and another. The lamps sway violently and two go out. The girls scream and grab each other.

'Mummy!' shrieks someone.

'Stay in your seats,' shouts Miss Daniels. 'We haven't been hit.'

These could be Alma's final moments. She must

think deep thoughts. But what about? Her brother Duncan? Her parents? Her friends? The future life that she might never see? How can she? If she hasn't seen it, she doesn't know how to think about it.

'Tally-ho!' yells Curls.

What's the matter with Curls? Why isn't she scared like everyone else?

Someone is reciting the same words over and over, only audible between the blasts, too indistinct to identify. Like a Catholic with a rosary, although this is unlikely, as Goldwyn's is strictly C of E – nobody's given a choice in the matter: it's decreed from on high. It sounds as if it might be Miss Rupin, but it can't be her because everyone knows she's an atheist.

The smell of damp concrete pours out of the walls, mixed with the tang of freshly dug earth, and thick, oily fumes from the lamps.

Another explosion.

Another.

In the pause between the explosions, a different banging starts up, sharp and regular.

'There's someone at the door!' says Giraffe.

Everyone freezes. They look at each other in horror.

'They've invaded,' shrieks a tiny girl from the lower fourth, who is wrapped up in a yellow blanket that she must have yanked off her bed and brought with her. 'They're parachuting in!'

'Don't be ridiculous,' says Miss Daniels. She goes to the door and opens it.

From her position near the door, Alma can see out, past the woman standing outside with two children. The sky is bright orange and a wall of fire fills the horizon. Exeter is burning. She tries to work out where her house in Norman Road would be but it's too difficult. There are no familiar landmarks. Her parents probably aren't there anyway. They'll be at the hospital.

Everything looks wrong. Merrivale, the boarding house, isn't where it should be. It's windy – she doesn't remember the wind when they dashed to the shelter – and everything seems to be on the move. The air is filled with smoke and sparks. She can hear glass breaking, bricks creaking, buildings collapsing–

Miss Daniels pulls the family in, slams the door shut and the dim dust of the shelter surrounds them all again.

Alma turns to Curls. 'Did you see?' she said.

Curls nods. She pauses, then brightens. 'Cable to Mr Hitler. Wrong date STOP Fireworks are November STOP May is apple blossom and bluebells.'

Alma wants to cry.

V

The woman and the two children stand just inside the door, transfixed with terror. Miss Rupin goes over and puts her hand on the woman's arm. 'Come and sit down,' she says. 'It's all right. You're safe now.'

But the woman doesn't take any notice of her.

‘Our house–’ she cries, her voice high-pitched and harsh, only certain words clear enough to understand ‘–on fire – burning – all our things – everything – everything–’

The two small boys are wearing dressing-gowns over pyjamas, their feet in wellington boots. They stare into space with blank, confused eyes, their hair tangled, as if they’ve only just woken up, their faces pale and streaked with dirt.

They’re like Bubble and Squeak, thinks Alma. Bewildered, not understanding what’s happening.

Miss Daniels approaches the woman. ‘It’s Mrs Shriver, isn’t it? You helped on the cake stall for the fête last year. Do you remember me?’ She holds out her hands for the two boys. ‘Come along,’ she says. ‘You come and sit over here.’ They stare at her, not moving, as if they don’t understand that she’s being kind.

‘My husband!’ cries Mrs Shriver. ‘Where is he?’

There’s a tense silence. A bomb explodes somewhere not far away and it’s impossible to say anything for a while.

‘He wasn’t with you when we opened the door,’ says Miss Rupin, in a dry voice.

‘Where is he? I must find him!’ shrieks Mrs Shriver, throwing herself at the door, fumbling with the catch.

‘No,’ says Miss Rupin, trying to pull her away. ‘You can’t possibly go outside again. Nobody could survive out there.’

They struggle for a few seconds until Mrs Shriver stops resisting and crumples. ‘It’s all gone,’ she says. ‘There’s nothing left. We only just made it to the Morrison shelter. My husband said it was too dangerous to stay there – the flames were spreading–'

Miss Rupin leads her to the wooden bench and sits down next to her. 'Everything'll be all right,' she says, putting an arm round her soothingly. 'You'll see...'

But everything won't be all right. Nothing will ever be right again. It's not just Mrs Shriver's things that have all gone. Alma's glimpse outside when they opened the door has shown her that the landscape has altered. Places are missing. All her possessions were in Merrivale. They must have been blown away into thin air. She tries to remember what she owned, what really mattered to her, but she can't recall a single item.

There's another blast and the last lantern swings wildly. The flame flutters for a few moments and dies. Thick, impenetrable darkness surrounds them once more.

'Can't we light it again?' asks Natalie, her voice strained and thin in the ensuing silence.

Miss Rupin has a torch. Why doesn't she use it?

'It might be better to wait for a while until the bombing has stopped,' says Miss Daniels. 'We don't want to risk fire.'

'Keep calm and carry on,' says a solemn voice.

'Oh, shut up, Stephanie,' says another.

'That's what it says on the posters,' says Stephanie. 'Are you suggesting Mr Churchill doesn't know what he's talking about?'

Curls's voice comes out of the darkness, clear and sweet and strong. 'Ten green bottles, hanging on the wall...' There's a piercing quality to her voice, a clarity that makes it impossible to ignore. It echoes through the space and fills he air around them. Alma joins in on the ninth bottle, Natalie and Giraffe on the eighth.

Curls is a musical prodigy, a pianist, but all four girls study music and are used to singing together, familiar with folk songs and madrigals, accustomed to three-part harmony.

Eventually most of the others sing with them.

By the time they've reached two bottles– '"And if one green bottle should accidentally fall"' – Miss Rupin has managed to turn on the torch again and two of the hurricane lamps have been relit. The air is once more filled with the murky comfort of fumes and half-light.

When there are no green bottles left, they start all over again with ten. Round and round, on and on, until everyone, even Miss Rupin, even the two small boys, joins in.

vi

They remain in the shelter long after the sound of the bombers has faded. Nobody wants to open the door to see the damage. Most of the girls doze, propping each other up on the wooden benches.

'Are you awake, Alma?' It's Natalie, propped against Alma's left shoulder.

'Yes,' whispers Alma, even though she isn't entirely.

'It's not fair. My parents said the Jerries wouldn't bomb Exeter. That's why they sent me here. So I would be safe. My uncle Billy and auntie Jean from next door were killed – they had to dig them out – but they weren't like real people any more, just grey, with their clothes all torn. The bombs missed our house, but the ARP wardens wouldn't let us go back in because it wasn't safe. You could hear Frannie, the baby from three doors down, screaming...'

Alma tries to listen – she wants to be sympathetic – but she can feel her eyelids drooping. She snaps awake once or twice, and on the last occasion, she realises that the heavy breathing in her ear is coming from Natalie, so she stops resisting and sleeps.

They're woken by loud thumps on the door. 'Is anyone in there?' A man's voice, loud and authoritative.

'Yes,' cries Miss Rupin, jumping down from her place on the bench. She staggers and takes a few seconds to stabilise herself before scrambling to open the door. 'We're all here.'

They emerge blinking into the pale light of dawn, barely able to recognise their surroundings. Merrivale has taken a direct hit. The front ivy-clad walls have gone, and the upper floors are open and exposed, a bedraggled skeleton dripping with water from the firemen's hoses. It has taken on the form of an ancient ruined monastery. The orange sky over Exeter outshines the rising sun.

Alma and her friends cling to each other, dazed and confused. Fires are burning wherever they look. Everything seems alive, groaning with the effort of remaining upright, teetering on the edge of collapse. Even the school buildings that are still standing seem to be hovering, testing their balance, unsure of their foundations. Walls are disintegrating, collapsing with a sudden roar, tumbling down on top of existing piles of rubble. Sparks flash from exposed cables, white cinders, driven by a strong wind, rain down like a blizzard.

'This is nothing,' says the ARP warden, an elderly, exhausted man. A rim of thin hair, blackened by soot, peeps out from under his helmet. 'You should see the centre of the city. High Street, Sidwell Street, South Street. They're all burning. Bedford Circus has been wiped out.'

'What about Paris Street?' asks Miss Daniels. 'My sister lives there with her children.'

He shakes his head. 'Can't say, I'm afraid. Everyone's out there fighting the fires. Students, fire-watchers, Home Guard, ambulance drivers. They've sent crews from Taunton and Torquay to help.'

There's a statue, not far from the entrance to Merrivale, that dates back to the founding of Goldwyn's in 1905 – a young schoolgirl with cherubic cheeks, ringlets and a very fetching floppy hat. It's still standing at the side of a mountain of charred bricks, miraculously undamaged.

Miss Daniels wanders away from the group of girls. She starts to call in a high, baby-like tone. 'Bubble, Squeak! Here, boys...'

'They can't possibly be still alive,' says Natalie.

Miss Rupin goes over to Miss Daniels and puts an arm round her. She talks to her softly for a while and walks her back to the group.

'She's crying again,' whispers Giraffe.

'So she's human, after all,' says Curls, but no one laughs.

'Come along,' says the ARP warden. 'We need to get you out of here. Follow me.'

He leads the boarders along a pathway through the rubble, between teams of men and women with shovels. The girls pick their way over broken glass and criss-crossing hoses, concentrating more on keeping their balance than working out where they are. 'Single file,' says the warden. 'As quickly as you can.'

They stumble after him, over stray bricks, shattered window frames, distorted cutlery, shards of crockery that must have been blown out of the kitchen in a fountain of exploding china and metal.

'Wait!' cries Miss Rupin. 'We must leave a message.'

'Not now,' says the warden. 'It's not safe to stay here.'

'The head won't know if we've survived,' says Miss Rupin. 'Parents will turn up.'

'We can deal with that later,' says the warden. 'It's more important to preserve human life than get messages to relatives.'

Mrs Shriver runs to the front of the line of girls and grabs the ARP warden by the arm. He stops. 'Please,' she says. 'My husband. I've lost my husband. Do you know where I can find him?'

The warden shakes her arm off. 'I'm sorry, madam,' he says. 'You'll have to wait. We must get these children to safety.'

'Children!' says Giraffe, who is about two inches taller than the warden. 'He thinks we're children.'

'It's less insulting to you than to us,' says Felicity, a sixth-former who's walking behind them. Alma has to agree. The sixth-formers wear skirts with blouses instead of the shapeless gymslips that the rest of the school have to endure and it's rumoured that one or two of them possess a pair of silk stockings. They're almost grown-up. Three sixth-formers left last term before their exams so that they could join the Wrens.

Mrs Shriver falls back, weeping softly, and Miss Daniels, treading delicately in her slippers, has to take her arm to make her carry on. Her two sons follow mutely, their pyjamas streaked with dust, their faces expressionless.

They walk for some distance, past burning homes, amazed by the gaps in a street where single houses have been plucked out in their entirety, leaving their neighbours intact. Eventually they reach a house at the end of a long road. Leaving them all on the pavement, the warden opens the gate, walks up the garden path and rings the doorbell. A woman in a flowery dressing-gown opens the door. 'Oh, you poor things,' she says immediately, coming out to them, examining them one by one as if she's searching for someone in particular. 'You must come in.'

vii

The boarders are led into a large drawing room with a pristine cream carpet and several large sofas. Nobody has the energy to speak. Exhaustion has soaked into them, like cold, numbing water, leaving them with no further resources. Alma's jumper feels inadequate after the journey here, too flimsy for the cool of early morning, damp from the water that hangs in the outside air. A blister has started to form on her right little toe, where the shoe's rubbing against her bare skin, lacking the protection of a sock. They seem to have been walking for ever.

'I'm Mrs Mayfield,' says the woman in the flowery dressing-gown. 'Now, you just make yourselves comfortable in here for the time being until we sort out where you're going to go.' She stops in surprise when she sees Mrs Shriver. 'Helen, what are you doing here?'

'We've been bombed,' says Mrs Shriver, in a flat voice. 'We've had to leave our home.'

The girls stand in awkward groups on the wooden floor around the edge of the room, fearful of venturing on to the cream carpet in their soiled shoes. Ash drifts from their coats and settles on to the floor. One or two, crushed with tiredness, lower themselves to the floor. Alma experiences an urgent longing for their lost worlds of sleep, those last dreams where they were all wandering separately, untroubled. She looks at Curls, Natalie and Giraffe, and all four of them sink to a sitting position against the wall.

'You remind me of my two girls,' says Mrs Mayfield, coming over to speak to them. She's talking unusually fast, as if she's lost control of her thoughts and the words are struggling to keep up. It needs concentration to follow what she's saying. 'They were both at Goldwyn's, you know, although it was a long time ago now and they were day girls. You probably wouldn't remember them. Sylvia and Francesca, they were called, Mayfield. Of course, they're both grown-up now. In London, doing important work, the details of which they can't possibly reveal to their mother. Coping with circumstances like this every day of their lives.'

Mrs Mayfield's face crumples briefly as if she's going to cry, then straightens itself.

'Now, come along,' she says. 'Take your shoes and coats off and sit on the sofas. You'll be much more comfortable there.' She helps some of the younger ones to shrug off their coats and leads them towards one of the large wide sofas. They climb on with her help and sprawl awkwardly among the enormous cushions.

'Do you know?' she says, talking faster and faster, her voice cracked and brittle. 'Nobody ever sits in here any more. My husband and I were wildly extravagant when we first bought the house, buying all these sofas, but we were always entertaining then. We had such a social life, you wouldn't believe it – parties, committee meetings, play-readings, family get-togethers. How strange it all seems. And now we have a use for them again. It's simply splendid that you're all here – so much more important...' She doesn't exactly stop talking, but her voice fades.

Giraffe rolls her eyes at Alma. 'She's nuttier than Miss Rupin,' she whispers.

'Will they send us home?' asks a girl with black plaits hanging down the sides of her white, pinched face. Maisie. Lower fourth.

'We won't have a choice,' says a girl in a navy jumper. Gwyneth, also lower fourth. 'If the school's been bombed.'

'It can't possibly be as bad as all that,' says Mrs Mayfield, recovering some of her earlier volume. 'I'm sure some of the buildings are still all right.'

Miss Rupin appears in the doorway. 'They didn't get the whole school,' she says, her voice even thinner and squeakier than usual. 'Plenty of the buildings are still standing. Latin lessons will proceed as normal.' It's probably an attempt to lighten the mood, but it doesn't work. They're all too worn out to notice.

There's room on the sofas for all the girls, who squash up together, sinking gratefully into the warmth and comfort. The adults take the armchairs. Mrs Mayfield gazes around with satisfaction. 'If only I'd realised,' she says. 'This is exactly what the room was designed for. I'm so thrilled that I can be of use to you all. Now, the kettle's been on for ages, and we must have a cup of tea.' She's talking more easily, getting control of her voice.

'Rosalind,' calls Miss Rupin. 'Sylvia, Felicity.'

The three sixth-formers climb wearily off their

sofa. 'Would you like us to come and help, Mrs Mayfield?' says Rosalind.

Mrs Mayfield's face lights up with pleasure. 'Well, thank you, girls. This is the spirit that proves we're fighting for something worth preserving. Come with me into the kitchen and we'll sort everything out.'

After a while, the girls return with cups of weak, milky tea and biscuits arranged attractively on plates. They offer them round.

Mrs Mayfield follows them in beaming. 'Well, you've obviously done this sort of thing before.'

Sylvia smiles. 'We're used to it. We do volunteer night shifts with the WVS, making tea for the soldiers in their mobile canteens.'

'Tuck in everyone,' calls Mrs Mayfield. 'Carrot biscuits. I made them myself for the evacuees, but this is just as good a cause. There should be enough for one each. Only half a teaspoon of sugar each, though, I'm afraid.'

The younger girls help themselves to the biscuits shyly, checking first with Miss Rupin and Miss Daniels to see if it's permitted. One or two hang back, obviously desperate to take one, but knowing they must mind their manners.

Alma's hands are hurting. She's amazed to discover deep scratches from the rose bushes across the palms. How could she possibly not have noticed the pain?

Curls sees the cuts. She gets up and goes over to Mrs Mayfield. 'Do you have anything for my friend's hands?'

Mrs Mayfield comes over immediately and assesses the situation. 'I have a first-aid kit,' she says. 'We'll soon fix that.' She fetches a little tin – white with a red cross on the front – and takes out a bottle of iodine. She pours some on to a wad of cotton wool and dabs at the scratches. Alma gasps with pain and blinks back tears.

'Sorry,' says Mrs Mayfield. 'But if it doesn't hurt, it won't heal.' She puts gauze over the worst scratches and wraps a clean bandage round Alma's right hand. 'There. That'll soon feel better, I think.'

Alma smiles carefully.

Mrs Mayfield suddenly sees Mrs Shriver, who's leaning against a wall, her arms locked round her waist, bent over as if she has stomach-ache. 'Helen,' she says, 'are you injured?'

'It's not me,' says Mrs Shriver, and bursts into tears.

'Oh, my dear.' Mrs Mayfield leads her to a chair and crouches next to her.

'It's George,' sobs Mrs Shriver. 'I don't know where he is.'

'But the children, where are they?'

'They're here. Robin? Jeremy? Where are you?'

The two boys creep up to their mother and Mrs Mayfield sweeps them into her arms. 'My darlings!'

'It's just that George...' whispers Mrs Shriver, starting to hiccup through her tears. 'He was with us when we left the house, but now he isn't.'

'You mustn't worry. I'm sure he's safe.'

Curls extricates herself from the tangle of girls on the sofa. Alma pulls herself upright and watches her go over to the two women. 'Mrs Mayfield?'

'Yes, dear?'

'Your piano – it's a Bechstein. Who plays it?'

'Oh – yes,' says Mrs Mayfield, turning around, as if the grand piano might not be where it should be. 'My sons, they play. Well, they used to, until...'

'Would you mind very much if I played something? It might help everyone calm down a bit.'

'Goodness,' says Mrs Mayfield. 'What a thoughtful idea. Of course, my dear, if you would like to. It would take our minds off our present circumstances. And it would be glorious to hear it again. My husband plays as well, you know, but he's in a prison camp in Germany. His regiment was taken at Dunkirk. I haven't heard from him for so long...'

Curls sits down at the piano and tentatively presses a key. The sound is soft and clear. She adjusts the stool, places her hands on the keys, pauses to think, her eyes looking inwards as she gives her attention to the music, and starts to play a Beethoven sonata. The music is like a song, the melody singing out over the dense chords of the accompaniment. The lower-fifths look at each other and relax a little. Ever since Curls came to the school, four years ago, she has been providing an accompaniment to their lives. They all know the story of how her parents found her, at the age of three, picking out 'Baa Baa, Black Sheep' on a friend's piano. Now she performs in concerts in London. Music lodges itself easily in her memory, so she can play whatever she wants wherever she finds herself.

There are photographs of two young men on the

mantelpiece, both immaculately dressed in Royal Navy uniforms with caps set at a rakish angle, their faces showing pleasure and delight in their new status. Alma turns to watch Mrs Mayfield, who is staring at their portraits, tears gathering in her eyes. They must be the sons who played the piano. She has been part of a family of six – one husband and four children. Her husband is in a prison camp, the daughters are miles away in London where bombs fall almost every night, and maybe the sons are dead. How does she keep going? How can she be so cheerful?

There's a loud rap on the door. Curls stops playing. Mrs Shriver leaps up. 'It's George! Someone must have told him where we are.'

But it's the ARP warden. 'I'm sorry, ladies,' he says. 'I'm going to have to move you on. The wind is spreading the fires in this direction and we've been asked to evacuate the entire street.'

'Oh, no!' exclaims Mrs Mayfield. 'Will I have to come too?'

'I'm afraid so, madam. Hopefully, the house will be safe, but we can't be certain.'

For a brief moment, an expression of panic, raw and uncontained, flits across her face. She straightens. 'We really are all in this together, aren't we? Have I time to pack a few bits and bobs?'

The warden hesitates, but nods. 'You might as well. Don't know when you'll be allowed back, or even if...' He doesn't want to finish and clearly Mrs Mayfield doesn't want him to say any more. 'As quick as you can, if you please. I have my orders.'

Mrs Mayfield runs upstairs but comes back down with an almost empty bag – just a few clothes thrown in as if she has taken the first things she could find. She gazes round the room looking for inspiration, but it's clear that she has no idea what to take. Alma gets up and goes over to her. 'Take the photographs,' she says, picking up the ones of the boys on the piano. 'Just in case it all goes up in flames. At least you'll have something then.'

'Yes, yes, of course,' says Mrs Mayfield, staring at her without seeing her. 'Thank you, my dear. Such a thoughtful thing to suggest.'

Alma and Curls go round the room with her, pointing out pictures and anything else that might have some value. She puts them all into the bag, hardly aware of what she's doing.

Miss Rupin and Miss Daniels organise the girls into an orderly crocodile. Everyone falls into line obediently, too tired to try to work out what will happen next. Miss Rupin and Miss Daniels take the lead, following the ARP warden along the road, with Mrs Mayfield and Mrs Shriver at the rear. As they head for the outskirts of the city, the roads become less damaged and most of the houses seem untouched, but every now and again a group of men rushes past them, carrying fire-fighting equipment. Eventually, the warden leads them up a garden path and delivers them to another large house.

They're invited into a downstairs room – but Mrs Bates, the owner, is less welcoming than Mrs Mayfield. 'I have to get to work by nine,' she keeps saying. 'It's the evacuees' centre. All those toddlers. They can't manage without me.'

'They might not be there any more,' mutters the ARP warden, but nobody has any inclination to comment.

viii

The doorbell rings. 'Thank goodness,' says Mrs Bates, who has dressed for work in a smart beige suit, immaculate hair and carefully applied make-up. She goes to open the door, expecting the ARP warden with instructions on where to send the girls. Instead, Miss Cunningham-Smith, headmistress of Goldwyn's High School for Girls, sweeps past her and into the drawing room, tall and solid, her large teeth protruding slightly and her short, straight hair as neat as always.

The atmosphere changes in an instant.

'Miss Cunningham-Smith!' cries Miss Rupin, with delight. 'You found us!'

'Of course I did,' says Miss Cunningham-Smith. 'I cannot believe you would doubt me. I've been to Goldwyn's, assessed the damage and followed your trail here, with the help of a somewhat pedantic ARP warden who kept muttering about not being allowed to share information with anyone. Infuriating man. Do I really resemble a German spy?'

Like the other girls, Alma has snapped awake at the sound of the headmistress's voice and is now shivering slightly, bewildered about her whereabouts, unsure if she is properly awake.

Miss Cunningham-Smith gazes round the room. 'Mrs Mayfield?' she asks.

Mrs Mayfield stands up, looking a little bewildered. 'Yes?' she says.

'I must thank you for your earlier hospitality towards my girls and the message from the ARP warden is that your house may well have been saved from the fires. They seem to have contained everything after all, although you will not be permitted to return for some time yet.'

'Oh!' says Mrs Mayfield, with a beaming smile. 'Thank you so much.'

'Now, girls, I must apologise for not being with you at the time of your greatest need. I was staying with my cousin in Topsham. She has not been well and needed a helping hand overnight. We heard the aeroplanes coming up the estuary. Of course, by the time we heard the bombs dropping, there was very little we could do except wait for the fireworks to end. The phone lines were down, so it was impossible to assess the severity of the situation for some time. But I can assure you that the moment it was safe I was on my bicycle, heading for Goldwyn's. Not as easy as you might think. There is a great deal of damage everywhere you go, broken glass and rubble making cycling extremely difficult. In the end, I chained my bicycle to an undamaged acacia tree and took a lift with an ambulance heading for the centre of Exeter.'

Alma smiles at Curls, who grins back. Everything will be all right. Miss Cunningham-Smith is in charge.

'I never thought I'd be pleased to see Miss Cunningham-Smith,' whispers Curls.

'I'm delighted to hear you've finally come to terms with the fact that I serve some useful purpose in your life, Jane,' says Miss Cunningham-Smith. 'Meanwhile, it gives me some satisfaction to notice that your experiences have not bowed your spirit.'

'Sorry, Miss Cunningham-Smith,' says Curls.

Miss Cunningham-Smith stares round at the boarders, examining each one carefully before moving on. 'I'm relieved to find that you have been so well looked after, girls. We must be grateful for the kindness of your various hosts.' She beams at Mrs Bates, who clearly doesn't know how to speed up the process of removing everyone from her house. 'Your ordeal is nearly over. I've already been up to Sherrard's and spoken to the headmaster. They're happy to take you in for the time being. It's all been arranged.'

The girls are all now wide awake. 'We're going to move in with the boys?' asks Natalie, her voice tight with excitement.

'It's only temporary,' says Miss Cunningham-Smith.

'What if parents come for their daughters?' asks Miss Rupin.

'I've left a large notice on the gate. ALL GIRLS SAFELY EVACUATED. They'll find us if they need to and we'll contact them as soon as the telephone lines are restored. Follow me.'

Miss Cunningham-Smith leads the boarders up the road in a neat, regimented line. Two by two, bare legs emerging from their regulation lace-up shoes, coats buttoned securely over their pale cotton nighties or jumpers pulled down as far as possible to protect their modesty. It's a dazzling, sunny day with an intense blue sky. Some of the streets are untouched while others are completely destroyed, without a single house left standing. There are people everywhere, digging, shovelling, pulling out bodies from the debris. Women and children stand in the middle of roads, wailing with shock and confusion. Shrieks of despair echo through the air as people identify the dead.

'Look straight ahead, girls,' orders Miss Cunningham-Smith, 'and keep going.'

Two old ladies join the crocodile for a while, dressed in their best clothes, hats with veils, white cotton gloves, smart buckled shoes. They wander away eventually, talking to each other with conviction, but not forming any real words.

The Sherrard's boys have all been woken early and given breakfast so that their beds can be taken over by the Goldwyn's boarders. Miss Cunningham-Smith supervises as the girls are allocated places, two to a bed, one at the top and one at the bottom. They creep between the still-warm sheets, not caring about the overcrowding, just glad of the comfort.

Alma places her throbbing hands carefully on top of the sheets. She's aware that Miss Cunningham-Smith is nearby, a calm and steady presence patrolling the dormitories, keeping a watchful eye over them. She falls into a restless, troubled sleep.

Part Two

i

15 August 1963

The taxi-driver changes down through his gears to first, roars up the steep driveway and takes the bend too fast, skidding as he rounds the corner. He straightens at the top and reverses to park, wrenching the steering-wheel clockwise, anti-clockwise, clockwise, until they are more or less at right angles to the edge of the shrubbery, with the tyres embedded in the gravel. He turns off the engine. They're facing the front of Goldwyn's Girls' School, Exeter. Red bricks, long windows, walls smothered by Virginia creeper.

Miss Wilhemina Yates, forty-three years of age, the newly appointed headmistress, steps out into eighty degrees Fahrenheit and gazes up at the scene of her future. She is replacing Miss Dulcie Cunningham-Smith, who died unexpectedly of a heart attack three months ago at the age of fifty-nine.

'A deeply regrettable death,' said the chairman of the governors at her interview.

'The school is still in shock,' said another.

'She was far too young.'

Miss Yates didn't think that fifty-nine was too bad an age to die. What about all those men who fought in the war, who hadn't even made it to twenty-five, twenty-one, nineteen? The future husbands whose absence had created an emptiness that still pulsated and echoed everywhere she went.

Miss Yates is a small woman in a navy suit. She looks as if she was born to wear a navy suit. The hemline of her pleated skirt ends precisely on the knee. The neat jacket is buttoned closely around her surprisingly ample bust, pinched in at the waist, ending with a short flare just above her hips. Her dark hair has been freshly trimmed just below the ears and permed into tight, manageable waves. Her lipstick, expertly applied in the cloakroom at Exeter Central station, is Stormy Pink, Revlon's latest.

The taxi driver, a tall man with loose, uncoordinated limbs, gets out and removes her suitcases from the boot. 'It's the school holidays, ma'am,' he says, looking around.

She stares at him, then softens her face. 'Well, of course it is. Every school has a holiday during August.'

He carries the cases to the top of the front steps and contemplates the closed doors. 'There's no one here,' he says, wiping the sweat off his forehead with his arm.

Miss Yates is opening her purse. 'Oh, don't worry about that,' she says, summoning a breezy confidence that seems appropriate. 'I'm expected. Rest assured, someone will be around somewhere. They're just a bit late coming to greet me.'

The driver stands next to her after she has paid him, a good two feet taller than her. He runs his eyes over the front of the building, then turns to examine the gardens on the steep slope back down to the road, narrowing his eyes to peer into the distance as if there might be reinforcements in sight, people running urgently towards the school to let her in. 'I don't know,' he says slowly. 'It don't look like–'

'Thank you so much,' says Miss Yates, smiling even more widely than before, letting a glimpse of her teeth appear between her lips to prove her sincerity. Her neck is aching with the effort of looking up at him. 'You've been extremely helpful. I can manage now.'

But still he hesitates. 'It's quiet. Too quiet.'

Why doesn't he go? His slowness is a torment. Miss Yates struggles with herself, longing to tell him to clear off but knowing that this is not the correct thing to do. 'Thank you *so* much,' she says again. She steps away from him and removes a white glove before pressing the doorbell with one finger. She concentrates on replacing the glove slowly and carefully, spending more time than is strictly necessary fastening the two buttons on the wrist of each one, hoping that the taxi driver will take the hint.

He moves reluctantly back to his cab. 'If it don't turn out – if there's no one here – there's a telephone box at the corner of the road. Turn right, bottom of the drive – you can't miss it. I'll come back and pick you up. I've written the number on the receipt.'

'Oh, I'm sure that won't be necessary,' says Miss Yates, with a confidence that is beginning to crumble as it becomes clear there is no response from inside the building.

The driver does a fast three-point turn, crunching the gears with nonchalant bravado, ploughing up the gravel as he heads towards the top of the drive. He toots briefly before descending and Miss Yates half raises her hand in response, but doesn't turn to watch him.

Oh, for a cultured, articulate, intelligent man.

But she's being unreasonable. They do exist. They just don't earn a living from driving taxis.

She rings the bell again and listens to it echoing through the building, a long, clear summons travelling into the empty interior. There's no sound of footsteps, no suggestion of life. She removes her glove again and tentatively reaches for the handle.

Ah, the door is not locked. They are clearly expecting her. There will be a good reason for no one being here to greet her. She steps in delicately and pulls her suitcases behind her. They're extremely heavy – she's been able to rely on taxi drivers and porters until now – and she finds she has to half drag them over the threshold. It is undignified. Not the way she had envisaged her arrival.

She is in the entrance hall, a generous space between the large double outer doors and a narrower windowed door into the main part of the school. It's comfortably cool after the outside heat. Leaving her cases in the hallway, she pushes open the inner door and surveys the territory she will command for the next few years – maybe for the rest of her working life. There's a smell of polish and dust, the calm, quiet patina of age. Corridors stretch out to the right and left, heading towards distant corners where they disappear into unknown territory. The floor is patterned with Victorian tiles – gleaming black, terracotta and white, polished or varnished to an unnaturally high gloss.

This will not do at all. Victorian tiles are not supposed to shine. Tradition must take precedence over utility. That is the whole essence of a school with history.

In front of her, a wide staircase divides halfway up into two flights, doubling back on itself and up to the first floor. The banisters, dark oak, are intricately carved, with a long, elegant rail curving round the bends.

'Hello!' calls Miss Yates, hearing her voice echoing through the empty spaces. She listens for signs of life, a distant reply, footsteps hurrying down the stairs, but she is met with total silence.

She remembers which direction she took when she came for the interview, following the deputy head. It had felt so different then. The bell had just been rung and girls were skidding along the corridors, leaping down the stairs, talking furiously to each other as they hurried to the next lesson, calling over their shoulders to friends who hadn't yet reached the bottom, shrieking with laughter, stuffing books back into their satchels, taking out the ones they would need, holding notes in front of them, mouthing words as they tried to memorise information for a test.

Potential disasters flashed before her eyes as she watched them. There could be collisions, girls losing their footing on the stairs, plunging to their deaths– This is not how it will be when I'm headmistress, she promised herself, already confident that she would be appointed. We will have an organised transfer of girls from one room to another. There will be no talking, no running, and a one-way system will have to be implemented on the staircase.

But which way had she turned at the top of the stairs? Left or right to the secretary's office where she had waited before being summoned to her interview? Next door to the headmistress's office.

When she'd walked in and found herself confronted by six governors, all seated round the substantial desk, she had been surprised and delighted by the elegance of the room. Wall-to-wall carpet and long, heavy curtains brought a respectful hush, masking the frenetic sound of the girls outside. A large vase of asters and delphiniums – blue and white – had been placed on the wooden filing cabinets. Out of the window, she could see Merrivale, the boarding house, which had been pointed out to her on arrival, and the netball courts, where a group of older girls were leaping around in their white Aertex shirts and loose, pleated navy shorts.

The board of governors consisted of five men, oddly similar in appearance, and one woman, all in their late fifties or early sixties, presumably contemporaries of the late Miss Cunningham-Smith. The men seemed small and shrivelled, reduced, perhaps, by their years of experience, their survival of the war, the hard graft required to keep their personal finances intact during periods of great upheaval. Hunched over the table, their backs fixed into permanent curves, their necks shortened by decades of supporting the weight of their distinguished heads, they gave the impression of being at a conference for gnomes. But she knew well enough that she shouldn't underestimate their intelligence, their enlightened attitude towards the education of girls, and their desire to safeguard the reputation of Goldwyn's as the most successful school in the region.

'I would put clear organisation near the top of my agenda,' she said, in answer to a question about her priorities. 'There must be regulations to ensure that the girls move quickly and safely around the school.'

'Splendid,' said the chairman of the governors, beaming at her like a benevolent uncle. She could see that he approved of her, but she suspected that he was a man who delighted in all women, regardless of their abilities.

'I wonder,' said Miss Jackson, 'if you could give us some idea of how you feel about rules. Can they not be too restrictive?' Miss Jackson, a bony woman whose wafer-thin skin sagged like crumpled tissue paper round her mouth and chin, sat up straighter than the men, and scrutinised her with sharp, penetrating eyes. As the only woman on the board, her influence would be proportionately greater, so convincing her was important. The others would expect her to have an instinct for female excellence.

'Oh, yes, indeed,' agreed Miss Yates. 'My view is that rules are necessary to bring order out of chaos, but they should be the oil that lubricates the smooth running of the school, not the driver.'

She could see that the governors were impressed and congratulated herself on her answer. They sat back and exchanged glances with each other. She decided to emphasise her vision of grasping hold of the reins of the school with firm, caring hands and leading it on to greater glory. 'I believe that we could make Goldwyn's the jewel not only of the south-west but of the entire country, a model school that will be admired for its traditional values and its forward-looking approach to girls' education. We should aim to attract more boarders. I would favour targeting the children of members of our armed forces who are stationed abroad. There is much scope for expansion in that area, I believe.'

The man next to Miss Jackson fixed one eye on Miss Yates. The other seemed to be studying something over her shoulder.

He has a wandering eye, thought Miss Yates. I must resist the temptation to turn round to see what he's looking at.

'You are aware that we are a direct-grant school?' he said. 'At least fifty per cent of our girls gain free places through the eleven plus.'

'Of course. But we need to fill the boarding house – the staff are excellent, I understand. A half-full house runs at a loss. Goldwyn's needs to make a profit, and a thriving, vibrant mix of boarders and day girls can only enhance the school's reputation.'

The chairman leaned forward as if driven by a greater sense of urgency than seemed necessary. 'But you do not intend to drop our standards, I trust, in order to fill these places.'

Miss Yates counted two seconds exactly before

answering. She wanted to appear intelligent and thoughtful. 'I cannot state strongly enough how important standards are to me. I shall be examining the entry exams for all local-authority-funded and fee-paying girls. We cannot allow profits to dictate standards. Our girls must shine as beacons of excellence.'

A governor who had not yet spoken, and seemed to have dropped off to sleep, unexpectedly shuffled the papers in front of him. The others turned to him in expectation, clearly accustomed to the signal that he was preparing to speak. He cleared his throat. Everyone waited. 'They are not your girls yet, Miss Yates,' he said, his voice low and gravelly.

I've overdone it, thought Miss Yates. I'm sounding over-confident. The opinion of this man clearly carried much weight. She smiled at them all, then directed her attention specifically to him. 'Of course not,' she said. 'I was speaking from the point of view of someone who has observed the school from the outside, admired the imagination of the previous headmistress, and would like to be part of its ethos.'

Miss Yates turns left and follows the corridor, reasonably certain that this is the way she went before. With luck she will meet someone who is expecting her.

As she walks, her heels click loudly on the tiles, tapping out the clear, authoritative message that she has arrived, that she is here to stay, that she expects attention from her staff and pupils, and that her will is the one that will prevail, should anyone wish to cross her. Every now and again, she stops and listens, certain that there are other people in the building and that they will become aware of her presence and rush out to greet her. As she reaches the end of the corridor and prepares to take another turning to the left, she finally hears voices in the distance, animated conversation, a sudden laugh. So she was right. There are staff here. Their organisation must have slipped so badly that they've managed to forget the arrival of their new headmistress.

Miss Yates quickens her pace, but now avoids putting her heels down too sharply. She would like to surprise these people who should be working, who should be waiting for her at the front door, who seem to be passing the time of day in frivolous chat. She reaches the point where the voices are loudest, stops to listen, satisfies herself that she has the right room and that they are still oblivious to her presence, then opens the door.

Inside, she finds two women. One, presumably the secretary, although Miss Yates doesn't recognise her from the interview, is sitting on the chair in front of the typewriter on the desk. She's wearing a pale pink and black checked dress, pinched in at the waist. Her hair is cut level with her chin, shorter at the back, with a thick fringe that almost touches her eyebrows. She's so young that she looks as if she should be wearing school uniform.

The other woman, in a sleeveless cotton shift with a scooped neck, is perched on the edge of the desk with her back to the door. She is older, in her thirties, perhaps. Her exposed flesh – there seems to be a great deal of it – is smooth and glowing, tanned to a warm brown. Her legs, which are crossed, gleam.

'Oh!' says the woman on the desk. She jumps off hurriedly and turns to face Miss Yates, smoothing down her skirt until it reaches her knees. 'You've taken us by surprise.'

'So I see,' says Miss Yates. 'You seemed to be having a...' she chooses her word carefully '...stimulating conversation. I trust you are exchanging the kind of intellectually challenging ideas that one would expect to find among the staff of a renowned girls' school.'

The two women glance at each other, clearly uncertain how to respond. 'Not that intellectual,' says the one who has jumped off the desk, suppressing a smile. 'We just didn't think we would be overheard.'

'Patently,' says Miss Yates.

Meanwhile, the other woman has had time to recover and now stands up, coming out from behind the desk and offering her hand. 'I'm so sorry. We weren't expecting anyone today. I'm Bridget Murphy. The new school secretary. Only started last week. Can I help you?'

'Yes,' says Miss Yates, without taking her hand. 'I think you probably can.' She pauses. The women begin to look uncomfortable. It's a technique that Miss Yates often employs. Silence tends to engender panic, and she has found that waiting before replying is an excellent way of establishing her authority. 'I'm the new headmistress.'

The secretary has let her hand sink a little, but

she's so shocked that she withdraws it completely and puts it behind her back. 'No, that can't be right – we weren't expecting you until tomorrow.'

'That is abundantly clear.'

'Are you sure? I mean,' she adds, looking flustered, 'of course you're sure of who you are, but – but are you Miss Yates?'

'I am indeed,' says Miss Yates, pleased with the effect she's having. It's extraordinarily satisfying to take charge. She now offers her hand, which Miss Murphy shakes gingerly.

'Well, that's a relief,' says the other woman. 'I think Bridget had a horrible suspicion that you were one of the unsuccessful candidates, turning up anyway to persuade us that the governors had made a mistake and you are the better prospect!'

'And you are?'

'Sorry,' says the woman, coming over with an outstretched hand. 'I'm Alma Braithwaite. Music teacher.'

Miss Yates shakes her hand, firmly and positively. She's not convinced by this pretence of mistaken identity. 'Well, I can assure you I am the successful candidate, and I would like an explanation of why no one was ready to receive me.'

'I can't understand it,' says Miss Murphy. 'I thought you were due tomorrow. I've asked the gardener to cut some roses in the morning and the housekeeper to prepare a bed for you in Merrivale. You are staying there, aren't you? For the time being?'

'I believe I am to be sleeping in the boarding house for a couple of weeks until the renovation of my house is finished. I'll need the porter to carry my suitcases over. They're in the entrance hall.'

'I can sort that out for you,' says Miss Braithwaite. 'I'll be going past Roy's cubby-hole on my way out. He's the porter and caretaker, by the way. How did you get in? I thought the front door was locked.'

'Am I to understand that nobody actually knew the front door was open?' says Miss Yates.

'Oh,' says Miss Murphy. 'It's not as bad as it sounds. Roy must have unlocked it this morning and forgotten to tell me. He checks all the entrances before he leaves at night, so there's no danger of anyone entering illicitly.'

'I'm sorry to contradict you,' says Miss Yates, 'but absolutely anyone could have come in. I simply opened the door and entered. There was no one to challenge me, even after I'd rung the doorbell. In future, please make sure that doors are only unlocked if someone is nearby to monitor them.'

'I'm sure nobody else would come in,' says Miss Murphy. 'After all, who would want to get into a girls' school?'

'Boys?' says Miss Yates, with a raised eyebrow.

'Oh!' say both women at the same time. They stare at her, obviously unsure if they should laugh. Miss Yates enjoys their embarrassment.

'Well,' says Miss Braithwaite, eventually. 'Since it's holiday time, and there aren't any girls here, I can't help thinking they wouldn't bother.'

'You'd be surprised,' says Miss Yates. She doesn't intend to offer any further explanation. She has found in her past job that being enigmatic is very effective. Nobody quite knows how to take her comments and nobody likes to ask for fear of appearing ignorant, so she succeeds in wrong-footing them.

'Here we are,' says Miss Murphy, producing an opened envelope from a side drawer in her desk. She pulls out the letter and peruses it quickly, her eyes scanning the handwritten script. 'Yes,' she says triumphantly. 'It says you'll be coming on the sixteenth.'

Miss Yates steps smartly over and takes the letter from her hand. Surely she hasn't made a mistake. She never makes mistakes. 'No,' she says with relief. 'It says the fifteenth, not the sixteenth. That is a five, not a six.'

Miss Murphy stares at the numbers in front of her and clearly doesn't agree.

'No matter,' says Miss Yates. 'I'm here now, so we'll have to make the best of it, won't we?' She allows herself a smile. A relaxing of tension is required at this point. She can see that Miss Murphy has a stubborn streak and is unwilling to concede that she has read it incorrectly. 'It is conceivable that you might have mistaken my five for a six,' she says. 'I will endeavour in future to make my communications clearer.'

Miss Murphy smiles nervously in return. She looks at Miss Braithwaite, who is gazing out of the window in an attempt not to interfere. Miss Yates considers showing her the letter and asking her opinion, but it would be humiliating if she sided with Miss Murphy, so she moves briskly on. 'Now, I wonder if you could show me my office,' she says.

'Yes, of course,' says Miss Murphy. 'It's just next door. I'll come and unlock it for you. We do keep all the offices locked when there's no one here, of course. We wouldn't want any confidential information to leak out.'

'Quite so,' says Miss Yates.

'I'll go and ask Roy to take your cases over to Merrivale,' says Miss Braithwaite.

'Thank you,' says Miss Yates. 'Before you go, I would like to point out that I expect my staff to be correctly attired at all times.'

Miss Braithwaite stares at her. 'I'm sorry? Have we done something wrong?'

Miss Yates enjoys her confusion. 'Your legs, Miss Braithwaite.'

'My legs?'

'I do not think bare flesh is suitable for someone whose job it is to guide young ladies towards dignity and moral strength.'

Miss Braithwaite is struggling to maintain a neutral look. 'You mean...?'

'I mean, Miss Braithwaite, that I do not consider it appropriate for you to be out in public without stockings. Our days of hardship and deprivation ended with the fifties, as I'm sure you know. We are entering a period of prosperity. Bare legs indicate poverty and loose living. I will tolerate bare arms in extreme heat when there are no girls present, but I will expect them to be covered at all times during term.'

She turns, opens the door, stands back to let Miss Murphy precede her, and leaves Miss Braithwaite to contemplate the new regime that she will soon have to help enforce.

ii

While Bridget Murphy shows the new head to her office, Alma waits, staring out of the window, tapping her toes in a silent rhythm inside her shoes. Right, left, right, hold for two seconds (a minim). Left, right, left... How dare this woman dictate what she wears? One, two, hold, hold...

Bridget returns and shuts the door behind her. They stare at each other and Bridget starts to giggle silently.

Laughing seems to be the only reasonable option. 'Is she real?' says Alma, letting go of her resentment and joining in.

'"I expect my staff to be correctly attired at all times,"' Bridget whispers with exaggerated enunciation.

'Do you think she ever removes the gloves?' says Alma.

Bridget rolls her eyes. 'Maybe when she goes to bed.'

'Not necessarily. She probably has a matching night cap.'

'And bed socks.'

In a brief pause, they hear the click of a door handle and sharp, urgent footsteps. There's just time to readjust their faces before the door opens and Miss Yates appears. She is not wearing her gloves.

'Miss Braithwaite,' she says, 'I thought you

were going to fetch the porter. There are certain documents I require immediately.'

'It's all right,' says Bridget. 'I'll go.' She turns to pick up a bunch of keys from her desk. As she does so, she mouths, 'Certain documents!' at Alma and raises her eyebrows.

'I'm sure you have more important things to do than stand around wasting time in my secretary's office,' says Miss Yates. 'I'm surprised to find you here at all during the holidays.'

'Oh, I have plenty to do,' says Alma. 'Swim the Channel, compose a symphony, write the last chapter of my tenth novel before the school term begins. Time marches on.'

She doesn't have things to do. She could have been touring Scotland with Maxine Wright (French) and Alison Wheatley (games) or staying in a caravan in Wales with Henrietta Fox (biology) but, as always, she's turned down all of the opportunities. It may be true that they haven't exactly issued invitations, but she knows that they would welcome her if she were to ask. She prefers to relax at home, in familiar surroundings.

'You write novels?' says Miss Yates, picking out the only feasible activity on Alma's list.

'I was getting a little carried away,' says Alma. 'It was a metaphor for all the urgent tasks that must be addressed.' She edges past and marches away along the corridor before she can be manoeuvred into any further conversation.

Alma throws her hands across the piano, brings her arms down with passion, crashes through the chords.

Rachmaninov. 'Polichinelle'. Loud, fast, aggressive.

Stockings? In this heat? What century does Miss Wilhemina Yates think she's living in? And as for covering arms... The woman's bonkers.

She ends with a furious, energetic blast of sound. Fingers in a flurry of activity at the top of the piano. A leap down with her left hand to the octave in the bass.

Missed.

Furious with herself, Alma refuses to correct it. The wrong sound echoes in her head, but it suits her mood. It must be over eighty degrees outside. The sun is blazing down out of a cloudless sky. She considers briefly whether it would be worth going to the beach at Exmouth this afternoon to sunbathe. But everyone else will have had the same idea and the trains will be overcrowded. The thought of all those hot bodies, damp with sweat, pressing up against each other is depressing.

She goes to the window and stares out. She can see Goldwyn's from here, the top of the reconstructed Merrivale, the dome above the school hall. It blocks the afternoon sun, creating a shadow across the bay window and wrapping the piano in a protective shade.

She often goes into school during the holidays, even at weekends, finding pleasure in the echoing corridors, the symmetry of the desks lined up in the empty form rooms, the uncluttered spaces waiting to be filled. It's the absence of the girls that she likes, and the fact that they will eventually return. There's an air of readiness, a sense of anticipation, that she finds exciting. The future is assured, but not yet. Sometimes she will go into a form room, check the distance between each desk and chair, make one or two small adjustments so that the patterns are perfect.

But now there's an intruder. The presence of Miss Yates is contaminating. She is the image of Hitler, Mussolini, Stalin (who may have helped the Allies win the war, but had not distinguished himself thereafter) transformed into female form in a navy suit. An expensive suit, moreover. Beautifully tailored, of course. Not that Alma is jealous. What else would you expect from a potential dictator?

There's nothing written down that forbids Alma to enter the school during the holidays, but is Miss Yates likely to introduce a new code of conduct for the staff? She's the kind of person who would insist on everything being documented and filed. A bureaucrat. *Certain documents*. The words carry ominous overtones.

Alma had heard the news of Miss Cunningham-Smith's death from a conversation among a group of lower-fourths one morning as she came into school. She found herself paralysed by shock, unable to express herself or even summon tears. Miss Cunningham-Smith had been the one stable presence in her life since she was eight years old and new at Goldwyn's. They had almost become friends in the later years, after the war.

Alma certainly hadn't wanted to engage in the orgy of emotion that had swept through the school like a contagious but very vocal disease. Even the dramatic displays in the staff room were somehow distasteful, as if they were all reverting to teenage behaviour, allowing the girls' hysteria to influence them. She had just carried on working, holding everything together, believing in the power of routine, habit.

And now Miss Yates.

Miss Cunningham-Smith's greatest strength had been her ability to remain the same. She never acted impulsively or allowed irrational thought to confuse things. She epitomised the tradition of Goldwyn's. Logical, strong, reliable. It was so unlike her to do something as unpredictable as dying.

Miss Yates, the unknown, the unknowable, the dangerous, will not be a natural successor to Miss Cunningham-Smith.

Alma swallows hard. There's a block in her chest, a hard, uncomfortable knot that's been a problem as long as she can remember, an impediment to eating, to talking. It seems to be expanding at the moment, upsetting her digestive system and waking her from complicated dreams in the middle of the night.

New routines, new methods, new rules.

The doorbell rings.

For a second Alma is confused, uncertain of where she is in the day. Has she forgotten something?

Could it be Duncan? Finally? After all these years?

The doorbell rings again.

'Antony!' she says, as she opens the door. She should have been expecting him. He'll be doing his grade eight next term and they've arranged an extra lesson. A few hours ago, she'd remembered he was coming, but he had slipped from her mind after the encounter with Miss Yates.

Antony steps in with a grin. He's seventeen, a tall, good-natured boy from Sherrard's, who spends most of his spare time playing cricket. 'Hello, Miss Braithwaite,' he says. 'Hope you didn't forget I had a lesson today.'

'How could I possibly forget you, Antony?' she says, leading him through the passageway between piles of discarded post. She'll clear it all away one of these days, but there never seems to be time. Her grand piano sits in the alcove created by the large bay window in the drawing room. She lifts off the books of music that are open on the stand and adds them to one of the many piles on the floor. 'Are you enjoying the holiday?'

He adjusts the piano stool while she fetches a chair to sit next to him. 'Too much to do,' he says. 'And Georgina's driving me mad.'

Alma teaches Georgina, his younger sister, a delightful child, full of chatter, hopeless at practice. 'You should be nice to her while you have the chance,' she says.

He looks surprised. 'Why? Is she going somewhere?'

'No, but you will, when you go off to university next year. Then you'll be sorry you didn't appreciate her while you could. C sharp minor, melodic, staccato.'

She relaxes into her chair and watches him play. His long back bends gracefully as he leans towards the top of the piano, strong and flexible, and settles easily into an upright position as he comes down again. She watches the ripple of his spine through his shirt, the wide spread of his shoulder-blades, the soft hair curling at the nape of his neck. She would like to lay her hand flat on his back, and hold it there to feel the muscles as he moves, investigate the latent power that is concealed behind the shirt. The easy strength that can hit sixes on the cricket field with effortless frequency or hurl a ball towards a batsman in a powerful, vicious arc. She wonders if some of his strength could flow from him to her.

An image of her brother, Duncan, pops into her mind, unexpectedly vivid, as he strides out for his innings, cradling the bat lovingly with one arm, his legs encased in white pads.

'Right,' she says to Antony. 'Let's look at the Mendelssohn.'

She sits up straight, the earlier lethargy evaporated, and her mind starts to hum with activity. She'll sort out some music for the chamber orchestra this afternoon, stock up her shelves from the Co-op and lie in the sun in the early evening, once the day has started to cool.

iii

Breakfast in the holidays. Robert Gunner, senior lecturer in mathematics at the university, reads the *Guardian* with his glasses pushed up. They hover at the top of his substantial forehead, ready to slide down as soon as he's forgotten they're there (he grunts with irritation when it happens, as if they've done it on purpose). He stirs Golden Syrup into the porridge that has been cooking all night in the bottom oven of the Aga. Godfrey, his thirteen-year-old son, is grilling toast, throwing away endless slices until he has exactly the right shade of brown.

'Try not to use up all the bread,' murmurs Robert.

'Is it OK if I go out for the day?' asks Godfrey, settling on a couple of slices and smothering them in butter.

'Try not to use up all the butter,' says Robert.

Pippa comes into the room wearing her new school uniform: a blouse with thin blue and white stripes; a navy tunic with flared skirt and tailored bodice; a blue and red tie; a navy jumper with a strip of pale blue set just inside the V. The Goldwyn's crest is embroidered on the pocket of the blazer, the colours fresh and shiny, proof of Pippa's step forward into senior school in September. *Per Ingenium Supero*: Through knowledge, I conquer.

Godfrey takes an enormous bite of toast and chews thoroughly for a few seconds before swallowing it. 'So can I?'

'Can you what?' says Robert.

'I want to go for a cycle ride with Bill. Up to Woodbury Common where we can make a campfire and cook sausages.'

Robert puts his paper down and stares at him. 'Did I know about this?' he asks.

'You do now.'

'I see,' says Robert. He can't decide whether it matters. 'All right,' he says eventually. 'Providing you're back in time for supper. Miss Dodds won't be happy if you're late.'

'Can I come?' asks Pippa. She's fiddling with the black velour hat on her head, turning down the brim at the front, examining her reflection in the small mirror propped up on the dresser.

'Dressed like that?' says Godfrey. 'Not likely.'

'I wouldn't wear this, silly,' she says. 'I was only trying it on.'

'Go and take it all off before you have breakfast,' says Robert. 'You don't want to spill porridge on it.'

'I'm not having porridge.'

'That's not the point. You shouldn't be wearing the clothes until the beginning of term.'

'It's a blokes' expedition,' says Godfrey. 'We don't allow girls.'

The doorbell rings.

'I didn't want to come anyway,' says Pippa, going out to the hall.

'Do you have any money for a packed lunch?' asks Godfrey.

'I thought you were going to cook sausages.'

'Yes, but we don't actually have any.'

Robert sighs and puts his hand into a pocket. This seems to be the only thing he's useful for, these days. He wonders if it would be any different if his wife, Grace, had survived. Perhaps she would have understood the children better.

Pippa comes in with a long box addressed to Robert. 'How exciting,' she says. 'Another lighthouse.'

'Eddystone, third version, designed by Douglass,' says Robert.

'But you've already got Eddystone,' says Pippa.

'This one is infinitely superior to my existing models,' he says, taking a sip of coffee. 'Handcrafted, built to scale.' He unwraps the brown paper and lifts the lid from the box. He removes the lighthouse carefully, checking for damage, then places it upright on the kitchen table.

Pippa picks it up and fingers the outside. The miniature bricks look as if they have been made individually and constructed by a real bricklayer, but they've been painstakingly drawn with a paintbrush. She peers in through a window. 'Why doesn't it have any furniture?' she asks. 'The least you'd expect would be stairs.'

'Think of what we could buy if we weren't slaves of the model-lighthouse industry,' says Godfrey, swallowing his last piece of toast.

'You've just had a brand-new ten-speed Raleigh,' says Robert. 'What more do you want?'

Robert, as the grandson of a lighthouse keeper, loves lighthouses. He uses the summer holidays to tour the coast of Britain with the children, drawing gradually closer to his goal of visiting every lighthouse in Britain. He doesn't mind what the weather is like and forgets that his children might, so he fixes them up with waterproofs, builds them a makeshift table of damp stones and hammers an imperfect corral of windbreakers round them. He then leaves them huddled together on the beach over a chess set while he investigates the nearest lighthouse. It's only possible to go into a few, but he likes to photograph each one, then sketch it to create a record of his observations.

There have been several memorable expeditions to Scotland, which has the greatest concentration of lighthouses in Britain, where the scenery is most spectacular. He first went there on his honeymoon.

'Couldn't you just settle for the photograph?' asked Grace. 'It would be so much quicker.'

'The light isn't usually good enough,' he said. 'Too much spray for clarity. Obviously. That's why they've put a lighthouse there. If I make a sketch as well, I can use a degree of creative licence and imagine a moment with no rain.'

'But it never stops raining in Scotland,' said Grace.

'It does,' he said. 'Although you have to be watching. Otherwise you miss it.'

Pippa replaces the model lighthouse on the table and puts some bread under the grill.

'Are we going into Exeter today?' she asks. 'We still haven't got the satchel or the Osmiroid pen.'

'I thought Miss Dodds was going to take you.'

'No, she thinks you're doing it.'

Robert sighs inwardly, trying to work out how to fit this in. He continues to go into the university during most of the holidays, but leaves later in the morning and comes home earlier. 'Well, we could meet up this afternoon. Round about four o'clock. Outside the station – good gracious.' He stares at a photograph in the paper. His glasses drop off, but he grabs them in time and puts them back up on his head.

'What?' says Pippa, about to leave the kitchen. 'Another lighthouse for sale?'

'There's a whole article here about Miss Cunningham-Smith, a tribute.'

'You mean the headmistress of Goldwyn's who died?' asks Pippa.

'The very same. I wouldn't have expected her to make the national papers, but it's pleasing to see she has. I'm surprised they're doing it so long after her death, but I suppose a tribute isn't quite the same thing as an obituary. They're looking back over her distinguished career. She was at Goldwyn's before the war, you know. Miss Yates, the new headmistress, will have a lot to live up to.'

'I hope she'll be as nice as Miss Cunningham-Smith.' Pippa had enjoyed her interview with Miss Cunningham-Smith. 'She wanted to know about my tortoises and what books I read. She was really nice.'

'Miss Cunningham-Smith will be irreplaceable, I'm afraid. She was a source of indefatigable energy, a formidable woman. Churchill should have come and observed her in action, seen how efficiently she could organise her girls. They'd have sorted out Hitler within in a year if she'd been in charge. She inspired absolute loyalty in her staff.'

'Did you know her before, then?'

Robert turns a page of the paper and doesn't answer.

Pippa leans over and bends down the front of the paper so he can see her. 'Miss Cunningham-Smith?' she says.

He puts the page back up again. 'Don't do that, Pippa,' he says. 'It's very irritating.'

'How do you know Miss Cunningham-Smith?' she says.

‘I just do,’ he says vaguely. ‘Have done for years.’

‘I didn’t know that,’ she says.

He looks up at her for a second. ‘There are lots of things you don’t know,’ he says.

Part Three

i

4 May 1942

The girls are woken at ten o'clock and go down for a late breakfast in Sherrard's dining room, watched over by a bleary-eyed Miss Daniels. Shortly afterwards, the first parents turn up. Rosemary's father has driven from Plymouth, where the bombing has been severe and everyone who can get hold of petrol escapes to the countryside before nightfall so they can at least get some sleep in the car. 'Darling girl,' he says as he comes through the door and catches sight of Rosemary eating a slice of toast and margarine. 'We expected you to be safe here.'

She drops the toast, leaps to her feet and flings herself into his arms. 'Daddy!' she shrieks, starting to cry, burrowing her face into his chest.

'She's overdoing it,' says Natalie. 'She was all right till he turned up.' But her voice lacks conviction and Alma wonders if they're all thinking the same as she is. I wish it was my father.

Stephanie's mother comes down on the train from Bristol, walks up from St David's station and encloses Stephanie in her arms as soon as she sets eyes on her. Stephanie, seeing over her mother's shoulder that her classmates are watching and not wanting to give the impression that this is normal behaviour, raises her eyes with despair at the overwhelming nature of her mother's hysteria.

Alma tries to phone her parents, but the lines are down. She knows they'll be working round the clock, ignoring their need for sleep. Her mother, the only female consultant obstetrician in the hospital, the cleverest student of her year when she qualified, will be brisk and efficient, in charge, handing out crisp, clear instructions, perhaps delivering babies for women who might have gone into premature labour as a result of the trauma of the bombing, or else working alongside her husband, exercising the general surgical skills she learned when training but had never needed, dealing with severe trauma, injuries beyond the power of imagination.

Mummy – no longer Mum. Alma reverts to the baby name, experiencing a great need to crawl into her mother's lap, feel her strong, capable arms circling her, making her safe.

She pictures her father, dressed in his white surgical attire in the operating room, calm and organised, every movement controlled. He's cutting, stitching, tying, his fingers moving with unnatural dexterity, blurring with speed. He only pauses between operations to gulp down a cup of lukewarm tea and a corned-beef sandwich, to sterilise his hands, before moving on to the next patient.

She sees his intelligent eyes above his facemask, assessing, calculating, his concentration absolute, calming any panic that his patient might be feeling.

'Daddy,' she breathes into the blank air. 'Where are you? I'm all right, but I want you to come and find me.'

A messenger, a fifteen-year-old boy, wanders into Sherrard's by mistake at eleven o'clock. He stops for some toast and tea, sitting in the Juniors' canteen on a chair that's too small for him. His clothes are thick with dust, streaked with black ash, and he has deep hollows of tiredness under his eyes. He tells the group of girls and boys who gather round him for news that one wing of the hospital has been badly damaged in the attack and more and more casualties are pouring in.

'Have you come across either of my parents?' asks Alma. 'Dr Braithwaite? They're both consultants and they have the same name.'

He looks at her for a while, apparently unable to focus properly on her face, then shakes his head. 'Sorry, I don't know them. If they're doctors, they'll still be working. It's terrible there – bodies everywhere...'

The girls grow silent. They don't want to think about dead people.

Alma is proud of her parents, but, at the same time, resentful. Shouldn't they come and check she's all right? Do they care more about strangers than their own daughter? Don't they realise that Goldwyn's has been hit?

The girls join the lower-fifth boys' English class at Sherrard's for the last double period of the morning. They're competing with them in a discussion about Wordsworth's *Prelude* when the door opens abruptly and Miss Daniels comes in, her cheeks flushed, breathing heavily as if she's been running. 'I'm so sorry to interrupt,' she says.

'She's just discovered the building's full of men,'

whispers Curls, and the girls giggle quietly.

'Alma,' says Miss Daniels, 'I wonder if you could come with me.'

Alma is confused by the unfamiliar softness in Miss Daniels's voice. 'Why?' she says. She wants to continue the analysis, read the words of the poem again, look for the puzzle within the poetry, the metaphors–

'Someone has come to see you,' says Miss Daniels.

A wave of relief. Her parents have come to fetch her, to take her home. Wordsworth can wait.

Dr Guest, an old family friend, is sitting in the small waiting room. Alma has known him since she was born, but she's never seen him like this, his black suit dusty and crumpled, his eyes red and swollen as if he hasn't slept for weeks.

He stands up when she enters the room. 'Alma,' he says.

She can't breathe. Her legs seem to have lost the ability to support her.

Dr Guest puts an arm round her and lowers her into the only comfortable chair. He moves one of the upright chairs so that he's directly opposite her. She doesn't know what to say. She's never done this before.

Her parents had both been on duty in the west wing when the ambulances arrived with the first casualties, even while the bombing was still going on. There weren't enough beds, so they started operating wherever there was space, in the emergency wards, in the corridors, in used offices. The bombers were still over Exeter, the roar of their engines, the blast of the bombs filling their ears as they worked. Some of the last bombs landed on the west wing. Direct hit. Twenty-three patients, six nurses, four doctors. Three patients survived and two nurses, horrifically injured. No doctors.

Dr Guest is saying something to Alma, but she no longer hears him. 'Thank you for coming,' she says, and pictures her mother standing at the door, talking to a door-to-door salesman, her hair pinned up carelessly, wisps escaping down her cheeks, wiping her floury hands on her apron. The heat of the kitchen; the smell of freshly baked cakes clinging to her clothes; the light from the open door giving her face clarity; the sharp sweep of her nose, the lips wide and friendly, the cheeks soft with tiny downy hairs that are invisible most of the time; her authoritative voice saying, 'Thank you for calling.'

After a while, Dr Guest gets up. 'You mustn't worry about anything, Alma. You will be taken care of. We'll send messages to your relatives, but you are most welcome to come and live with us if you prefer.' His voice sounds as if it's a long way away, at the far end of a tunnel.

'Duncan...' whispers Alma.

'He will be contacted.'

And now he's talking to someone else – Miss Daniels must have come back into the room: 'I have to get back. I'm needed at the hospital – not enough of us – my wife will be in touch.'

She remains in the waiting room for some time. She feels that she should be thinking of her parents, going over everything that she knows about them so she doesn't forget them, but she can't. She's wrapped in a deep, cold silence. Miss Daniels comes to see her and tucks a blanket round her, but she's too exhausted to search for words. Someone produces a cup of tea– 'Here you are, dearie. Three spoonfuls of sugar. Try and get it down you. It'll do you good.'

Good? What is she talking about?

She forgets the cup of tea. When she finally remembers and picks it up to take a sip, it's lukewarm and unappetising.

Then Curls appears at her side. 'Shove up,' she says, and squeezes herself into the armchair next to Alma, putting an arm round her. '"Roll over,"' she sings softly, '"Roll over. There were ten in the bed and the little one said, Roll over, roll over..."'

They sit there together until Curls reaches '"One in the bed, and the little one says – Goodnight."' When she stops, the silence seems slightly less dense, less intense. Alma wasn't even listening properly, but some of Curls's heat has begun to transfer to her and the ice inside her feels slightly less solid. Her mind starts to grope its way back to a land she knows.

'I don't mind if you want to cry,' says Curls.

But Alma shakes her head. She's not sure what she wants to do, but she knows she doesn't want to cry. 'What lessons are we missing?' she asks, her voice dry and husky.

Curls shrugs. 'Nothing important. The lower-fifth boys are so immature. A school full of boys and we end up with that lot. Now, if they'd let us join the sixth-form lessons, that would have been a different kettle of fish altogether.'

Alma allows herself a small, weak smile. Curls's familiarity and her refusal to change when everything else has been blown up and vaporised in a short conversation with Dr Guest is unexpectedly comforting. 'What time is it?' she asks. 'Have we missed lunch?'

Curls looks around. 'There's no clock in here,' she says. 'It's probably meant to confuse the Nazis if they invade. I hope they appreciate that the head will only see them if they have an appointment and even then they'll have to wait, just like everyone else.'

'Aren't you hungry?' Alma doesn't mind missing lunch – there's no sensation in her stomach and the thought of eating makes her faintly nauseous, but she knows that food is important to Curls.

'I'm starving. Let's go and find out what they've got to eat. We might just bump into the head boy. He's frightfully handsome.'

Alma stands up carefully. Her legs feel odd, as if they don't belong to her, and she's not quite sure if she can make them work. She pushes out her right foot. It moves. She puts weight on it and moves the left foot. She can still function, after all. Nothing has changed.

For a few seconds, she is swamped by a volcanic anger. Everything just carries on as normal. How can this be? It's not possible, not right. The world should be different, everyone in it should know that they can't continue in the same way now that her parents have died.

But she's still breathing, the air flows past her when she moves, the floor remains solid and real under her feet.

Curls touches her on the arm. 'Are you all right?'
Alma swallows and nods. She has no choice.

ii

At five fifteen p.m., Robert Gunner, twenty-seven years old, junior lecturer in mathematics at the newly established University College of the South-west, swings his right leg over his bicycle while it's still moving, balances both feet on one pedal and brakes gently. He is the warden of Mortimer Hall (named after the benefactor who bequeathed his ten-bedroom house and garden on the edge of the Streatham estate to the university in 1922). Robert glides to a halt in front of the two Home Guards who are standing at the end of Sidwell Street, preventing a small group of people from going down the road.
He finds cycling more manageable than walking as he has a pronounced limp, caused by a life-changing collision with a horse-drawn milk-delivery cart when he was a child. The milk had poured out over the road in vast quantities, much to the consternation of the unfortunate employee of the dairy and the expectant housewives, but, even worse, the horse had had to be put down. As a result of the carelessness of one milkman, a colossus of a carthorse was destroyed and an eight-year-old boy was compelled to spend months in bed. For Robert it had a bene-

ficial effect. Having nothing else to do all day, he devoured every book put before him, and embarked upon a lifelong love of learning, which culminated in a scholarship to the new University College of the South-west. (There was no beneficial result for the horse, but everyone who worked for the dairy was supplied with an unusually large quantity of unidentified meat and thrived for days on rich, tasty stews.)

Like most of the inhabitants of Exeter, he hasn't slept for more than thirty hours, and everything around him has started to glow with an unreal aura, as if he's sitting in a darkened room, watching a lit screen from a distance. He has stopped thinking about the possibility of sleep. Everyone else is working, so it would be unacceptable to complain or collapse.

Robert had been fire-watching in the early hours of 4 May, believing he and his students could be of use. They were stationed at one of the highest points of the university campus, scanning the night sky with binoculars, when they heard the aircraft flying in low along the Exe estuary. They recognised the sound of German aircraft, but thought they might be heading for Bristol. When the magnesium flares emerged from the darkness and started to drift down, bathing the city in a greenish glow, Robert sent two of his students down the hill to phone Headquarters. Then there was very little else they could do except watch the torrent of bombs that followed the flares. As they hit the ground and exploded, dazzling displays of light ripped the sky apart, and the hillside shuddered with the force of the impact.

Robert and his students were compelled to remain where they were, itching with frustration and impotence, having to accept that they could be of no use until the bombing ended. Only after the aircraft had left and the all-clear was sounded could they scramble down from their position and join the teams of volunteers manning the stirrup pumps as the centre of Exeter burned. At half past five, reinforcements arrived from towns as far away as Torquay to help fight the fires. At eight o'clock, Robert returned to Mortimer Hall, washed and shaved, and was in the undamaged lecture hall by nine o'clock. Three hours later, he received a phone call from the vice chancellor.

'Ah, Gunner. I'm told you have some spare beds at Mortimer Hall.'

'We're not at full capacity, sir,' he said cautiously.

'Been speaking to a Miss Cunningham-Smith, headmistress of Goldwyn's, the girls' school. Do you know it? Carstairs has three girls there. Anyway, they've been bombed out. Found places for most of their pupils but got a problem with the last four. Can Mortimer put them up?'

Robert hesitated. Children? At Mortimer? 'Yes, sir. Anything we can do to help.'

'Good man. Pick them up this evening. After four thirty. Go to Goldwyn's and they'll tell you where the girls are billeted for the time being. Let me see...' Robert can hear him shuffling papers on his desk. 'Yes, here it is. Alma Braithwaite, Jane Curley – well, you don't need the names. They'll tell you when you get there.'

Crossing Exeter on his way to Goldwyn's has

been more difficult than he anticipated and the bicycle is proving to be an impediment. While other people are able to pick their way through the piles of bricks, he has to find a more circuitous route.

'Sorry, mate,' says one of the soldiers stationed at the entrance to Sidwell Street. 'Can't go up here. Too dangerous.'

A shop front remains intact, its window in one piece, the poster on the wall above – **'FRY'S COCOA makes LESS MILK into MORE FOOD'** – as clean and normal as it was yesterday, while the entire building behind has collapsed into itself.

Robert looks past the Home Guards at ghosts of buildings that are only half there, leaning forward, hollow-eyed. A demolition squad has fastened a steel rope to one of them and, as he watches, the rope is pulled tight by a winching device. There's a sound of creaking, a scattering of bricks, a tense pause, then the entire wall gives up and crumbles to the ground. The small crowd watching at the end of the road cheers.

'Can I go through now?' asks Robert.

The sergeant shakes his head. 'Sorry, mate,' he says. 'No can do.'

Two young boys dart past them, nipping round the winch and heading down Sidwell Street, jumping over the jagged shards of broken glass, whizzing past the demolition squad.

'Oi!' yells the soldier, and races after them. 'You can't go down there!'

'Got your work cut out,' says Robert to the sergeant.

'Them're just lads,' he says. 'No skin off my nose. I'd be doing it meself if I was their age.' He looks too old for the job, his face drooping wearily, a victim, like everyone else, of lack of sleep. Dust has turned his skin a dirty, muddy grey, clogging the stubble on his chin and coating his helmet.

A woman in WVS uniform approaches them with two mugs of tea in her hands. 'Here you are, lads,' she says, in an educated voice. 'This should keep you going for a bit.'

The sergeant takes the mugs from her. He sips cautiously from one and breathes out, letting the steam escape from his mouth. 'Just the job, Mrs T. Did you find your lassies?'

She stares at him for a few seconds, her eyes dark and still. 'They were in the air-raid shelter on Sidwell Street,' she says, turning away.

'Oh,' he says. He offers the second mug of tea to his mate, who has just returned.

The woman walks back to the mobile canteen, upright, dignified, picking her way through the mounds of earth and rubble with meticulous care, as if she is concerned that she will damage her shoes.

'Direct hit on Sidwell Street shelter,' says the sergeant to Robert. 'No survivors. She left her little girls with a neighbour while she went out on a night shift. They was only ten and eight.'

Robert watches her, the way she talks to the other WVS workers, the way she behaves the same as everyone else, chatting, accepting a cigarette, lighting it with a cupped hand. He thinks of her still eyes and shudders.

'Husband's a colonel,' says the other soldier,

following Robert's gaze. 'Nice lady, not lah-de-dah at all.'

Robert checks his watch. It's getting late. They'll be wondering where he is. 'Any ideas how I can get to Goldwyn's School?' he asks.

'You got lassies too, then?'

Robert smiles. How old does he look? 'No, no. I just need to get there, that's all.'

The sergeant pushes his helmet back and scratches his head. 'They took a hit at Goldwyn's.'

'Yes, I know. I've been asked to help.'

'Dunno how you'll get there, mate. It's pretty bad all round these parts. What d'you reckon, Alf?'

His companion thinks for a while. 'Bampfylde Street's out, and Summerfield. You'll have to double back, go round the edges.'

'Thanks, lads.' Robert turns away, visualising a map of Exeter in his mind, trying to plan an alternative route. But whenever he tries to follow a normal pathway, it doesn't work. Nothing is where it should be. Without the familiar landmarks and the streets laid out as they used to be, he finds it difficult to know which direction to take. He feels as if he's wandering through a massive building site with no markers, no signs to indicate his current location.

An army clearance squad is standing round an empty safe that they've just prised open. It's the only object still intact in a desolate, crushed wilderness.

'Empty,' says one.

'It can't be,' says a man in a suit streaked with dust, who must be the owner. His voice is hoarse, horrified. 'I locked it myself, the night of the raid. There was money in there. A lot of money.'

'It's vaporised,' says the soldier. 'That's what heat does.'

Interesting, thinks Robert. I must remember to discuss that with someone from the physics department.

A well-dressed elderly couple are rooting through the rubble, picking up bricks by hand, moving them to one side as they search for their possessions. A small pile of salvaged objects is accumulating – one high-heeled shoe, a charred copy of *Grimm's Fairy Tales*, a necklace, two forks, a metal basin. Behind them, an entire bathroom has slid to the ground intact, the bath poised at the top of the sloping floor like a ship waiting to be launched.

Robert removes the cycle clips from his trousers and pushes the bicycle up the steep drive to Goldwyn's School. He stands at the top for a few moments and contemplates the front aspect, which has not been damaged. Edwardian, he guesses, *circa* 1908.

He leans the bicycle against the front wall, chains it to a drainpipe with the padlock and walks round the side of the building, wondering where he's supposed to go. He is immediately confronted by a now familiar scene of destruction. One building, the boarding house presumably, has been damaged beyond repair. Two walls are still upright, clinging together at one corner, solid enough but blackened from fire, while the other two sides have been swept away, as if by a giant wave. Identical fireplaces, one on every floor, are lined up above each other. The exposed rooms, cracked open for public display, glistening with water from the firemen's hoses, still bear traces of their former inhabitants: pink rosebuds on shreds of wallpaper; a bed tipped up on its end, the springs transformed into twisted sculptures of tangled wire; a small blue and white striped blouse, childlike, apparently perfect, suspended from a jagged. splinter of wood; piles of books tossed into a corner by the blast of the bomb, like a carefully constructed bonfire waiting for a match.

Several other buildings have been damaged. Bricks lie in vast piles, some fractured and crumpled, others sharp and clean, as if they've come directly from the factory, discarded by mistake. Rubble fills every space: pipes half melted by the heat; shattered roof tiles; distorted window frames; steel girders tossed aside as if they were weightless.

There are women everywhere, in loose trousers or knee-length skirts, solid lace-ups, their hair tied back in headscarves. They're clearing pathways, bringing some order to the chaos. They seem well organised. Some are shovelling bricks into wheelbarrows. Others remove the full barrows and take them away. Empty ones take their place without a break. Some women, in thick gloves, are moving bricks by hand or sweeping the cleared sections. They must have been there for most of the day and their efforts seem futile amid the mountains of destruction, but they don't look defeated. One woman is singing a Vera

Lynn song softly, under her breath, as she wields her broom.

Robert approaches one of the women nearest to him. 'Excuse me,' he says.

She pauses, leans on her broom and kneads her back with one hand. 'Who are you?'

He smiles nervously and offers her a hand. 'I'm Robert Gunner from the university. Can you tell me where I can find Miss Cunningham-Smith?'

She shakes his hand firmly. 'Cressida Davies, head of maths, currently engaged in the distinctly unmathematical task of demolition and disposal. Have you come to lend a hand?' She regards his suit and shoes with amusement. 'You'll need overalls.'

He flushes, conscious of his civilian clothes, his age. 'I'm sorry, I'm not really here to help clear up. We – the university – are supposed to be taking some of your pupils for a while, some boarders who need accommodation.'

She beams. 'Ah, of course. We've been expecting you. Miss Cunningham-Smith is over there, other side of Merrivale – the boarding house which is no more. You'll know her when you see her.'

'But how will I recognise her?'

Miss Davies regards him with a gentle smile. 'Believe me, you will know her.'

She makes him uncomfortable, as if he's said something foolish. 'Thank you for your help,' he says.

'My pleasure,' she says.

She stands and watches him as he walks off. He can sense her eyes on his back and knows exactly what she is thinking. Where's your uniform? Why aren't you out there with our boys? Men like you should be helping the war effort, fighting with the rest of them, not basking in the gilded, protected life of university.

He doesn't attempt to disguise his limp.

As he turns the corner, stepping awkwardly over piles of rubble that have not yet been touched, he discovers that Miss Davies is right. He knows immediately which one is Miss Cunningham-Smith. In the middle of all the devastation, surrounded by women who are picking out anything that might still be usable and putting it into empty pillowcases, stands a tall woman whose round, substantial knees are gleaming whitely in the gap between the top of her wellington boots and the bottom of a black skirt, rolled up at the waist. She is clearly in charge. She's holding a large list pinned to a board and keeps consulting it, continuously adding notes while simultaneously engaging in an earnest discussion with a fireman.

'The site's unstable,' he is saying. 'Your workers are going to have to move out.'

She contemplates the remains of Merrivale. 'It looks safe enough to me,' she says. 'What precisely are you suggesting will happen?'

'It will collapse,' he says, with a curiously pleased smile.

'It's managed to remain standing for the last twelve hours and I fail to see any reason why the situation should change.'

'I have orders to get everyone off the premises.'

'Go back and tell your superiors we're not going,' she says. 'There's far too much to salvage.

This is a boarding house, you know, not an empty building. We, the staff of Goldwyn's, are obliged to save as much as we possibly can for the sake of our girls. There are personal possessions here, equipment that we will need as soon as lessons resume tomorrow.'

The fireman looks appalled. 'Surely you're not expecting to carry on as usual.'

'Clearly not as usual,' she says, 'but it is my intention that we should fulfil our duty to teach as soon as humanly possible. The main building is still intact, and we'll rebuild at the first available opportunity, so I cannot countenance your suggestion that we abandon our school to scavengers. If an army demolition squad turns up, I am prepared to discuss their intentions with them. In the meantime, it's all hands on deck.'

'And what if the Nazi baby-killers come back?'

She fixes him with a penetrating stare. 'To which babies are we referring? Do you have evidence that they target babies deliberately? Can you be certain that no babies are killed in Allied raids?'

He backs away from her, bewildered. 'That's what the newspapers call them.'

'Do we infer from this that you are not capable of thinking for yourself?'

He takes a deep breath. 'I was just asking what you'd do if they bomb us again tonight.'

'I imagine we'll do what everyone will do, wherever they are, and take shelter. It seems unlikely that the Germans have specifically targeted Goldwyn's, and if your theory about the babies is correct – a matter about which I have severe misgivings – even "sausage-eating Nazis" could manage to work out that we wouldn't have babies on the premises. Nowhere is safer than anywhere else. Meanwhile, we have much work to do, so I suggest you allow me to carry on.'

The fireman withdraws. 'I'll be speaking to my boss,' he mutters.

Miss Cunningham-Smith doesn't even look in his direction. 'You do that,' she says. 'I'll be more than happy to discuss the situation with him.'

Robert hesitates, nervous now at the prospect of approaching. She is what one would describe as a formidable woman. She looks around as if she's searching for someone, sees Robert and fixes him with a steely glare.

'Who are you?' she says.

He steps forward. 'Miss Cunningham-Smith?' he says.

'Of course,' she says.

He puts out a hand. 'Robert Gunner,' he says. 'From the university.'

'Ah,' she says. 'Mr Gunner. Just the man. Why didn't you say so before?' She takes his hand in hers and squeezes, hard.

'I've come for the children,' he says, withdrawing his hand. He resists the temptation to rub it to restore the circulation.

'Children? Oh – you mean my girls.'

Robert nods vigorously. 'Yes, that's it. Your girls. Are they here?'

'Of course not. They've been billeted at Sherrard's for now – the boys' school up the road – but they can't stay there. It's unsatisfactory. I fear for their moral safety.' She pauses and looks at him for a few seconds, as if she expects him to challenge this statement. 'Now, I've placed most of my girls locally, but I am hoping you can help me with the last four. Delightful girls. Several of our boarders have returned home to their parents, a course of action of which I am not in favour. In my opinion, it is even more essential in these difficult times that they continue with their education. However, since this is not possible in all cases, we must concentrate on the ones who remain. We intend to keep the school running, of course, so they'll need to be able to travel to and from their accommodation easily and have access before and after the school day.'

'I think we can manage that,' says Robert. 'The university is not running at capacity, so there are rooms available in my hall of residence.'

'Oh,' she says. 'But you are the warden of a men's hall. Have I not made it clear that these are girls?'

'We have female staff at Mortimer's,' says Robert. 'I have arranged for Mrs Anderson, our housekeeper, to be on the premises to look after them from five o'clock in the afternoon until half past eight in the morning. And, of course, during the weekends.'

Miss Cunningham-Smith scrutinises his face for a few more seconds and Robert can feel himself blushing. Has he said something wrong? She reminds him of his primary-school headmistress, who had not been kind to him because, according to her, he was too clever for his own good. She didn't like clever children. They knew when she made mistakes, and she was not prepared to accept correction from a child under eleven.

But Miss Cunningham-Smith is better than that. She can read thoughts. 'I see that you are an honest man, Mr Gunner, so in the present circumstances, I will have to believe in your sincerity. Since the beginning of the war, we have all been obliged to place our trust in strangers and, by and large, that trust has not been misplaced. Curious, don't you think, that we should feel safer with someone merely because we speak the same language than we do with foreigners who might think like us but cannot express that common link in words?'

Robert avoids dealing with women if at all possible. Ever since his mother died, two years ago, he has found himself more and more confined to male company. When compelled to communicate with university staff or female students, he copes by treating them as if they are men. For some reason, when he'd agreed to take in four children, it had not occurred to him that this isolation might be a problem. It had not seemed relevant that they were girls.

'They're expecting you at Sherrard's. I can't let them know you're on your way, I'm afraid – the telephone lines are still down. I would appreciate it if you could inform them that we propose to recommence teaching tomorrow. Nine o'clock.'

Robert cannot see this as a realistic possibility.

Miss Cunningham-Smith anticipates his scepticism. 'There are plenty of undamaged rooms. We will be using the science laboratories for most classes – completely untouched by the Nazi baby-killers...' She pauses and an expression of amusement drifts across her face. 'It might be necessary to remove our specimens of dead frogs – we use them for dissecting, of course – I'm not sure that focusing on death is entirely appropriate in the circumstances. The Bunsen burners will cause a problem, but there will be strict rules governing their use. Our numbers are down, but most of the day girls will continue to attend, and the handful of boarders whose parents have had the wisdom to leave here will bring some normality to the situation. We are most grateful for your generous offer of help.'

By now, Robert is experiencing the heated discomfort of embarrassment. The decision to accept the children had not been his. It would not have occurred to him to refuse the vice chancellor's direction. 'We all have to do our bit for our country,' he says, hearing hypocrisy in his voice.

She studies him. 'We do indeed, Mr Gunner,' she says. 'But jargon is wearing. I expect people to express what they are thinking, not use the words they have been fed by others.'

'Of course,' says Robert. He finds himself in agreement with her, but wonders how easy it would be to converse without recourse to the many phrases and expressions that have been in everyday use for the last couple of years.

'Thank you for coming to our rescue,' she says, turning away. 'There is still a great deal to do here if we're to resume teaching by tomorrow. I trust you can find your own way to Sherrard's.'

By the time Robert reaches Sherrard's, it's well after six o'clock, much later than he'd intended.

There's no danger it will get dark before they arrive back at Mortimer Hall – they're in Double British Summer Time to save energy – but the diversions around the bombsites will delay them. He worries that it's getting late, that the children will be too tired and distressed to walk far.

He sits down in the small waiting room and rubs his left knee, which is aching more than usual. There's a cup of tea on the side table, next to an unopened copy of the *Express and Echo*, as if someone has come in here for a few moments of relaxation, only to be swept away almost immediately, summoned by an unknown emergency. He touches the side of the cup. It's stone cold. Whatever happened took place long before he set off on his journey around the city.

The door opens and a tall, skinny woman enters. Her black hair is scraped back, coiled at the nape of her neck, and she has very large feet, which are severely laced into brown leather army shoes. 'Mr Gunner,' she says, her voice high-pitched and penetrating, 'I am Gertrude Rupin, the girls' housemistress. I look after the boarders.'

Robert shakes hands. Her palm is uncomfortably clammy and she clings to him longer than is appropriate, as if the contact reassures her in some way. 'You appear to be temporarily out of a job, Miss Rupin,' he says.

'Difficult times,' she says. 'But we mustn't complain. No one was hurt and there's still plenty to do. The welfare of the boarders remains my priority. Do you have an air-raid shelter at your hall?'

'Yes, we've had one built at the bottom of the

garden. Not terribly comfortable, but it will do. Of course, many of our students are out fire-watching at night, so there'll be plenty of room.'

She ushers him through the open door. 'Please come with me, Mr Gunner. We have four girls from the lower fifth whom we should like to keep together. I shall introduce you to them immediately and then you can organise their transfer to your hall of residence. Sadly, one of them, Alma Braithwaite, has just lost her parents so she needs to be treated delicately. Do you have transport?'

Robert flushes, aware of the inadequacy of his provision. 'We'll be on foot, I'm afraid, although I may be able to carry some luggage on my pushbike.'

Her face becomes grave. 'I fear they have precious little to take with them. We all have nightwear, of course, since we were summoned from our beds by the sirens, and Sherrard's have been kind enough to provide shirts out of their small surplus. Some of our staff have brought in skirts for them, but of course there is a problem with sizing.' She smiles briefly. 'The wonder of the safety-pin, Mr Gunner. You would not believe the significance of its place in history.'

Robert is finding this conversation embarrassing. He's not sure how much information he requires.

'Miss Cunningham-Smith has managed to collect together our clothes coupons – luckily the school office wasn't damaged – and she intends to buy them all a change of underwear. Colson's will almost certainly have to sell off stock. The

Church Army Home at the back of them took a direct hit, you know, and they lost the top floor to fire – it's still burning, I gather – but the clothes they're wearing will have to do for the time being. We've asked the parents of day girls to see if they have any items of uniform they can spare, but that will take a while to organise. I imagine you will be able to provide towels, bedding, that sort of thing.'

'Yes, of course,' says Robert. 'We have adequate resources.'

He follows her into a room where several boys and girls are sitting quietly at their desks, doing prep. They stand as he and Miss Rupin enter the room.

'Sit down, sit down,' she says irritably, flapping her hands in the air as if she's been confronted with a swarm of midges. 'Girls, will you come with me, please?'

A girl with short straight hair and a large nose puts her hand up. 'What shall we do with our books, Miss Rupin?'

Miss Rupin stares at her, hovers indecisively, then shrugs. 'Leave them here, of course, Jane, since they're the property of Sherrard's. Now, come along, all of you. We've found you some alternative accommodation.'

The girls leave their desks and head towards the door.

'Jane has already made her presence known,' says Miss Rupin to Robert, as the girl with straight hair walks past them. Jane sweeps her gaze over him, her face impassive.

'This is Marjorie.' Marjorie is unusually tall,

towering over the others and her face is tanned, as if she spends a great deal of time out of doors. She smiles briefly and follows Jane out of the door.

'Alma.' This is the one whose parents have just died. She's dark, with a long, serious face and a nose that is slightly off-centre. She walks past him without looking up.

'And Natalie.' Natalie is strikingly attractive, with bushy red hair. She studies Robert as she passes him, narrows her eyes, then winks at him. He stares at her in astonishment, but she continues walking and doesn't look back.

Robert finds himself gripped by a mounting sense of horror. These are not the children he had envisaged. They are young ladies, almost women, their developing bodies threatening to burst out of the inadequate shirts that have been provided by the boys' school. Their busts protrude alarmingly. The curves of their hips sweep out from their ill-fitting skirts – held up by safety-pins – roundly and provocatively, while their long, well-shaped legs defy the childhood image engendered by their ankle socks and sandals. There's something about them that is extremely alarming: the glow of nascent womanhood; a warm, ripe scent that reminds him of something, something he can't put his finger on – a certainty about their movements, as if they already know the secrets of their bodies. It's a world of which he is entirely ignorant.

Can he really take them back to Mortimer Hall? It's such a correct establishment, where he has worked hard to cultivate the hushed, austere atmosphere of academia, where he expects his young men to behave with impeccable manners. They eat meals in near-silence, breaking it only to examine some philosophical subject with cautious, disciplined thought. How can he release these girls into his precious intellectual world? What chaos might they unleash on the young men in his care?

Before leaving the form room, he looks back at the boys at their desks. He can see glances passing between them now that they think they're unobserved, knowing grins, eyes rolling, excitement crackling between them like static electricity. They've already been contaminated by these young women. He has no doubt that they were once as calm and disciplined as the students in his hall, and now there is something restless about them, a tension that's bouncing around the room, stuttering and flashing through the spaces left by the girls. His face burns and he becomes aware of the sensation of sweat trickling down his back, soaking into his shirt.

It's becoming increasingly clear that he has made a serious error of judgement in agreeing to take in these girls at Mortimer.

iii

Miss Rupin sends Alma, Curls, Giraffe and Natalie upstairs with spare gas-mask bags. She's told them that they're about to be moved elsewhere and they must pack as quickly as possible. Alma watches her friends gathering up their meagre possessions, debating where they're going, and feels she's lost her connection with them. She doesn't care what happens next. One place is the same as any other.

A low-wattage light illuminates the dormitory, adding to the unreal quality of the day, as if none of this is actually happening and she's viewing a film through a flawed, scratched lens. Sounds are muffled, voices sometimes confused and indistinct. She tries to shift herself back to a time before the war, when homework was the only thing worth worrying about, when discussions were about who was playing in the school hockey team, who had snitched on the sixth-former who'd had a secret rendezvous with a boy from Sherrard's, whether boiled cabbage was better or worse than lumpy swede. She's half expecting to wake up and find that everything has been a dream.

'Why do we have to leave?' says Natalie, attempting to tie back her unruly red hair with a strip of white ribbon. Nobody has supplied them with hairbrushes. 'I like being at Sherrard's.'

'You just like the boys,' says Giraffe.

'And you don't?' says Natalie. 'I hope we don't have to share beds where we're going. Your legs are too long.'

'Who do you think he is,' says Curls, 'the mysterious stranger with the limp?'

'Goodness only knows,' says Natalie.

'Oh, come on,' says Giraffe. 'No one's going to tell us what's going on. It's a case of "Keep mum and do as you're told." Same as always.'

Mr Gunner had introduced himself, but not offered much explanation. 'I've been asked to take you to a safe place until your – Miss Cunningham-Smith – can arrange for you to return to Goldwyn's. I need you to collect all your – um – belongings as quickly as possible. It's quite a long walk. Come back down as soon as you're ready.' His voice had faltered, he'd mumbled and stuttered, and he'd been unable to look any of them in the eye.

'He seems nice,' says Alma, trying to pull herself into the present. She felt drawn to the man with the awkward limp, identifying with his awkwardness, the burning heat of embarrassment that radiated from him. She'd liked his little speech, the neutral, stilted tone. He reminded her of herself, nervous, uncertain of his place in the world, but trying very hard.

Curls shrugs. 'Well, no doubt we'll soon find out.'

Miss Rupin's voice calls along the corridor, shrill and urgent: 'Do hurry up, girls. There's a long way to go.'

They've packed their nighties, and the toothbrushes and flannels provided by the Sherrard's boys. There isn't much else.

Curls has some bent forks and spoons that she picked up when they first emerged from the bomb shelter. 'Part of history,' she'd said. 'I'll show them to my children when I'm telling them the story of the war.'

Alma remembers the souvenirs her father had collected from the First World War: bomb casings he'd brought back from the front; a small German leather wallet with nothing in it except a train ticket; a Tommy's helmet, blackened and battered. He'd shown them to Alma only once, and she'd understood that they were very important to him. 'It should never have happened,' he said. 'People shouldn't fight. They should talk.' His work was essential to the war effort so he hadn't been required to fight this time, but he'd told Alma he wouldn't have gone even if he was conscripted. 'I'm dedicated to saving lives,' he'd said. 'I'd rather go to prison, even be executed, than have to kill another man.'

Alma used to be impressed by this, but she's not sure if she agrees with him any more. The idea of getting behind a machine gun, lining it up on the air crew who had come over Exeter to kill her parents, and raking them with bullets appeals to her. She's seen this kind of avenging bravado in films. She knows how it works.

'Make sure you've got your masterpiece, Nat,' says Curls.

'Of course,' says Natalie. She's been jotting down their experiences. She says she'll have it published when she's older and the war's over.

She'd read out extracts to them during afternoon break:

'The bombs rained down like hailstones, deliberately targeting Goldwyn's School as the pearl of Devon, the repository of the most elegant, most sophisticated, most delectable schoolgirls in the whole of Britain. These girls remain undaunted, determined to stand up to the bullying of the Nazi war machine. While the rest of Exeter burned, they sat in their bomb shelter and sang, embodying the spirit of Gracie Fields, emulating the brave survivors of the London blitz, refusing to be bowed. Thus are born true British citizens, heralds of a brighter dawn, a future world where oppression is defeated for ever.'

The girls waited nervously to see how the others would react.

'I like the bit about standing up to the Nazi war machine,' said Curls at last.

'It's a bit ... flowery,' said Giraffe.

'You have to write like that,' said Natalie. 'It's literature, so you can't just make it into an adventure story. Can you imagine Byron saying "The Germans bombed Goldwyn's. We hid in a bomb shelter"? You have to find poetic words, get the atmosphere right.'

'It's not an adventure story anyway,' said Curls. 'It's real.'

The four girls hoist the canvas bags on to their shoulders, put on their outdoor shoes and walk down the stairs to meet Mr Gunner, who's waiting for them outside the front door with Miss Rupin. Most of the other boarders have already left in twos or threes, some to another girls' boarding school, others to private homes. The lower-fifths are almost the last to go.

'Come along now, girls,' says Miss Rupin, bustling, officious. 'Mr Gunner is in a hurry. He's taking you to Mortimer Hall – it's a university hall of residence, where the students usually stay. I'm expecting you to behave like well-brought-up young ladies. Be polite, gracious and co-operative, and remember that Miss Cunningham-Smith will find out if your behaviour has not been exemplary. Lessons will resume at Goldwyn's tomorrow after an assembly of thanksgiving at nine o'clock.'

'What are we giving thanks for?' asks Curls.

Miss Rupin glares at her. 'Our salvation,' she says. 'Nobody was hurt in the bombing, and we must show gratitude for our lives, even if buildings and possessions have been destroyed.'

'How can you say that?' says Curls. 'What about all the other people who've died? What about Alma's parents?'

Miss Rupin blinks rapidly, then turns to Alma. 'Of course, Alma, our thoughts are with you,' she says, in a gentler voice.

Alma stares at her, confused by the sudden attention. What's the point of a service of thanksgiving? Her parents have gone. They'll never come back. That's all that matters. Desolation settles on her shoulders, presses down on her head, forces her to keep her mouth closed.

Somewhere, underneath the weight of it, there's a small thought that it's a terrible mistake, that her parents are waiting somewhere for the moment when they can come and find her, calm in their belief that all will be well.

They walk in pairs, Alma and Curls together, Giraffe with Natalie, while Mr Gunner leads the way, pushing his bicycle. He occasionally puts both feet on one of the pedals, freewheels down a hill and waits for them to catch up at the bottom. He's offered to let them have a ride, but they refuse, anxious to stay together.

Everyone they pass seems to be possessed by a nervous urgency, walking as fast as possible, glancing nervously at the sky, as if they're expecting the return of the bombers at any moment.

Alma also peers upwards every now and again, searching for black specks in the distance, seeing shapes that disappear and rearrange themselves every time she blinks, her eyes watering with the brightness. 'What time does it get dark?' she asks.

'Not for ages yet,' says Giraffe.

'There's no need to worry,' says Curls. 'The Luftwaffe are hardly likely to be flying in broad daylight. They'd be shot out of the sky long before they reached us.'

Two small boys race past them, fast and nimble as they dodge through the collapsed buildings, jumping over the piles of bricks, gas-mask bags clutched tightly in their hands. A policeman follows a short distance behind, blowing his whistle. His boots strike the ground heavily, the sound ringing out hard and metallic. 'Come back here, you little varmints!' he yells, as he removes the whistle from between his lips.

But they're faster than he is, nipping between mountains of bricks and clambering over fallen masonry, as if they're familiar with the layout, as if it's always been like this. They look back to check the whereabouts of the policeman and tumble straight into the arms of a large airman in a blue-grey uniform with a dark blue cap. 'Gotcha!' he says. He picks them up, tucks one under each arm, and carries them back to the policeman. The boys squirm and struggle to get away. 'OK, lads,' the policeman says. 'You'll be coming with me now.' He turns to the girls and Mr Gunner, who have joined the group of onlookers. 'Looters,' he says. 'Think they can take advantage of other people's suffering.'

'They're only children,' says Mr Gunner.

The boys are not very old and their knees, poking out from their ragged trousers, are thin and bony, marked with scars, cuts and grazes.

'That's right, mister,' one says to Mr Gunner. 'Our family's starving, bombed out, nowhere to go. We was just trying to help–' He squeals as the policeman cuffs him on the ear.

'See?' says the boy to the onlookers. 'He don't care if we live or die. It's all right for you lot. You've got things. We ain't got nothing.'

'That'll do, Johnny,' says the policeman. 'These folks here aren't going to believe all your stories.' He addresses Mr Gunner directly, recognising some authority in him. 'I know the family. Generations of petty crooks. And you don't want to believe this homelessness lark. Their house is still in one piece, over by Pennsylvania – you know the area? – when the homes of more decent folk have been flattened.' He puts a hand on the shoulder of each boy. 'It's down to the station with you two to see what you've got in those bags.' They march away.

'Who do you believe?' asks Natalie.

'I'm not sure,' says Curls.

'You mustn't concern yourselves,' says Mr Gunner. 'They can't prosecute the boys and they have to guard against looters – a lot of people's property is just lying around in the streets. It needs to be protected.'

The airman who caught the boys grins at everyone. 'Keep city safe,' he says, in a strong accent and then he starts to laugh, his shoulders bouncing up and down. He shakes hands vigorously with Mr Gunner, then works his way through the watching crowd, including the girls. 'Lieutenant Kowalski,' he says. 'I Polish. From the base at Exeter airfield.'

'Hello,' says Natalie, looking up at him through her eyelashes.

'Come, ladies,' he says. 'I escort you to your destination, save you from evil thieves.'

The girls watch Mr Gunner, wondering how he will react to this interference, but he doesn't seem to mind. 'Thank you,' he says. 'We're later than I'd intended. It's so difficult to get round the city.'

'*Tak*,' says the airman. 'These Germans, they are dratted nuisance, heh?' He slots easily into place alongside Mr Gunner, occasionally taking the handlebars of the bicycle and lifting it up to negotiate awkward piles of rubble.

'Over here!' shouts a man, his voice shrill and harsh in the unnatural stillness that envelops the whole area. The girls and Mr Gunner stop to see what's going on. Two Home Guards who have been digging through a mound of shattered bricks and broken glass put down their shovels and start lifting debris more carefully. A limp hand is visible, attached to an arm encased in a yellow flowery sleeve. It's a dressing-gown, pretty and lacy, presumably thrown on hastily when the sirens started, the buttons fastened in the light from the falling incendiaries.

'She's moving!' shouts a woman, rushing over to help. 'She's alive.'

Several others join in the rescue, throwing bricks out of the way, until one of the soldiers is able to bend down and pull her out. She's an old woman. Some of her thin grey hair is still wound into curlers while the rest hangs down in long wispy tendrils. Her face is black and swollen, and it's only the curlers and the dressing-gown that identify her as female. As the men ease her out, it becomes apparent that she has only one leg. She's very, very dead.

'Mother!' shouts a woman, who is rushing up behind them. 'No!'

'Stand back,' orders one of the soldiers.

But the woman throws herself on to her mother, wailing with grief.

'I'm sorry,' says the other soldier. 'She can't have known what hit her.'

'But her hand moved,' says a man next to the girls. 'She waved.'

The soldier shakes his head. 'I've seen it before. You think they're waving, but they aren't. As you shift all the rubble on top of them, their position changes and it just looks as if they're moving.'

Natalie starts to cry.

'Come along,' says Mr Gunner. 'We must carry on. We're only halfway there.'

They follow him away, glancing back as they leave the men and the body and the daughter. They don't talk for a while.

I've never seen a dead body before, thinks Alma. She stops abruptly, struck by a thought.

'Come on,' says Curls. 'What's the matter?'

'They're still digging people out,' says Alma. 'They must be expecting some of them to be alive.' Maybe there's something to hope for, after all. She shouldn't have been so quick to accept Dr Guest's explanation. He might not know as much as he thinks he does. Some of the weight that's been clamped tightly over her shoulders for the last few hours eases a little.

They start walking again, rushing to catch up with the others. Mr Gunner has turned round, his face creased with concern. 'Please hurry, girls,' he says. 'We really shouldn't be out so late.'

'It's all right for him,' mutters Curls. 'He can just hop on his bike any time he wants to.'

'To be fair,' says Giraffe, 'he's offered to let us have a go. And he does wait for us.'

His limp is more pronounced the further they walk, but he keeps going, leaning heavily on the bicycle, lurching from side to side, only once in a while allowing Lieutenant Kowalski to help.

'Do you think he was injured in the war?' asks Natalie.

'Maybe the First World War,' says Giraffe.

'He'd have to be a soldier with a name like Gunner,' says Curls. 'Army. Artillery, don't you think?'

Natalie nods. 'It makes sense.'

Alma pulls at Curls's arm. 'You've got to help me,' she whispers urgently. 'I have to get to the hospital.'

Curls stares at her. 'Why? Are you injured?'

'I've just realised. My parents – they might not be dead. They could be buried underneath all the bricks, waiting to be rescued. Like that woman.'

'She was dead.'

'But she might not have been.'

'Surely they'd contact you if they were alive, wouldn't they?'

'I know that, but I have to go and find out. I want to see for myself how much they've cleared, how much is left. I need to be sure.'

Curls looks around, as if she's assessing their chance of escape. 'It could be really difficult to go now. We'd be in no end of trouble. Tomorrow, perhaps, after school. No one would be checking up on us then.'

'No,' says Alma. 'I can't wait until tomorrow.'

'But you don't know the way.'

'Yes, I do. I know where we are. It's only about ten minutes to the hospital from here. You could pretend I'm still with you, divert Mr Gunner and the lieutenant if they notice I'm missing.'

'Don't be ridiculous,' says Curls. 'I'm not going to let you go without me. If you're going, I'm coming too.'

Alma tries to smile at her.

Curls taps Giraffe on the shoulder. 'Alma and I are going to take a diversion,' she says. 'You have to carry on without us and pretend not to notice.'

'*What?*' says Natalie.

'Alma needs to know what actually happened to her parents. We're close to the hospital, so now would be a good time to go.'

'Wouldn't it be better if we all went?' says Giraffe. 'We could ask Mr Gunner.'

Alma doesn't want them all to come. She's trying to cling to the surge of hope that's just hit her, but a tiny seed of doubt has already drifted in, threatening to undermine that moment of optimism. If she's wrong, she doesn't want anyone to witness her distress.

'He'd never agree to it,' says Curls.

'But what on earth can we tell them when you've disappeared?' asks Natalie.

'Say we had to go back for something,' says Curls.

'There isn't anything to go back for,' says Giraffe. 'It's all been destroyed.'

'They don't know that, do they?' says Curls. 'Unless you tell them.'

Giraffe lowers her eyes. 'No,' she mumbles. 'I wouldn't do that.'

'I can't believe you'd think we'd betray you,' says Natalie. 'We're your friends.'

'I think you'd be best to say you don't know where we've gone,' says Curls. 'Then you're not implicated and it will buy us extra time.'

'Do you know the way?' says Giraffe.

Alma nods. 'I've been to the hospital loads of times on my own.'

'No, I mean to Mortimer Hall. Where we're going now.'

Alma looks at Curls. She hasn't considered this.

'How difficult can it be to find?' says Curls.

'We'll head for the university and ask for Mortimer Hall. Someone must know where it is.'

'Please don't take too long,' says Natalie. 'You'll get into frightful trouble.'

'We will anyway,' says Curls. 'Time won't make much difference.'

'I hope everything goes all right,' says Giraffe.

Mr Gunner and Lieutenant Kowalski are engaged in a complicated discussion. Giraffe and Natalie speed up and narrow the distance between them. Alma veers off to the side and starts to run. She can hear Curls's feet behind her, quiet and intense.

Part Four

i

5 September 1963

Alma sits at her desk in the clean, silent, well-ordered form room, waiting for the nine o'clock bell, and reads through the list of upper-third girls. It's the first day of the autumn term. Two-thirds of the girls will be new, while the rest are coming up from the junior section, but they will all be overwhelmed by senior school. Half of them will be in Alma's form and the other half will go to Upper Third P (Parallel), with Cressida Davies as their form mistress. Parents have been asked to drop their daughters off in the gym, which is easy to find, and the girls will be accompanied from there to the school hall for the first Assembly, after which Alma and Cressida will lead them back to their form rooms.

This is Alma's first year as a form mistress, an appointment made by Miss Cunningham-Smith at the end of last term. It's been accepted by Miss Yates, although Alma suspects that it's more a matter of convenience than a sign of approval.

In normal times, she would have examined the list of pupils long before now and familiarised herself with the names of the eleven-year-old girls who are about to become her responsibility. Miss Cunningham-Smith used to spend most of

August studying photographs of all the new girls, memorising them as if she was expecting to be examined on them at the beginning of term. Once she'd committed a girl's name and face to her memory, she never forgot her. Mind like a razor.

Alma's attention wanders and she stops reading the list. This term will never be normal. She's not at all sure how long she will be able to tolerate the new regime.

She gets to her feet and walks up and down between the desks, making sure that each row is exactly the same distance from the next. She examines the blackboard and flicks away stray flecks of dust, satisfied by its smooth, untouched surface. Twenty-five yellow pencils are lined up in front of her, HB, all the same length, pointed and pristine. To the left of the pencils are twenty-five unused rubbers, fresh from the box, constructed into a white, gleaming wall and on the other side, a pile of red exercise books, their immaculately cut edges clean and aromatic, their covers stamped with the school crest and motto.

Why is she so jittery? Is it the prospect of being a form mistress and her inevitable rise in importance, or is she taking on the anxiety of the new intake? Is it the presence of Miss Yates and the certainty that things are going to change?

She reads through the list of girls again, making a serious effort to concentrate.

Her mouth goes dry.

Philippa Gunner.

It's a trick of the light, a warning that it's time to have her eyesight checked.

The name is very clear on the list. Why has she not seen it before?

He'd have to be a soldier with a name like Gunner. Curls, clear and certain, standing just behind Alma's shoulder, her voice travelling through the twenty-one years from then to now, unchanged. *Artillery, don't you think?*

Philippa Gunner. Ninth on the list, immediately after Henrietta Garnet and just before Naomi Isherwood.

Alma's mind slips backwards to the other Exeter, the ruined city, which no longer exists. After the war, architects and designers developed a grand plan, which was admired by everyone until it was contracted by the inevitable reduction in budget. Everything has changed: a larger Colson's and the introduction of an escalator in Exeter for the first time; Bedford Circus redesigned and Princesshay created in some of the empty space left by the bombing; a new Bobby's being built on the corner of Sidwell Street and High Street. In twenty-one years, the city has transformed itself. It has shovelled away the blackened shells of the past, the remnants of homes and businesses, the acres of destruction.

Is Philippa Gunner the daughter of Robert Gunner?

Alma's right foot starts to jiggle with a mind of its own.

She was sure Mr Gunner had left the area. Whenever she'd met anyone from the university, they hadn't seemed to know him. Even the university librarian she'd sat next to at a concert, who was on first-name terms with most of the lecturers, hadn't heard of him. It's true that she worked in the arts faculty, but she'd said she would know. Maybe he's moved away and come back. Or maybe the librarian wasn't as knowledgeable as she claimed.

And now he has a wife and at least one child.

The school bell rings.

It's not unreasonable that he's married. There were so many women, grown-up women, left over after the war, abandoned and spare, ready to run the moment any man raised his eyes and started looking. Curls would no longer have seemed important. He must have been snapped up and spoken for even before Alma had had time to become an adult.

Ha! says Curls, in her ear. *Nobody ever does what you expect.* Music is echoing around the room. Schubert. The first Impromptu.

Cressida Davies puts her head round the door. She's older than Alma, an unmarried leftover from the First World War, grey-haired, five foot one, all leathery skin and sharp, jutting bones. 'The bell's gone,' she says. 'Didn't you hear it?' She's always been generous with her time, having known Alma as a pupil and seen her return as a teacher. She's a formidable force in the school, her presence always stable and predictable, living proof that the years under Miss Cunningham-Smith were good, settled years.

'Yes,' says Alma, leaping up quicker than she intended, anxious to show that she's functioning normally. She bangs her knee on the side of the desk.

'Ouch!' says Cressida.

'Oh, it's nothing,' says Alma. 'Absolutely nothing.'

The bell has stopped ringing and a vibration drums through the building, set off by the movement of hundreds of feet. Girls are pouring out of their form rooms, fresh in their new indoor shoes, clean and shining, probably for the only time during the school year, and filing into the hall.

Miss Yates's instructions to her staff have been very precise. She's asked them to assemble by the upstairs banisters overlooking the stairwell. From there, they can look down to where the three flights of stairs – two from above, a single wider one from below – meet in the middle, at the entrance to the hall. Most of the other teachers are present when Alma and Cressida arrive, neat in their newly dry-cleaned suits, hemlines exactly on the knee. Miss Yates is wearing a mortarboard and black gown over her clothes.

She's clearly making a point, since most of the staff have teaching diplomas rather than degrees. Alma composes her face to demonstrate her lack of interest.

'Which university did you attend, Miss Yates?' asks Maxine Wright.

Typical Maxine, Alma thinks. Already trying to make an impression.

Miss Yates hesitates before answering. 'St Anne's, Oxford,' she says eventually. 'Can we pair up, please, ladies, ready for our entrance?'

Alma senses something reluctant about her reply, not connected to her need to get the staff organised. Nothing obvious, just a small pause, as if she had to think carefully before speaking.

They watch the girls swarm into the hall, guided by Edith Smalley, games. Her assistant, Catherine Edgington, brings the new upper-thirds, all of whom appear nervous and bewildered, across from the gym. She herds them ahead of her, settling them in front of the platform. Every other teacher is with Miss Yates, at the top of the stairs.

The doors to the hall swing shut.

'Are we ready, ladies?' says Miss Yates.

There are several silent nods.

'Very well, follow me. In twos, if you please.'

She steps forward and descends the stairs, followed by her staff in orderly pairs. An adult crocodile, capable of showing teeth, but docile and obedient for the time being, jaw firmly closed.

Miss Yates pauses at the doors, then pushes them open dramatically.

Miss Smalley's sharp, authoritative voice from inside the hall: 'Quiet, please.'

The shuffling and murmuring stop as they process down the centre. They walk with their heads up, eyes to the front, and ignore the girls who've turned round to watch their entrance.

It's impressive. There's dignity to the occasion, a solemnity that's pleasing. Quite a good idea, after all. But will it last? It's all well and good for the first day of term, but will they continue to command all this silence and respect?

They climb the steps to the platform, Miss Yates in the lead, and the staff arrange themselves in front of the semi-circle of chairs set out behind her.

When everyone is settled, Miss Yates leans forward over the rostrum. 'Good morning, girls,' she says, in a clear voice. 'I'm your new headmistress, Miss Yates. I've not yet had the opportunity to meet many of you, but I'm hoping we will rectify this in the next few days and weeks. All of you will be aware of the sad and unexpected death of your former headmistress, Miss Cunningham-Smith, last term and I know you will be joining me in my sorrow at her abrupt departure from this world.'

You didn't know her, thinks Alma. What gives you the right to express grief?

'Now, we have some practical matters to discuss, so please be seated.' There's a rumbling and shuffling of shoes, a rustling of skirts, indistinct whispers. The older girls, from the lower fifth upwards, have chairs at the back of the hall. The younger ones sit on the floor.

'Before we start our morning service, I would like to draw attention to your conduct on the school premises. I am introducing a new rule concerning the manner in which you walk along the corridors. In future, running – for any reason whatsoever – is forbidden. You must walk at all times. Anyone who disobeys this rule, anyone, without exception,' she seems to be looking directly at certain girls, and the teachers on the platform follow her gaze with interest, wondering if she has already encountered some of the more difficult girls, 'will be placed in detention after school. It is essential that your parents know about this possibility and that you are prepared to remain here for an extra hour. You may well consider that you will never find it necessary – and I sincerely hope you are all thinking this – but I want you to go home and discuss the alternative forms of transport you would require, should you find yourselves in this position. I will not accept any excuse, whether you have a piano lesson or you are playing Titania in *A Midsummer Night's Dream* or you have an appointment with Her Majesty the Queen.' There's a cautious ripple of laughter from the back that dies away before it has the chance to reach the younger girls. 'I trust I make myself clear.'

Every girl in the hall has her eyes on Miss Yates's face. The silence has a tangible quality. It's heavy with fear of the unknown. Miss Yates is unfamiliar to everyone present, and even the older girls appear to be affected by a sense of unease.

'There will also be a change in the way you negotiate the main staircase. I wish to introduce a one-way system. If you are at the bottom of the stairs and you want to come up, start on the left and keep to that side, remaining on the left once you have reached the middle landing and carry on up. If you are at the top, take the right stairs down and then the left side of the lower flight.'

Several of the girls have lifted their hands and are moving them from right to left. They can't work it out, thinks Alma. It's going to cause chaos.

'Finally, there will be no talking as you transfer from one form room to the next.'

There are shocked exchanges of glances between some of the older girls. They've been accustomed to a more relaxed regime.

She's not going to be able to enforce this, thinks Alma, with a growing sense of pleasure. She'll have a mutiny on her hands. She can hardly expel them all.

'You may be feeling that these rules are unnecessarily harsh,' says Miss Yates, in a softer tone. 'But you must always remember that I act in your best interests. I have confidence in you all and I must ask you to have confidence in me.' She takes time to look around at their faces before continuing.

Alma stops listening. She finds herself scrutinising the faces of the upper-thirds at the front, searching for familiar features, a fleeting expression she might recognise. What would Robert Gunner's daughter look like? Would she have his curly dark hair, those almost black eyes that wavered and shifted to the side when he was faced with anything remotely confrontational?

Curls is playing again, in this hall before the bombing, on the old upright piano that has now been replaced by a baby grand. A Chopin Prelude as the girls file in for Assembly.

The new girls look so young, diminished by the older pupils, stiff and uncomfortable in blazers that have been bought to last. Those who have come up from the lower third are wearing blouses with limp collars, ties faded from washing, jumpers with threads pulled, but they're still overawed by their surroundings. They've been protected by the smallness, the cosiness, of the lower school. Now they've joined the senior school, they're frightened.

Which one is Philippa Gunner? One of the two

girls at the end of the second row perhaps, or the one sitting upright with her eyes rigidly fixed on Miss Yates? Maybe it's the girl gazing round the hall, not concentrating, reading the names of past head girls that are carved on the wood panels that line the walls.

Which one? Surely she should be able to recognise her.

'Please stand up,' says Miss Yates.

Everyone, including the staff, stands.

'I'm delighted to see you all this morning, so well dressed, so cheerful, and I hope you appreciate the challenge of this new term as much as I do. The sun is shining, the sky is blue, and we are fortunate in this country to have plenty to eat. Raise your hands if you believe that it is good to be alive.'

What is this? A test to see how much authority she has? The staff eye each other nervously and come to a tacit agreement that it would be beneath their dignity to respond to this direction.

But nearly every girl – the few exceptions are the over-dramatic sulky teenagers who make themselves uncooperative as a matter of principle – raises her arm.

'I am pleased to see that the verdict is almost unanimous.' Miss Yates's voice is strong and clear, the voice of someone who expects to inspire her listeners. Alma studies her back and wonders if she has grown a moustache since her entry into the hall. Black, small, with straight edges. Surely, she is only a short step from asking the girls to raise their voices in unison.

'*Heil*, Miss Yates.'

ii

Pippa bursts through the front door after her first day at Goldwyn's. 'I'm back!' she shouts.

Robert Gunner is in the glory-hole. He keeps his tools there, in the cupboards with ill-fitting doors and on the shelves above the stained, battered workbench. It's a space where he's always contented. Nobody knew the glory-hole was there until he knocked through a wooden panel one day and found it, a secret room full of broken dolls and random pieces of jigsaws from long ago. He told everyone it was a mistake when the wall panel caved in, that he hadn't meant to damage anything, just put in a few nails to hang up pictures, but he had suspected the existence of a secret room for some time. He'd measured the walls, drawn a diagram of the ground floor of the house and concluded that there were several missing square yards. Now it is crammed with his carpentry projects and everything he didn't want to throw away.

'In here!' he calls.

Miss Dodds is in the kitchen on the other side of the partition wall, preparing the evening meal. He can hear her talking to Pippa.

'Hello, dear,' says Miss Dodds. 'How was your first day?' Her voice is dry and worn, as if she's squeezed out all of her saliva earlier in the day and hasn't been able to refill her supplies.

'It was OK, actually,' says Pippa.

Miss Dodds comes in to help with the housework – or, more accurately, do the housework, since no one else seems to be capable of much – and cook the evening meal. She's been around as long as they've lived here, even when Grace was still alive. Small and dressed in black, always suntanned, even in the middle of winter, hardly taller than Pippa, she's not exactly a mother-substitute, but at least she's comfortingly present when she's needed, a woman who can do the useful things that women do to keep a household running.

'School was brilliant,' says Pippa. 'I need brown paper, or wallpaper or both. Any idea if we've got any?'

'Whatever for?'

'It's my homework. We have to cover our books.'

'Why don't you ask your father? He'll know if we've got any.'

'Hello, Daddy,' says Pippa, appearing in the entrance to the glory-hole, stuffing a Garibaldi biscuit into her mouth and chewing rapidly.

'Try over there,' says Robert. 'I think there's some old wallpaper you can use.'

Pippa jiggles one of the rickety drawers until it opens and pulls out a pile of assorted scraps. 'Hey!' she says. 'Look at this – my bedroom paper. It's so clean.'

Robert smiles. 'Wallpaper weathers when it's been up for years.'

'Maybe it's time for a change. We could make it all new again.'

'Maybe.' Robert remembers how he and Grace

tackled the house when they first moved in, the exhaustion of the decorating, the missed meals, the bone-aching collapse into their bed every night. 'How was school?'

'OK.' Pippa stuffs another biscuit into her mouth and chews thoughtfully. 'My form mistress is a bit odd. She's really thin and ancient and does her hair in a bun – can you believe it? She's got a funny soft voice so we couldn't hear what she was saying a lot of the time.'

'I'm sure she's perfectly normal,' says Robert.

'She kept looking at me as if she wanted to say something, then changed her mind. I thought there must be something wrong with my uniform or I was sitting at the wrong desk.'

'You were probably imagining it.'

'No, even Roberta who was sitting next to me noticed. She thought I must be in the wrong form room.'

'Did you catch the train all right? I finished early this afternoon and needed to get back. I thought you were old enough to manage on your own.'

'Easy,' says Pippa. 'Piece of cake.'

'Well done,' he says. 'I don't suppose there's a pot of tea, Mrs Dodds?' he calls.

They can hear her grunt with irritation. 'The kettle's just about to boil.'

'And how were things without Miss Cunningham-Smith?' asks Robert.

Pippa stops on her way back to the kitchen and turns to stare at him. 'Come on, Daddy, that's a daft question. I only met her once. How would I know what it's like without her when I don't know what it was like with her?'

'No, of course not,' he says. 'It's just hard to believe she's not there.'

'Miss Braithwaite said the same thing. It must be something to do with your age.'

He looks up at her with amazement. 'Miss Braithwaite? Alma Braithwaite?'

'She's my form mistress. She's hardly going to tell us her first name, is she? We're the pupils, she's the teacher.'

'Well, how extraordinary,' he says. 'I wouldn't have expected her to be still there.'

'Don't tell me. You used to know her too.'

Robert nods thoughtfully. 'She was only a girl then.'

iii

Miss Yates leans over the banisters on the first floor and watches her pupils as they walk up and down the main stairs in silence, neat files of girls, subdued, calm and controlled. The spectacle creates an intense satisfaction in her. She has given instructions and been obeyed. Within three weeks, she has transformed disorder into discipline.

She fixes her gaze on a girl – Beatrice Willoughby, she thinks – who is turning to talk to someone behind her. The friend senses they're being watched. She glances up, flushes and shakes her head briefly at Beatrice. Beatrice also looks up, meets Miss Yates's eyes for a second, then continues on her way. A touch of defiance?

She'll have to be monitored.

'Miss Yates!'

She turns. Alma Braithwaite is standing behind her. 'Ah, Miss Braithwaite.'

'Might we speak?'

Miss Yates sighs inwardly. Alma has presented herself as a problem since the day they first met. She has consistently refused to consider new ideas. She's never prepared to try them out, let them settle before passing judgement. No doubt she's here to take issue with yet another of Miss Yates's initiatives, determined to engage in skirmishes over every innovation, big or small, as if it threatens the very survival of the school. 'Look,' she says to Miss Braithwaite, gesturing at the girls below, 'efficiency in action. A simple one-way system and our safety problems are resolved in an instant.'

Miss Braithwaite leans over the banisters and watches the orderly transference of the girls from upstairs to downstairs, downstairs to upstairs. 'Very impressive,' she says.

Miss Yates waits for the 'but'.

'But I can't help thinking it's too quiet. They don't seem as cheerful as they used to be.'

'The girls are here to learn,' says Miss Yates, 'not to enjoy themselves.' She envisages future glory for Goldwyn's girls, scholarships to Oxford and Cambridge, top jobs across the country. They will distinguish themselves as adults, carry their learning with pride. Miss Yates has no intention of allowing them to be diverted by a misguided attempt to entertain them along the way.

'In my opinion,' says Miss Braithwaite, 'they

should be allowed to do both. Learning should be fun.'

Miss Yates is not convinced that Miss Braithwaite believes this. It's the kind of theory you might read in the education pages of the more liberal newspapers, a vague, woolly idea that is impossible to implement. And 'fun' is not exactly something she would associate with Miss Braithwaite, who rarely smiles. 'Perhaps you could come to my office this afternoon after the girls have left,' she says. 'Shall we say four thirty?'

'It will be a pleasure,' says Miss Braithwaite, icily polite.

Miss Yates watches her walk away, tall and angular, her head set very firmly on her narrow shoulders. Gone are the bare arms and legs, the flowery summer dress. She wears a dull suit, conservative in style, for her teaching, as if it gives her gravitas. Her dark hair, very thick, is scooped into a severe bun at the back of her head, which makes her look older than she is. She doesn't know how to dress.

Does she cultivate the image of a difficult woman on purpose? She lives alone, apparently in a large house that she has never shown any desire to share, even when other teachers have been looking for digs. She was a pupil at Goldwyn's during the war and takes a proprietorial interest in keeping the school the same, in harmony with her schoolgirl memories. It's not a happy situation. She should have moved on, found new opportunities, but she clings to tradition. She seems unable to shift her thinking to the present, unwilling to accept that you have to embrace the future in order to progress.

Perhaps if she had been married, with children, she would be a different woman, but she probably never had a choice. The war took away her chances and forced her to become someone she should never have been. It occurs to Miss Yates that she and Miss Braithwaite are more alike than she would like to admit, trapped in the limiting environment of a girls' school, surrounded by single women who all face the same lonely future.

Alma sits stiffly upright, facing Miss Yates across the headmistress's vast desk, refusing to lean back. Occasionally she smiles, but the movement is hard and unconvincing and her eyes remain unnaturally still.

Miss Yates relaxes into her new swivel chair – leather, padded arms – and breathes easily, hoping to conclude this meeting as quickly as possible. She's learned that the best way to deal with confrontation is to enjoy the experience, ride the wave of anger from the other person, and maintain her grip on authority throughout. She has a set of rules that have served her well over the years:

Smile and remain calm.
Never accept that you can be out-manoeuvred.
Remain polite, regardless of the other person's attitude.
Always look directly into the eyes of your opponent.
Don't give in unless you want to.
Savour the thought of the cup of tea that awaits you when it's all over.

She has written out this list and pinned it up in her bathroom where she finds the reminders comforting. She has developed the habit of having a bath at the end of every day, regardless of the lateness of the hour, extravagant with the hot water and the bath salts – it would have been an unheard-of luxury once, but she can afford it now. It's an opportunity to take stock of the day, work out what's gone wrong and why. She's good at her job – she's usually right about most things – but she has no wish to jeopardise her success by alienating her staff.

'So, Miss Braithwaite – Alma – how can I help?'

Alma shifts uncomfortably, examines her hands and looks up again. 'Well – you may not be aware of this, but I always arrange the term's concerts in advance. I choose the music during the holidays and start to rehearse immediately we return to school…' She produces one of her unconvincing smiles.

'I'm delighted to hear it,' says Miss Yates. 'Being prepared is a most commendable quality.'

A flush is spreading up to Alma's face. It starts in her neck, works its way through her chin, and comes to rest in the centre of her cheeks, forming circles of darker pink. 'I overheard the girls talking. I'm sure it's just a mistake but they seem to think we're going to be performing "Zadok the Priest" at the end of term.'

Ah. Now it's clear what this is about. Miss Yates sits back and folds her hands without saying anything.

Alma watches her for a few seconds, clearly confused by the silence. 'I was under the impression that my duties as head of music would remain unchanged.'

'As indeed they do.' Miss Yates smiles amiably.

'Is it true? Have you made this decision without consulting me?'

Miss Yates decides that it's unnecessary for her to do more than nod in acknowledgement.

The colour in Alma's cheeks becomes more concentrated. She can't maintain her direct stare, so she looks past Miss Yates towards the window. 'So not only have you decided something of great significance without my knowledge, you have also made this known to the girls before consulting me. Were you deliberately trying to humiliate me?' Her voice trembles slightly with the effort of trying to remain calm.

'I'm so pleased you have come to discuss this with me,' says Miss Yates. 'Let's take one point at a time. First, I have no intention of humiliating you. Of course not. But I must own up to the fact that I am particularly fond of "Zadok the Priest" and felt it would be appropriate for the school to perform it for my first concert at Goldwyn's.'

'You didn't think you should discuss this with me first?'

'Of course I intended to seek your opinion before making any clear decision. Which brings me to my second point. It seems that a girl, maybe more than one, has been eavesdropping while I've been mulling over ideas with a colleague. This information has subsequently been passed on, leading to the most unfortunate course of events that you have described to me. It is completely unacceptable that you heard my thoughts from someone other than myself.'

Alma relaxes a little, clearly relieved that a full-blown argument is not going to be necessary. 'Even so, I admit that I am still...' she struggles for the right word '...disappointed that you felt another colleague should be the first person to hear your thoughts on the matter, and not me.'

'A perfectly reasonable reaction, I would say.'

'Miss Cunningham-Smith always consulted–'

Miss Yates raises her voice very slightly. 'But I am not Miss Cunningham-Smith, Alma. I am Miss Wilhelmina Yates.'

Alma seems ready to say something, but changes her mind. The temperature in the room is dropping, and while the sweat on her cheeks still glistens, her skin is fading to a chilled white, making the red circles even more startling.

Miss Yates sits forward. 'How long do you think it takes to perform "Zadok the Priest"?'

Alma shrugs, then concentrates as she makes some calculations. 'I don't know – between five or ten minutes, perhaps, depending on how fast it's taken.'

'Exactly. And how long are your concerts, usually?'

'Well, about an hour, an hour and a half maybe. I realise of course that "Zadok the Priest" would be only a small part of the concert, but there would be difficulties...'

'And what would they be?'

Alma spreads her hands, clearly not accustomed to negotiating. 'Well, we don't have any tenors or basses for a start.'

'I'm sure Sherrard's would oblige.'

'But that's exactly what concerns me. You're taking the decision out of my hands. If we ask Sherrard's to come and help us with the concert, we introduce a whole new element. Where do we put the choir? Have we enough good players for the orchestra? What about the instrumentalists who also sing in the choir? Will there be enough room on the platform? If boys come too, we would have to accommodate their parents – there simply isn't enough room.'

Miss Yates smiles. 'Don't you think, perhaps, you're allowing the negative aspects to override the positive? I know from experience that taking part in "Zadok the Priest" can be a life-altering experience. I used to sing in a choir when I was at school, you know. Before the war. I have never forgotten the thrill of singing with men's voices for a centenary concert we did in our local concert hall. Ever since I arrived here and discovered that we have a thriving music department, I have been longing to offer the same pleasure to our girls. There must be ways round these problems. Perform on two nights, expand the choir and orchestra, ask staff to sing, or even parents – be innovative. Think beyond the obvious.'

Alma glares at her. 'But what I've been trying to say is that the decisions have always been mine.'

Miss Yates stands up. They've covered this ground already. 'Alma, if we did things in exactly the same way as they've always been done, we would stagnate. We have to consider new ideas, new possibilities, let our minds roam in new directions.'

Alma doesn't stand up, clearly determined to say more. But Miss Yates walks over to the door and opens it. 'Now, if you'll excuse me, I really am very busy...'

She still doesn't get up. 'Miss Cunningham-Smith always trusted me and valued my expertise.' She's talking to the empty chair in front of her.

'I also value your expertise.'

'Then why are you overriding me?'

'I have no intention of doing that, I assure you. But I believe in looking for new approaches. Sometimes we need someone to point out to us that we have become entrenched in certain ways of doing things, someone to shake things up a little.'

'Miss Cunningham-Smith was always very satisfied.'

Miss Yates allows a note of impatience to creep into her voice. 'But Miss Cunningham-Smith is no longer with us, Alma. If she were, we would not be having this conversation. I'm afraid I have another appointment.'

Alma finally gets up. She pulls her skirt down, picks up her handbag and walks to the door. As she draws level with Miss Yates, she stops and looks at her directly without speaking. You will not continue to ride over me like this, she seems to be saying. I will not be intimidated. Then she turns and walks away along the corridor.

Miss Yates receives and understands the message. She watches her for a few seconds before going back inside her room and shutting the door. She calculates the level of her success. Seventy-five per cent, she decides, give or take five per cent.

The first battle has been won, but she knows it is the first of many. Alma Braithwaite will be back. But Miss Yates is confident that she will prevail.

The headmistress's house is situated on the edge of the school grounds, the front gate opening on to Buttermere Road, an elegant street lined with plane trees. The back garden lies adjacent to Goldwyn's hockey pitch. The house is large and robust, as if the Edwardian trustees had in mind an early superwoman who could take on the post of headmistress at the same time as managing her own large family. Why else would there be five bedrooms and a substantial garden that would require the attention of a gardener for three days a week? As every headmistress since the founding of the school has been single, their forward thinking would seem to have been misplaced.

A second house for the bursar was built alongside, but hierarchy demanded that it should be smaller, so a succession of male bursars with large families squeezed into the limited space until Black Tuesday of 1929, when the stock market failed and plunged the world into the Great Depression. The trustees had invested heavily in an American company that manufactured office equipment for left-handed people. Since nobody could spare their limited resources for innovative devices for a minority group, the firm collapsed and Goldwyn's had to sell off the bursar's house in order to keep afloat.

Once Miss Yates had accepted the post, near the end of the summer term, Miss Jackson, the only female member of the board, had invited her to come and inspect her new home. 'Now, please don't concern yourself about the state of it,' she said. 'It will have been modernised by the time you move in.'

Miss Cunningham-Smith had been appointed headmistress in 1934 at the age of thirty, so she had lived in the house for twenty-nine years, during which time nobody had considered the necessity of refurbishment. There had been two heads before her, both intellectuals, concerned more with affairs of the mind than the more frivolous matter of décor.

Miss Yates and Miss Jackson, who was surprisingly fast on her feet despite her advanced age, entered through the front door into the bright and spacious hall. Light seeped in through panels of stained glass above every door that led off the hall. Art-nouveau roses: red, yellow, blue blossoms; green stalks curving and swirling through a background of plain glass. The effect was of a static kaleidoscope, richly coloured and dazzling.

'I've always loved this hall,' said Miss Jackson.

A smell of dust greeted them as they opened doors and discovered rooms crammed with enormous sideboards and sofas, richly patterned Indian rugs and books. If the dark, solid furniture had been fashionable once, it had long ago lost its charm and gave the impression of function rather than elegance; the rugs were faded, worn to grey threads in areas that had seen heavy traffic; every available wall was occupied by bookshelves. Overflow piles of books were scattered around the room as if they were waiting for a librarian to appear, expecting to be indexed, catalogued, put in their rightful places.

'All this clutter,' said Miss Yates. 'It absorbs the light.'

'The books will have to go,' said Miss Jackson.

'Indeed they will,' said Miss Yates.

'Do you think she'd read them all?' asked Miss Jackson.

'Unlikely,' said Miss Yates, who understood the compulsion of buying something for its rarity rather than its function. She picked a book out of a shelf at random and turned to the front pages. 'Yes, I thought so. This is a first edition.' She examined one or two more from different shelves and confirmed her suspicions. 'Miss Cunningham-Smith was a collector.'

'I didn't know that,' said Miss Jackson. 'And I thought I knew her.'

Miss Yates smiled. 'You can only ever know what someone is prepared to reveal.'

'She was a remarkable woman. She did wonders for Goldwyn's.'

Wait and see what I will do for Goldwyn's, thought Miss Yates. There are even more remarkable achievements ahead of us. 'But what happens to her possessions?' she asked. 'Are there any relatives?'

'Apparently not. She left everything to the school in her will, so I imagine we'll have to organise a sale and put the money into some special fund. A scholarship or two, perhaps.'

'Excellent,' said Miss Yates. 'I couldn't think of a more worthwhile way to profit from Miss Cunningham-Smith's appreciation of valuable objects.'

Miss Jackson beamed. 'Do you think they're all first editions?'

'Unquestionably.' Miss Yates knew exactly how the mind of a collector would work. 'She wouldn't have settled for anything less. Apart from the books she was using for teaching, of course.'

'So they would be worth a lot of money?'

'I suspect there will be serious collectors interested in this library, judging by the sample I've just seen.'

'I suppose Miss Cunningham-Smith felt safer investing in books than banks.'

'Oh, she wouldn't have been interested in their value. She would have collected them for love.'

'Really?' Miss Jackson's eyes opened wide with astonishment, as if the concept of putting Miss Cunningham-Smith's name and love into the same sentence was beyond her comprehension.

Miss Yates had an idea. 'Why don't we make a small collection of some of the more interesting books, and display them somewhere in the school as a memorial? We can call it the Cunningham-Smith Collection. Have a specially made bookcase.'

'That would be a splendid way of remembering her.'

'Meanwhile,' said Miss Yates, 'do you think we could arrange to have them all packed safely away so that we can see the walls and let in a little light?'

Work started almost immediately, before the end of term, and builders moved in. Miss Jackson reported to Miss Yates regularly on the telephone, confirming that the work was proceeding correctly. Apparently there was an atmosphere of suppressed tension among the pupils, which was exacerbated by the heat. Despite several entreaties from the staff, the builders persisted in removing their shirts in the sunshine. Their burned-brown backs shone with sweat as they filled skips and shifted supplies of bricks, bags of plaster, fresh planks of wood. They cooked breakfast on portable gas grills, timing it so that they would be sitting and eating when the bell rang for a change of lesson and large numbers of girls would be moving from one building to another. A collective shiver of excitement was spreading through the school, a realisation that the male world was encroaching on their territory, a delicious sensation of the forbidden. Finding plausible excuses to wander over to the hockey field became a daily preoccupation and the words 'rape and pillage' echoed in whispers among the girls as they lined up for Assembly.

'Someone needs to address the problem,' said Miss Yates. 'Would you like me to come down?'

Miss Jackson was reassuring. 'We'll be breaking up soon and the men will be gone by the beginning of next term. There'll be no lasting harm done.'

Twenty books were selected for the Cunningham-Smith collection – more for their interesting appearance than for any monetary value or academic worth; the rest were packaged up and sent to specialist book dealers. Everything else was removed by house-clearance specialists.

Miss Yates now has a house of light and colour – sage green in the sitting room, lemon in the kitchen, dusky pink in her bedroom – and beige carpets have been fitted throughout, right up to the skirting boards, an unfamiliar luxury that adds a pleasant warmth. Sunshine pours in through freshly painted window frames on to her china cabinets. Where Miss Cunningham-Smith had books, Miss Yates has china. Royal Worcester. She has crates of plates, cups and saucers, gravy boats, teapots, coffee pots, figures of birds, of children, of animals, all wrapped by hand in layers of tissue paper, ready to increase in value as time goes on. Much of it is antique while some of it is new, bought at vast expense in anticipation of her future salary. There hasn't been time to unpack all of it, so the new pieces remain cocooned in satin in presentation boxes, waiting for her attention.

Miss Yates loves her new home. She's a long way from her last school in East Anglia, separated from her past.

On the mantelpiece in the living room, she has placed two large framed photographs. One is of Mr John F. Kennedy, the American president, whom she greatly admires for his strong character and ability to negotiate difficult situations in the interests of world peace. There had been such a fine photograph of him in *The Times* on the day of his inaugural speech that she had been unable to throw it away. In the end, she had taken a watercolour of Tenby out of its frame and replaced it with the President of the United States. She was proud to hang it in her sitting room. 'This is the man who will bring security to the free world,' she tells everyone who visits. 'We must never forget to show him suitable respect.'

The other photograph is of a young man in an RAF uniform. Only his head and shoulders are showing. He has high cheekbones, a long, straight nose and a finely sculpted chin. His sad, taut eyes are gazing out, past any observer, as if his mind is in the skies, his thoughts on flight. Thick dark hair, parted on the left, escapes from his cap and sweeps jauntily over his forehead. Miss Yates often studies his face and imagines how he would look now, even talks to him when she is on her own.

'A difficult day, Raymond. How do you persuade staff that they're stuck in the old ways?'

'You'd love the weather today. Blue skies, no cloud, perfect for flying.'

'You should be grateful you're no longer here. The world's such a disappointment now, you know. They don't deserve your sacrifice. Nobody wants to work together any more. The war's already forgotten, and they've abandoned the old spirit of co-operation.'

He gazes back at her, his face calm, his thoughts far away.

When people come to visit, Miss Yates tells them about Raymond. 'He flew Spitfires, defended us all in the Battle of Britain. Didn't survive, I'm afraid.' Then she would pause for a few seconds, looking down at the floor, remembering, accepting their sympathy.

What she doesn't tell them is that Raymond was not hers to mourn. That he had been engaged to her childhood friend, Betty. That all through that time of fast living and fast dying, Wilhelmina Yates had never managed to find an admirer. During the war, she was plumper than she is now, didn't know how to dress, and she was too shy to flirt. Like everyone else, she had lost loved ones, but not a fiancé or even a boyfriend. She had only ever admired Raymond from afar.

'Still, never mind,' she would say brightly, smiling and brave. 'We must carry on, mustn't we? Can't live in the past. Would you like another slice of fruit cake? I made it myself.'

She doesn't want to live in the past anyway. There's already too much from that time that she'd rather forget. Raymond died in a dogfight over Dover, but she wasn't the one who had gone to the memorial service in the absence of a body, the one who kept referring to her deceased fiancé, the one who wore black for years. She cried privately for the relationship with Raymond that had been only imaginary, mourned the great hole in her life that had never been filled and secretly thought that Betty was making too much fuss over someone she had known for just six months.

iv

Alma's drawing room is large and imposing with wide windows that look out over the garden and enough space for several sofas. The oak-panelled walls give the room a dark, slightly oppressive atmosphere, but this is how it was when her parents were here, so nothing will change.

It is, of course, far too big for her. She doesn't

need a five-bedroomed house. It might have been sensible to sell it after the war, but she preferred to stay. The house survived the war even if most of its inhabitants didn't, so it symbolises permanence to her, the triumph of solid structure over the fragility of flesh and blood. Remaining in the family home means she won't forget anything.

There are advantages to a house of this size. It doesn't matter if it gets a little untidy. Or even very untidy.

There's no one to say: 'Why don't you decorate your front room, Alma? Let the light in.'

'If you picked up some of the clothes on your bedroom floor, you'd see what a nice carpet you have. It's not a bad colour, is it? A little worn near the door, perhaps, and on the right side of the bed, but that's to be expected. Axminster, of course. Tough as old boots.'

'It would be easier to wash up the saucepans every time you use them. They're only black because the dirt gets cooked on. Not that you cook often, of course.'

The voices are there, in her head – in fact occasionally they seem to be outside her head as well – but she knows they're not real. They sometimes sound like her parents, sometimes even her grandparents, whom she remembers vaguely from before the war, or Dr Guest and his wife who gave her a home but never managed to replace her parents.

They'd suggested she should sell the house. 'It's full of memories, Alma. There's no need to go back there after all this time. You can stay with us, you know. We'll always be happy to have you.'

But she'd wanted to go home. As soon as she was old enough, she'd returned and set up residence where she belonged. She has never regretted it.

Today she paces through the ground-floor rooms, picking her way through piles of unwanted or abandoned items, going over and over the conversation with Miss Yates. The woman is poisonous. She does whatever she wants. She has no respect for tradition, no consideration for her staff. She acts as if she would prefer to run the school without assistance.

All those girls with their arms in the air at that first assembly. Miss Yates the dictator. She's frightening.

Every Monday, in a meeting during morning break, she pretends to consult her staff, asking for suggestions to improve the daily running of the school. Everyone's keen to contribute, tell her what they think. She listens, comments, writes down their ideas, then pursues her own agenda. Every adjustment in the timetable, the length of the school day, rules for improving behaviour, awards for good work, scholarships, comes from her.

The other teachers have not yet discovered that she's not interested in their opinions.

'It's about time we had some changes around here.'

'At last, someone with common sense.'

'Miss Cunningham-Smith had common sense,' says Alma, indignantly.

'Yes, but she was very old-fashioned.'

'That's ridiculous. If it works, it works.'

'It sometimes takes a new person to see where things can improve.'

'She's very on the ball, isn't she? I can see why she got the job.'

'A new broom...'

Alma is infuriated by their naïvety, Miss Yates is not what she seems. She has delusions of grandeur. But when she tries to point this out, they all groan.

She puts on a record and lies down on one of the sofas, flat on her back, and looks up at the ceiling. After a little preliminary scratching, Beethoven's seventh symphony begins, and Alma stops thinking. Her feet tap compulsively. Right two three four, left two three four. The energy reinvigorates her, more powerful than a glass of wine. She moves her eyebrows up and down with the rhythm, taps third fingers against thumbs, nods her head up and down.

Rhythm forms naturally within her, alongside the pumping of her heart, a central, stabilising force that constantly regenerates itself, pulsing through her body with urgency, compelling a physical response. It's so fundamental to her existence that it creates an accompaniment to everything she does, the incidental music of the film of her life. It even penetrates her dreams. In primary school, when the children sat at their desks and listened to *Singing Together,* Alma was the first to join in, knowing by instinct where each verse started, while the others waited for the lead from the singers on the wireless. Her teacher noticed that her feet were always in time when they danced the Virginia Reel or skipped through 'Oranges and

Lemons' in the playground. 'You should learn an instrument, Alma,' she said. 'I'll speak to your parents.'

So Alma went for piano lessons and discovered that she was good at it – although never in the same league as Curls.

And when she was fifteen, she discovered the Lindy Hop.

Part Five

i

4 May 1942

Curls and Alma approach the hospital along roads that look exactly the same as they always did. It seems as if the bombs that fell on the west wing were dropped by a single plane, separated from the organised formation of the rest of its squadron. An afterthought. An incompetent pilot losing his companions, not sure where to go, turning and heading for home, then deciding that he had several bombs left and couldn't possibly take them back with him. This'll do, he thought (in German). Bombs away.

The hospital is in the grip of ongoing chaos. They're still pulling people out of the rubble, and ambulances roll up continuously, driven by women in uniforms, while soldiers leap out, lifting stretchers, shouting instructions. Doctors and nurses rush past Alma and Curls as they stand contemplating the scene, wondering where to go.

Everyone has that wild expression on their faces, the same as the woman who came into their shelter with her two children and without her husband, the bewildered old women they saw wandering about when they walked up to Sherrard's. It was the look they had seen in each other's eyes inside the bomb shelter, before the lights went out – shock, terror, but also excitement. It's as if they are all living through their own action film, as if they are actors in their own lives. The soldiers' uniforms are grey with dust, their helmets tilted back over flattened hair, their faces dirty and exhausted. The doctors and nurses remain calm, although there are streaks of blood on their white coats and uniforms, and exhaustion in their movements. They look as if they've been awake for several days, as if this has become a way of life that will never end.

A soldier walks towards the entrance, guiding a mother with a baby in her arms. He approaches a nurse who has come out for a quick cigarette. 'Please, can you help?'

The nurse hesitates. 'What?' she says, her voice dull and unwelcoming. 'Admissions are over there.' She gestures vaguely and moves away from the soldier, but he grabs her arm.

'Hang on,' he says quietly. 'Could you just look at the baby? We're not sure – she won't let anyone take him away from her.'

'I'm sorry,' says the nurse. 'I can't– I have to–'

The soldier takes her to one side, away from the mother and baby. 'Their Anderson shelter was picked up by the blast, thrown about five hundred yards away from its original position and set down in one piece.'

The nurse's eyes widen in astonishment. 'And she's still walking?'

'When we opened the door she just stepped out, as if she was in her back garden. Didn't even notice the change of scenery. Asked us for a nappy for the baby. Said she couldn't find her supplies.'

The nurse hesitates, then makes a decision and stubs out her cigarette. She goes over to the woman who's standing on her own, oblivious to everyone rushing past. 'Hello, love,' she says. 'Would you like me to help you with your baby?'

The woman doesn't respond at first, but then raises her eyes and studies the nurse's face, as if she's surprised to see her. 'He's all right,' she says. 'We don't need to see a doctor.'

'Of course not,' says the nurse. 'Why don't you come with me and we can find somewhere for him to settle? I expect you're both exhausted after all this time.'

The woman allows herself to be led away, the baby silent and motionless in her arms.

The soldier takes his hat off and scratches his head, sighing. He catches sight of Alma and Curls watching him and his expression changes. 'It's all go,' he says, winking at them, and sets off back down the road.

Alma avoids looking at Curls. She's afraid she might cry.

The bombed part of the hospital is the familiar scene of destruction that they have seen in the centre of Exeter. There's no longer any need for firemen – everything is blackened, twisted, disintegrated, but the fires have been extinguished. Army demolition experts are engaged in collapsing the remains of the building, clearing everything into a convoy of lorries that come and go in an orderly queue.

It's hopeless, thinks Alma, rooted to the spot, struggling to take in the extent of the destruction. She has known this hospital all her life – the buildings, the doctors, the nurses, the receptionists. She used to accompany her parents here when she was younger – she still does occasionally, during half-terms and holidays. She usually curls up in a corner of her father's office with a book, chats to her mother's secretary, accepts sweets from a junior doctor while she waits for one of her parents to finish for the day. It's always been a friendly place. Heat belting out of white-painted radiators, shiny green walls and brown lino on the floors coming up at the edges. Beds that can be wheeled about like prams by cheery porters, who wink at her as they pass, nurses who smile and bring orange squash, an elderly patient in stripy pyjamas who draws pictures for her on a spare piece of paper.

But the entire wing has gone. Nobody could still be alive in this. There's nothing left, no trace of the world that was once so comforting, so busy.

A soldier is coming towards them. 'Come on,' says Curls. 'Let's ask.' She steps forward and approaches him. 'Excuse me,' she says.

He looks at them with amazement, as if they're the wrong characters, placed on the wrong board, in the wrong game. 'Are you injured?' he asks, his voice thick and puzzled.

'No,' says Curls. 'No, not at all.'

'Then you shouldn't be here.' He attempts to herd them towards the hospital gate, as if they're naughty children or animals in the wrong place. Alma finds herself remembering a flock of geese landing in her garden, her mother dashing out to shoo them away, her arms flapping urgently. 'Go away, go away. You can't land here. This isn't your home. Take off again, fly away to where you belong. You can't come here.'

'Wait,' says Curls, refusing to move. 'We need to know.'

He drops his hands and stares at her.

'Did some people survive the bombing at the hospital? What happened afterwards? Did you dig anyone out?'

He stares at her again, his face tight and unrevealing. 'Of course we dug people out, dozens of them, haven't stopped all day – we're still finding them, bits of them, arms, legs–' He suddenly seems to notice who he's talking to and stops in mid-sentence.

Alma steps forward. 'Was anyone alive?'

He turns his gaze towards her. 'Alive? No, of course not. Nobody survives that kind of blast.'

'Nobody?'

He shakes his head. 'Nobody.'

But Alma can't let it go. 'What about the people on the edges, the ones who weren't at the centre of the explosion? They can't all have been dead.'

'Well, there were some injured–' He stops again. 'Why are you asking? Who wants to know?'

'I want to know,' says Alma, although as soon as she says it she decides she doesn't want to know. It's much better not to be certain. That way you can still pretend.

'You need the office,' he says, turning away.

'I'm sorry,' says Alma, wanting to go after him, wanting to tell him that she wouldn't have bothered him if it wasn't important, but Curls is pulling her arm.

'Come on,' she says. 'He doesn't know. We'd better find the office.'

The rest of the hospital has also changed. There are too many people: stretchers placed in the corridors; confused, bandaged patients sitting on chairs outside rooms, their faces grim and tight, oblivious to everything going on around them. The girls walk up and down a few corridors, following arrows and hastily erected directions, until they reach a glass window with a person behind it who is prepared to take them seriously.

'We're looking for Alma's parents,' says Curls, with authority, as if she does this sort of thing all the time.

The woman's face is pale and haggard, her eyes red-rimmed and watery, and she keeps swallowing, as if she has a sore throat or is trying not to cry. 'What are their names?' she asks, in a soft, husky voice.

'Dr Braithwaite,' says Alma. 'And Dr Braithwaite.'

The woman shakes her head. 'This is the wrong place for a doctor. You need to go to Admissions.'

'They're her parents,' says Curls. 'Her parents are doctors. We want to know where they are.'

We know where they are, thinks Alma. They're dead. It's obvious. We should never have come.

'Oh!' says the woman. 'You mean Dr Giles Braithwaite?'

Curls nods eagerly. 'Yes, and Dr Ellen Braithwaite.'

The woman's face sags suddenly. 'I'm sorry, dear,' she says, softening her voice.

'What's that supposed to mean?' asks Curls.

'They were in the West Wing. The one that was bombed.'

'We know that. But there must have been some survivors.'

The woman's head bobs up and down. Alma's hopes rise slightly. 'No,' says the woman. 'They didn't survive.'

'But how can you be sure?' asks Curls.

The woman stops nodding. 'I've spoken to the doctor who examined the bodies.'

'They actually saw them, dug them out?'

'Well, dearie,' says the woman, 'not the bodies, exactly. Just bits of them, enough to identify...' She glances at Alma and stops abruptly. 'Look,' she says, 'you'll have to come back later when we're not so busy. When we've had time to record everything properly. They haven't filled in all the forms yet.'

But Alma knows it would be pointless. Someone has seen her parents after the bombing, someone who knows for certain that it was them. She turns away. 'Come on,' she says to Curls. 'We'd better get back.'

'Alma!'

A doctor is striding towards them, a tall stringy man with a beard. Dr Perkins, her father's senior registrar. 'What are you doing here?' He stops in front of them, suddenly silent, unable to say anything.

Alma faces him squarely. Better to sort it out once and for all. She raises her eyes to his. 'Were you there?' she asks.

He nods slowly. 'I'm sorry,' he says.

'Alma, Jane!' A voice booms out from behind

them. 'I have found you. At last!'

Alma turns in astonishment and sees a huge man thundering down the corridor towards them, his grey jacket unbuttoned and billowing behind him, inappropriate laughter pouring out of his open mouth.

'Who in the world is he?' asks Dr Perkins. Even the woman behind the glass window is sufficiently surprised to raise herself slightly out of her seat to peer at him.

'It's Lieutenant Kowalski,' says Curls.

He stops in front of them, takes Dr Perkins's hand in his and shakes it vigorously. 'Polish Air Force. I thank you for taking care of girls. They wander off. Very unwise. We think we lose them.'

Dr Perkins stares at him, unable to retract his hand.

'How did you find us?' asks Curls.

'Soldier by ambulance. Very helpful.'

'I mean, how did you know we were at the hospital?'

'Your friends. They tell us.'

Curls raises her eyebrows at Alma. 'You'd think they'd hold out a bit longer than that, wouldn't you?'

But Alma doesn't care any more. She has found what she came for. Nothing else seems to matter very much now.

Lieutenant Kowalski lets go of Dr Perkins's hand and shakes his forefinger in Curls's face, just in front of her nose. 'Mr Gunner not a happy man.'

'Well,' says Dr Perkins, rubbing his knuckles, 'I have to get on. There's far too much to do.' He turns back to Alma and touches her arm gently. 'I'm so sorry, Alma,' he says. 'I'll be in touch.'

She half smiles but doesn't manage to speak. There's an enormous lump in her throat, as if she has tonsillitis. She can't swallow.

'Anyway,' says Curls, 'I bet you don't know how to get to Mortimer Hall any better than we do.'

Lieutenant Kowalski shrugs. 'I know university. We ask someone the way.'

It's well past ten o'clock by the time Alma and Curls finally join Giraffe and Natalie in the common room at Mortimer Hall. It's comfortable, with a record player, a piano, table tennis and several sofas. A group of young men, who are discussing Churchill's latest strategy in low, restrained voices, seem confused by their presence – two girls must be acceptable, four too many – and they depart one by one, leaving them on their own.

'What did Mr Gunner say?' whispers Giraffe.

Curls shrugs. 'Nothing too ghastly. Except that he'll have to tell Miss Cunningham-Smith.'

'Oh,' says Natalie. 'Not good.'

'You'd make useless spies,' says Curls. 'How long exactly did it take before you broke down under interrogation?'

'We were worried,' says Natalie. 'We thought you might not find us.'

'Mr Gunner was awfully nice about it,' says Giraffe. 'He said you wouldn't get into trouble if we told him where you were.'

'Well, he would say that, wouldn't he?'

The door opens suddenly and Mr Gunner puts

his head round. The girls stare at him in guilty silence. 'Miss Curley and Miss Braithwaite, Mrs Anderson has prepared a late supper for you, after which I think you should all retire. It's been an exhausting day, and it must be well past your bedtime.'

He withdraws and Curls rolls her eyes. 'Anyone would think we're children,' she says.

'If he thought that,' says Giraffe, 'he'd hardly call you Miss Curley.'

'You behaved irresponsibly,' says Miss Cunningham-Smith, the next day. She's standing behind the dust-strewn desk in her office because there's no longer a chair to sit on.

Alma knows she should offer an explanation, but it all feels too complicated.

'We had to do it,' says Curls. 'Alma needed confirmation about her parents.'

'Leaving aside the issue of showing trust in the authorities when they give us information, did it not occur to either of you how distressing it must have been to Mr Gunner? He offered you sanctuary, gave up his spare time to come and fetch you, then lost you. The very least you could have done was to ask for permission.'

'He wouldn't have given it,' says Curls.

'Since you didn't ask,' says Miss Cunningham-Smith, 'you cannot make that assumption.'

'But we needed–'

'I have heard enough from you, Jane. Have you anything to add, Alma, in your defence?'

Alma shakes her head.

They stand in silence for a few seconds while

Miss Cunningham-Smith gives the matter some thought. 'Very well,' she says eventually. 'I accept that compassion is in order, and I'm reluctant to ask too much of you, bearing in mind the difficult work we all have ahead of us in clearing up. I shall therefore require you to arrive ten minutes early every morning and report to me, so that I can assign to you any extra tasks that might present themselves.'

As they leave the room, Curls smiles at Alma and rubs her arm. 'Not too bad. It could have been so much worse.'

'I know,' says Alma. 'Thank you.'

The girls adapt to living at Mortimer Hall more easily than the students adapt to their presence. At first, it's frustrating that these young men in suits and ties, with sharp left partings in their sleek hair, in black laced shoes shiny with polish and elbow grease, all so full of potential, refuse to communicate beyond the polite 'Good evening,' as they hold open doors, or 'Please could you pass the salt,' when they sit at the same table in the dining room. But after a few days, the men become more accustomed to their presence and start using the common room again, still not exactly talking to them, but at least asking which records they would prefer. The students are not aware of it, but they are being very closely observed.

'Mr Hitchens,' says Curls, in their bedroom. 'Jack. Have you seen his eyes? They're *enormous*. And that lovely Irish accent.'

He's over here from Ireland with Dennis Thwaite to study maths, taking advantage of the extra places left vacant by students who have given up their right of exemption and enlisted. They're not part of this war – there's no conscription in Dublin. They both have courtesy and charm and seem slightly alien, foreigners who talk in the same way as they do but are somehow different. They have been more aware of the girls than the English students, directing them to the dining room when they were lost, enquiring politely after a few days if they have settled in.

'I prefer Geoffrey Harris,' says Giraffe. 'He stutters when he talks – as if he's nervous of me!'

'He would be,' says Curls. 'You're taller than him.'

'Eric Westland reminds me of Bing Crosby,' says Natalie. 'There's something about Americans, isn't there? Who do you like, Alma?'

Alma, who has always had the same taste as Curls, has been studying Jack Hitchens, touched by his thoughtfulness. She's fascinated by the waves in his hair, which manage to escape from his regular combing and spring up with a joyful freedom. 'I don't know,' she says. 'All of them, really, I suppose.'

One evening in the common room, Curls decides that she can ignore the piano no longer. They have been staying behind at school to practise, but it would be so much more convenient to play at Mortimer Hall. They haven't been able to decide if they need permission.

She sits down, adjusts the height of the stool, checks the position of the pedals and tries a few keys. The other three are involved in a game of table-tennis, compensating for the lack of a fourth player by circling the table, keeping the ball in play by running to the other end after each go and waiting for the ball to be returned to them. It's good fun, but impossible to score, since no one stays in the same team. Curls starts to play the first movement of a Beethoven sonata, *allegro*, with plenty of *crescendos* and *diminuendos, sforzando* chords. The other girls run faster, hit the ball harder, bump into each other more, until the music stops. They collapse on to the sofas, breathless and giggling, while Curls brings the Beethoven to a close.

Geoffrey Harris, a short, thickset man, Eric Westland, the American, and Colin Streetly, a first year physics student with blond hair and serious blue eyes, are sitting in a corner, talking intently. They look up briefly when Curls starts playing, but return to their conversation almost immediately. Tristan Watson, an earnest young student who looks younger than the girls, ignores the music and continues to read his book.

'I've played that,' says Natalie.

'Not as fast as Curls,' says Giraffe.

'So what? Speed isn't everything.'

'But it's not so good if it's slow.'

Curls plays a few notes, a tune with a syncopated rhythm, and unexpectedly changes a flat to a natural, crushing the notes together.

Alma looks round at her. 'I like that,' she says. 'What is it?'

'Not sure,' says Curls. 'I heard it on the wireless.' She adds a left hand, and suddenly she's playing something wild and daring, swinging the rhythms, introducing unfamiliar harmonies. It's the kind of music that forces you to tap your feet, impels you to get up and dance.

The three men, who have successfully ignored the Beethoven and the noisy enthusiasm of the table-tennis, stop talking to stare at Curls.

The door opens. Jack Hitchens and Dennis Thwaite burst in, transformed astonishingly into dancers. They're bouncing from the knees, leaning backwards as if they're about to sit down on an invisible chair, while their feet form steps that are clearly familiar, their arms opened wide, fingers clicking.

The girls stare at them. Still dancing, Jack struts over to Alma, who happens to be nearest to him, and takes her by the hand, pulling her up from the sofa.

'Come on!' he says. 'Let's swing.'

Alma doesn't need any further encouragement. Her bones are vibrating in time with the music, her feet itching to move.

'Forward!' yells Jack and she finds herself advancing in a row, Natalie on the other side of Jack, then Dennis, then Giraffe, all linked by hand, their arms outstretched. She tries to imitate Jack's steps, not keeping up, stumbling slightly. Jack swings her round so they're facing each other and grabs her other hand. 'Step, step, triple-step!' he shouts. 'Watch my feet. Step, step, triple-step.' Alma copies him and they go forwards and backwards, jutting their chins out towards each other like hens. Her knees, supple and fluid, bounce her into the movements and they circle, side by side, back to back, round to the front again. Jack lets go of one of her hands and they swing apart, still connected on one side, while the free hand rushes out into the space. 'One, two, three-and-four, step, step, triple-step–'

Alma almost loses her balance, but Jack grabs her and they move together again. She watches him, follows his movements, breathless with excitement. She's conscious of Giraffe and Natalie nearby with Dennis, while Eric, Geoffrey and Colin have abandoned their discussion and leapt up to join in.

The beat, the beat. It's pounding through her, while the tune belts out, high up the piano, and she's alive in a way she's never experienced before. She can't resist, can't stop–

'Swing your arms,' yells Jack. 'Feel the rhythm!'

Alma's legs are moving faster than her thoughts, her arms swooping through the air, her body twisting and turning–

Curls stops playing.

They stand in the middle of the floor, breathing heavily.

Blood is cascading through Alma's veins at a dizzying speed. 'Why have we stopped?' she asks. 'Can't we carry on?'

'Our pianist has run out of steam,' says Jack. He's grinning, his cheeks scrunched into cheerful mounds beneath his eyes, his mouth stretched so wide that his face is split into two by a mouthful of straight, perfect teeth.

'What's the dance called?' she asks. She has never experienced this kind of dancing before, never imagined it was possible. The music is in her head, the beat has become her pulse – she can't slow down. She didn't know it was possible to generate such excitement.

Jack raises his hands above his head and claps. 'You don't know? Really?'

Alma looks round at Giraffe and Natalie, whose faces are flushed, their shoulders still rising and falling as they struggle to get their breath back. They are as confused as she is.

'No,' says Curls. 'We don't know what it is. Tell us.'

'It's the Lindy Hop,' says Jack. 'Everyone's doing it in the States – I lived there for a few months before the war.'

'Oh,' says Giraffe, suddenly excited. 'It's in the film – *Hellzapoppin'*.'

'That's right,' says Dennis. 'You've got it, girl.'

'Have you seen the film?' Natalie asks Curls. 'Is that where you heard the music?'

She shrugs. 'No. I just heard the tune on the wireless, then made the rest up.'

Alma has never met anyone else who could just hear a piece of music once, remember it without even knowing where it came from, then sit down at the piano and reproduce it. She couldn't do it. She wouldn't even be able to pick out the melody with any degree of accuracy, let alone get the rhythms right and add harmony.

'You've been improvising!' says Jack. 'Now, that's class. A natural-born jazz musician.'

'She's not like normal people,' says Natalie. 'She's got perfect pitch.'

'Will you teach us the steps?' asks Giraffe. 'So we can do it properly?'

'You bet,' says Jack.

'But I only know one tune,' says Curls. 'And,

anyway, I want to join in.'

'We've got records,' says Geoffrey. 'Glenn Miller. Louis Armstrong. Jack's been teaching it to us all at Mortimer.'

'Really?' says Curls. 'Everyone?'

'Well, nearly everyone.'

Jack twirls round, knees bent, feet moving in rhythm. They can hear him counting under his breath, barely audible, the beat somehow within him, as he bounces into a series of steps. 'One, two, three-and-four, five, six, seven-and-eight.' He stops and talks normally again. 'Some of the students are not doing too badly,' he says, 'although they're not exactly Ole Olsen or Chic Johnson.'

Curls glances at Alma and mouths, 'Who?'

'They're in the film,' says Giraffe.

'If you're all so good at it, why haven't we seen you dancing before now?' asks Curls.

'You've only been here for a few days,' says Jack. 'Wait for the weekend.'

'We don't include Mr Gunner, of course,' says Geoffrey. 'In fact, we keep quiet about it when he's around. Not at all sure he'd approve.'

Alma and Curls glance at each other and a smile passes between them. Mr Gunner and the Lindy Hop? It's not just the limp. Mr Gunner, whose English is always formal and correct, who thrives on near-silence, who is too embarrassed to look you in the eye when he's talking to you and prefers to focus on something over your shoulder, is not a dancer.

'I'd like to see him have a go, though,' says Curls.

Alma hasn't had so much fun in her whole life

as she has in the last five minutes. The music is still inside her, beating away. Her feet are tapping with the memory, her legs aching with the frustration of not moving. 'Can we do it again?' she says. 'I want another go.'

'You'll have to put on a record,' says Curls.

'That's fine,' says Jack. 'Let's just go over the steps first.'

They line up in front of him and he takes them through some basic steps. It doesn't seem so complicated when they go slower and watch him doing each movement first.

'You're all going to be good,' he says. 'Let's do it in pairs.' Four of the men step towards the girls and Alma finds herself opposite Geoffrey Harris.

'Men, put your hand on the lady's waist,' says Jack. 'Ladies, put your hand on his shoulder. If you haven't got a partner do it side by side. Music, Dennis.'

Dennis goes over to the shelf and selects a record. He removes the paper sleeve, places the disc on the turntable and winds up the handle with several vigorous turns. Then he lowers the needle on to the first groove. There is a preliminary scraping, a buzzing of sound.

Alma, conscious of Geoffrey's hand snaking round her waist, doesn't know where to look. She can smell the soap on him, feel the weave of his herringbone jacket under her fingers, hear his breathing above her head. Heat rises through her, steaming up into her face, continuing to the hairline and beyond, forming pinpricks of sweat on her head.

The music starts. 'Let's do it!' shouts Jack.

A clarinet wails enticingly, then the band tumbles in and winds itself up, a complicated beat from the drums, the snap of a bass, the high, frenzied semiquavers of a trumpet. Rhythm and melody explode around them.

'Forwards!' shouts Jack. 'One, two, three-and-four–'

It's impossible not to be taken over by, the music. It has more drive than the piano, more colour, a rhythm and tempo so compelling that Alma feels as if she can never sit still again – ever – that her feet have taken over, that there's nothing else that matters outside the music, nothing except the dancing–

The music stops.

One by one, they come to a standstill, swaying in the sudden silence.

Mr Gunner is standing by the gramophone, his hand lifting the needle from the record. 'Good evening, ladies and gentlemen,' he says quietly.

ii

Robert Gunner remains uncomfortable about the invasion of Mortimer Hall. He finds the presence of young ladies disruptive in a way he cannot precisely categorise. The deep, satisfying hush of Mortimer Hall has always been a haven for him after long days of lectures, seminars and tutorials. He is accustomed to coming home, joining the students for supper, then retiring to his study before going out to do his fire-watching shift. There are always papers to mark, lectures to prepare, ongoing research he is planning to publish on the subject of convex and discrete geometry, and if there's any time left after that and he's not too tired, he turns his attention to his personal project. In a series of exercise books, he's writing down as much as he can recall of his grandfather's life as a lighthouse keeper, much of it related to him by his mother. His grandfather had not been a talkative man, so Robert knows he will have to find much of his information from research. He has a plan to travel to the locations of his grandfather's assignments, experience the places in person. The prospect excites him.

He has always been content to hear murmuring and footsteps as students pass his study, the occasional dry laugh in the distance, even a snatch of music, and he doesn't mind being interrupted occasionally by a student with a problem. Indeed, he enjoys sitting down with one of his young men, offering him sherry, helping him to sort out his study programme or, more frequently now, discussing whether or not it would be wise for the young man in question to abandon his studies and enlist in the army, the navy or the RAF.

Robert has applied to join the navy three times since the beginning of the war, and been rejected three times. Not fit for active service.

'We require our sailors to walk upright on a rolling deck,' said one doctor.

'You wouldn't even spot the target with your eyesight,' said another. 'Let alone hit it.'

'I've got my glasses,' he said.

'And what would happen if they blew off in a bomb blast? Where would you be then?'

He has tried to persuade them that he could do a desk job. 'You're a mathematician,' said the officer in charge. 'The country needs your brain in place, fully functional. We'll get in touch with you if something comes up.'

Nobody has ever been in touch. The least he can do is train his students to the highest level possible so that they can offer their services to their country.

He is conscious of a shift in the atmosphere at Mortimer Hall, a vigilance that is unspoken but somehow present, a disturbing alertness among his students, which reminds him of the boys at Sherrard's when he picked up the Goldwyn's pupils. It's puzzling to him that four young ladies should have such a powerful effect.

He has spent more time than usual on his lighthouse project in the last week, unexpectedly finding his memories more soothing than his maths research. He stayed with his grandfather twice when he was a child, before his grandfather's mysterious disappearance. The lighthouse where he was serving at the time was on a remote part of the Welsh coastline, and the only way to reach it was along a coastal path, two miles from the station.

At the end of the path, a gap had been blasted out of the cliff and steep, rock-carved steps led down to a bridge over the narrow channel between the lighthouse and the mainland. PROPERTY OF TRINITY HOUSE, said the sign on the gate. ENTRY IS FORBIDDEN TO THE PUBLIC. In a way, that was the most exciting part of the holiday. He was allowed to go somewhere that was forbidden to everyone else. The first time he went, when he was about ten, it had been a relief to reach the gate after the exhausting walk over the cliffs. He and his mother had left his father, who had been blinded and mentally damaged during the First World War, in the care of a neighbour. They carried as many supplies as they could manage – fresh vegetables, coffee, butter, milk. 'No point in going all that way empty-handed,' his mother had said. But the bags were heavy and Robert's lame leg threatened to let him down. He didn't complain. His mother would have sighed and added the bags to her already heavy load.

They opened the gate and climbed down the steps to the unsteady wooden bridge. Clumps of heather, part of the vast carpet that wrapped the cliff in a purple-pink haze as far as the eye could see, were inching their way over the edge of the steps in an attempt to reclaim the land. When he looked through the planks of the bridge beneath his feet, Robert could see the sea forcing its way through black, seaweed-covered rocks, compressed in the narrow passageway, stirred into milky foam, booming as waves from opposite directions collided with each other. Each time this happened, even on a hot, still August day, the spray shot into the air, almost as high as his feet. It made him feel like an explorer or an adventurer somewhere in the continent of Africa, but he couldn't deny a sense of relief when they reached the other side.

Until he confronted the 162 steps ahead. He

counted them as he climbed, putting his weight on his stronger left leg, then bringing up the right to join it. He paused frequently, standing still and turning to admire the view. It was a way of pretending. He didn't want his mother to know that he couldn't do it in one go, that the bag of apples was heavy, that his legs were still trembling from the terror of the bridge. He knew what she would say to his grandfather: 'Robert found the steps difficult, poor lamb. He'll suffer from that injured leg till the day he dies, bless him.'

His memories of the lighthouse holidays centre on silence, on hours alone or with his grandfather, gazing out to sea and watching the weather change, the dark, smooth swirl of underwater currents, harbour porpoises swooping up and over the waves in glistening arcs, seagulls whirling and screeching, heads of seals bobbing up and shaking the drops off their whiskers, cormorants settling on the rocks below. Will, his grandfather's assistant, a brooding, large-boned man with tangled blond hair and a speech impediment, spoke even less than his grandfather. His sole contribution to the human language consisted of an enquiry every morning: 'D'you want sugar on your powwidge, Wobert?' The answer was always 'Yes, please,' but he kept asking anyway.

Sometimes Robert climbed up and down the steps to the bridge, trying to beat his own record, believing he could make his weak leg stronger. He even clambered down to the rocks below when the tide was low, moving slowly, dodging the spray, careful not to slip on the wet seaweed.

His grandfather was not a talkative man. He

spent much of the day watching the horizon, outside if the weather was fine, behind a window if it was stormy, chomping on the stem of his pipe, which seldom stayed alight for longer than half an hour, but never left his mouth. He should have had a beard – it would have been much easier in the absence of running hot water – but shaving was a ritual he enjoyed every morning at seven o'clock precisely. Seven bells, he called it, as if he was on a ship, although Robert had read enough books about ships to know that seven bells didn't mean seven o'clock in the morning. He'd tried to tell his grandfather and Will. 'There are eight bells, one for each half-hour of a watch, so seven bells in the middle watch – that's the middle of the night – is three thirty in the morning.' But he'd seen his grandfather's eyes stray towards the sea at the first mention of numbers, so he hadn't finished his explanation.

So they sat together, and the silence sank into Robert, changed him, taught him the value of not speaking. He learned nothing about his grandfather, beyond what his mother had already told him, but he knew everything about him that mattered. He was a presence in Robert's mind, lodged there with a certainty and a solidity that had no need for words.

When his grandfather was later posted to a rock lighthouse, a mile and a half offshore, the plan was that Robert should visit him during the summer, when the weather was calm enough for him to row out with a local fisherman.

But it never happened. Three months after his grandfather had moved there to join two other keepers, the coastguard went out on his monthly visit to replenish their supplies. When he landed, tied up his boat and climbed to the entrance, the place was deserted. There were two places laid for breakfast, cornflakes poured into a bowl, milk curdled in a blue and white striped jug and coffee stone cold in a pot. Slices of home-made bread lay on a plate, solid and dry as biscuits.

It was February and there had been several fearful storms. It was thought that something must have diverted the attention of the three men: they'd gone out to cope with an emergency, a fishing boat, perhaps, veering off course and failing to notice the danger – although no one ever came forward to report a missing boat – and a wave had swept them off the rocks. But why were all three of them down there? Regulations decreed that two should be on duty at all times. The third should have been off-duty, probably asleep. All three sets of waterproofs were gone from their pegs by the door. Perhaps one had been ill – appendicitis, heart attack, burst ulcer – and they had intended to launch the boat, row to the mainland for treatment. They'd closed the door neatly behind them, but the boat was still secure in the shed and they had disappeared without trace. Perhaps they'd had a fight, fallen out over whose turn it was to make the bread, who had left their muddy footprints on the stairs, who had finished the last of the butter. Irritating habits can become overwhelming when you're trapped in close proximity with two people you can't stand, in a landscape of extreme isolation.

Whatever the reason, they had disappeared and

nobody ever found out what had happened to them.

His mother wept quietly, almost non-stop, for many weeks. Her visits to her father had been important to her, giving her a break from her husband.

Robert wishes he could have written all this down before his mother died. She would have loved it. He's never forgotten the satisfaction of silence, the way it can wash over and through you, cleansing and rinsing until time takes on a different meaning and you discover something inside that you never knew was there. He kept it with him when he went home from the holidays to his father, who was always angry, and his long-suffering mother, who oppressed him with her quiet, patient love. The silence of his grandfather and the sharp logic of mathematics kept him sane and gave him purpose. He believes he can pass on the gift of silence to his students.

He is sitting at his desk one evening, his mind on the next day's lectures, when someone taps on his study door.

'Come in!' he calls.

It's Mrs Anderson, the housekeeper. 'I've rung the bell for supper,' she says. 'I can't keep it hot for ever.'

Robert pushes his chair back in surprise. 'I'm so sorry. I was distracted.'

Mrs Anderson, a short woman with arms built for wielding a rolling pin and carrying gigantic dishes from the stove to the table, sighs. 'Well,' she says, 'how unusual. But I'm talking about everyone else, not you.'

'No one has turned up for supper?'

She shakes her head solemnly.

'How very odd. Where are they all?'

He becomes aware of the sound of music in the distance. But they can't all be in the common room. Where's everyone else? 'Are the young ladies back from school?'

'Ages ago. They've had tea and biscuits. And all of your students have signed in. It's shepherd's pie – a small cut of real beef that the butcher put aside for me specially. To feed up the girls, he said. I need everyone to come at once.'

'Of course, of course,' says Robert. 'Don't worry, I'll sort this out. You go back to the dining room and prepare to dish up. I'll send them all down immediately. They probably didn't hear the supper bell.'

'I rang it twice,' she says, making her way down the corridor to the stairs, her large, apron-clad body casting sinister shadows in the dim, low-wattage light.

He can hear the music more clearly now. It's unusual, bouncy. Dance music? Here in Mortimer Hall? Surely not. His students are serious young men, chaps who value their opportunity to study, who have postponed their chance to join the army so that they can do something worthwhile first. Or, like Robert, they've failed to be accepted by the armed forces, but believe they can contribute to the body of knowledge and invention that may lead to victory. They are never frivolous and never allow themselves to be caught up in the kind of irresponsible activities that seem to be diverting so many young people nowadays.

And yet, as he descends the stairs behind Mrs Anderson, it's impossible to ignore the compulsive rhythms that are coming from the common room, music so frantic that it's difficult to understand how the musicians find time to breathe.

When he opens the door, he's astonished to find all ten of his students present. Most of them and the four schoolgirls are leaping around with an energy and athleticism that he wouldn't have believed possible after a hard day's work. They're jumping, hopping, strutting, their feet moving so fast that they should be tangling, their arms swinging out, sometimes colliding, but usually just missing. There's a wild joy on their faces that he has never seen before.

Robert, whose experience of music has been restricted to classical concerts, doesn't know how to classify the sound. He has occasionally listened to jazz concerts on the Home Service, but the style is not entirely to his taste. He prefers Bach. This music is so energetic that he feels exhausted just listening to it. And yet he can't seem to prevent his toes tapping inside his shoes.

The men, who have all removed their jackets, have lost their normal inhibitions and become children. Mr Hitchens, a second-year student from Ireland, who is always so calm, so polite, so courteous, is leaping into the air with extraordinary agility, swinging his arms and clicking his fingers. Mr Harris, a final-year chemistry student with a fine mind – his latest assignment is sitting at the top of a pile in Robert's room waiting to be marked – is twirling, moving freely, not entirely managing to keep up with everyone else, but nevertheless transformed into a Dervish in shirtsleeves, an expression of unguarded excitement transforming his face.

And then the girls. They're jumping around with the same energy, their faces radiant. Two are following Jack Hitchens, their heads down as they concentrate on the steps, then laughing uproariously as they nearly fall over, flinging their heads back and their arms out as if they no longer care about anything. They've rolled their skirts up round their waists so that their knees are showing and they can move more freely. The other two are dancing with partners, linked as if they're going to do the sort of dancing Robert knows about – a waltz, perhaps, or a foxtrot – but there's no sign of the formality he would expect. They're rolling their shoulders, swinging their hips, bouncing with the rhythm. Only Tristan Watson remains unaffected. He is sitting in a corner with a book, ignoring everybody.

'Ladies and gentlemen!' calls Robert. But no one hears him. No wonder they missed the dinner bell. He edges round the room to the gramophone, takes a breath and lifts the arm. The men stop first, one by one, their faces reflecting their embarrassment as they become aware that Robert is in the room. The girls respond less guardedly, unable to let go of the dance so easily. They continue to sway, as if the rhythm is still echoing inside them, still beating through their bones.

Robert would like to react with exasperation at the way they've all abandoned their dignity so enthusiastically, but as they face him, the sweat shining on their faces, their eyes bright and aroused, he can't find the words.

'Good evening, ladies and gentlemen,' he says.

They're still breathing heavily and nobody speaks. The atmosphere is heated, overexcited, and he can smell the girls again, that unfamiliar, earthy smell that disturbs him every time he catches a hint of it in the corridors of Mortimer Hall.

'It seems that you didn't hear the gong for supper. Could you please make your way to the dining room as quickly as possible? Mrs Anderson is on the verge of mutiny.'

He watches as the men straighten their ties, put their jackets back on and smooth their hair with their hands. They pick up their books and papers, tuck them under their arms and leave the room without a word.

It's possible that Mr Hitchens winks at the girls before he leaves, because a grin passes between them before they unroll their skirts.

Robert clears his throat. 'I assume you've done your homework?'

He's unsure if they're nodding or not. They move their heads, but they're sending each other sidelong glances at the same time, as if wild giggles are concealed somewhere within them and they're struggling to contain them.

'I have taken on the responsibility of overseeing your care and your education outside school hours,' he says, knowing he sounds pompous but unable to avoid it. 'I'll be answerable to Miss Cunningham-Smith if you neglect your work.'

He's interrupted by the sound of the gong. 'Your supper is getting cold. We must proceed to the dining room immediately.'

He watches them leave and remains to look around the common room. Nothing has changed. The books are neatly lined up on the bookcases, the table-tennis bats and balls have been replaced in the rack on the side of the table and the piano lid has been closed. But there's a raw energy in the atmosphere. It seeps through his skin, burrows its way in, stirring something deep inside him, filling him with a sense of unease.

He turns and makes for the dining room. 'Keep calm,' he says to himself, thinking of the poster on the door of the maths department. **Your Courage, Your Cheerfulness, Your Resolution, will bring us Victory**.

Maybe those poster designers knew what they were talking about.

iii

'No one, I repeat no one, will touch the Bunsen burners,' announces Miss Cunningham-Smith.

Alma, at the end of the row of girls sitting along the science bench, watches Curls exchange glances with Natalie. She recognises the way her mouth alters its angle on her otherwise impassive face, the faint scrunching of the skin at the corner of her eyes, and she knows that Curls is not taking the situation seriously. I should be in on Curls's planned rebellion, she thinks. We should be plotting together to turn on the Bunsen burner when no one's looking.

But she's too tired. She has spent most of the last few nights awake, learning to identify the noises of Mortimer Hall, listening for creaks that might become familiar by repeating themselves, hearing the bombers return, the deep, heavy drone of their engines growing louder and louder, only to jump violently and discover that she had dropped off and was dreaming. She dozed briefly until someone in the unknown depths of the building went to the lavatory and woke her again. She could hear the chain being pulled, the sudden activation of the cistern, the movement of the pipes as the water flowed through them, along the walls and under the floorboards. The blackout curtains took away all sense of the present, wrapping Alma's new home in a dense blanket of nothingness. It tucked itself round every surface, pressing down, blunting her thoughts.

They've been having lessons now for several days and most of the day girls have managed to come in to join the boarders. Some of them have lost their homes and need to be in school while their parents struggle with the complexities of finding somewhere else to live. Most of the teachers have turned up, but there aren't enough classes for them to teach so Miss Cunningham-Smith has organised some of them in the clearing-up work. Keeping the flag flying.

Curls puts up her hand.

'Yes, Jane?' says Miss Cunningham-Smith.

'When you say nobody will touch the Bunsen burners, is this a statement of fact about the future, i.e. a prophecy, or do you mean that you hope nobody will touch them?'

Miss Cunningham-Smith fixes Curls with a hard, penetrating stare. She does not reply.

But Curls is strangely oblivious. It must be the lack of sleep, the changed circumstances, the need to adapt to the new situation. 'Should you state it as an absolute fact when you can't actually be certain?'

By now everyone is holding her breath. Miss Cunningham-Smith smiles without humour. 'You raise an interesting point, Jane. You are correct that one cannot be certain, but one can make the statement as a fact if one wishes to emphasise the seriousness of the situation. You may, if you wish, reach out and touch the Bunsen burner, and thus prove my statement invalid, but one would like to think you have more intelligence. Some situations are worth challenging – Hitler's desire to subjugate the world being a case in point – others are not. I would consider disobedience in this matter to be unnecessary and wasteful of your resources. In short, Jane, should you wish to challenge my authority, I would advise you to pick something of greater significance. You should bear in mind the gravity of the times in which we live.'

Curls thinks for a moment, clearly tempted to touch the Bunsen burner anyway, just for the fun of it, but then says, 'I take your point, Miss Cunningham-Smith.'

Miss Cunningham-Smith's smile relaxes – a rare thing. 'You have demonstrated admirable restraint, Jane,' she says. 'I have high hopes for your future.'

Alma sees a look pass between the two of them,

a clear message of understanding, and she experiences a pang of jealousy. Something has happened that gives Curls an advantage, a signal of her growing maturity. In comparison, Alma feels slow, heavy, stupid.

The girls have been divided into three groups. The gym, the science lab and the hall are still in use, and two form rooms. There are several broken windows, but the weather is warm and Miss Cunningham-Smith believes in fresh air. Each class therefore includes more than one form and normal lessons are impossible. The upper fourth, the lower and upper fifth have been spending the last few days acting out *The Merchant of Venice* in the hall, but have now been assigned to the science lab.

At half past two, after Miss Cunningham-Smith has left and Miss Jenkins, the English teacher, has gone to check where they need to go next, Curls lights a Bunsen burner. She slips over to Miss Jenkins's desk and takes the box of matches lying next to the slide rule. She strikes a match on the box, watches it flare, and shields it with her hand to prevent it going out. The rest of the girls watch in horrified but admiring silence as she turns on the Bunsen burner and moves the match steadily into its stream. It lights instantly with a roar. She fiddles with the hole on the side, opening it as far as possible and the combined gas and air turn the flame blue, tight and noisy.

Curls turns it off again, her face impassive, replaces the matches on the desk and goes back to her seat.

Miss Jenkins returns and sniffs the air. She

looks around suspiciously, studying the face of every girl individually. 'Has anyone been striking matches?' she asks.

'No, Miss Jenkins,' they reply.

She frowns, sniffs again, but clearly doesn't know how to proceed. 'Very well. Last scene, please. We're in Portia's house...'

iv

Dr Guest and his wife, kind people, old friends of the family, arrange the funeral, so when Alma first sees the coffins, they are sealed and anonymous, unrelated to her memories of her parents. Occasionally, she still finds herself believing that it's all been a terrible mistake, that they might have been elsewhere at the time of the bombing and the bodies in the coffins are imposters, but she knows she's being unreasonable. Her father's senior registrar identified them. There is no alternative story.

When Alma tells Dr Guest that she would prefer to continue boarding rather than stay with his family, he's happy to accept her decision. 'You'll be welcome at any time if you change your mind,' he says. 'And we'll be expecting you for the holidays, of course.'

She longs for her brother, Duncan, to come home. She's written to him, and thinks Dr Guest has as well. She addressed the letter to the training camp near Durham, his last known address, but he can't still be there. She thinks of him often, somewhere in the world, fighting Nazis, ignorant of the death of their parents. She imagines him crouching behind piles of sandbags, occasionally peering over the top, fixing his rifle on an enemy soldier, pulling the trigger, notching up his tally on a list in a notebook, like a cricket score. She wonders if he has a blanket made up of knitted squares, like the ones they produce at school in domestic science.

She can't pay attention during the funeral. Her mind is on the Lindy Hop. They've started to organise regular practice sessions – once during an evening after school and twice at weekends. Waves of excitement pulse through her every time she thinks about it – the all-consuming beat, the freedom of her body as she allows it to find its own strength. It's as if she was never really alive until she discovered dancing, as if her previous life was a preface, an introduction. All day, she waits for the evenings when she can practise. During the night, whenever she wakes, snatches of tunes echo through her head and she rehearses the steps in her mind, feverish with anticipation.

At the end of the funeral, in the open air of the graveyard, they sing a madrigal, conducted by Jack Hitchens, who used to be a music scholar at a cathedral school. The four girls and three other men have rehearsed under his direction, learning the parts, discovering the pleasure of four-part harmony. Alma and Natalie sing soprano and Curls and Giraffe sing alto. John Dowlands's 'Flow My Tears':

Flow my tears, fall from your springs,
Exil'd for ever let me mourn;
Where night's black bird her sad infamy sings,
There let me live forlorn.

The sound echoes into the open sky and at the end the mourners, some of whom have travelled long distances to be there, seem to be holding their breath. There's a long, long silence, interrupted only by the chattering of blackbirds in a nearby oak tree.

It seems appropriate to sing, to balance the excitement of dancing with the sober, thoughtful songs and memories of her parents.

Miss Cunningham-Smith works tirelessly to restore the school day to normality, or as close as possible. Two of the day girls were killed in the bombing, but after the special assembly that was held for them, they have been allocated their place in folklore, romanticised by their early deaths, and now it is hard to talk about them any more. Like Alma's parents, they've sunk into the category of the unmentionable. Too much emphasis on them would be bad for morale.

'We're living through our own history,' announces Natalie, one afternoon, as they come out of their last lesson of the day, an analysis of the causes of the Wars of the Roses.

'Obviously,' says Curls.

'It's different from how it used to be,' says Natalie. 'We weren't at war then.'

'Everything's history,' says Curls, 'once it's gone.'

‘Nobody will be interested in us,’ says Giraffe.

Alma’s toes are tapping inside her right shoe. One, two, three-and-four–

‘You don’t know that,’ says Natalie. ‘In two thousand years, they’ll be digging up strange mounds of earth and one of them will be Goldwyn’s. “Aha,” they’ll say. “A school. One of those quaint little institutions where twentieth-century girls were taught about things that didn’t matter.”’

‘They’ll already know about Goldwyn’s,’ says Curls. ‘Miss Cunningham-Smith will be a famous figure from our period. Her name will remain long after she’s gone. Like Florence Nightingale or Emily Pankhurst.’

‘Why would anyone remember a headmistress?’ asks Natalie.

‘Oh, come on,’ says Giraffe. ‘Nobody would dare forget Miss Cunningham-Smith.’

The girls have been experimenting with hair-styles, examining pictures in magazines – Greer Garson, Deanna Durbin, Katharine Hepburn – trying to work out how to produce suitable curls. Natalie, whose red hair is naturally curly, has been the most successful. She’s used a small clip to pin up one side behind her ear so that the hair swoops and swings in exactly the right shape. Giraffe, Curls and Alma have struggled with overnight curlers, waking up every morning in keen anticipation, desperate for manageable curls that will hang seductively over one cheek, but somehow never achieving the effect they want.

Curls’s hair is a complete failure, too strong-willed to conform. It’s been possible to see signs of a few bends and kinks at breakfast, but by lunchtime they've nearly all gone, leaving her hair fluffy and uneven. She has become sensitive on the subject and is guaranteed to react with indignation if anyone says, 'Have you been trying to curl your hair, Curls?'

She's decided to give up trying. 'Hollywood will have to manage without me. Who wants curly hair anyway?'

Giraffe now puts on lipstick every afternoon before walking back to Mortimer Hall, keeping her head down as they leave the school, while the other girls keep a lookout for Miss Cunningham-Smith. They know there will be serious trouble if Giraffe gets caught. Miss Cunningham-Smith's scathing opinions about makeup are well known to every Goldwyn's pupil.

The lipstick was sent by Giraffe's sister, who works at Bletchley Park doing something top secret. 'My lips are sealed,' says Giraffe, if anyone asks, giving the impression that the lipstick is an important part of the sealing. The other girls suspect she doesn't know anything. They've all seen the poster outside Exeter Central station. It shows a shapely woman – amazing curls, very red lipstick – surrounded by admiring, uniformed men: **'Keep mum. She's not so dumb! CARELESS TALK COSTS LIVES'**.

Alma follows the other girls out of the side door and watches her feet move, one in front of the other. One, two, three-and-four. Step, step, triple-step. She's hungry for the dancing, her pulse racing as she runs through the steps in her mind.

'Alma!' calls a voice, from somewhere to her side.

She turns and sees a soldier standing back, almost hidden behind the bushes, unnoticed by most of the girls as they emerge from the school. He looks familiar, but she doesn't know any soldiers.

'Alma,' he says again.

She examines him more closely. 'Duncan!' she cries, and throws herself into his arms.

After a few comforting moments, she pulls herself away and examines him carefully. His face is sunburned, leaner than she remembers, like a real man, not her brother. Now that they have spent time apart, she's conscious, for the first time, of the ten years between them. 'They sent bombers – the Luftwaffe...' she says slowly. She doesn't know how to tell him.

He smiles and looks exactly like their father. 'I know,' he says.

He can't have received her letter. If he had, he would have been back in time for the funeral. 'Did you get my letter?'

He shakes his head. 'I've been abroad,' he says. 'It takes for ever for post to reach us.'

He doesn't know they're dead. He can't know. What words can she use? 'Mum, Dad–'

But he stops her. 'A message got through to me,' he says. 'From Dr Guest. Why do you think I've come home?'

'You're too late,' she says. 'They've been buried.'

'I'm sorry. I did my best, but you can't rush the army. I'm lucky to get back at all – they let me cadge a lift on a transport plane but I had to beg.'

'I needed you at the funeral,' she says. Then she does something she hasn't done before. She bursts into tears.

V

When Robert realises that there are only three girls at supper, he wonders if he has already been told why and forgotten. He turns to Mrs Anderson. 'Who's missing?' he asks.

'Goodness,' she says. 'It's Alma. I hadn't noticed. Let me ask the girls if they know where she is.' She goes over and talks to the other three.

Of course, he should have known it was Alma. The one whose parents have died.

'Apparently her brother's home on leave, the one in the army. He's turned up unexpectedly. The girls aren't certain where they are, but think they've probably gone into Exeter to get something to eat.'

'They really should have asked permission,' says Robert. 'We can't have them wandering around without telling us. What if we were to have another bombing raid?'

'What indeed?' says Mrs Anderson.

When Robert returns to his room after supper he can hear the sound of the piano in the common room and recognises the music of Bach.

Robert is fond of Bach. When he was growing up in Manchester, he used to attend concerts in the

Free Trade Hall with his mother. They would climb the steps (he'd had plenty of practice at this during his holidays at the lighthouse) to the cheapest seats under the roof and their view was often blocked by pillars, but nothing could prevent them hearing the soaring sounds of the Hallé Orchestra or the rise and fall of voices in performances of the St Matthew Passion, the St John Passion, the Peasant Cantata. He has heard Horowitz and Moszkowski performing Bach on the piano. Preludes and fugues, toccatas, three-part Inventions. In those years between the wars, as he grew into an adult, he learned to delve deeper into his inner world for inspiration. While he pondered the magical patterns of geometry theorems, algebraic formulae, the secret joys of calculus, he also found himself learning to appreciate Bach more and more. A composer who could see the mathematical possibilities of form, who could weave together intricate patterns of melodies with a rigorous exactitude, compromising nothing, yet produce a work of intellectual and aesthetic beauty.

So when he hears the sound of a Bach fugue, he is sufficiently interested to stop and listen. He knows it well and immediately recognises that an expert is playing.

The music is coming from the common room. Robert makes his way along the corridor, reaches for the handle, pauses, then turns it slowly and carefully, not wishing to interrupt the music.

He assumes that it's one of his students playing, a young man who perhaps plays for pleasure but whose great love is really physics, mathematics or chemistry, who would not necessarily have revealed that he could play the piano. It hasn't occurred to Robert that the performer could be one of the schoolgirls from Goldwyn's. The background noise they've generated so far is one of high-pitched voices and odd little shrieks of laughter. It reminds him of his mother, the only female presence he has ever known.

He knows Mrs Anderson can deal with the girls, but he can't quite remove them from his consciousness. He is pleased he can contribute to the war effort, but he would prefer not to run into them when going down for breakfast in the morning, or meet them along the corridors, in the garden. He suspects that the episode with the dancing has been repeated but they shut the door, turn the music down a little, protect him from the worst excesses. He is grateful for this. He wouldn't welcome further confrontation.

So he is not prepared for the discovery that this lyrical, gifted performer of Bach is a girl. It's the thin, confident one with angular limbs and a long neck, her thick, straight hair cut short in line with her chin and a severe fringe across her forehead. The one they call Curls.

He stands and listens. There's no one else in the room – the rest must be doing their homework – and she clearly believes herself to be alone. She moves with the music, her back soft and supple, her arms youthful and fluid, her head dipping and soaring with the ecstasy of the music. She looks as if she should be sharp and tight, but she is not. She is so absorbed in her playing, her fingers moving with dazzling speed, that her body is a manifestation of the music itself. Robert finds that he's as moved by her physical movements as by the music. He can't separate the two.

The music reaches further inside him than he could ever have imagined. It breaches his silence, arouses more emotion than he thought he possessed. He's always understood that music has the power to move – he has experienced it many times before – but never like this. Never with this extraordinary depth.

The music draws to a close. The girl remains with her head bowed over the piano for some time, as if she's unwilling to leave the world she has created. Robert can't move either. He doesn't want her to know that he has witnessed her performance but, equally, he finds it impossible to leave the room. His throat is swollen, aching with the strain of the unaccustomed emotion.

Then she turns and sees him. She claps a hand over her mouth. 'Oh,' she says. 'I didn't know you were there. I hope you don't mind, only I needed to do some practice. I have a concert in a few weeks' time.'

'You play in concerts?' he asks, his voice dry and unfamiliar.

'Yes, I'm afraid so. I've been doing it for years. Everyone says I'm a prodigy. But I don't think that's really true. I just like playing.'

He stares at her. 'I didn't realise – nobody told me.'

'Why should they? It's a bit boring, really.' She laughs. She's so normal. And yet her playing transforms her. Just watching her, seeing her eyes when she first turned round – so wide and expressive – has aroused in him a sensation he has never before experienced.

'You have a great talent, Miss Curley,' he says. 'I can see why you're in demand for concerts. I'm only sorry that I hadn't known about this earlier.'

She laughs again, so natural, so childlike. 'Ah, well, it was just something I was born with. I'm not sure if it's a good or bad thing. But you have to go along with it, don't you? Otherwise it would be wasted.'

He finds himself smiling. She's a fifteen-year-old girl, not a grown woman. Why does he feel so clumsy, so inadequate?

'Is it all right?' she says. 'To play the piano sometimes?'

'My dear,' he says, 'you have my permission to play any time you wish.'

Part Six

i

9 October 1963

Wilhelmina Yates surveys the twenty-one members of staff sitting round the polished walnut table in the boardroom and offers them a warm, welcoming smile. There's a cup of coffee in front of each one and three plates of assorted biscuits – custard creams, ginger snaps; the chocolate digestives have already disappeared. These weekly staff meetings during Monday-morning break have proved to be invaluable. While the girls stroll around outside with their buns and bottles of milk, lightly supervised by two members of staff, the teachers gather for precisely thirty minutes to discuss procedures and innovations. The ghost of Miss Cunningham-Smith is fading, thinks Miss Yates. My staff are beginning to work with me rather than against me. Only Alma Braithwaite remains determined to resist at all costs.

Alma is sitting at the far end of the table, as far away from Miss Yates as possible, refusing to make eye contact. Why can't she acknowledge that some changes are worth making, that new ideas are not necessarily always wrong?

Does she simply require more patience and kindness? Not that Miss Yates has ever been unkind. But maybe she needs a different sort of kindness, a prolonged interest in her affairs. Maybe they should sit down regularly together, over afternoon tea, to discuss the policies of Miss Cunningham-Smith and the possibilities of moving on from some of them, taking Alma's suggestions into account.

It all sounds so cosy, so feasible, but it's difficult to imagine it having any success. And there simply isn't enough time in the day.

Miss Yates turns to the woman sitting next to her. 'Now we are all settled, I would like you to welcome a new addition to our staff. Fräulein Adelinde Bauer. It has been suggested to me recently by one of our governors that we should be offering a second language to our girls and I agreed. That is why Fräulein Bauer is with us today.'

Fräulein Bauer, a woman with wide shoulders and solid arms, lowers her head in a nod of greeting to the other members of staff. 'Good morning, ladies,' she says, in an amiable voice, which gives the impression that a deep chuckle is lurking inside her chest, waiting for the opportunity to emerge.

Alma stares at Adelinde Bauer. 'We're going to teach our girls to speak German?' she asks.

Miss Yates smiles. 'Yes. I thought it would be appropriate in today's climate of *entente cordiale*. This by no means reflects any dissatisfaction with Maxine's excellent teaching of French' – Maxine Wright looks up at the mention of her name, with a slightly cold smile that fools no one – 'but our girls should have the opportunity to expand their talents whenever possible. We have some gifted linguists among them, I believe,' Maxine's smile softens as she acknowledges the truth of this, 'and I would like to feel we can open up greater job opportunities for them in the future.'

There are several nods around the table by now and Miss Yates can sense a gradual warming of the initial frosty response that had been voiced by Alma.

'But how will we manage the timetabling now that we're halfway through the term?' asks Cressida Davies. 'There's very little room for manoeuvre.'

Miss Yates beams at her. She likes Cressida, who has a logical mind and rarely wastes time passing judgement, preferring to address the matter as if it's a maths problem that needs to be solved. 'Well, I thought Fräulein Bauer could come in for a few hours a week to start with. Some sixth-formers might relish the prospect of taking an extra O level and we could probably squeeze some lessons into their free periods. It would be more complicated lower down the school, but we could certainly manage some lunchtime lessons, or after school. If the take-up is significant, we could juggle the timetable a little in time for next term. It may even be possible to–' She stops. She had been about to propose that some girls could miss a non-academic lesson, but she realises that music lessons would be at risk for those girls who weren't doing O-level Music. Alma would be outraged and her resentment could easily spread to domestic science, games or art. 'Well, let's see how things develop. A letter to parents would seem to be the first step – to assess the amount of interest.'

'Do you seriously think we're ready for German lessons?' asks Alma.

Miss Yates examines the faces of the women round the table. Only three are in their twenties, newly appointed teachers who wouldn't have significant memories of the war. 'Most of the grammar schools now offer German. We mustn't lag behind. I think we should remember the words of President Kennedy at the Berlin wall. "*Ich bin ein Berliner*," he said. I am a Berliner. Can we not all be Berliners?'

Fräulein Bauer clears her throat. 'We in West Germany do not believe that we should be constantly looking backwards. We are Europeans. We would like to believe that we are welcome in your country, just as you are welcome in ours.'

'After all,' says Miss Yates, 'the war ended eighteen years ago.'

'There were twenty-one years between the First and Second World Wars,' says Alma Braithwaite, softly.

'You can't seriously be suggesting we'll continue to fight wars with Germany every twenty-odd years,' says Maxine Wright, staring at Alma with barely concealed hostility.

Alma looks directly back at her and there's a noticeable drop in temperature. 'Of course not. I was merely pointing out that it's not long since the end of the war and we should bear in mind that many of us here remember it well.'

There are several murmurs of agreement around the table from the more senior members of staff. 'Indeed,' says Miss Rupin. 'It isn't easy to forget.'

Miss Yates would like to encourage Miss Rupin into early retirement. She was originally part of the boarding staff, but now unsuccessfully teaches Latin – she lacks the necessary authority, by all accounts – and she is too willing to side with Alma.

'Well,' says Henrietta Fox, biology. 'If we teach our girls German and there's another war, we'll be thanked for creating a potential source of new spies.'

'Don't be ridiculous,' says Maxine Wright.

Miss Yates would prefer not to remember the war. She frequently wakes at around two o'clock every morning to the sound of nightmare sirens. She finds herself standing by the side of her bed, rocking backwards and forwards, paralysed by waves of fear, her feet numb with cold and her legs unable to function. She knows it's not real, that the sirens were dismantled long ago, but it takes her for ever to breathe normally again, to persuade herself that there's no danger to her except from lack of sleep. By the time sensation has returned to her legs and her heart has stopped pounding, she is wide awake and has to go and make herself a hot cup of Ovaltine before she can go back to bed.

'I see a danger and self-indulgence in dwelling in the past,' she says. 'We're living in the sixties, a time of exciting change and innovation. That's one of the reasons why I have decided to appoint Fräulein Bauer. To iron out any of our lingering prejudices.' Unfortunately, she can see from the expressions round the table that Alma Braithwaite is not alone in her doubt.

'What part of Germany do you come from?'

asks Cressida Davies.

'Lübeck,' says Fräulein Bauer. 'I don't know if you are familiar with my home town. It's on the north coast, beside the Baltic Sea, built in the twelfth century as part of the Hanseatic League. We are now the second largest town in Schleswig-Holstein and an important port.' Her voice is low-pitched and the words seem to come from her chest, as if her throat is sore and she needs to bypass it. There is still a suggestion of humour underneath. Can she see something amusing in the conversation, which she is not prepared to share with them?

'Ah,' says Cressida. 'Lübeck.'

'We know about Lübeck,' says Alma after a moment's silence.

Miss Yates stares at her staff with some bewilderment. What is the significance of Lübeck? 'I'm sorry?' she says. 'Is there some connection with which I am not familiar?'

'The Baedeker raids,' says Alma, her voice icy.

'Ah, yes,' says Fräulein Bauer, with a slightly twisted smile. 'Of course.'

'Lübeck was a port. There was at least a reasonable motive for the British bombing.'

'Like you, we all suffered,' says Fräulein Bauer. 'I lost my entire family.'

There's another awkward silence.

'Well,' says Miss Yates, anxious to move on, 'hostilities ended a long time ago. Let us remember President Kennedy's hand of friendship.'

'Miss Bauer seems to be under the impression that we were the aggressors,' says Alma.

'No,' says Fräulein Bauer, gravely. 'I did not

mean to give that impression.'

'Could someone explain to me exactly what this is about?' asks Miss Yates, realising that the subject is not going to go away.

'The Baedeker raids,' says Cressida Davies, the maths teacher, the analyst, 'were the result of the RAF bombing Lübeck and Rostock. Hitler was so furious about the RAF attack that he vowed to destroy historic cities in Britain with three stars in the *Baedeker Guide*. It's a tourist guide, you see, so it highlights the highlights, as it were. Exeter, Bath, Norwich, York and Canterbury were the ones chosen.'

'I see,' says Miss Yates. She should have known this, of course, and been prepared. 'Nevertheless, we must move on. We cannot allow ourselves to indulge in a competition for who suffered most.' There really is nothing more to say. She would like to quote President Kennedy again, but feels she's already made that point. If they want to compare experiences, she could tell them that she was in Coventry at the time of the bombing. Nothing can compare with the bombing of Coventry. The only astonishing thing was that anyone had survived at all. Bombing is bombing, whether you are German or British. If you lose your family, everything else becomes irrelevant.

'Is Lübeck in West Germany?' asks one of the younger teachers.

'I would not be here if it was in the GDR,' says Fräulein Bauer.

'Are you close to East Germany? Can you see the wall?'

'The wall is in Berlin. In Lübeck we are separated by the river. There's a crossing in the south of the city.'

'You are that close?'

'We are that close.'

'Can we talk about the parents' evening for the upper third?' asks Pauline Adams, the new English teacher, fresh from Leeds University with a first. 'It's only three weeks away.'

Miss Yates smiles at her gratefully. 'That was the main point on my agenda,' she says, and distributes copies of her information sheet. She has listed timings and general advice. 'I would like to say how pleased I am that you have all embraced the idea of a parents' evening so enthusiastically.'

'I think it's an excellent innovation,' says Cressida Davies. 'Parents should be involved with their daughters' education.'

'Personally, I think parents should be kept as far away as possible,' says Henrietta Fox. 'They cause nothing but trouble.'

'I think we can all sympathise with that view,' says Miss Yates with a gentle smile. 'But we have to bear in mind that they pay the fees.'

'We might well find that the girls work better if their parents know what we expect,' say Cressida.

'Let's see how it goes before we get too carried away,' says Maxine Wright.

Alma Braithwaite is looking out of the window, her eyes still, her mind elsewhere.

ii

This is Alma's first parents' evening as a form mistress. She has spent the last few days organising her pupils, making sure the insides of their desks are immaculate, their rough books presentable, and there are no surplus items of games kit cluttering up the form room. Every detail has been attended to with military precision and she can find any child's record within seconds. She's been staying late at night, imposing a greater order over a space that has always been well ordered. Pencils are arranged according to height in the holder, inkwells contain the same amount of ink, the pictures on the walls are lined up exactly. It's all very pleasing. The elegance of control.

The last girls have left and the building settles into an untroubled silence.

Cressida Davies comes in. 'All set?'

'I think so,' says Alma. 'Is there anything that I'm likely to have forgotten?'

'I suspect I should be asking you that question. You're always much more efficient than I am. I found two appointment slips yesterday that the girls had forgotten to take home, so I've had to phone the parents. Not a satisfactory process. They pick my brains there and then, over the phone, and still want to come in for their rightful allocation of my time.'

'I've spent hours trying to please everyone, but

it's impossible. They all want to come at the same time.'

'I've had the same problem. All that work, just to please a handful of people.'

Alma looks at Cressida. Is she implying that it's really just to please Miss Yates? She has never voiced any dissatisfaction before – in fact, she gives the impression that she's broadly in favour. Alma runs a finger along the neat edge of a pile of papers arranged on her desk and resists the temptation to become openly critical. 'I'm not convinced it was necessary to give appointments. People are used to queues.'

Cressida smiles. 'It's almost anarchical, isn't it, avoiding queuing? Changing the habits of a generation. Miss C-S must be turning in her grave.'

Now she's referring directly to Miss Cunningham-Smith. Could she be trying to tell Alma that she's on her side? An alliance? Miss Braithwaite and Miss Davies versus Miss Yates? Or could Cressida be a spy? Sent to lure Alma into indiscretions that could lead to her dismissal? It's impossible to know for certain and she doesn't want to say anything incriminating. 'The old ways are often the best,' she says cautiously.

'Well,' says Cressida, turning to the door, 'I'd better get off. I've got a nice stew in the oven – good nourishing fodder before we go over the top – and I don't want to be late back. Mustn't be seen to be neglecting one's responsibilities in the face of enemy action.' She stops on her way out. 'It's immaculate in here, Alma. One of these days you'll have to tell me how you get fifteen delightful eleven-year-olds to resist their natural inclination to clutter up the immediate environment with every conceivable unnecessary item. It's a skill I've never mastered.'

'It's not me,' says Alma. 'They seem to want to do it themselves...'

But Cressida has gone and Alma is talking to herself.

Alma has memorised the details of her appointment list.

Robert Gunner asked for a late appointment and signed his name in a tight, neat signature. She's kept his note, studied his ticks on the small slip of paper, wondering if he wrote them with the black enamelled fountain pen with the gold-rimmed cap that was always clipped into the top pocket of his jacket.

He still turns up in Alma's dreams occasionally, always charming and correct with his quiet concern.

She's discovered that his wife died eleven years ago. It was easy to get hold of the information. As a result of Miss Yates's determination to remove all clutter from her room, the tall filing cabinet that contains the pupils' details has been moved into the secretary's office and the staff now have access to the records.

Alma wonders what his wife was like. Did she appreciate music? Did she play an instrument?

Curls at the piano, leaning over, her fingers fluttering, like leaves on a tree in the wind. Light, agile, brilliant.

She's given him the second last appointment. Eight-forty. If it was the last one, she might find herself in an embarrassing position, having to continue talking to him while she clears up. This way, she can show him out courteously and demonstrate her professional manner.

Will she recognise him? Will he recognise her? Will he mention Curls?

All after-school activities have been cancelled. No orchestra practice, no netball matches, no hockey coaching. After Cressida has left, Alma remains in her form room for a while. She tells herself that she needs to go over her last-minute arrangements, but in reality she just wants to sit on her own, listening to the sounds of the building, hearing nothing. The silence pleases her.

She has no reason to go home. No one waiting there for her. She's brought some sandwiches – mackerel paste from the Co-op – and an apple, which she'll eat in one of the music rooms, once she has taught her private pupils. They're coming to Goldwyn's for their lessons today. As she leaves her room, she passes Roy, the caretaker, and his assistant, John, who are removing a few chairs from each form room and placing them in rows along the corridors so that parents can sit down while they wait for their appointments.

'Whose idea is this?' asks Alma, stopping in front of them.

'Give you three guesses,' mumbles Roy, who never speaks unless he has to. He has trouble forming his words properly. His lips seem to lack the necessary tension.

'Our esteemed headmistress?' suggests Alma.

They exchange a moment of eye-contact. Alma turns away with a sense of satisfaction.

She heads for the Vaughan Williams Building, the new music block that was finished shortly before Miss Cunningham-Smith died. It won't be open this evening, since the visiting music teachers won't be attending – too inconsequential, not significant enough for contact with parents – but Alma, as head of music, will be available in her own form room if any parents want to speak to her about their daughter's musical progress.

Her pupil, Antony, who has walked down from Sherrard's, is waiting for her. He grins at her in his easy, relaxed way as soon as he sees her and she responds with a smile. 'You're on time,' she says, as she unlocks the door.

'How could I be late for you, Miss Braithwaite?' he says, standing back to allow her to enter first.

Is he being cheeky? She hesitates, uncertain, but the moment passes before she can decide how to respond.

She enters the building, sensing his towering presence behind her. He hovers politely, giving her space, treating her with respect. She has taught him since he was eight and seen him transformed from a shy, earnest child to a confident young man with much natural ability. He is so uncomplicatedly, so authentically masculine that his presence always brings her a warm rush of pleasure.

'Let's play the Steinway today,' she says. 'Everyone else has gone home so we'll have the place to ourselves. It'll be useful for you to get used to the piano before the exam.'

She flicks on all the lights. The grand piano, left to Goldwyn's in the will of an Old Girl who had caught TB in her thirties and died young, is standing to one side, its dark wood gleaming. The large, pleasant room has a wooden floor and tall windows that look out over a softly sloping grassy bank. At the top of the bank, it's possible to see the rose garden and the statue of the Goldwyn's girl that used to stand outside Merrivale. An iconic photograph of this statue was published in the *Western Morning News* after the bombing. The young girl stood triumphantly in the midst of chaos, miraculously untouched, a symbol of Exeter's ability to survive and rise again.

Antony goes over to the piano, raises the lid from the keys and presses a few notes around middle C. The quality of the piano is immediately apparent. 'I'd forgotten how good it was,' he says.

'Let's have the lid up,' says Alma. 'Can you hold it for a minute?'

She finds the supporting rod and fixes it into place, admiring Antony's casual strength, the simple way in which he takes over the weight of the lid.

'Try it,' she says. 'Why don't you play the Bach?'

He sits down, adjusts the height of the stool unhurriedly, putting out his right foot to find the pedal, glancing down to make sure he's lined up properly.

For a brief second, Alma is reminded of Curls, cool and level-headed, who always did exactly the same thing in the few tense moments before starting to play in a concert. Alma often used to wish she could emulate Curls's calm maturity, knowing that she would sit down and start too quickly, later discovering that the pedal wasn't where she'd thought it was. Even now, when playing in Assembly, she sometimes forgets to check.

Antony begins to play the B minor prelude. *Allegretto*, sonorous, the *sostenuto* chords filling the space of the room with a warm, rich sound. Alma has intended to pull up a chair so that she can correct him where necessary, but she finds herself standing back and watching, startled by the strength of his playing. His performances have never been this good in the past. A new sensitivity seems to have come from somewhere inside him, as if he's discovered a new source of emotion, not waited for her advice but moved to a higher level on his own.

He starts on the fugue, faster, more frantic, the semi-quavers rushing to trip over each other, but never out of control. Each time the subject appears, he brings it out resolutely, even when it takes the middle voice, a single line of melody singing out through the complexity of the other parts. Not quite up to Curls's standard, but still extraordinarily good.

She steps forward to turn the page, but she's too far away and Antony attempts to manage for himself, flapping it over with his left hand while trying to keep going with the right.

The music flies off the stand and lands on the floor with a dull thump.

The interruption is ugly and uncomfortable for a few seconds. Then Antony laughs. 'Oops,' he says. 'I hope that doesn't happen in the exam.'

Alma goes to retrieve it, finding herself almost

giggling, exhilarated by the intensity of his playing. 'Never mind,' she says, 'but you'll have to work out how to do it. Since you've stopped anyway, let's go back and examine a few details. Lovely playing, by the way. You've been practising, haven't you?' Her praise seems inadequate, but she doesn't know how to make it sound more convincing.

'It's Mum's fault. She's been standing over me with a whip – well, not quite, but she says she's not going to pay all that money for an exam if I don't make an effort.'

'Has she bribed you?'

He nods, a little sheepish. 'She says I can have driving lessons if I get a merit or a distinction.'

'Excellent!' says Alma. 'Now, let's go back to the first page. I thought the semi-quavers here were just a tiny bit leisurely – not noticeably so but enough to disturb the flow. They need to sound effortless.'

'It's a difficult section – there's so much going on.'

'Let's have a look at the fingering.'

They work for about half an hour, examining details, polishing, improving. Just before they finish, Alma becomes aware of noises outside. She turns and sees a group of four girls staring in through one of the tall windows. Their faces are close to the glass, their eyes fixed on Antony. They haven't even noticed that they've been seen.

Irritation spreads through her. What are they doing here? Why haven't they gone home with the rest of the girls?

She recognises one of them. Janice Goodwin

from the lower fifth. A boarder. Her father is with the army, stationed in Germany. Alma goes over to the window and taps on it sharply. Antony stops in mid-phrase, turning to see what's going on. The girls outside stare at Alma, their eyes wide and uncomprehending. She flaps her hands at them to shoo them away, but they remain fixed to the spot as if they don't understand.

'Go away!' shouts Alma. She waves again, but they still don't react. 'There's going to be trouble,' she mutters, as she strides to the door.

Antony gets up uncertainly. 'No,' she calls, over her shoulder. 'Carry on playing – do some scales. I won't be long.'

She leaves the building and circles round the side of the music block to the rear. Standing at the top of the bank, she has a clear view of the girls, all of whom are still peering in through the window. They're from the upper fourth and lower fifth. Fourteen and fifteen years old. Not girls who have displayed much interest in music in the past.

It's not the performance that interests them. It's Antony.

One of the girls sighs, a long-drawn-out release of breath. 'He's gorgeous,' she says slowly, spreading out the sound of the vowels.

'I thought you only had eyes for Cliff Richard,' says another.

'Oh, there's room in my life for the real thing. Cliff will still be around tomorrow–'

'Janice!' calls Alma, sharply.

Janice turns. She's tall and well developed; her gymslip is struggling to accommodate her progress towards maturity. Her tight brown curls are held back by a regulation navy hairband.

'What exactly are you doing here?' demands Alma.

'Nothing,' says Janice. 'We're just music lovers.'

'Nothing what?'

Janice makes a great show of sighing heavily. 'Nothing, Miss Braithwaite,' she says.

There are giggles from the others.

'Be quiet!' says Alma. 'The next person who encourages Janice's rudeness by laughing will get an order mark.'

There's an intake of breath from all four, followed by a shocked silence. Order marks are rarely given, usually only for potentially expelling offences. Any girl who gets one achieves instant notoriety and is spoken about in whispers, admired for her cheek.

Alma knows she's overreacted. She's never been able to command the kind of respect that she would like from the older pupils. In the past, she's always assumed that it's because she teaches class music, an unexamined subject for most girls, a slot in the timetable for relaxation only. Her new appointment as form mistress should change that, but the upper-thirds are still the only ones who take her seriously. Cressida Davies can silence a room just by walking through the door. When Alma walks in, the older girls don't even notice she's there.

'Will you please come away from the window immediately and go back to Merrivale? Surely it must be time for tea.'

'No, Miss Braithwaite,' says another girl she

doesn't recognise. 'Tea isn't for an hour.'

Alma is not familiar with the boarders' timetable so she can't argue. 'Nevertheless, I want you to allow us to continue our lesson in peace. I am extremely displeased by your lack of consideration.'

'Who is he?' asks one of the girls.

'He's really dishy,' says another.

'What's his name?'

They still don't move.

Alma is swamped by her usual sense of inadequacy and frustration. She's no different from any of the other teachers but for some reason she can't get the girls to co-operate. She raises her voice. 'Will you please leave?'

Nothing happens.

'Move!' She's shouting now and the girls finally respond. One starts to back away.

'What exactly is going on here?'

Miss Yates is standing at the top of the slope, her feet planted firmly apart, staring down at them. She's shorter than Alma, but she seems to fill more space. The girls turn towards her instantly, their defiance changing abruptly to fear.

'Nothing to worry about,' says Alma. 'Everything's under control.'

Miss Yates doesn't answer, but watches while the girls climb up the bank without another word. They huddle together at the top and watch her nervously.

'Sorry, Miss Yates,' says one, and the others join in: 'Sorry, Miss Yates.'

'Go straight back to Merrivale and report to me first thing tomorrow morning. I expect a full explanation of your behaviour from each one of you. And there is to be no comparing of your stories. I always know when there has been collusion.'

The girls shuffle away and Alma takes a breath, conscious that her cheeks are burning. 'There wasn't a problem,' she says. 'Nothing I couldn't handle.'

Miss Yates studies her for a few moments. 'I'm sure there wasn't, Alma,' she says. 'The boarders do get a bit carried away, though, don't they? Lack of parental discipline, presumably. I always think it's worth having two voices of reason. Adds extra weight to our authority.'

She's patronising me, thinks Alma. She thinks I can't control the girls.

But Miss Yates gives no visible sign of contempt. 'Are you using the music room?' she asks.

'Yes. It's a boy from Sherrard's. I've had to teach him early because of the parents' night, and it was easier for him to walk down here than to come to my house.' Why does she sound as if she's making excuses? 'Miss Cunningham-Smith always said she liked to have other children come into the school. She enjoyed hearing music in the distance.' She shouldn't have mentioned Miss Cunningham-Smith. She knows it annoys Miss Yates. But the present situation would be more manageable if Miss Yates were to express some irritation. Her determination to be fair is unconvincing and humiliating.

'I see,' says Miss Yates. 'Well, as long as it doesn't interfere with any of the girls' activities, I see no harm in it.' She turns to go. 'And it's true, the music is pleasing.'

Antony's mother comes to pick him up. She usually drops in at the beginning of term to pay the fees and occasionally they talk on the phone if Antony or his sister need encouragement to do more practice before an exam, but most of the time, she waits in the car and Alma rarely sees her. She's a tall, imposing woman, with grey patches in her wavy, permed hair, a little old to be the mother of Antony and Georgina.

'We're just finishing,' says Alma.

Mrs Crewe is looking through the windows with interest. 'Well, Goldwyn's has changed a bit, hasn't it?'

'Do you know the school?' asks Alma. Is she an Old Girl? She's never mentioned it before.

'I'm afraid the last time I came here was not a happy period in my life,' says Mrs Crewe.

'Really?' says Alma, reluctantly. She would prefer not to hear about Mrs Crewe's tragic past.

'It was during the war, the night of the bombing. When they destroyed the city. You probably wouldn't remember – I don't imagine you were in Exeter at the time.'

Alma stiffens. What is she talking about? How could Mrs Crewe have possibly been at Goldwyn's then? She would have known her. 'I was here,' she says. 'At Goldwyn's. I was a boarder when the old Merrivale was destroyed. We were in the bomb shelter.'

Mrs Crewe stares at her. 'Really? What a coincidence. I went to the bomb shelter too – we joined the girls. That's the only reason I'm standing here today.'

'I don't think–' says Alma. 'It was just the boarders there. Miss Rupin, our house mistress, and Miss Daniels, the matron.' She doesn't want to think about that time.

'Oh, yes, of course. Gertrude Rupin and Carole Daniels. They were so kind. Do you know, this is the first time I've set foot on the school grounds since then? So painful, all of that.'

Alma studies Mrs Crewe's face, trying to understand why she would lie. Is there something familiar about her after all? Has Alma forgotten something about that night that she should try to recall? She experiences a faint stirring of recognition. Something about the way Mrs Crewe is standing, her face turned slightly away to the side as if she finds it too difficult to look directly at her, a fleeting expression–

Miss Rupin opening the door and letting in two small boys, silent and confused, staring around with large eyes – their mother–

'Mrs Shriver!' she says.

Mrs Crewe smiles brightly. 'You do remember!'

Alma stares at her. 'Yes, but–' She turns to look at Antony, making calculations, trying to work out if he could be one of the boys. He can't be. He's too young.

'Oh, no,' says Mrs Crewe, following the direction of her gaze. 'I married again, after the war, then had Antony and Georgina.'

'So your husband...'

'They never found him.' She shakes her head. 'Never. They thought perhaps he'd been blown to pieces, bits here, bits there, impossible to put back together again.'

Alma doesn't know what to say. How can she comment on the horror of knowing your husband has disintegrated, disappeared into thin air, the terror of having no home to go back to, with two young children? But underneath these thoughts there's a sharp, barbed needle of resentment at the unfairness of it all. How could this woman marry again so easily? There were so few men left after the war, and most of them were already spoken for, yet Mrs Shriver had managed to find a second husband and start another family. 'What happened to your sons, the boys?' she asks.

'Oh, they're fine. The loss of their father changed them, of course, but they've always been very close to their stepfather. I was lucky – he's such a good man.' But her face doesn't reflect her belief in her good fortune. Sadness has descended over her and she leans a hand on one of the chairs, as if she's finding it difficult to hold herself up. 'I'm sorry,' she says, with a nervous laugh. 'Coming here has brought it all back.'

Once again, there's no obvious answer. Alma turns to Antony. 'Have you got everything?' she asks.

He comes over to them. 'Will the next lesson be at your house?'

'Yes.' Alma starts to walk towards the door, hoping to encourage Mrs Crewe to leave, but she seems reluctant.

'Are Gertrude and Carole still here?' she asks. 'I'm afraid I lost touch. I wasn't at my best for a long time.'

'Miss Daniels retired a few years ago,' says

Alma. 'Gertrude Rupin is still here – she teaches Latin now.'

'I should make contact with them. Talk about old times, thank them for their kindness.' She pauses. 'Maybe not. It wouldn't be wise, would it, to go over it all again?' She wanders to the door with Antony. 'Lovely to see you again, Miss Braithwaite. Who'd have thought it? We knew each other all the time.'

iii

Robert Gunner is reluctant to go to the parents' evening. He arranged for Pippa to attend Goldwyn's by corresponding with Miss Cunningham-Smith, who, surprisingly, had remembered him as well as he remembered her. Her letters were littered with moments of sharp, iconoclastic wit, which gave him much pleasure. He still thinks of her with admiration, as a woman who could accomplish anything. But he was unwilling to return to the school itself, not wishing to reawaken memories. He's managed to avoid visits until now by entrusting Pippa to family friends with two daughters already at the school for a guided tour, then transport to and from the entrance exam.

On Pippa's first day at school, he walked with her from the station to show her the way but didn't go in. He stood at the bottom of the hill and watched her climb the steps behind a group of other girls. Nothing about their uniform seemed to have changed, and it was hard to distinguish between then and now. Robert raised his hand when Pippa turned at the top of the steps, and she waved back to let him know all was well.

Miss Cunningham-Smith in her wellies. Mountains of rubble. The bicycle firm in his grip as he walked back to Mortimer Hall, followed by four girls he didn't know. Their voices behind him, shocked and subdued. The panic when he discovered two were missing and he thought he'd lost them.

'There's a new headmistress,' he says to himself, as he prepares to leave his study in the Washington Singer building at the university. Miss Yates. He picks up a pile of papers from his desk, taps them until the edges are lined up, and slides them neatly into his briefcase. 'The school will be completely different. I probably won't even recognise it.'

But there's the worrying fact that his daughter's form mistress is Miss Alma Braithwaite. Alma and Curls. The dancing. The music. Curls.

Miss Braithwaite will be professional, of course. From Pippa's descriptions, she's the kind of woman who likes to have everything organised. It shouldn't be necessary to go backwards at all.

He sighs and sits down again at his desk, mentally examining a procession of faces that were so familiar twenty-one years ago, all of which have been pushed away by the complexity of his family life. Promising young men who came under his charge in Mortimer Hall, most of whom he never saw again.

So many didn't survive: Tristan Watson, the socially awkward young man who seemed too young to be a student, who'd already been injured, was killed in a motorcycle accident in France, delivering messages to the generals; Geoffrey Harris died in Africa; Dennis Thwaite volunteered and died in the Normandy landings; Eric Westland, the American – he's not sure what happened to him, injured, he thinks, although he can't remember the details. Jack Hitchens, who took his advice thank goodness, and didn't enlist until he'd finished his degree, is still alive and well, now a Professor of mathematics. At least someone benefited from the education.

The telephone rings and he picks it up, pleased to have his thoughts interrupted.

'Daddy?'

'Hello, Pippa. Everything's under control. I'm just leaving.'

'Don't forget to ask Miss Braithwaite about the ink. I've got really muddled about it.'

'Don't worry, I won't forget. I need to get on, though, or I'll be late and won't be able to ask her anything.'

He puts the phone down, moves his finger over the pile of books and documents on the side of his desk, making sure everything is in the correct order for tomorrow, and checks there's nothing outstanding in the in-tray. He opens and closes the venetian blinds several times, ensuring there are no gaps that anyone could see through from outside, then turns off the Anglepoise. He picks up his briefcase and takes his raincoat down from the peg, folding it over his arm. At the door, he looks back into the room. He's reluctant to leave the study, his sanctuary on a cold, dark night.

He turns off the light, locks the door and walks through the corridors of the deserted maths department, switching lights off behind him as he goes.

Robert sits on one of the small, inadequate chairs outside Pippa's form room, his raincoat and briefcase perched on his lap. He's already spoken to the subject teachers and everything seems fine. There's nothing to worry about. He plays over some words in his mind, trying to formulate a few sentences that would discourage Alma Braithwaite from talking about the past. Will she even recognise him? It's possible that she might not have made the connection. He could pretend that he doesn't recognise her – after all, she was only a girl when he knew her and her appearance must have changed – but she is certain to recognise him. Perhaps he should have disguised himself, grown a beard.

This is ridiculous. She's probably as reluctant as he is.

A large, blonde woman, in a tight-fitting green woollen suit, sits down heavily on the chair next to him and crosses her substantial legs. 'They're a bit small, these chairs, aren't they?' she says.

He smiles. 'I think they're probably meant for eleven-year-old girls, not adults.' The chairs are a reasonable size. She's just too big for them.

She starts to search in her handbag, eventually producing a lipstick and a small mirror. Holding the mirror with her left hand and peering into it with slitted eyes, she applies the lipstick with a curious dabbing technique, placing small spots at regular intervals. She smacks her lips together, rolls them around, and uses a finger to remove any surplus. Then she puts everything away and snaps her bag shut.

'What time is your appointment?' she asks Robert.

'Twenty to nine,' he says.

She wrinkles her nose and puckers her mouth. 'Bother. That means Miss Braithwaite's running late. My help starts to get annoyed if I'm not back on the dot, as if I've done it on purpose. I don't suppose...'

But Robert's mind is not on the conversation. He's checking his watch. A man and a woman are sitting on the other side of the door, not communicating. Are they together or not? Either way, he needn't have hurried.

He has some assignments from his second-years in his briefcase and considers starting work on them. He likes his marking to be thorough, explaining every point, ensuring that his students understand every process. It would be useful to make a start, but he has to consider the awkwardness of putting the papers away when it's his turn to go in.

A couple emerges from the form room. 'Well,' says the mother, letting out a huge sigh as if she's been holding her breath for the last ten minutes, 'Not as bad as the history mistress said.'

'I told you she'd be fine,' says the father. 'But you wouldn't listen.'

After a couple of minutes, Miss Braithwaite puts her head round the door. Robert can see the back of her head. 'Mr and Mrs Acton?' she murmurs to the couple opposite. They stand up together and go into the room. The door shuts behind them.

Was the colour of her hair the same? She doesn't appear to be much taller than she was when she was fifteen. Her voice – hushed, respectful. Was that how she used to speak? Maybe it's not her at all.

'Jolly good,' says the woman next to him. 'Nearly there.'

He'll be as brief as possible. There won't be much to say – it'll be about Pippa settling in. She's a clever girl. She's not struggling in any way.

He looks down and sees that his left foot is jiggling. He places both feet firmly on the floor.

What is it he has to ask about the ink?

The woman next to him sighs loudly, uncrosses her legs, then crosses them in the other direction. Her left knee is now almost touching him. 'I suppose a parents' evening is a good idea,' she remarks, 'but I can't really see the point of having it so soon after they've started.'

Robert smiles politely, but can't think of a reply.

'My husband refused to come. He says it's my job to make sure the girls are being educated properly. Did your wife twist your arm?'

'I'm sorry?' says Robert.

'How can I persuade my husband to come next time without me?'

He's not sure what she's talking about. 'I'm

afraid I can't help you,' he says and tries to turn away. It's not easy. He's trapped by her leg.

She opens her bag again and takes out a green Penguin paperback. Dorothy L. Sayers, *The Nine Tailors*. She starts reading, licking her finger every time she has to turn a page, occasionally breathing in sharply, as if something has shocked her, sometimes letting her gaze wander from the book and rest on the wall opposite, presumably trying to work out who is the murderer.

Robert glances down at the book. She turns the pages faster and faster. Is she just pretending to read?

The form room door opens and the couple come out, their faces composed.

Robert puts his hand on the briefcase, arranges his mac on his arm, prepares to respond instantly.

After a few moments, the door opens again and Miss Braithwaite puts her head through again, facing him this time. 'Mr Gunner,' she says, looking straight at him, a faint smile on her lips.

The woman next to him uncrosses her legs and releases him. He stands up, takes a step forward, longing for a genuine excuse, a reason not to go in. He catches the door as she withdraws her head and follows her.

Once they are both inside, she holds out her hand, composed and fully prepared. 'Mr Gunner,' she says. 'How nice to see you again.'

He takes the hand. It's warm and slightly damp. He squeezes firmly – one second, two – before releasing it. She doesn't respond with any reciprocal strength.

He is wrong-footed, unprepared for such a direct approach. 'I hadn't realised you were teaching here,' he says.

She gestures at the empty chairs in front of her desk. 'Do sit down, Mr Gunner.'

He sits and studies her without saying anything. Feathery wisps of hair have escaped the clutches of the pins from her severe bun and bring to mind the disordered arrangement that used to bush out round her fifteen-year-old head. The long, serious face with downward-looking eyes and pale skin is now imprinted with fine stress lines; the straight nose, slightly off-centre, remains strikingly individual; her unusually narrow shoulders and back would still stand out in a crowd. She must be about thirty-six. She is undoubtedly the adult version of the Alma Braithwaite he knew in 1942. He would have recognised her immediately if they had passed in the street.

'You'll be pleased to know that Pippa has settled down very well,' she says, interrupting his thoughts.

'Good,' he says, nodding vigorously. 'Good.'

'She's made several friends and is already a popular member of the form.'

'Excellent,' he says.

There is silence for a few seconds.

He wonders why she didn't marry.

'Do you have any questions you would like to ask?' she says. 'About Goldwyn's?'

He pretends to think. 'No ... no, I don't think so.'

'Well, in that case–' She starts to rise.

'Oh – I nearly forgot. The ink. I'm supposed to

ask about the ink.'

She sits back down again. 'Yes?' she says, apparently pleased that there is something more to say.

But he can't remember what he's supposed to ask. 'I'm not quite sure what the problem was. I just know that Pippa insisted I should mention it.'

'Oh dear. Can you remember any details?'

'Perhaps you could tell me what instructions they've been given about ink and I can go over what she needs to know when I get home.'

She smiles and, for a brief moment, loses the teacher's veneer. 'Of course – a sensible idea. Well, for the time being, they're required to use the dip pens and ink provided by the school, rather than their own fountain pens.' She indicates the inkwells that have been fitted into the holes to the right of each pupil's desk. 'When Miss Jenkins, the teacher who takes their weekly calligraphy lesson, considers their handwriting to be acceptable, she writes "Osmiroid" in their books. At that point, they may bring in their own fountain pens – the Osmiroid that appears under "Essential Equipment" on the list we sent out before the beginning of term. The girls will then have to supply their own ink, but it must be Quink, royal blue, washable. They may then use the pens for all their lessons. Biros are, of course, banned.' She pauses. 'That's the general situation. I can't really think of anything else she might be worrying about.'

Robert nods. 'It sounds as if washable blue is the answer we require.'

They look at each other and half-smile. He gets

to his feet.

Miss Braithwaite stands up opposite him, no longer the quiet, sad schoolgirl who resides in Robert's memory but a grown woman with authority. 'I'm so pleased to have met you again,' she says.

He feels he should say something positive, but nothing seems appropriate.

She puts out her hand again and he shakes it. 'Pippa is a lovely girl,' she says. 'You and your wife must be so proud of her.'

'Well...' he says, wondering if he should mention the death of his wife. 'Quite so.' He turns towards the door. When he reaches it, he hesitates, wanting to offer something else, but not knowing what he can say. 'I'm so glad–' he says.

'Thank you for–' she says at the same time.

They smile. 'I'm pleased to see that things have worked out well for you,' he says.

'Thank you for coming,' she says.

He opens the door.

'By the way,' she says, 'Miss Yates, our new headmistress, is in her office if you want to speak to her. She wishes to meet as many of the parents as possible.'

He nods again. He has nodded so much in the last five minutes that he can feel his brain loosening. 'Very well,' he says. 'I might go and introduce myself.'

iv

Alma struggles with her last appointment. They've already met several times: Mrs Robinson is one of those mothers whose existence seems to depend entirely on her daughter. She comes in almost every morning to search for missing games kit, and often pops in after school as well, to check that Tina has her homework written down correctly. 'I'm sorry,' says Alma, every time. 'You'd have to talk to Tina's maths teacher/history teacher/French teacher. I can't help you with homework set by other teachers.'

Twenty-one years seemed to have had no visible effect on Robert Gunner, although he was less remote than she remembers, prepared to accept her as an equal. When she first saw him waiting outside the room, she experienced something most unexpected: a frisson of excitement and warmth, as if she had made contact with an old friend. It should have been embarrassment, but felt like pleasure, an alien sensation that worried her.

Everything should be safely catalogued and filed away. She shouldn't be reverting to her teenage impulses so eagerly.

'Tina has specially asked me to ask you if she could sing in the choir, Miss Braithwaite. She has a lovely voice.'

Tina does not have a lovely voice. She's already

had an audition. She can only sing three notes in the vicinity of middle C. 'I think she needs a little more experience before we can consider her.'

'But how does she get that experience if she isn't in the choir?'

'I assure you, the girls have plenty of opportunity to sing. I'm a great believer in singing.'

Why didn't she manage to conduct a sensible conversation with Robert Gunner? She had ideas lined up, prepared speeches intended to demonstrate that she's a competent teacher, but the words had simply abandoned her and she had reverted to the incoherence of a fifteen-year-old. She had given him the opportunity to tell her about his wife. Why hadn't he said anything?

'The thing is,' says Mrs Robinson, placing her large handbag on the desk, 'Tina feels that she's being left out of everything. Can't you make the other girls involve her more?'

A widower, a man she once knew. And now it's too late. She's let herself down. Why was she not sparkling and witty?

She studies Mrs Robinson in front of her and fights an overwhelming desire to sigh. 'I'm sure there's nothing to worry about. She just needs time to settle down.'

He didn't start conversations easily in the past so why should she assume he had changed? He obviously still needs some gentle nudging. How could she be so hopeless? He didn't even use up his full ten minutes.

Mrs Robinson leans forward. 'She doesn't seem happy. She had far more friends at her old school.'

'She's with a nice group of girls. I'm sure she'll

integrate better once she gets to know them.'

Mrs Robinson leans back and sniffs. 'She should never have been put into the same form as Beverley Wilson. That girl can be really spiteful underneath all her so-called innocence.'

Alma suspects that Tina is the one who is spiteful and would like to say so but knows she can't. 'I'll keep an eye on them both,' she says, standing up and offering her hand to Mrs Robinson. 'Please don't worry about Tina. I'm sure she just needs to find her place in the form and then she'll be happy.'

Would she even notice if something was going on? Are there undercurrents that she is completely unaware of, festering beneath the surface? Has she been looking closely enough?

Mrs Robinson shakes her hand reluctantly. 'I don't know how you managed to get behind on your appointments when you spend only five minutes with each of us.'

Alma ignores the criticism. 'Miss Yates would like to meet you in her office if you have time. I'm sure she'll be prepared to discuss Tina's problems with you.'

'I can't possibly stay a minute longer,' says Mrs Robinson. 'My help will be having kittens by now. I'm already running late.' She goes over to the door and pauses. 'Anyway, we've had enough letters from Miss Yates recently to light a bonfire. Hockey matches, concerts, and now a parents' night, if you please. She's got grand plans, I'll grant you that, but a swimming pool? Where's the money coming from? That's what my husband would like to know. She tells us she's going to extend the school day, offer German lessons. As if anyone in England would want to learn the Nazi language.'

At least there's one thing they can agree on.

'She's too ambitious for Goldwyn's. If she's that good, why's she come here? Why doesn't she go somewhere where they're used to new ideas and they've got loads of spare money?'

Alma smiles. Why does she dislike the woman when they agree on so much? 'It probably depends on what vacancies come up.'

'She'll be off before you know it. You'll see. Goldwyn's is just a stepping stone for her.'

Mrs Robinson needs encouragement to go so Alma walks to the door and opens it. 'Thank you for coming,' she says. 'It's always a pleasure to see you.'

It worries her that she has to lie, that this is what you have to do as a form mistress. Wouldn't it be better to tell parents the truth about their daughters? How can it help them to have all these illusions? Of course there's a need for tact, for politeness, but should it outweigh honesty?

The trouble is, Alma doesn't like Mrs Robinson – she doesn't like fifty per cent of the parents she's met today. Is this what she will have to endure for the rest of her working life?

She walks around the form room, nudging the desks back into position, then stands at the front and assesses if they are lined up exactly. She removes everything from the surface of her desk. The room is calm, correct, organised, although the chairs are not identical. There's a recent ink stain on one of the desks. She'll ask the cleaners if they can do anything about it.

At least Mr Gunner didn't mention Curls.

She has never before questioned her future as a teacher, but things have changed recently. Miss Yates's iron fist has pushed too hard and she's been compelled to resist. And now Mr Gunner has reappeared. She's conscious of sitting on a swing that has been steady for a long time and is starting to move again, gently but perceptibly, backwards and forwards, disturbing her equilibrium.

Why can't all the chairs and desks be identical? These battered desks from different periods in the past, stained with ink spills, rickety on their uneven legs, need to be discarded and replaced with something more modern. Why should the girls have to put up with these relics?

It would be pointless to raise this issue in staff meetings or in private. She has to learn not to speak. Not to express her views. It's the only way to survive. Just get on with things. Don't argue. Just do it.

She turns off the lights and closes the door behind her, knowing that the caretaker will come round and check everything when they've all gone, but preferring to do it herself. Ahead of her, along the corridor, she can see Mr Gunner sitting on a chair outside Miss Yates's office. His feet are arranged symmetrically in front of him and he's holding the handle of his briefcase, firmly, his mac folded and draped over his arm. She likes this neatness in him, his ability to be ready for action immediately he is required. When Miss Yates emerges from her office, he jumps to his feet and they shake hands as he introduces himself.

She can hear Miss Yates's voice: 'How lovely to meet you, Mr Gunner. Do come in.' Her outline seems softer and more fluid than usual, her smile broader, and her voice warmer. She ushers Mr Gunner into her office.

Alma experiences a moment of alarm. Will he see through Miss Yates's charm to the manipulating woman underneath?

Part Seven

i

27 May 1942

Alma watches Duncan as he puts the key into the lock and pushes open the heavy door to their house on Magdalene Road. She has not been able to persuade herself to go back since her parents died, even though Dr Guest and his wife have offered to accompany her, so it's remained shut up since the night of the bombing. 'I don't want to go in,' she says.

'Nonsense,' he says. 'It's our home.'

It *was* our home, she thinks. It isn't any more.

'Come on.' He takes her hand and pulls her into the hall.

The house seems to be the same as always: sun shines through the window above the front door, illuminating banks of dust motes in the open space of the hall: hats and coats dangle from their pegs, outdoor shoes are stacked in the corner and the curved handles of umbrellas lean over the side of their stand below the mirror.

'Something smells,' says Duncan, letting go of Alma's hand and heading for the kitchen. She follows him in, half believing that she will find her mother there, her hands in the mixing bowl, rubbing flour and fat together to make pastry, the air warm and sweet with the scent of freshly baked cakes.

Duncan opens the door to the larder and a stench of overripe, rotten food gushes out into their faces. 'It must be the milk,' he says, holding his nose with one hand and picking up the jug with the other. He rushes to the sink and turns the tap on, pouring out the liquid. Furry grey and brown fragments wash to the side of the sink and remain there. He pokes at them with a wooden spoon until they dissolve in the running water and finally disappear down the plughole. The smell lingers.

'The jug needs washing,' says Alma pushing him out of the way and taking it out of his hands. She swills water round several times until it is cleaner.

They look at each other. 'Phew,' says Duncan. 'Is that it?'

Alma goes back into the larder and finds cheese, blackened and crumbling, butter melted into a pool of separated liquids that have solidified again and the remains of a tin of corned beef, blue with spidery mould.

'Open the back door,' she says.

Duncan reaches up for the key that's always left at the top of the china cabinet. He unlocks the door and throws it wide open, letting in fresh, cleansing air. Alma hands him the plates of ruined food and he takes them outside, away from the house, throwing them into the bushes and scraping off as much as possible with dock leaves. He brings the plates back in and rinses them under the tap.

'There! That's everything, I think,' says Alma, fanning the door backwards and forwards.

'We probably shouldn't leave the food so close to the house,' says Duncan. 'We'll get rats. But we can sort that out later.'

Alma starts to open the windows, replacing the odour of decay with the delicious scent of lilac and apple blossom.

They go into the drawing room. Chairs and sofas are scattered around, bright with cushions, and the coffee-tables are piled with newspapers, medical notes, reference books. A volume of Mozart sonatas sits open on the piano, at the exact page where Alma left it when she went to school at the beginning of the summer term. Her mother had clearly not found time to play. Her spare reading glasses rest against the base of a lamp. A paperback lies on the table by her father's chair near the fireplace, pages down, open at page 127. *For Whom the Bell Tolls*. He liked Hemingway. His pipe lies on the tiles of the hearth in front of the fire, the ash tapped out into the nearby ashtray. The room is still heavy with the calm, restful smell of pipe tobacco.

'It feels,' says Alma, 'as if they have only just left. As if they're coming home this evening.' She watches Duncan, wanting to see how he reacts, so that she can know what she should do or say.

For a while he doesn't say anything, just looks around and sniffs the air. Then he walks over to the french windows and opens them. 'Come on,' he says. 'Let's have a game of tennis.'

'I'm not wearing the right shoes,' calls Alma, as she chases him through the garden, past the vegetable patches, where peas and beans are sending delicate tendrils up into trellises of bamboo poles.

'Doesn't matter,' he shouts, over his shoulder. 'We'll just have a quick knock around, get all that mould out of our lungs.'

They grab a racquet each from the small hut at the edge of the court and unscrew the wooden clamps, leaving the holders discarded on the floor. There's no one to tell them to put them away neatly, or to shut the door after them so the rain won't get in, or to insist they're wearing the right shoes.

Duncan removes his khaki jacket and hangs it up on the corner of the shed door, then he picks up four balls and stuffs two into his pockets. They stand side by side at the edge of the tennis court and examine the grass. At first sight, it's perfect, lush and green, immaculate, but when Alma puts a foot out to tread on it, they discover it's about four inches long.

'Ah,' says Duncan. 'Obvious, really, I suppose.'

'What do you think's happened to Fred?' asks Alma. When things are normal, he's out here most days, pruning, digging, cutting the grass.

'I'm not sure.'

'Maybe he knows what's happened and he's found another job. He wouldn't keep coming if he didn't get paid.'

'I can't believe he'd just give up,' says Duncan. 'It's too soon. Surely he'd hang around for a bit longer to see what we wanted to do.'

'Or he died in the bombing too,' says Alma.

Duncan nods.

'We'll just have to volley,' says Alma, who doesn't want to lose the momentum. 'Like badminton.' She grabs a ball and attempts to bounce it in front of her. It falls into the grass with a quiet plop and makes no attempt to come back up again.

Duncan winds up the net to its full height and they stand a reasonable distance on either side. The chalked lines are still visible on the tips of the grass, so they can tell if the balls land in or out.

They volley a ball backwards and forwards a few times, and each time they miss, they have to hunt for it in the long grass. Duncan starts hitting harder, and they run further, reaching out more urgently, laughing as they stretch for the shots, leaping into the air, twisting into impossible contortions, determined to keep the ball in play as long as possible. Alma sends a ball high up into the trees and they watch it soar over the wall into next door's garden.

'Crazy!' shouts Duncan. 'I was never going to get that.'

'That's why I did it,' says Alma, gasping for breath. 'I play to win.'

'Losing the ball doesn't win,' says Duncan.

'No, but it's very satisfying.'

After half an hour, all the balls have disappeared into the undergrowth and Alma and Duncan collapse exhausted on the ground. For a while, they lie on their backs, cushioned by clover and thick grass, gazing up at the sky.

'I keep waiting for someone to call us in for supper,' says Alma.

'I know,' says Duncan.

'It's odd being here on our own. As if it's not real.'

Duncan reaches out and takes her hand. His is

warm and damp after the game, but Alma can feel the strength in it, the calluses, the evidence of hard work. She strokes his fingers, remembering how he used to throw her up into the air when she was little, how he used to sneak into her bedroom at night and tell her scary stories, then stay with her until she slept, huddled in a chair by her bed, wrapped in a blanket, smiling at her every time she opened her eyes. Her brother has been a man for some time, qualifying as a solicitor just before the war, but now he's a soldier too, someone who has travelled a long way to fight.

'What's it like?' she says.

'What's what like?'

'Fighting, killing, being so far from home.'

He pauses. 'I don't know,' he says. 'You just get on with it.' He raises his head and props himself up on an elbow, his face in front of Alma's eyes, blotting out the sky. 'I've been to places I didn't know existed, but – it's OK. I've got friends – we've had some good times. Most of the men, they'd never left England before. Some of them hate the heat – they burn and peel – it makes them irritable and angry. Others, they thrive on it, as if they were born to live in the desert. I like it – should have been an Arab. But you don't think about things, you just do as you're told, follow orders. It all feels a long way from here...' His voice trails away. It's as if he can't say what he wants to say, as if it's too difficult to think about on their tennis court, in their garden, in the place where he grew up.

'Can I stay with you here while you're home?' asks Alma, softly.

'Of course you can,' he says. 'I'm an adult, aren't I? I'm allowed to look after you. It's not for long, though. I've organised a lift back and I can't miss it – I'd be in serious trouble if I did.'

The idea of being here together is strange. Just the two of them in their own home. With half their family missing. They'll have to go indoors again soon, and at some point enter their parents' bedroom, see the abandoned clothes in the wardrobes, do something with all the unwanted possessions.

'But when the war's over,' says Alma, 'we can go on living here together, can't we? I won't have to stay with the Guests for ever?'

'Don't worry. I'll look after you. Don't you want to stay with the Guests? There's always Aunt Janie and Uncle Brian. Or if you don't want to leave Exeter there are loads of people who would love to have you. You don't have to keep boarding if you don't want to.'

'I do want to – then I can be with my friends. And I like the Guests. But I'd prefer to live at home. With you.'

'It will happen,' says Duncan. 'Just you wait and see. Everything'll go back to normal one day – well, as normal as it can be – and I'll be home for good.'

Alma gazes past him at the line of elms that edges the garden. 'I thought it was all a mistake at first,' she says. 'I even made Curls come to the hospital with me because I thought they'd just be wounded – you know, nothing important – and we'd find them sitting in a waiting room with bandaged legs or something like that. But that part of the hospital wasn't there any more. It was just bricks, huge piles, as if it had never been anything in the first place. Then I met Dr Perkins. You remember him? Dad's senior registrar?'

What a ridiculous question. Of course Duncan knew Dr Perkins. They used to visit his house, have lunch with his family, play table-tennis in his games room with his children.

'Have you seen Bedford Circus?' she asks, thinking of the first time she went into the centre of Exeter after the bombing.

He shakes his head, as if he doesn't trust himself to speak.

'It's not there any more, either. It doesn't exist. You can't work out where the roads were, or the shops, or anything. It's like a different place, where you've never been before. How can the Jerries do that? I can't see why they bombed us.'

'It's the same for them as well, you know. We bomb them. And most of them are just ordinary people like us, trying to get on with everyday life.'

'It's not the same. They started it.' Alma doesn't want to think about them as real people.

'This is what I hate,' says Duncan, in a low voice. 'The way you get used to it, the way you think it's good to kill other people, because if you don't they'll kill you. It starts to be acceptable, as if it's the only way you can think. I really, really hate it.'

He stops, as if he's struggling to draw breath.

'That's what Daddy said,' says Alma. 'He didn't want to fight again.'

They're silent for a while and she can hear his breathing slowing, becoming more regular, calming. After a while, he jumps to his feet again.

'Come on,' he says. 'We've got to cook.'

'I'm no good at cooking,' she says. 'Not on my own.' She needs her mother at her side, explaining, giving instructions, keeping an eye on things.

'We can do it, I'm sure. There must be cookery books.'

'But we won't have any of the right ingredients.'

'There'll be something we can use.'

They walk back towards the house. Looking up, Alma can see the window of her parents' room looking out over the garden, dazzling in the reflection of the lowering sun. 'The room with a view', her mother used to call it. The curtains are still closed, the blackout blinds still down from the night of the raid, when her parents would have been summoned by telephone in the early hours of 4 May and asked to come in to deal with the casualties. They would have dressed hurriedly, probably without talking, aware of the chaos going on in the city, taking the car, heading for the place where they knew they could be most useful, demonstrating the same dedication to their work that they had always shown, until the bombs had fallen and they'd disappeared. If they hadn't responded so promptly, if they'd stayed here and gone in later, they would still be alive.

'Have you heard of the Lindy Hop?' she asks.

ii

The students always knock on Robert Gunner's door softly, as if they share his desire for silence and hesitate to break it.

Mr Harris, speaking barely above a whisper: 'I'm sorry to d-disturb you, Mr Gunner. The telephone seems to have jammed.'

Mr Hitchens, his voice soft and melodious: 'Excuse me, Mr Gunner. I wonder if you would mind if we took the wireless into the common room.'

'There doesn't seem to be any hot water today, Mr Gunner.'

Robert will stop writing, screw the top back on his fountain pen – a present from his mother when he was awarded his scholarship to the university – stand up, stretch his legs and consider the problem. He doesn't mind giving permission to move the wireless, as long as it's returned correctly; he can go and check the immersion heater, which usually just needs a hearty bash to jerk the connections back into place; he's used to unscrewing the outer casing of the pay-phone and inserting his penknife into the slot, wiggling it up and down to see where the coin has jammed. It's usually a ha'penny, bent slightly out of shape as if someone has tried to distort it and make it resemble a penny. But Robert trusts his students. He believes in their intrinsic honesty. He assumes that someone has made a mistake.

This evening, when there's a knock on his door, he freezes for a few seconds. Could it be Curls? He can see no reason why she should want to speak to him but, despite a deep sense of embarrassment, he's finding it difficult to ignore in himself a growing urgency to be in her presence. Whatever has come over him? His mind is full of the Bach, the perfection of her playing – but at the same time he keeps seeing the way she sat at the piano, the way she moved. This response embarrasses him. It would be better to avoid her. But he wants to see her, hear her play Bach again.

He listens intently for a few seconds, waiting for a quick shuffle of movement that would suggest restless female youth, but there's nothing out of the ordinary. 'Come in,' he says.

The door opens and Alma enters. She's accompanied by a young man in uniform, with serious eyes and a small neat moustache – presumably the brother. He's a lieutenant and has the worn, jaded appearance of a man who has seen action. He moves with confident ease, knowing what's worth worrying about and what isn't.

Robert stands up. 'Come in,' he says, moving two chairs for them. 'Sit down.'

'I'm Duncan Braithwaite, sir,' says the soldier. 'Alma's brother. Home on leave for a few days.' He's well into his twenties, perhaps the same age as Robert.

They all shake hands and sit down with the barrier of the desk between them. Alma clearly adores her brother. Her face softens every time she turns to watch him, the muscles round her mouth losing their iron grip, her eyes becoming wider as she lets them relax. 'You have been fortunate to get leave at this difficult time,' says Robert.

He nods seriously. There's a pause.

'So, how can I help?' Robert asks.

'We were wondering if you would give us permission for Alma to come and stay at home with me for the few days I'm here. So we can sort out the house.'

Robert clears his throat. 'I'm afraid you'll have to check with Alma's headmistress,' he says. 'She has entrusted her pupils to my care for the time being, but she has overall responsibility for their welfare.'

'OK,' says the young man. 'I'll go to Goldwyn's with Alma tomorrow morning and speak to Miss Cunningham-Smith. It'll only be for four nights. I'm due back after that.' He doesn't offer any further information. 'Would you mind if I stay here this evening? Alma would like to introduce me to her friends, and...' He hesitates. 'She wants to teach me a dance they've all been learning.'

'Ah.' The dancing.

Robert has become accustomed to the sound of the music. It serves the useful purpose of keeping everyone occupied, and the sound of it in the background has become almost comforting. There's no evidence that it affects anyone's work, and as long as it doesn't interfere with fire-watching duties, he's willing to let them enjoy themselves.

Alma's brother is on active duty and only here for a short time. He deserves some recreation.

'You'll be welcome at any time during your leave,' says Robert, 'providing you sign the book in the hall and let our housekeeper know if you wish to eat in. I shall expect you to restrict your presence to the common room and dining room. We pride ourselves on an orderly, well-run establishment at Mortimer Hall.'

'Of course.'

'Meanwhile, if you'd like something to eat now, it's possible that Mrs Anderson has something left over from supper.'

The two of them look at each other. 'Well, we've–' says Alma.

'That would be most welcome,' says Duncan, at the same time.

They both laugh, but don't explain.

'Off you go, then,' says Robert. 'I hope you enjoy your stay back in England, Lieutenant Braithwaite.'

Later, on his way to speak to Mrs Anderson, he hears the dance music and finds himself drawn towards it. The door has been propped open, and heat generated by the activity, sealed in by the blackout blinds, wafts out of the room in thick, sweaty waves.

Robert peers into the room. Everyone from Mortimer Hall seems to be present and on the move. As the music blasts out, far too loudly, their feet move together, faster and faster, like a visible manifestation of semi-quavers, clustering, tapping, jumping. Four of the men pick up a girl each (at this point Robert prepares himself to walk in and demand an end to such madness, but he is diverted by the need to see the girls safely back on the floor) and throw – literally throw – them into the air. They're almost flying, but they come down again, competently snatched from their freefall by the men, their legs stretched out briefly on either side of the men's bodies before they jump to the floor with an agile, rubbery bounce. Robert is mesmerised by the brilliance of this. What he sees and envies is their energy. The lithe athleticism of the men, the way they plunge into movements without inhibition. They are simultaneously barbaric and exhilarating. Every action, however small, is rhythmic, following some preordained pattern, slotting into the whole with extraordinary precision. They click their fingers, move their arms, shape their hands, swivel their feet, strong and controlled, their resources limitless.

And Curls is there. She's thrown up by Alma's brother and lands in his arms, gazing at him with adoring eyes while still concentrating on the movements, her face alive and breathless. Robert stares at her, mesmerised, captivated by the delight on her face.

The trouble, he realises, is that the girls are not girls, not children, although not women either. Women would never move with such unchecked abandon. They're in a transitional stage, a moment between child and woman, where they can be either or both.

Robert steps backwards with a deep breath. He shouldn't be there.

He tries to not leave his study unless it's absolutely necessary, determined to avoid any further contact with the girls. He goes for his breakfast as early as possible, eats rapidly and sets off towards the university soon afterwards. At supper time he finds himself acting in a way that he would consider suspicious in anyone else. He lingers in his study, interpreting the sounds of the building, and judges when most of the students have left the dining room. Then he opens the door and peers into the gloom of the corridor, his eyes and ears straining for evidence of another human presence. If the coast is clear, he creeps down the stairs silently, stopping to listen every now and again, hoping to eat alone.

Jane Curley is fifteen years old. He has no right whatsoever to think of her in any way other than as a child. His response to her shocks him.

Whenever a distant laugh ripples along the corridor and seeps under his study door, he can feel the blood accelerating in his veins, his vision blurring, and he has to take off his glasses and wipe them – breathing on them, then polishing them with the lintless cloth that he keeps in the inside pocket of his jacket. He knows it's Curls because of the quality of her laugh, a cascade of minor thirds, rising and falling with the elegance of a phrase shaped by Chopin. She seems to laugh more than the other girls, as if she can see beyond the prosaic inconvenience of their bombed-out existence and wants to spur them on to greater girlishness. It's a more musical laugh than he's ever heard before – well, it would be, wouldn't it?

He immerses himself in his investigation into lighthouses. Recently, he's moved on from his grandfather's history, diverted by the wonders of other lighthouses: the locations, the shipwrecks, the stories. He's piling up knowledge like layers of sediment, preserving and fossilising, forming rock formations. The research limps on without purpose, an almost deliberate reflection of his own life. At the moment, he's interested in an early Eddystone lighthouse – Rudyerd's Tower, built in 1709, which survived for only forty-seven years.

As with most lighthouses, especially from the early days when the lights were fuelled by candles and there was a constant risk of fire, there's a good story to tell about Rudyerd's Tower. In 1755, the lantern caught fire. The keeper on watch at the time, a certain Henry Hall, who was a remarkable ninety-four years old (or maybe eighty-four, depending on which account you read), tried to put out the blaze by throwing water upwards from a bucket. But the lead on the roof melted and, because his mouth was open, some of it poured down his throat. He and the other keeper continued to battle the fire, but it was burning from the top downwards and failure was inevitable. They were eventually driven out on to the rocks, where they were rescued eight hours later. The sea was too rough for the boat to land, so the men were dragged through the sea on ropes to safety. The lighthouse smouldered for another five days (although it's difficult to understand how a wooden structure could last that long) until it was completely destroyed. Henry Hall, who was badly burned, didn't die for another twelve days and a post-mortem discovered a flat piece of lead in his stomach that weighed seven ounces. The doctor who found this was ridiculed by the Royal Society, who refused to believe anyone would survive at all after swallowing lead, and spent the rest of his life pouring lead down the throats of animals to prove that they wouldn't necessarily die straight away. The piece of lead can still be seen in the Edinburgh Museum.

Robert likes stories like this, stories that demonstrate the dedication behind the great engineering feats of the past and the perils of lighthouse-keeping: some men went mad; some hanged themselves; some, like his grandfather, disappeared without trace and without reason; and one died with seven ounces of lead in his stomach. Robert understands these men from the past, their desire for isolation battling with their need for human connection, an inner conflict that could send them mad. He is reassured by the long-service keepers, knowing that there were other men like him and his grandfather and his grandfather's assistant. Men who liked silence but were prepared to share it with each other.

It's a different kind of silence from that of his father, the survivor of a mustard-gas attack. That silence meant intolerable oppression, a heavy build-up of pressure that could only be broken by violent explosions of anger, and it cast a pall over Robert's childhood. It came to a merciful end when Robert was a teenager, when bronchial-pneumonia released his father from further torment. His memories linger on in suffocating nightmares where he is hiding in the dark space of his childhood wardrobe, hearing his father rampaging blindly through the house, knocking everything out of his way with superhuman strength, the hacking of his cough getting closer and closer.

'He was a good man,' his mother told him, after he'd died.

Not in Robert's memory.

'He joined up just before you were born, so you couldn't know what a kind man he was once. He wasn't the same when he came back.'

Robert wished he had known him before he became a soldier. He would have liked a more positive memory.

'He was all set to be a hero,' said his mother. 'He enlisted with the best of intentions. It wasn't his fault that he was gassed, that nobody was interested in heroes once they stopped being useful.'

Robert's father was never a hero for him. The word itself seems absurdly optimistic now. He sees uniforms everywhere, of course, and he recognises the necessity of soldiers and the concept of heroism. But the presence of khaki makes him uneasy.

iii

There are eight of them. Alma and Duncan, Curls, Natalie, Giraffe, Geoffrey Harris, Jack Hitchens and Dennis Thwaite. The men are all musicians, ex-choristers. Jack and Dennis are violinists – they've already spent an evening entertaining the girls, alternating freely between Beethoven sonatas and Irish jigs; Geoffrey plays the French horn;

Duncan grew up, like Alma, learning the piano.

It's a Saturday – hot, still, blue-skied – and they have decided to take a bus out of the city for the day. It might be their last opportunity for freedom before the students leave. Geoffrey has been offered a research post at Farnborough, but he's considering joining the RAF instead. They've all been to see the documentary film *Target for Tonight*, sitting in the darkened cinema and chewing their nails, worrying about whether F for Freddy will make it back, fretting at the mist that's rising over the sea, rejoicing when the Wellington finally lands. Geoffrey was particularly affected by the film and has been debating the relative merits of bombers and fighters ever since. Dennis and Jack are wavering on the issue of whether or not they should enlist.

Mrs Anderson, who is always susceptible to a little gentle persuasion from the young men, has prepared a picnic: sardine sandwiches; corned-beef pie, with carrots, potatoes and leeks to make up for the lack of meat – not very large, but enough for a small slice each; an eggless cake, which is a bit heavy but interestingly flavoured with some early gooseberries from the garden. Mortimer Hall has been following government guidance **(Dig for Victory; Lend a Hand on the Land)**, and when the students are not fire-watching they do their patriotic duty in the garden. So far, they've dug up the rose borders and removed large numbers of bulbs, storing them in sacks in the outhouses and replacing them with fruit and vegetables. It has not all gone according to plan – the entire greenfly population of Exeter seems to have homed in on Mortimer – but at least the gooseberries have been successful.

The men spread out the blankets while the girls divide the food into equal portions. There's a short but comfortable silence as they force themselves to eat slowly, making everything last as long as possible, licking their fingers and dabbing up the last crumbs. Then they smooth out the sheets of greaseproof paper and fold them carefully so they can be used again. The war seems far away and irrelevant.

Alma lies back, sighing contentedly, and watches a small brown aircraft with red, white and blue circles on its wings circling above them. She sits up. 'Is that a Hurricane?'

Geoffrey spreads his fingers in front of his eyes to reduce the glare and studies it. 'Definitely,' he says. 'Coming in to land.'

They watch it lose height rapidly, almost scraping the top branches of a group of elms not far from where they're sitting until it drops out of sight.

'Are we by an airfield?' asks Natalie, in surprise.

'Didn't you know?' says Jack. 'It's just behind the trees.'

'Can we go and have a look?' says Curls.

'I don't see why not,' says Dennis.

They jump up and fold the blankets, stuffing them into bags that the men hoist on to their shoulders. Heading in the direction of the airfield, they pick their way through the small wood, breathing in the rich scent of damp earth where the dryness of summer hasn't yet penetrated. In front of them, between the last of the trees and the airfield beyond, there's a tall wire-netting fence. They can see the three runways, but there's no sign of the newly landed Hurricane, which must have taxied behind one of the hangars in the distance. Groups of aircraft have been left on the grass between the runways. They're leaning backwards on their rear wheels, their noses pointing at the sky, immobile but restless, birds testing the air. A hangar, monstrously big, has been erected near the fence. The place appears deserted, still and shimmering in the heat of the day.

'Where is everyone?' asks Giraffe.

'They'll be around somewhere,' says Dennis. 'They have to be on permanent alert for incoming aircraft. They cover the whole of the West Country from here, including Plymouth.'

'Look!' says Curls. 'You can get through.'

A part of the fence seems to have been left unfinished, one section of the wire-netting overlapping another without being properly attached. Curls pulls away the flap and walks in. They wait for alarms to go off, for someone to challenge her, but nothing happens.

'Do you really think you should?' asks Alma.

'Why not?' says Curls. 'No one knows I'm here. Look!' She performs a few steps from their latest version of the Lindy Hop, her legs, thin and ungainly, becoming elegant with the rhythm of the steps. 'Come on,' she calls. 'It's quite safe.'

The men, who have turned out to be less earnest and less fond of silent meditation than Mr Gunner has led the girls to believe, file through the hole in the fence, followed by Natalie and Giraffe. Alma hangs back.

'We can't leave you behind,' says Curls.

'But what if we get caught?'

Duncan comes back through and draws her forward with an arm round her shoulders. 'Don't worry,' he says. 'Nobody will see us.'

Alma takes a deep breath and follows them, with a sense of guilt that she can't quite shake off. Might they get into serious trouble? For a few seconds, she hesitates again, then realises, with an odd sense of liberation, that there's nobody left to care. Her parents are gone and her brother is with her, therefore equally culpable, and he's about to leave again anyway. She's nobody's responsibility any more. There's Dr Guest and his wife, but she's not strictly answerable to them yet since she hasn't spent any time under their roof; they can hardly reprimand her at this point. I can do what I want, she thinks. Just like Curls. Curls has parents, it's true, but she always manages to do whatever she wants without worrying about the consequences.

She runs after the others as they make their way along the side of the hangar towards the front.

'The side door's open,' says Geoffrey. 'Let's go in and see the planes.'

'If the door's open,' says Natalie, 'that means someone has opened it. They must be inside.'

'Not necessarily,' says Curls.

The men are striding ahead.

Alma follows them into the hangar. No one's there, but the lights have been left on. It's completely empty, except for various climbing structures placed along the sides. No people, no aeroplanes, just a vast space that soars up to the ceiling.

'It's enormous,' whispers Natalie.

Her words echo out and around them, reaching up to the distant ceiling, over to the far corners.

Curls sings a scale – 'Do re mi fa so la ti do.'

The notes follow each other into the space, gain tone and volume, and return in stages, round and full, amplified by their travels, each sounding over the top of the previous one, like a choir.

'We should sing,' says Curls. 'It would be extraordinary.'

'No,' says Giraffe. 'Someone might hear us.'

'We have to sing,' says Alma. 'We might not come across acoustics like this ever again.' She's not afraid any more. She wants someone to find them, someone who will be angry with them, who will report them to Mr Gunner or Miss Cunningham-Smith. She wants to make a fuss, cause disruption, disappoint everyone she can think of. They need to know that they can't expect her to continue to be obedient or even amiable. She's a changed person and it's only right that everyone knows this. 'We could do "Now Is the Month of Maying".'

'Yes,' says Duncan. 'Let's do it.'

They shuffle themselves into a semi-circle, the girls on the right, Alma and Natalie together as sopranos, Curls and Giraffe altos, the men grouped into tenors and basses.

Jack, at the end of the semi-circle, studies the floor for a few seconds, concentrating, nodding thoughtfully, a stray lock of hair springing up and waving in time with his beat.

'Give us a C, Curls,' he says.

She hums a high C instantly, with no hesitation. They all hum their notes and for a brief moment a C major chord hangs in the air, strong and clear.

Jack raises his right hand, they breathe in. He brings his hand down.

Now is the month of Maying, when merry lads are playing! Fa la la la la!
Each with his bonny lass, upon the greeny grass! Fa la la la la!
The Spring, clad all in gladness, doth laugh at Winter's sadness! Fa la la la!
And to the bagpipes' sound, the nymphs tread out the ground! Fa la la la!
Fie, then, why sit we musing, youth, sweet delight refusing? Fa la la la la!
Say, dainty nymphs and speak! Shall we play barley break? Fa la la la la!

Alma imagines the Elizabethans singing these words, a cheerful band of men and women, perhaps with tankards of beer in their hands, perhaps with Thomas Morley conducting his own music, outside among the apple blossom and amaryllis. She's seen the only surviving picture of Thomas Morley, his long, thin face with its pointed beard and neat moustache mirrored by the two sharp points of his collar, and wondered if he was a likeable man. He was a contemporary of Shakespeare – he even set some of his words to music. Did they know each other? Could they have met and been friends, even? The words, like Shakespeare's, are full of *double-entendres* – a barley break, a roll in the hay. The singers and their listeners would undoubtedly have appreciated the implications. She suspects that somehow it would have been less refined, more raucous.

The *fa la las* bounce off the ceiling, come back down, wrap themselves round each other in a staggering wall of sound, until they finally come to rest in simple unison on C.

They stop and look at each other, overawed by the resonance of their surroundings, the sound still ringing in their ears.

'Well,' says Duncan, with a twisted grin, 'that was remarkably good.'

'Let's sing another,' says Alma. The building remains still. Nobody has appeared at the door.

'They'll hear us,' says Natalie. 'We'll get into trouble.'

'Who cares?' says Curls. 'Let them come and find us. Lucky them. They can have a free concert.'

'Yes,' says Alma. 'Who cares?' She's watching Duncan opposite her in the semi-circle. He's older than the students, a man who has been out into the world. Does he demonstrate his experience in some mysterious, unspoken way? Is it possible to read his knowledge and proximity to death from the lines on his face, from the manner in which he stands, from the way his eyes seem to reflect more than his immediate surroundings? He's almost a stranger to her, like a friend of her parents she might meet at a concert, who might make polite conversation with her. A man who understands things that she can't even imagine, who would see her as a young and naïve school-girl.

But this intriguing, masculine, unfamiliar man is her brother, the brother who used to throw her up into the air when she was little, catch her again, put her down on the floor as if she was a piece of delicate china and check that she was still in one piece. It was the checking that she remembers now. It moves her. That he cared about her, really cared, so that even if he was having fun, he was aware that she was precious. She mattered to him.

He looks across and winks. She smiles back, but then realises he's not looking at her. The wink was aimed at Curls. Curls shakes her head, flicking her hair round her cheeks, grins and looks away quickly when she sees Alma watching. A gentle pink is creeping up her cheeks.

Alma stares at her, unable to believe what she's seeing. Curls never blushes. She can walk on to a platform in front of thousands of people and begin a Rachmaninov piano concerto (far beyond Alma's ability) as if she's performing in her own drawing room. She can produce the final flourish of a concerto, leap from the stool, bow deeply, accept bouquets, smile and walk off, not tripping over her long silk dress, grinning as if she has just performed for her friends. Why would she blush when Duncan winked at her?

'Let's do "The Silver Swan",' says Giraffe. 'It would sound beautiful in here.'

No one disagrees. They reorganise themselves so that they can sing in five parts and Curls provides them with an F. Once again, they take time to find their opening notes, then Jack brings them in together. This is slow music, more thoughtful, every note holding on longer than usual, setting up suspensions that resolve themselves into clear, pure chords.

The Silver Swan, who, living, had no Note,
when Death approached, unlocked her silent throat.
Leaning her breast upon the reedy shore,
thus sang her first and last, and sang no more.

A swansong. The myth that a swan can only sing just before it dies. This is someone's final performance. But whose swansong is it? Alma focuses on the silver swan. Tears are swimming in her eyes.

'Farewell, all joys! O Death, come close mine eyes!
More Geese than Swans now live, more Fools than Wise.'

All the tragedies she has ever known about are filing through her mind. Byron in Greece, dying of a fever; the death of David Copperfield's mother and the subsequent tyranny of Mr Murdoch; Schubert succumbing to syphilis at the age of thirty-one, with all those future masterpieces lost to the world; poor mad Ophelia floating on the river. And, finally, finally, the death of her parents, people who devoted their lives to saving others.

A nudge to her side from Natalie breaks her concentration. She blinks to clear the tears. Three men in uniforms are standing in the entrance to the hangar, silhouetted against the brightness of the outside. They're holding guns in front of them, pointing them at the group of singers. Alma falters, but the men are not coming towards them. They're motionless, watching – as if they, too, have glimpsed some greatness in the music and cannot bring themselves to interrupt.

The singing continues, more intense. Alma is sure that if she were to look, she would see tears on everyone's cheeks. The emotion is frightening, too alien to cope with. Now she can't think of anything except the sound of her voice, soaring above the others, while the lower voices move away, filling the centre, creating a rich texture. The lines of music thread round each other, blending into a greater whole.

When they reach the final note, they watch Jack, who brings his right hand up and holds it steady for a second, two seconds, three. They listen to the final pure tone of their voices, then he shuts them down by closing his fingers. Nobody moves. They are conscious of an enormous silence that matches the size of the building.

After a long, long pause, one of the airmen clears his throat. He steps forward smartly. 'Who are you?' he says. His voice is so small that they have to strain to hear him.

Everyone turns to Jack, expecting him to offer an explanation, but he's having trouble finding words.

'Are you aware that you are on military premises? This hangar is the property of the Royal Air Force and you are trespassing in a highly sensitive area. I hope you have an explanation.'

'We were just singing,' says Curls. 'That's all.'
'We noticed that.'
'You let us finish,' she says. 'You must have been enjoying it.'
The soldier stares at her. 'Name?' he says.
'Jane Curley,' she says. 'Spinster of this parish. Pupil of Goldwyn's High School for young ladies of reputable families.'
There's a flutter of amusement from the girls, but the faces of the men remain serious.
Duncan steps forward. 'Look, chaps,' he says, 'we shouldn't be here, we know, but we haven't done any harm. The acoustics were just too good to be true.'
The three men scrutinise his army uniform. 'Who are you?'
'Lieutenant Braithwaite, 7th Armoured Division of the British Eighth Army.'
They eye him with suspicion. 'Shouldn't you be on the other side of the world?' says one.
'I'm on leave. My parents were killed in the bombing.'
'Can we see your papers?'
Duncan hands over his documents and they spend some time examining them, studying his face, then checking every detail. 'This doesn't explain why you were here in the first place.'
The girls and the students look at each other. They don't really have an explanation for why they crept through the fence and came into the hangar. It's beginning to appear as a foolhardy course of action. Whose idea was it? Alma thinks back, trying to work out why they decided to trespass, who took the first step, why they all

followed, but there doesn't seem to be a rational explanation. Just the atmosphere, the sense of adventure, the desire to do something different.

'We were testing your security,' says Curls. 'You'll have to do something about that fence. It was dead easy to get in.'

'I think,' says Jack, 'we got a bit carried away.'

'Just a bit,' says the soldier. 'You are all under arrest.'

iv

Robert receives the telephone call from the Military Police at the airfield in the middle of the afternoon, but he has to attend a meeting of the local fire-watching service, presided over by the ARP wardens, before he can go to the airfield. He stands at the bus stop, fretting about the work waiting to be marked. The bus, when it finally arrives, is full, so he stands on the platform at the back, clinging to the pole with one hand, hemmed in by a group of subdued, weary factory workers who have just finished a weekend shift. The clippie struggles to reach each person on the platform, edging through them, taking their money and punching the tickets with some difficulty. She refuses to allow anyone on at the next stop.

'Sorry!' she shouts. 'You'll have to get the next one.' She rings the bell twice and they move off. The people in the queue watch them go, their faces set in well-practised resignation.

At the airfield, Robert is stopped at the gate by two airmen and asked for his identity card. It's scrutinised by one of the airmen, who then opens the barrier and allows him in. 'I'll take you over, sir,' he says. He sets off rapidly towards a group of buildings in the distance while Robert limps along behind him, determined not to let on that he's finding it difficult to keep up.

He still doubts that the officer who spoke to him on the phone has understood the situation correctly. Why would his students be trespassing on a military airfield? They're young men with superior minds, destined for significant careers, loyal citizens who volunteer for fire-watching shifts on a regular basis. There has unquestionably been a mistake.

He is led into one of the offices where he meets Squadron Leader Mulligan, an unusually tall man with a large floppy blond moustache but a completely bald head. 'Look, old man,' he says to Robert, once they are seated in his office on opposite sides of the desk. 'I don't seriously believe that your chaps are fifth columnists – they seem too naïve for that – but you know how it is. We should follow procedures strictly, report all incidents, fill in forms, but I'm rather hoping to avoid some of the tedious stuff.'

'I completely understand,' says Robert. 'Vigilance is essential.'

The squadron leader clears his throat and lowers his voice. 'Actually,' he says, 'we are not entirely blameless. The hangar should never have been left unattended. We have rectified the situation immediately, of course, but it would seem wise to reduce the fuss as much as possible.'

'Are you absolutely certain my students have been trespassing? It seems very out of character.'

'I think you'll find that one can never be absolutely certain–'

He is interrupted as the door opens abruptly and Miss Cunningham-Smith walks in. Both men rise hastily to their feet.

'I'm sorry, sir,' says the young lieutenant behind her. 'She was unstoppable.'

This should be interesting, thinks Robert. He can't decide if he's pleased to see her or not. On the one hand, his position has been usurped and his presence is probably now redundant, but on the other, the situation will almost certainly be sorted out more satisfactorily than he had hoped.

'Miss Dulcie Cunningham-Smith,' she says, advancing on the squadron leader, her hand outstretched, her head tilted to take in his great height. 'Headmistress of Goldwyn's Girls' School. And you are?'

'Squadron Leader Mulligan, ma'am,' he says, offering his hand.

'Well, it's a pretty kettle of fish we have here,' says Miss Cunningham-Smith, making a swift examination of the office and apparently finding nothing of significance. 'Ah, Mr Gunner, we meet again.'

'Good evening, Miss Cunningham-Smith,' he says. 'A most unfortunate set of circumstances.'

'Indeed. Correct me if I'm wrong, Mr Gunner, but I believe my young ladies were in your care when this incident took place.'

He nods nervously. 'I'm extremely sorry.'

'As am I, Mr Gunner.' She turns back to the squadron leader. 'And have they an explanation for their extraordinary behaviour?'

Squadron Leader Mulligan pulls up another chair for Miss Cunningham-Smith. 'Please sit down,' he says, folding his abnormally long legs like the parts of a crane and arranging them under the desk. 'They say they were just messing about.'

'Messing about? I take it you've threatened them with ghastly punishments – thumbscrews, the rack, that kind of thing? They should not conclude that this is an acceptable way to carry on during a war.' She makes it sound as if a war is a passing inconvenience, a situation that has to be acknowledged but not allowed to take precedence over good manners.

'They have been interviewed individually, and their stories tally, so we're inclined to–'

Miss Cunningham-Smith is not prepared to wait for details. 'Good, good. I'm assuming I can take them away with me. Mr Gunner will be responsible for the young men and I believe you also have a member of our armed forces in your care, who will presumably be returned to the correct authorities. Rest assured that action will be taken over my girls' part in this. They will not escape punishment.'

'I wouldn't be too hard on them,' says the squadron leader. 'I've been persuaded that it was just high spirits. We must make some allowances for youth.'

Miss Cunningham-Smith stares at him so hard that he has to look away. 'You may consider high spirits to be acceptable, Squadron Leader, but I do not. I expect my young ladies to behave with absolute decorum at all times, and especially in public.'

Does she know about the dancing? Robert thinks not.

'However,' she says, 'it seems to me that there is something alarmingly inadequate about your security. I trust that this will alert you to errors in your organisation.'

The squadron leader bows his head and chooses not to answer for a few seconds. 'I understand that their singing was rather good,' he says eventually.

Miss Cunningham-Smith stares at him. 'Singing? What in the world are you talking about?'

'They were singing. Madrigals, I've been told. Sixteenth century–'

'Young man, I know what madrigals are.'

'Quite so.' He clears his throat. 'They were singing in one of our aircraft hangars. That's how we knew they were there. They tell me that the acoustics are exceptional. According to my lads, we should have let them go on a little longer. Quite an acceptable performance, I gather.'

'I would expect nothing less. Now, would you fetch them for me so that I can return them safely to Mortimer Hall?' She turns to Robert. 'I assume you'll be following shortly with your young men.'

'I sincerely hope so,' he says.

Squadron Leader Mulligan rises from his chair, comes round from the side of the desk and opens the door to his outside office. 'Captain Richards,' he says to his adjutant, 'could you take Miss Cunningham-Smith to where our young trespassers are waiting? I believe they're in the mess. She has my permission to take them home.'

From Robert's position, he can see the squadron leader's face. He's reasonably sure that he catches the ghost of a wink and a faint twitching of the lips, the suggestion of a smile – visible to him but not Miss Cunningham-Smith, who is facing the opposite direction.

Miss Cunningham-Smith sweeps out. 'Come along now,' she says to the captain. 'It's getting late and we need to make sure we're all safely behind blackout curtains before there's any possibility of another raid.'

The squadron leader closes the door behind her. He looks at Robert and allows himself a more overt smile. 'Crikey,' he says. 'I think we should wangle her a position in the War Office. We need people like her in charge. I'm just relieved I'm not one of her girls.'

'Will Captain Richards be able to cope with her?' asks Robert.

The grin on Squadron Leader Mulligan's face expands. 'Not my problem,' he says. 'Now, I assume you're going to take the students off my hands?'

'Have you given them a serious lecture?'

The squadron leader nods. 'Gave them a pretty furious dressing-down – told them they'd endangered national security and it must never happen again. They were fairly contrite, I'd say.'

'Thank you for your understanding.' Robert gets to his feet. 'They should be ashamed of themselves, wasting everyone's time like this.'

'They're only young,' says the squadron leader.

'You put young men of that age into aeroplanes and they risk their lives for us every day. My students have no excuse for their appalling lack of forethought.'

The squadron leader looks down at the desk and moves pieces of paper around without any sense of direction. His smile has faded. 'I sometimes think we're asking too much of my lads.'

They are both quiet for a few seconds.

'Can you take the lieutenant chappie with you as well?' says Squadron Leader Mulligan. 'Different service. Not our responsibility–' He's interrupted by the sound of a siren. 'What the–' He jumps out of his chair, goes to the window and pulls back the blind. People are dashing across the airfield, searching for shelter or diving to the ground as the blast of an explosion rumbles through the air. The floor rocks under their feet.

The door opens and one of his staff steps in smartly. 'Sir, it's a lone Stuka – Ju-87 dive bomber – having some fun at our expense on its way home, probably. Or he's just got lost and wants to give us a bit of a fright.'

'Well, he's come to the wrong place if he thinks he can get away with that,' says Squadron Leader Mulligan. 'Why can't I hear the anti-aircraft guns?'

'Just getting him in their sights now, sir. He caught us napping, I'm afraid. And we've scrambled the air crews – we're trying to get some machines in the air before he comes round again.'

'Has he hit anything?'

'No, sir. I can see why he's got lost. He's a bit of a loose cannon. Doesn't seem to have any sense of direction.'

Robert follows them out of the office. The Stuka is circling in the distance preparing to make another pass over the airfield.

'He's got a death wish,' says one of the mechanics, standing at Robert's side, gazing up at the sky, a hand shading his eyes.

Miss Cunningham-Smith and her four girls have been caught out in the open, crossing the road from the mess, and they've thrown themselves to the ground. They're pulling themselves upright, preparing to run towards a building.

'Someone get those women out of here!' roars Squadron Leader Mulligan.

Men are pouring out of the buildings, heading for the stationary Hurricanes. Propellors start to turn and the throaty roar of engines fills the air as three taxi to the runway, ready for take-off.

'Hit the deck!' yells someone, as the Stuka gets into position and dives down towards them again, engine shrieking, wings rocking wildly as he drops another bomb. He's aiming randomly, not even targeting the waiting Hurricanes on the runway. Robert throws himself down, and feels a rush of air and the heat of the engine as the plane climbs back up, swinging from side to side. One of the Hurricanes is hit by a stray tile from a damaged roof and careers off towards the grass, a plume of smoke coming from its engine. The pilot leaps out and runs for cover just before the engine explodes with a dull thump. Fire engines appear from nowhere and race towards the conflagration, their sirens ringing. As the Stuka circles again, the remaining two Hurricanes take off.

As soon as the enemy plane has passed over, Robert lifts his head and is appalled to see Curls jumping to her feet and racing over to where Alma is still lying motionless on the tarmac. She leans over. 'Alma!' she screams. 'Are you all right?'

Alma's head pops up from the ground. 'Yes,' she says. 'I'm fine.'

Curls sinks back on her knees and laughs. She turns to stare at the plane, as if she's trying to understand the mind of the pilot. Why would you threaten me and my friends when we've done nothing to you? she seems to be saying.

Robert takes a deep breath. Curls reminds him of the woman on the poster – **Serve in the WAAF with the Men Who Fly** – but without the curly hair. Chin up, gazing at the sky, steely eyes. The backbone of England.

Slowly, everyone gets to their feet. The two Hurricanes, which have taken off, are now chasing the Stuka over the trees. There are sudden bursts of gunfire and they can see all three aircraft shooting upwards into the blue of the sky. They soar and swoop with energetic grace, birds engaged in a light-hearted game of tag. They can hear anti-aircraft guns, see the white puffs of smoke in the sky. A Hurricane fixes itself on the tail of the Stuka, refusing to be shaken off, firing into its tail. Finally, the nose of the Stuka turns upwards in a slow-motion gesture of defiance. Then it plunges towards the ground, pursued by an ever-thickening wake of black smoke.

They feel the impact as it hits the ground. More fire engines spring into action, their sirens wailing as they drive out of the gates and head in the direction of the crash.

'Goodness me!' says Curls. 'Who'd have thought we'd see that?'

Robert examines himself to check that he is intact. His legs are trembling, but he ignores them. He dusts down his jacket, straightens his tie, looks around for his students.

All of the girls, except Curls, burst into tears.

V

Miss Cunningham-Smith would never allow the distraction of an air raid to divert her from her mission to mould her girls into obedient, honourable members of society. The next day at school, she summons the four girls to her office.

'This must never happen again,' she says. 'It was an appalling waste of my time – and that of Mr Gunner, who has more important things to do – to have to go all the way out to the airfield to fetch you.'

Alma examines the dark wooden floor under her feet and tries to listen to the reprimand. But her mind is wandering. Duncan left this morning – thank goodness they hadn't been held any longer at the air base – at five o'clock.

As they'd waited outside the house, hearing the oily rumble of the jeep approaching and waking up the neighbourhood, he'd put his arms round her and pulled her off her feet. 'I'll soon be back,' he said, 'so make sure everything's ready next time. I expect the grass to be cut, the hedge trimmed and a lamb stew simmering in the oven. You'll have to find some onions this time, whatever it takes.'

She clung to him, the coarse khaki material of his uniform prickly against her skin. 'Don't do anything stupid,' she said fiercely. 'You mustn't get killed.'

'Who – me? I'm immortal, you know that. Anyway, I've got a little sister to look after.'

The driver of the jeep hooted as he pulled up outside the house.

'Got to go,' said Duncan. 'Make sure they can see you giving me a kiss. They'll think I've got a sweetheart. Gives me a bit of credibility.'

He set her back on her feet and she reached up to kiss his cheek. Then he turned and ran towards the jeep, throwing in his kitbag and leaping in. He barely had time to sit down before they skidded away. Her last glimpse of him was his arm, lean and tanned, waving out of the back of the vehicle as it rounded the corner at the bottom of the road. She stood there for a long time, listening to the sound of the engine dying in the distance, carrying Duncan away.

'You are young ladies,' says Miss Cunningham-Smith. 'You must take some responsibility for your own behaviour.'

'We're sorry, Miss Cunningham-Smith,' says Curls, in a small voice.

'Good. Whatever were you thinking? Do you realise how serious this could have been? How important security is in these dangerous times?

They could have arrested you, put you in prison and thrown away the key. They have far more important things to deal with than schoolgirls on a prank. You will stay for an hour at the end of every school day for the next fortnight, writing lines. Is that clear?'

An hour, thinks Alma, plus the extra ten minutes in the morning. A long day, but it could have been so much worse. She risks a glance at Curls whose eyes are down like her own, studying the carpet, her whole appearance one of remorse and repentance. Very briefly, Curls returns her look, a flash out of the corner of her eye. Alma resists the temptation to smile.

They turn to file out of the room, their heads still down and their cheeks burning.

'Incidentally,' says Miss Cunningham-Smith.

They stop.

'I hear the singing was of a very high quality,' she says.

They leave the room, carefully shutting the door behind them. 'Phew!' says Natalie, once there is some distance between them and Miss Cunningham-Smith.

'A whole hour after school,' says Giraffe. 'What a bore.'

Curls grabs Alma and whispers in her ear, 'I've got something to tell you.'

Instantly Alma feels better. Things are slipping back to normal. Secrets with Curls, not involving the others; lectures from Miss Cunningham-Smith; detention at the end of school. The world is beginning to feel a warmer place again. She follows Curls to the girls' lavatories, not saying anything, pleased at the prospect of a conspiracy.

Once they have checked that no one is there, Alma turns to Curls. 'Well?' she says. 'What is it?'

Curls hesitates, almost as if she regrets having said anything.

'Come on,' says Alma. 'We'll be late for history. What's happened?'

'Well,' says Curls, 'you know Duncan?'

This is to do with Duncan? Alma's brother? What can Curls know about Duncan that she doesn't?

'He kissed me,' says Curls.

What is she talking about? She's got the wrong person. She must mean Jack. 'Who?' she asks.

'Duncan,' says Curls, quietly.

They face each other for some time without speaking. Alma is trying to sort out her thoughts, make sense of what Curls is telling her. Duncan kissed Curls? 'Why?' she asks eventually.

Curls starts to speak, then changes her mind. She shrugs. 'I don't know,' she says lightly, then turns away. 'Come on, we'd better get going.'

But Alma follows more slowly. Duncan kissed Curls. That was what she'd said. Not 'I kissed Duncan.'

It can't be right. She must have misheard.

A churning knot of distaste is forming inside her at the thought of her best friend and Duncan together. It's all wrong, she wants to say. You can't mean it. We always like the same boys. Duncan's my brother. He belongs to me. It doesn't make sense.

The telegram comes a week later.

Alma and Curls have not spoken about Duncan again. A barrier has grown between them, which Alma can't quite understand. She wants to ask again – why did he kiss you, was it more than once, did he mean it or was it a joke? – but she's afraid that the answers may not be right. She's afraid of what she may find out.

The doorbell rings at Mortimer Hall at seven fifteen one evening while they're having supper in the dining room. Mrs Anderson goes to answer it and comes back almost straight away, followed by Miss Cunningham-Smith in her black cycling coat. Her hair is dishevelled and she's breathing heavily.

The girls stand up in alarm. She's never been to Mortimer Hall before.

Miss Cunningham-Smith approaches Alma and hands her the telegram. 'My dear…' she says, and seems unable to continue.

'What is it?' asks Curls.

'It's a telegram,' says Alma, staring at it, not able to think clearly. She sits down and studies it in her hand. The word 'Priority' is written at the top.

'Open it,' hisses Curls. Her voice is tight, tense, urgent. 'If you don't, I will.'

'No,' says Alma. Nobody else can do this for her. She slides a finger under the flap and rips it open.

Duncan's transport plane was shot down off the coast of France. Three airmen, four soldiers. Including Duncan. All seven are missing.

Part Eight

i

23 October 1963

It's after ten, long after the last parents have left, when Wilhelmina Yates returns home. She switches on all of the downstairs lights, draws the curtains in the sitting room and kneels down to light the fire with a match. The gas leaps up with a little *whoomph* of pleasure, catching the flame and spreading rapidly until the radiants start to glow. Miss Yates watches it for a while, listening to the putter of the gas, enjoying its comforting rhythm, allowing her skin to absorb the heat. Once she's warmed up, she goes into the kitchen to make a bedtime drink.

She's exhausted, but not yet ready to relax or to assess the success of the evening. She was up for most of the previous night preparing, examining the file of every girl, memorising details of their hobbies, their strengths and weaknesses in the entrance exam. Now she sits down with her Ovaltine and goes through the files again, tucking her perceptions of their parents into her mind, making notes about her conversations, analysing the information. She can recognise faces without effort – after one short meeting she will remember them for ever – but she has to go over other details more carefully. If she does this soon after she's met them, she can later summon the information in a second, as easily as if she's pulling out a file on them. Name. Father's profession. Approximate age; summary of every conversation she has ever had with them.

'You'd make a good teacher,' her mother said to her once. 'My junior school teacher was like you. Mr Jarvis. He knew every child in the school. He would gaze into space for two seconds – his eyes went off to the right – and you'd think he'd forgotten you were there, but then he'd look back and he knew everything about you. A clever man, he was. Very clever.'

I wish you could see me now, thinks Miss Yates.

Nobody in her family has lived to see her rise from the bonfire of their damp, overcrowded home and end up in this light-filled house, which is far too big for one person. Her mother, father, brothers and sisters remain in Coventry. When the bulldozers removed the rubble and levelled the ground, traces of her family would have fallen through the cracks and embedded themselves into the dirt. Charred bones, rotted flesh pummelled into a solid base, moulded into foundations for new buildings. You can't possibly collect every single bit of a person when they've been blasted by a bomb. There'll always be something left even if you can't see it.

There's a restaurant there now, and a funeral parlour, built over the old street in Coventry that had once been lined on either side with terraced houses.

Wilhelmina Yates, the nervous young woman with acne, who didn't have the necessary skills to make friends, who had no real experience of life, was not there on the evening in question. She was living at St Anne's College, Oxford (curfew ten o'clock, no gentlemen visitors at any time), studying for a degree in mathematics.

Miss Yates, headmistress, is no longer the young woman who came home to discover she had no family. She has learned exactly what she has to do to be successful, how to be self-sufficient, how to use her life in the most efficient way possible.

She finds herself staring into space.

Robert Gunner. There was something so familiar about him. His earnestness, his scrupulous manners. He reminded her of her father, a clerk who worked for the railway, an honourable man who believed that outward appearance should reflect the decency within. A good man. Her brothers, George and Herbert, younger than her, had been the same. Small replicas of her father, calm, contained, impeccably polite.

'Wilhelmina Yates,' she said to him, offering her hand when she came out of her office. He was the last one. He had a firm handshake. Exactly the right amount of pressure, which she was able to reciprocate. 'Gunner,' he said. 'Robert Gunner. Pippa's father.'

She had already worked that out. The only man without a wife. She found herself wanting to hold on to his hand longer than usual.

She let go.

She ushered him towards the door of her room, but he stood back to allow her to go first so she led the way in and he shut the door quietly and firmly before limping towards the two chairs placed before the desk. A war wound, perhaps?

'Please take a chair, Mr Gunner,' she said, indicating with her hand where she was expecting him to go. They sat down at exactly the same moment.

'Pippa is a delightful child,' she began – as she had with every other parent. 'We're so pleased that you decided to take up our offer of a place at Goldwyn's.'

His face was tanned and weathered, as if he spent a lot of time outside. Was he a gardener in his spare time, a sailor? 'I'm afraid I didn't have much choice,' he said. 'Pippa made the decision to come here when she was about five years old and saw a group of Goldwyn's girls getting off the train in their uniforms.' He stops for a moment, then continues, 'I knew the school many years ago – during the war. Miss Cunningham-Smith was headmistress in those days.'

'Ah, yes,' said Miss Yates. 'Miss Cunningham-Smith. Her presence has cast a long shadow over the school.'

He smiled. His eyes were dark brown, almost black. 'A benign shadow, I believe. I've always had the greatest admiration for her.'

'Benign, of course. But a good school should never stand still and eventually we have to throw off shadows from the past, do you not think? We must have aspirations, ambitions for our girls.'

He inclined his head. 'Indeed we should, Miss Yates, and I have every confidence that Goldwyn's will be safe in your capable hands.'

Miss Yates was conscious that they were saying nothing of significance. She contemplated the heap of files arranged on the side of her desk and made a decision to be bold. 'I wondered, Mr Gunner, if I might ask a personal question – in Pippa's interests, of course – so that we can treat her in the most sympathetic manner possible.'

A faint frown creased his brow. 'I'm afraid I don't quite...' Then his face cleared. 'Oh, yes, I see. Pippa's mother.'

It was a pleasure to talk to a man who could follow one's thoughts without requiring everything to be explained in detail. 'I hope you don't mind me asking. It's always helpful to understand family circumstances.'

'Not at all, not at all.' The slightly nervous repetition seemed to imply that he did mind. 'Well – my wife died shortly after Pippa was born.' He paused for a few seconds, as if he was sifting through the details and deciding which ones were relevant. 'Complications in childbirth,' he said eventually.

Excellent. No scandals. No secret mistresses. No mad wife in the attic. Miss Yates beamed at him. She had only his word for it, of course, and he was hardly likely to give out genuinely private details, but she had seen his eyes when he told her this, heard the certainty in his voice, and she trusted her instincts. He was an honest man. 'And do you have help? I'm thinking of emergencies, of course. Not that it's likely she would have an accident – the safety of my girls is always uppermost in my mind – but one cannot control the spread of measles or whooping cough, however hard one tries.'

She was watching his face, noting his reactions.

He nodded seriously, responding correctly, smiling when she smiled. His round glasses were too large for his face, and she could see from the thickness and distortion of the lenses that the right eye was the weakest, probably with some kind of astigmatism. He was leaning forward, his back slightly hunched, in the manner of a man who spends a considerable amount of his time at a desk.

'You should contact me in an emergency,' he said. 'At the university. I can arrange for Miss Dodd, the lady who comes in to help, to look after Pippa if she's ill. She's very amenable.'

'Splendid,' said Miss Yates. 'I understand you're a lecturer. In what subject?'

'Mathematics.'

She was delighted. 'How interesting,' she said, deciding that this accounted for her ability to communicate so easily with him. She was about to reveal that she had studied mathematics at Oxford, but thought better of it. 'Does Pippa share your talent?'

He shuffled awkwardly in his chair. 'I'm not sure I would call it a talent,' he said. 'It's more a matter of discipline and application. A need for concentration is the most significant requirement, and I'm not sure Pippa has acquired that yet.'

'I think you're probably doing yourself an injustice,' said Miss Yates, smiling at him. 'Talent is an essential ingredient.'

A flush was creeping over his face. Genuine humility? Embarrassment? This was an unusual response to a small compliment.

They sat and studied each other thoughtfully for

a few seconds. Mr Gunner was the first to speak. 'I hadn't expected to find Miss Alma Braithwaite here,' he said.

A jolt of surprise disturbed Miss Yates's contemplation of the pleasure of sharing the room with an educated and modest man. 'Why? Do you know her?'

He crossed his legs and one foot started to jiggle. He seemed reluctant to continue. 'I used to – the university took in some of the Goldwyn's boarders for a while during the war, after the bombing. Their boarding house was completely destroyed.'

Miss Yates nodded encouragingly, intrigued by the prospect of a portrait of Alma Braithwaite from the past. 'How interesting! I knew Alma had been a pupil here during the bombing, but I hadn't realised she'd been evacuated to the university.'

'I was the warden of Mortimer Hall at the time and we were asked to accommodate four girls. Alma was one of them.'

'How old were they?'

'About fifteen, I think – lower fifth. It was a departure from our normal routines. I was accustomed to having young men in my care, but we had a housekeeper and a cook, so we were able to take them in. It was a difficult time for all of us.'

It had been harder in Coventry. She had returned home immediately after the first terrible night, the night of more than five hundred bombers and fires that would burn for days to the accompaniment of further raids, and discovered how difficult it was to find out if missing family members were dead or just relocated. So she was there for the next night of bombing. And the next, and the next. Wave after wave of aircraft. Crammed into bomb shelters, shivering with fear as the ground shook. The government were watching the people of Coventry. To see if they could be broken by mass bombing.

Why was she thinking of this now? It wasn't appropriate. 'Hopefully, our present girls will never have to face a similar situation.'

'Indeed. I was delighted to hear of your plans for expanding the curriculum, especially the provision of German lessons.'

'Yes, German will be offered as a choice when the girls make their selections for O levels.' She looked down at the papers in front of her, shifted them around, pretended to read something of significance. 'What was Alma Braithwaite like when she was younger?' She tried to keep her voice casual, her enquiry neutral. A matter of passing interest.

Mr Gunner seemed reluctant to give any more information. He gazed past her at the window, but his eyes were turning inwards, as if he was running through a memory he rarely visited. 'I'm not sure I could really tell you much about her. I didn't know the girls well – they were in the care of the housekeeper, you understand. I remember that they were very engaged in their music – and dancing.'

'Dancing?' Miss Yates was astonished. Alma? Dancing?

'Yes. Several of my students turned out to be keen dancers and they taught the girls. I'm afraid

I found it a little too much, but the young people had to let off steam. They needed a way to cope. You must have been aware of this yourself. They sang too. More serious music.' He smiled unexpectedly. 'They almost caused an incident at the RAF base. A group of them somehow managed to get through the perimeter of the airfield – it was not entirely their fault, the fencing wasn't secure – and decided to sing madrigals in an aircraft hangar. It wasn't exactly sensible, drawing attention to their presence by singing, but apparently the acoustics were first-rate and they didn't consider the consequences of being caught. Fortunately, the RAF overlooked the incident and didn't proceed further. High spirits, we all agreed. Probably not high treason.'

High spirits? Alma Braithwaite? It was difficult to imagine. 'Well, I must confess I'm seeing Alma in a new light.'

He smiled, a little sadly, she thought. 'She lost her parents in the war, you know.'

'I wonder if that's why she's reluctant to accept change. She seems unnaturally attached to the memory of Miss Cunningham-Smith.'

He looked at her sharply. She tried to undo what she had said. 'We all admire what Miss Cunningham-Smith accomplished in her time here as headmistress, but it must be better to think forwards than backwards.'

'Of course,' he said. 'We're living in an age of great change.'

She smiled, pleased at his willingness to see past her moment of unguarded honesty. She had a sense that they'd reached an understanding.

That their ability to communicate went beyond the mundane.

The sitting room has warmed up nicely. The knowledge that she no longer needs to worry about the gas and electricity bills is a source of enormous pleasure to Miss Yates. Indeed, she often leaves all the lights blazing simply because she can. But now she turns on two lamps and switches off the main light so that the atmosphere is gentler, with soft shadows gathering in the corners. It reminds her of her childhood and the cramped living room where everything took place. She and her five brothers and sisters – Avril, George, Herbert, Barbara, Thelma – would sit round the dining-room table to do their homework, next to the range, their faces burning on the side facing the fire, freezing on the other, tilting their books towards the single source of light in the middle. The older ones helped the younger. All six were clever, encouraged by their parents' love of learning, and competitive, winning scholarships to the grammar school, peering through the gloom to wrestle with calculus, memorise the weather statistics of Chile, find out if Pip marries Estella in *Great Expectations*. As the only survivor, Wilhelmina owes it to the others to be successful.

She rarely allows herself to return to the past like this. There's nothing to be gained from it.

The Royal Worcester china – sets of teapots, milk jugs, sugar bowls, cups and saucers, placed in cabinets around the room – come to life in the soft glow of the lamps. Tiny points of light glisten through the glass. Paper-thin bone china, delicately patterned with flourishes of flowers or fruit, gold rims catching the light. She goes to one of the cabinets and takes out an accent plate – she has not yet unpacked the rest of the set – an antique Regency design, with rich, intricate colours. It gleams, sheer and unblemished. She runs a hand over the smooth surface, feeling the warmth of the lustre through her fingertips. She lifts the plate to her face and lets the edge touch her lips, the most sensitive part of her body, where she can accurately assess the quality of the glaze.

She never buys seconds. She examines every item thoroughly before she pays for it, taking it out of the presentation box, running her fingers over the surface. She requires a perfection that she knows she cannot find elsewhere. Every piece is a small victory. Proof that she has succeeded.

She thinks of Robert Gunner in her office, sitting opposite her. An intelligent man.

ii

Bridget Murphy and Alma are on their knees on the office floor, stifling their laughter as they pick up and sort out files that have fallen off the side of the desk. Alma has started to visit Bridget regularly, enjoying her company, possibly because they share the same healthy lack of respect for Wilhelmina Yates. It's odd that they should have become friends – Bridget is considerably younger than her – but it always feels as if they're on the same side. There's never the sense of caution that hovers, like an unseen cloud, over her conversations with the other teachers, the consciousness that their loyalties might be divided, that they could be spies for Miss Yates.

'Have you come across Philippa Gunner's father?' she asks casually.

Bridget sits back on her shoes – two-inch stacked heels, black bows on a white fabric background – her brow creased with concentration. 'Pippa Gunner – oh, I know, the one with bunches, a bit cheeky, scored the highest mark for maths in the entrance test. Why are we interested in him?'

'I used to know him,' says Alma. 'Once. A long time ago.'

Bridget's eyes widen. 'Oh, do go on. What's the story?'

'There isn't one,' says Alma. 'We met during the war, that's all. And then he turned up for Pippa's parents' evening last week.'

'Did he remember you?'

'Yes, surprisingly, considering I was only fifteen when I knew him before.'

They stand up, clutching the files. Bridget holds open the drawer of the filing cabinet and Alma slips them in neatly, all in order. 'Is there something you want to tell me?' says Bridget.

Alma hesitates. Where could she begin? Bridget would know nothing about the war. She hadn't even been born then. 'No, of course not.'

Bridget makes them some tea with a small electric kettle in the corner of the room. She stirs milk and sugar into each mug and brings them over to the desk where they sit down next to each other, looking out over the school grounds and the netball courts. The lower-fourths are playing an after-school match against St Margaret's. Loyal supporters in regulation school macs and hats are gathered behind the wire-netting, cheering for Goldwyn's.

Alma blows on the surface of the tea and takes a sip. 'How's life with the sergeant major?' she asks.

Bridget shudders. 'She's changing everything. Filing systems, procedures, contact with parents. It's as if she has to be ten times better than Miss Cunningham-Smith. You wouldn't believe how much work she's created. I'm thinking of asking for an assistant.'

'An assistant to the assistant?'

'I'm not an assistant. I'm the secretary. The only one. Of course, I should be promoted to personal assistant since I'm doing all this extra work, but that's not likely to happen. She'd have to pay me more.'

'Not even the satisfaction of a posh job title, then?'

'Quite.'

They're listening for footsteps along the corridor. Miss Yates is in a meeting with the governors, but they know from experience that she might emerge when they're least expecting it. It's almost as if she does it deliberately, creeping up on them, hoping to catch them out in some conspiracy. Mutiny, plotting a coup, an assassination attempt.

'You know when she applied for the job – Miss

Yates?' says Alma, lowering her voice to barely above a whisper. 'Do you still have her application form?'

Bridget's eyebrows almost disappear under her fringe. 'Why?'

'I was just wondering...'

'Yes?'

'Is she as squeaky clean as she pretends she is? I bet there's something in her past that she'd rather we didn't know.'

'Like what?' whispers Bridget.

'I'm not sure. I was just wondering...' Of course she's only feeling her way in the dark, hoping to stumble across something interesting. 'Well, it occurred to me she might have a guilty secret – something she'd rather we didn't find out.'

'Ooh!' says Bridget. 'A shady past. How exciting.'

Alma makes an effort to grin, to lighten the conversation. 'I'd just be interested to find out where she was teaching before here and see why she decided to move on. Look at her references.'

'You can't tell anything from references. If they're really positive, it might mean that the candidate is brilliant, but it's more likely that her present school is desperate to get rid of her.'

'Even so, you've got to admit it would be interesting.'

Bridget puts her mug of tea on the desk and frowns. 'Do you really think we should? It seems a bit...'

'Do you know where her application form is?'

Bridget's eyes slide sideways to a small cabinet in the corner of the room.

'Is it locked?'

Bridget's gaze moves in the direction of a bunch of keys in an ashtray adorned with the words 'Ashes to Ashes'. 'It's the small silver key,' she says. 'Are you sure this is a good idea?'

'Tell you what,' says Alma, 'why don't you go to the lavatory? I'll mind the desk while you're gone and answer the phone.'

'I could get into trouble.'

'That's ridiculous. Everyone's allowed to go to the lavatory. You'll only be away for a couple of minutes.'

'OK,' says Bridget. She picks up her bag, hoists it on to her shoulder and heads for the door. She pauses on her way out. 'I won't be long,' she says, in a normal voice. 'Can you watch the phone for me?'

'Of course,' says Alma. 'I'm always happy to help.'

As soon as Bridget has left the room, Alma grabs the keys and heads for the filing cabinet. It takes a few seconds to slot the key into the hole, turn it and pull out the top drawer. The files are not in any kind of order – Bridget probably does need an assistant – and she riffles through it hurriedly, increasingly aware of the passing of time. She tries to listen for footsteps, but the noise of the paper moving and the thumping of her heart make it impossible. Hurry, hurry... If I'm quick enough I can't get caught. Where is it? Her breathing becomes louder and sweat is breaking out on her forehead.

A door opens and closes in the corridor. At precisely that moment, Alma finds a file marked

'Headship Applicants'. She grabs it and slips it under some papers on the desk, pushing the drawer shut at the same time. She turns the key and replaces it in the ashtray just as Bridget dashes back in, her face flushed and anxious.

'Quick!' hisses Bridget. 'She's coming.'

Alma drains her mug and replaces it on the table by the window.

Miss Yates enters the room. She looks at Bridget, frowning slightly. 'I don't think I've ever seen you running before, Bridget,' she says. 'Is there something urgent you have to attend to?'

'No,' says Bridget. 'I just thought I could hear the telephone.'

'Hmm,' says Miss Yates. She studies her for a few seconds, then turns to Alma. 'Ah, Alma, there you are,' she says, as if she has been looking for her for the last ten minutes. 'I wonder if you could go outside and investigate what's happening under my window. Several girls are engaged in a heated argument. Something to do with hockey sticks and bruised ankles. They're disturbing our meeting.'

'Isn't anyone supervising them?' says Alma. She dislikes aggressive situations with the girls.

Miss Yates studies her for a few seconds, as if she suspects she's making excuses. 'I really don't know, but I'd be most grateful if you could see to it.'

'Of course,' says Alma.

'By the way, I met an old friend of yours last night.'

An old friend? What is she talking about?

'A Mr Gunner, Philippa Gunner's father. I

gather you knew each other some time ago – during the war.'

Alma doesn't want to talk about Robert Gunner with Miss Yates. 'Yes,' she says.

'A charming man, I thought.'

They become aware of dangerously raised voices outside.

'I'll go and sort it out,' says Alma, picking up the papers on the desk and sweeping past Miss Yates, hoping desperately that the file isn't visible. She doesn't look at Bridget's face.

iii

Robert is digging a new vegetable patch when Pippa comes to tell him about the concert. He spends much of his free time gardening. He enjoys the solitude, the distance from other people and a calmness that comes from not needing to find words. Silence settles around him as a welcome barrier from the world of people, although of course it's never entirely silent. There's almost always a flutter of breeze. Birds come surprisingly close without apparently recognising he's alive, while insects crawl above and below the soil beneath his feet.

As Pippa and Godfrey's wireless and record-player now operate without a break, and the desire for continuous noise has escalated in the world around him, Robert has come to understand that his pleasure in silence is unusual.

There's more traffic on the roads, more music everywhere he goes, and students now seem convinced that talking is a viable alternative to thinking. A large garden dampens some of this noise, keeps it at bay.

Silence was the quality that attracted him to Grace, his wife, although, curiously, once they were married, she started to talk more, chattering away without caring if he was listening or not. When he thinks back to his marriage, it seems so fleeting, just a few brief years.

She was a typist in the science-faculty office at the end of the war. The first few times Robert encountered her, he could see only her head as she bent over the typewriter, dark, curly hair that he later discovered was natural and not permed. She had an unusual crown and hairs swirled round its centre like water circling a plughole. Then, one day, she glanced up at the precise moment he was observing her and their eyes made contact. She looked away immediately, but he was left with a lasting impression of soft brown eyes and a gentle flush creeping up her pale cheeks.

Only a couple of weeks after that brief moment of contact, Robert attended a concert at the cathedral. Three Beethoven string quartets. He sat on the uncomfortable wooden seat, drew in his elbows so he wouldn't knock the people next to him, squeezed his feet close together and absorbed the sound. He allowed the music to transport him to a world where the mathematical precision of chords and the symmetry of melody collided, resulting in a sensation of enormous pleasure. When the first movement of the first quartet ended, he stretched his legs, looked around and saw Grace sitting in the row in front of him, five seats to his right. She would know he was there if she turned her head very slightly. During the following three movements, he struggled to follow the progression of the themes. He and Grace seemed to drift towards each other in the interval as if it had been arranged.

'Hello,' he said, aware that he was blushing.

'Mr Gunner,' she said.

They shook hands. 'I'm so sorry,' he said. 'I'm not sure that I can remember your name.' This was not strictly true. Bowers, a senior lecturer, had given him the information. He had raised an eyebrow when Robert asked, but made no further comment.

'Miss French,' she said. 'Grace.'

They didn't speak for a while.

'Wonderful concert–' said Robert.

'Glorious music–' said Grace, at the same time.

They discovered that when either of them had something to say the other was usually about to say almost the same thing.

His mother would have approved, he thought, and Robert wished she had been there to help with the wedding arrangements when the time came. He would have liked someone to tell him what to do. When Godfrey was born eighteen months after the wedding, he discovered in himself a variety of new emotions. Enormous pride (he had to fight the urge to go out and tell everyone he was now a father), great tenderness for Grace and his new son, a desire to save as much money as he could for his son's future and, strangest of all, an unexpected emptiness.

He realised eventually that he was missing his mother.

Godfrey's birth was straightforward, almost easy, but Pippa caused complications. Robert went with Grace to the hospital in a taxi, out in the world together for the last time, aware of the distressing nature of her contractions but unable to help beyond carrying her small case through the doors of the hospital. He had to keep Godfrey occupied in the waiting room before being told to go home and wait for news. They never saw her again.

When he was summoned by the phone in the middle of the night, he had to call in a neighbour to mind Godfrey and cycle to the hospital through dark, empty streets, unable to comprehend what had happened. Eclampsia, they said. The baby had survived but Grace hadn't. He understands the scientific details of the term – he had gone to the university library and read up the relevant medical textbooks – but he has never been able to relate it in any meaningful way to Grace. Even now he can't understand why it happened to her, what they did wrong, how a child as sunny as Pippa could be the product of such a secretive, sinister condition. When he brought Pippa home to meet Godfrey, Grace had already disappeared without trace and they carried on as if she had only ever brushed against the edges of their existence. Godfrey adjusted, Pippa had never known her anyway, and Robert was thrown into the hectic routine of childcare without having time to fix her in his mind.

They had said so little to each other.

'I thought we might go to Dorset for a holiday this year. Go and see Portland Bill.'

'I don't think I'm familiar with Portland Bill. Was he at university with you?'

'No, darling. It's a lighthouse.' But when he looked up at her, he saw that she knew this. She had been making a joke.

So they had laughed together, privately, as if they'd discovered humour for the first time.

He had never spoken to her about Curls. Why not? It wasn't as if he had anything to be ashamed of, yet he knew that he couldn't share his experience with Grace. That short period in his life had become more a dream than reality, yet another manifestation of the irrational nature of war. Thinking about it made him feel disloyal.

He struggles to equate the figure of Grace that appears in photographs with his memory of her: small; hair held back on one side with a little clip; clothes hanging fluidly from her tiny, bird-like frame. She was twenty-eight when she had Godfrey, thirty when she died, a fully grown woman, yet in the photographs she retains the childlike appearance that never left her. She was seven years younger than Robert when she was alive, but now the gap has grown and stretched.

He'd bought this house for her.

She'd raced through it on their first visit, impatient to see it all. 'I love the morning sun in the kitchen.'

'We'll need a total of fifteen light bulbs that will probably need replacing every six months. It will be an expensive venture,' he said.

'We could plant lilies in the garden. Hundreds of them. There's so much glorious space.'

Every now and again he would examine his life and marvel that he'd ended up as a married man with a house and a garden. Later, after she had died, he dug up the lilies and redesigned the garden so that he could grow vegetables. He was more comfortable with practicality.

He can't recall experiencing a violent passion for Grace, and yet somehow they'd been drawn together, pulled in by an invisible magnetic field. She'd been married before, lost her husband in the Dunkirk evacuation, and clearly craved the comfort of physical touch. She would insist on holding his hand when they were out, much to his embarrassment, and she was always flapping around him at home, patting his arm, leaning on his shoulder, snuggling up to him on the sofa and messing up his papers, checking he was still there.

'Godfrey will need some shoes soon. He's just taken his first steps without support.'

'You'd better get his feet measured.'

They shared pride, pleasure, enthusiasm, but most of the words came from Grace.

Why had a woman to whom physical contact was so important married a man who was content with his own company? She must have seen something in him that he couldn't identify for himself, something that had gone back into hibernation after her death.

He has never allowed himself to make a comparison between Curls and Grace. It would be unfair to try. Curls could produce sublime music while Grace was a warm, loyal wife and mother. She enjoyed music, but was never completely transported by it, never moved beyond expression. He can't decide if this affected their relationship. Is it possible to experience passion with someone who cannot fully appreciate the complexity of Bach fugues?

Does he miss Grace? He is uncertain about this. Pippa has taken over the house, her female presence fluttering around, filling the spaces, chattering good-naturedly to anyone who will listen, making up for her mother's absence.

He bends over to ease out a large dandelion, careful to pull up as much as possible, shaking off the loose earth. The black soil crumbles in his hand and slips easily off the roots.

It's more than three weeks since the parents' evening but ever since, he's found his thoughts have been slipping backwards.

Mortimer Hall, 1942, digging up the garden with his students, preparing the ground for vegetables. The rich, damp smell, amiable banter between the students.

'Here, Jack. Another worm.'

'Ah, meat. Terrific.'

'I'll inform Mrs Anderson of your preferences, shall I?'

Chuckles, a few thrown worms, the sun warm on their faces, Mrs Anderson with a large tray containing mugs of tea and Madeira cake, otherwise known as the Yellow Peril. They would look up every now and again, checking the sky, listening for the sound of engines. The world was enclosed, protected by routines, separate from the war. It was before the bombing, before the girls arrived.

Curls at the piano, playing a Bach Prelude; his precipitous tumble into the precarious world of emotion; the panic when he discovered that he was attracted to a fifteen-year-old girl.

A sense of unease stirs somewhere inside Robert. He tries to ignore it, but it persists. Has Curls somehow re-established her presence in his consciousness? Sneaked back in when he wasn't looking?

He would prefer to remember the sedate, cerebral world that he knew before the war, the world that he has tried to re-create at the university, where his relationships were all civilised, wrapped up in the comfort of politeness.

Here comes Pippa, pounding up the stone steps at the back of the house. 'Daddy!'

He straightens and leans on the spade as she races along the path towards him. She emerges from behind the line of laurels that guard his new vegetable patch.

'It sounds urgent,' he says. 'Have you phoned the Fire Brigade?'

'Ha, ha, very funny. I'm going to Alison's tonight, remember, for her party and staying the night.'

'Yes, yes, of course.' He'd forgotten. He always forgets, but he prefers to give the impression that he can keep track. 'Who's going?'

'Honestly, Daddy, I told you.'

'Tell me again?'

'Just me and Alison, and Celia and Margaret,'

she says. 'Only I need you to sign this. It's for the concert next week. We forgot to send back the slip and Miss Braithwaite is getting annoyed.'

Robert takes the piece of paper from her. 'When is it again?'

'Daddy, you're hopeless. I must have told you millions of times. It's the twenty-second of November, next Friday. You've got to sign to say you're coming.'

'It says here that I'm invited to pre-concert drinks with the headmistress.'

'Oh, yes. I forgot that.'

He's not sure that he wants to go.

'You haven't got a silly work meeting, have you?'

'No, no meeting, silly or otherwise.'

'Come on, then. Stop making excuses. I'm going to be late.'

He sighs. 'Give me the pen.' He scribbles his signature at the bottom of the page.

'Thanks, Daddy,' says Pippa, grabbing it and flashing a grin. 'See you tomorrow evening.'

'Make sure Miss Dodds knows you won't be here for supper.'

'Oh, she knows already. I told her last week.'

'And don't forget to move the tortoises before you go.'

'I hope you're not suggesting I neglect them.'

He watches her disappear, hearing her progress through the garden, crunching the gravel, brushing against the shrubs, clattering down the steps. He smiles to himself. Pippa is never invisible, even when you can't see her. Unlike Godfrey, who manages to slink through the garden and house on silent feet, not even making the floorboards creak. Godfrey is like him, while Pippa is like no one else he knows. He wonders sometimes why she doesn't resemble Grace and whether there was another side to his wife that he didn't discover, which never had the chance to blossom.

No problems with Pippa, though. She makes friends wherever she goes, sprinkling chaos and excitement in her wake.

He starts to dig again. He's not sure yet what he's going to plant here. Maybe potatoes, maybe carrots. Miss Dodds complains that he produces too many vegetables, but he doesn't mind if she gives them away to friends or relatives. It's good to have an abundance. There have been too many times in his past when there wasn't enough.

iv

Alma plunges through a Beethoven sonata – C minor, Op. 27, number 1, 'Quasi una fantasia' – her mind elsewhere but her fingers searching out the notes with reasonable accuracy. She puts the weight of her arms into the pounding chords, draws out long *crescendos*, emphasises *sforzandos*, sudden explosions of sound.

She knows something. She manoeuvres round clusters of semi-quavers and reaches for chords. But she doesn't fully understand what she knows.

She has received two letters this morning. One was from Lillian, an old college acquaintance.

Lillian has invited her on a trip to America, on the *Queen Elizabeth*. 'I need a companion,' she wrote, 'and I thought you might be interested in an adventure.'

Why me? thought Alma with growing cynicism as she read through the letter. Has she fallen out with everyone else?

She can see the other letter out of the corner of her eye, sitting on the coffee table. A reply to the enquiry she sent two weeks ago. A crest from St Anne's College, Oxford, imposing against the white of the paper.

She's memorised the words:

Dear Miss Braithwaite,

Thank you for your enquiry. I am sorry to have to disappoint you, but I'm afraid no student with the name of Wilhelmina Yates has ever graduated from St Anne's. Might you perhaps be mistaken about which college she attended? Lady Margaret Hall, St Hilda's, St Hugh's and Somerville all took women undergraduates during the war years. Could she have registered under a different name? I have found that people change their names for all sorts of unexpected reasons. If you find that she attended St Anne's under an alternative name, I would be pleased to check again for you.

I hope that you manage to trace your old friend, and I'm sorry that I have not been able to be more helpful.

Yours sincerely,

Catherine Wilson (Miss)

Alma starts the last movement, attacca, without a pause, as Beethoven intended, knowing that she should go slower if she wants to avoid mistakes, but needing the fast, furious effect that will bring it alive.

This is not the response she was expecting. She'd hoped to find out something from Miss Yates's past, some scandal that had led her to apply for a job where she would not be easily found, but all of her references imply that her conduct has been exemplary in every school where she's worked. There's no suggestion of scandal or incorrect behaviour.

The evidence from St Anne's implies that she doesn't exist. Is it possible that she's changed her name? But why would she do that if she had nothing to hide?

Or she didn't go to Oxford.

Why would she lie? To increase her chances of getting the job, of course. An Oxford degree would carry more weight.

Maybe she doesn't have a degree at all.

The unexpected return to the theme from the first movement, gentle and thoughtful, followed by the cadenza and the Presto – fast – finale, reflects Alma's mood. She comes to an end with a final flourish of chords and sits back, breathing heavily, her mind still reverberating with the thrill of it.

What should she do with this knowledge?

What knowledge does she actually have?

She can see the garden through the french windows, now no longer recognisable as the place where she played as a child. The tennis court, the vegetable patches, the lawns, the flowerbeds are completely overgrown, impossible to identify.

Nettles and brambles are growing freely. Fast-growing, well-established plants are the only ones to have survived – climbing roses, ivy, honeysuckle – pushing themselves forward and up towards the light. Bindweed has advanced and conquered.

The correct procedure would be to confront Miss Yates and give her the chance to explain. After all, she might have a perfectly reasonable explanation. Alma doesn't want to go to the board of governors with incorrect information.

There have been complaints from the neighbours about the garden – the trees are overhanging and blocking the light, the bindweed is invading – but Alma hasn't taken much notice. She still uses the patio, where she half-heartedly swipes heads off dandelions and flattens a patch of weeds so she can set up her deckchair and sunbathe whenever possible. Everything else remains as it was twenty-one years ago. Indoors, she cleans the surfaces, never bothering to move furniture, tidies the downstairs rooms and makes sure the passageway to the piano is clear for her pupils.

Acquaintances from her student days used to write and ask if they could come and stay. They wanted a break somewhere by the sea, or they needed an overnight stop on their way down to Cornwall. But she always refused. 'I'm so sorry,' she wrote. 'I'm away that week. Have you thought of a hotel? Some of them are lovely, I believe. A bit expensive, perhaps, but it's nice to have a little luxury, isn't it?'

They've stopped asking. Most of them have stopped writing. Which is why Lillian's letter was so unexpected.

She's wrestling with her motives, ashamed of the underhand way in which she borrowed Miss Yates's application form. Why did she write to St Anne's? What was she expecting to find? When did she turn into this sneaky person who plots to bring about someone's disgrace? Her embarrassment makes her reluctant to do anything about it.

I'll hold on to the information for now. See how the situation develops.

The trouble is, Alma is finding that music no longer satisfies her. In fact, nothing satisfies her. Even food is losing its attraction, and cooking, just for herself, seems pointless. She doesn't want to peel potatoes or carrots any more or grill a chop or bake a cake. It's so much easier to make a sandwich, a mug of tea and have a Kit-Kat.

She sighs into the emptiness of her house. Dust hovers in the air, on the surfaces, on the floor. She's just one more speck of dust in a houseful of neglected objects.

She makes a cup of tea and takes it back into the drawing room, switching on the Home Service before she sits down. She wants to listen to the news, but she's disturbed by music from somewhere outside. At first she attempts to ignore it, but the music grows in volume until it reaches the point where she can't concentrate. She switches off the wireless. The sound is coming from next door.

Puzzled, she goes upstairs to her bedroom and pushes all the empty mugs to one side of the sill so that she can open her window. She looks down into next door's garden.

How strange. They're having a party. On a Thursday evening. The parents must be away. Alma stands behind her curtain in the darkened room and watches. The garden is full of young people who have spilled out through the open doors of the drawing room. The girls' brightly patterned dresses flutter as they're illuminated by the light from the house. They scream with laughter as they collide with the young men. There seem to be about a hundred of them. Girls with bare arms, boys in open-necked shirts, all oblivious to the autumn chill.

The music is coming from a record player set up just inside the patio doors. Alma recognises the music. She knows about the Beatles.

Everyone in the garden is dancing. They jerk up and down, moving freely, fast and frenzied, some in rhythm, some hopelessly not. There is little to compare it to the dancing of Alma's youth. No proper steps, no overall structure. It can be done without expertise. Unlike the Lindy Hop.

Alma hasn't danced for years. They tried every dance in existence at Mortimer Hall before they all went their separate ways: the Jitterbug, the Beer Barrel Polka, the Pennsylvania Polka, Tin Pan Alley, Praise the Lord and Pass the Ammunition, the Victory Walk. But she always preferred the Lindy Hop. It was the dance they continued to practise, improving and polishing. She would lie awake at night, reliving the excitement, running through the steps in her mind, while still straining her ears to detect the sound of aeroplanes approaching, the herald of more air raids. Nowadays, she drops into a deep, dreamless sleep and rarely wakes. It's as if all her energy was concentrated into those few short months, as if she'd used up her entire quota of life in one go.

Once or twice they were woken by sirens and had to rush downstairs to the Anderson shelter at the back of the garden, squashed up with the students and Mr Gunner, listening to the engines of approaching aircraft, trying to interpret their tone so that they would know if they were British or German.

Alma watches the young people next door for a long time. She likes the ease with which most of them move, their lack of self-consciousness. Were we like that? she wonders. She has clear memories of the beat burning inside her, the sense that nothing mattered except the ability to fling herself across the floor, fly through the air higher and higher, strain every ounce of her energy into improving. As if she had been possessed, as if the power of the beat had removed her inhibitions and led her by the hand to a wild and wonderful world that wasn't real.

For such a very short time.

Her feet are tapping, her knees bouncing, and she's mirroring some of the movements of the young people. The beat can provoke a response even now, entice her to twist her body, swing her arms–

What is she doing? What if someone sees her? Pupils from Goldwyn's could be there in that garden, looking up, seeing her pretending to dance.

She closes the window. The school concert is tomorrow and she needs to go to bed. The noise from the party is going to be a nuisance.

She wants to impress Miss Yates with this concert. It won't be easy. Three girls in the upper sixth who have held the orchestra together for the last few years have just backed out, making the excuse that they want to concentrate on their A levels and university interviews. The orchestra is now woefully inadequate. Four first violins, three seconds (one of whom has only just passed grade one and doesn't know what is going on most of the time), no violas and one cello. The woodwind section has four flutes, an oboe and a bassoon. One trumpet makes up the brass section and a girl who plays the piano has volunteered to do percussion – she can manage to bash the cymbals and tap the triangle with a surprisingly good sound, but she has difficulty counting the long rests and tends to come blasting in at the wrong moment.

'Hilary!' cried Alma, during their last afternoon rehearsal, after the cymbals had crashed a bar early for the fifth time and made them all jump. 'You must watch me.'

'Sorry, Miss Braithwaite,' said Hilary, blushing furiously.

'"Sorry" won't save us if you do it on the night.'

At least the choir will be good. They're going to sing three-part arrangements of English folk songs – 'The Raggle Taggle Gypsies', 'Dashing Away With the Smoothing Iron' and 'She's Like the Swallow'. The programme will be filled out with a piano trio, two piano duets and three soloists on oboe, violin and piano.

They'll have to bring in extra players for 'Zadok the Priest' at the end of term.

Maybe there's been a genuine mistake. Maybe Miss Yates really did have a different name once and there was a reason for it, or maybe the college records are incorrect.

Miss Yates has invited the board of governors (of whom only Miss Jackson is likely to attend), a select number of parents and a few local dignitaries to pre-concert drinks. She's told the staff that she would like as many as possible to attend and hopes that they will respond to the encouragement.

She's bought a new outfit from Colson's for the occasion. She's been modelling herself on Jackie Kennedy's style ever since she first saw her photograph in a copy of *Life* magazine at the dentist, and this A-line suit with three-quarter-length sleeves, set off with a new pair of white gloves, makes her feel like a president's wife. She's also purchased a matching pill-box hat, which nestles charmingly among the curls of her new perm and pleases her enormously, but it will have to wait for an outdoor event.

At six thirty precisely, she leaves her office, descends the main staircase and makes for the sixth-form common room where they're holding the reception.

Adelinde Bauer has already stationed herself at the doorway, ready to accost every parent who appears. Miss Yates is beginning to tire of Adelinde, who is always present, always first in the queue, always stepping in with her own opinions, which seem deliberately designed to conflict with any that Alma Braithwaite might express. The two of them dominate almost every staff meeting, and several of the recent discussions have deteriorated into an excessively polite exchange of words, heavy with unspoken fury, compelling everyone else to either take sides or sink into resentful silence.

Cressida Davies sidles up to her, thin, angular, in a cream woollen suit, her eyes twinkling. Miss Yates has already grown fond of Cressida, who manages to tread the difficult path between opposing views without alienating anyone. It sometimes feels as if she would make the better headmistress, a consummate diplomat, a teacher with years of experience and liked by everyone. 'Good turnout already, Wilhelmina,' she says. 'Rather a cunning wheeze to invite them all for drinks. It guarantees a decent audience for the concert. By the way, steer clear of Adelinde. She's campaigning for a tuck shop.'

Miss Yates examines Cressida's face and tries to work out if she's joking or not. 'A tuck shop? Surely not.'

'I'm afraid so. She has decided that it's in keeping with the spirit of the times. Why shouldn't the girls have easy access to pleasure like everyone else? I think that's her line of reasoning.'

'Her desire for influence far outweighs her presence in the school,' says Miss Yates. 'She is, after all, only part-time.'

Adelinde Bauer appears at her side. 'Good evening, Headmistress,' she says. 'Everything is warming up well.'

'Fräulein Bauer,' says Miss Yates. 'How good of you to come.'

Adelinde beams. 'It is a pleasure to be here. I

enjoy so much seeing my pupils taking part in school events. It is important to me that they are happy, you know. I am so fond of them.'

'As we all are,' murmurs Cressida. Is there a hint of mockery in her voice?

The door opens and Robert Gunner steps into the room. He walks over to greet Miss Yates.

'Mr Gunner,' she says, with pleasure, holding out her hand.

Alma Braithwaite appears unexpectedly on his other side. 'Mr Gunner,' she is saying with her hand outstretched.

Mr Gunner contemplates the two of them with bemusement. He hesitates, turns first to Miss Yates, then to Alma, then back to Miss Yates. He comes to a decision, presumably based on seniority. 'Miss Yates,' he says, shaking her hand first. Then, 'Miss Braithwaite.'

There's an awkward silence between the three of them. 'I'm so pleased you could make it,' says Miss Yates. 'You must have a drink.'

Alma follows them and takes a glass of sherry from the table. Mr Gunner picks up a glass with one hand, a cube of cheese and pineapple on a stick with the other. There's a slight tremor in his fingers as he pops the cheese and pineapple into his mouth and chews rapidly, while tipping his glass at a precarious angle. He notices at the last minute and brings it upright with an apologetic smile. Miss Yates is unexpectedly moved. So like her father. A serious man with a good brain who's nervous in public. How endearing.

Alma is wearing a sleeveless dress with a full skirt, covered with large red poppies. Has she learned nothing? Bare arms are not appropriate for an occasion like this. Especially without gloves. Miss Yates decides that she will have to issue a dress code for staff. She cannot have them attending official events looking as if they are about to go to the beach. She remembers what Mr Gunner told her about Alma and her fondness for dancing. Does she still have a yearning for frivolity? Or is this a deliberate attempt to undermine Miss Yates's authority, to show that she will act as she wants to, rather than follow advice?

'Did we get the right information about the ink?' asks Alma.

Whatever is she talking about?

But Mr Gunner knows. 'Yes, yes,' he says, a little over-enthusiastically, 'it was a lucky guess. She seemed entirely happy with it. I gather she's about to progress to an Osmiroid.'

'Oh, I am pleased,' says Alma, sounding quite unlike herself. 'I'm afraid I'm not usually told when it happens. It's entirely up to Miss Burns, her writing teacher.'

'Our girls are lucky to have Miss Burns,' says Miss Yates. 'Her calligraphy skills are much sought after across the whole of the south-west, you know. She has been approached by several local schools for her expertise, but she has chosen to remain with us.'

Adelinde comes up behind Miss Yates and makes them all jump. 'Miss Yates,' she booms. 'About the tuck shop.'

'Tuck shop?' says Miss Yates. 'I wasn't aware we had a tuck shop.'

'And this is the problem–'

'Tell me, Mr Gunner,' says Miss Yates, ignoring Adelinde. 'What is your view on girls taking a degree in one of the sciences? I have found surprising opposition among parents. They're concerned that there will be no jobs for their daughters in the scientific world.'

He looks startled, as if he was not expecting to have to give an opinion. 'Well, of course they're perfectly capable – my university is, of course, always in favour and there are jobs available, but the numbers are very small.'

'I would like to introduce a little sweetness to our hardworking girls,' says Adelinde. 'It will increase their energy, keep them amiable–'

Cressida comes up. 'I think perhaps we should take our seats, Miss Yates,' she says.

Alma examines her watch with surprise. 'I must go,' she says. 'The girls should be tuning up.' She turns to Mr Gunner. 'It was lovely to see you again,' she says. 'Perhaps we'll meet after the concert. I do hope you enjoy it – we're a little short of strong musicians this year.' She downs her drink in one gulp, hovers for a few seconds more, clearly unwilling to leave, puts the glass on a nearby table and dashes off.

Miss Yates smiles at Mr Gunner. 'Let's go and sit down. I believe some seats have been saved for my guests at the front, so if you'd care to join us...'

'Thank you,' he says. 'It will be a pleasure.' He stands back to let her lead the way.

The orchestra are already on the stage. The coloured-glass window behind them, depicting Marie

Curie, Florence Nightingale and Mary Wollstonecraft, reflects the warmth of the interior lights against the darkness outside. The audience takes time to settle, shuffling, filling the empty chairs, chatting.

Alma walks on with her conductor's baton. She faces the audience and smiles. 'Good evening, ladies and gentlemen. Thank you so much for attending our concert tonight. We will be starting with the March from *Carmen*.' She turns back to the orchestra, holding up the baton. There is a moment of uncertainty, then she lowers the baton and taps the rostrum. 'Flutes!' she says, in a sharp voice that everyone can hear. 'Please pay attention.' She raises the baton again and brings it down firmly.

The music is not bad, although the violins struggle with some of the semi-quaver passages. Alma has imported a trombone and a tuba, and Miss Upton (history) has stepped in with a clarinet. Alma's dress is proving to be even more unsuitable than Miss Yates thought. She's probably not aware of it, but when she leans forward, the dress tips up at the back, exposing the tops of her stockings. And it rustles. In the pauses, or during the long, quiet passages, you can hear the lining moving, the brush of nylon against cotton.

Miss Yates is very conscious of Robert Gunner at her side. He is sitting very still, his attention on the music, but she can see his toes tapping inside his highly polished black shoes, and she can just see the curl of hair that is brushed immaculately away from the side parting. She can feel him breathing...

Something is happening at the back of the hall, movements, people talking in low voices. Miss Yates turns to glare at the offenders, but she can't see where the noise is coming from. She decides to ignore it. Someone walks up the central aisle, their heels clicking on the wooden floor. This is disgraceful behaviour. Someone will pay for it.

It's Bridget, her secretary. She's agitated, her breathing rough and uneven. 'Miss Yates–'

'Miss Murphy,' she whispers, indignantly. 'What–'

Bridget bends down so that she will not block anyone's view. 'I'm sorry, but I thought you should know. I've just heard on the wireless...'

What can possibly be so important that it can justify interrupting a performance?

Alma falters as she becomes aware that something is happening. She half turns, but keeps conducting. The orchestra follows the beat imperfectly.

Bridget whispers into her ear.

'What?' Miss Yates's voice echoes through the hall. The music continues, but members of the audience are talking to each other now, murmuring, getting gradually louder and the musicians gradually fizzle to a halt. They gaze round in confusion, their faces panicky and scared. The leader is the last to notice that everyone else has stopped and she continues to play for a while, every note clear and perfectly in tune (she is Goldwyn's most talented player, on course for a scholarship to the Royal College of Music), unaccompanied by any other instrument. When she finally peters out, Alma turns with an expression of outrage. 'What's going on?' she asks, her voice icy.

Miss Yates is struggling to maintain a calm exterior. She's shaking in a way she wouldn't have believed possible. An unbelievable scenario is cascading through her mind, like several films trying to play at the same time, colours and movements colliding and confusing her. I must take control, she says to herself. This is an important moment. I have to show leadership. I must not allow my personal emotion to affect the way I behave. She stands up and ascends the stairs at the side of the stage.

She faces the audience. 'Ladies and gentlemen,' she says, hearing her voice ring out, strong and authoritative, 'I apologise to our young players for having to interrupt the concert, but I have just had some very disturbing news.'

All noise ceases. Miss Yates is conscious of the quality of the silence. It's true, she thinks, you really could hear a pin drop.

'President Kennedy has been shot. It is not thought that he will survive.'

There's a pause as every person in the room stops breathing. Then Alma drops her baton, a flute clatters to the floor and a girl in the choir shrieks.

Part Nine

i

20 June 1942

'We shouldn't have sung "The Silver Swan",' whispers Alma to Curls, sitting on the edge of her bed, rocking backwards and forwards. 'In the aircraft hangar. It wasn't meant to be Duncan's swansong.'

Curls climbs out of bed and sits down next to her. Her face is red and puffy. 'He'll come back,' she says. 'The telegram only said "missing", not "dead".'

'The plane came down in the sea,' says Alma. 'People die when planes crash.'

'Not always,' says Curls. 'The sea isn't as solid as land.'

'They just drown instead.'

'I won't believe it,' says Curls. 'He was too alive.' She puts her arms round Alma and they rock together. Curls keeps sniffing. Alma thinks she should cry too, but she feels empty and dry.

Later she lies on her back and stares up into the solid and impenetrable darkness produced by the blackout blinds. It's an almost tangible presence, whose touch she can feel on her face, which retires in the early mornings when the sun somehow manages to creep round the edge of the blinds, squeezing through tiny pinholes, poking its fingers into unseen, unsealed cracks and forcing them apart.

If she hadn't woken Duncan on the day of his departure, the pick-up jeep would have gone without him and he wouldn't have been on that plane.

She can't see the ceiling, but she knows what it looks like. There's a brown stain in one corner, evidence of a recent leak, which stops abruptly just before the picture rail. Someone must have been up on the roof and dealt with it. Alma tries to imagine Mr Gunner climbing a ladder, moving a foot up one rung at a time, pausing, dragging his injured leg behind him, reaching the top and moving very slowly on to the roof.

It's an unlikely scenario. He'd have sent up one of the students. Jack perhaps, who understands mechanical details, or Dennis, who is very fit and energetic. Either of them would have climbed the ladder in a matter of seconds, crossing the roof with calm assurance, knowing exactly how to stop the leak.

Duncan was like Jack and Dennis. Alma can picture him in the desert: leaping into a tank; driving a jeep through the sand; cleaning his rifle, slotting everything back into place, confident of his ability to make things work.

He can't be dead. It's not possible. He's too useful, too valuable. They've made a mistake. Got the wrong man.

Plenty of soldiers come back, even during the war; airmen return to their airfields, battered but intact; ships sail into ports all around the country, loaded with sailors and soldiers. Any one of them could be Duncan.

The unfairness of everything takes her breath away. She lies still for a long time, her thoughts churning. Something about Curls's breathing suggests she's awake too, staring into the darkness like Alma, unable to believe they won't see Duncan again.

They've all wept for him. After Miss Cunningham-Smith left, the girls huddled together for comfort on a sofa and sobbed. Mrs Anderson brought in cups of sweetened tea and sat with them for a while. The men came into the common room in twos and threes to offer reassurances, then withdrew. 'He'll be back,' said Jack, his Irish accent soft and reassuring. 'You'll see. One of these days he'll walk in that door and we'll wonder what all the fuss was about.'

'D-don't worry too much,' says Geoffrey. 'If he makes it to the coast of France, he'll be fine. The Resistance have networks. They smuggle our lads out through Spain and Portugal.'

'Worst-case scenario,' says Colin, sitting next to her, his blue eyes serious and thoughtful, 'the Jerries have captured him and he'll spend the rest of the war in a PoW camp.'

It seems that she's not going to sleep ever again. She tries to sort out the tangle in her head about Curls and Duncan. She wants to ask Duncan if he kissed Curls, but now she can't.

Does it matter?

If they'd been sleeping in Merrivale, safely back in their dormitory, Alma would get up and go downstairs where she could read a book, do some homework, even play the piano out of earshot of everyone else, but up to now she hasn't felt comfortable enough to risk leaving the bedroom in Mortimer Hall, let alone find her way around in the dark. She doesn't know which of the stairs creak, if it's all right to turn on any lights. She misses the familiarity of Merrivale. Miss Cunningham-Smith has told the boarders that they will be able to sleep at Goldwyn's next term, but her plans involve converting another part of the school. Not the same, but better than nothing.

What she really wants to do is go home.

If she could just get downstairs, she could practise her steps for the Lindy Hop. She's pretty good, these days – better, probably, than the others because she practises more, although not as good as Jack, whose energy seems limitless. But she's going faster, knows more routines, can introduce more complexity to each movement. As she thinks about it, music starts to beat in her head and her legs move restlessly, itching to get started.

She sits up and throws off her blankets, pushing them with her feet to the end of the bed. She can't lie here any longer. She has to move, do something. Her feet, as she lowers them to the floor, are shaking with the desire to dance. She's not sure if she has full control over them.

She tiptoes through the darkness, hoping there's nothing in the middle of the floor that she can trip over, gropes for the door handle, not finding it where she thinks it ought to be, hitting it with her hand and stopping as the sound reverberates through the silence of the night. Has she woken anyone? Curls remains motionless, and the sound of her breathing continues uninterrupted. She must have finally dropped off. After a long pause, Alma opens the door very slowly, very quietly. It groans in protest. She waits again and listens. The whole building is shut down, snoring gently, dreaming deeply, making the most of a night without air-raid sirens or fire-watching. Even the water pipes are resting, pausing before their next bout of activity.

Rock step, kick step, kick and kick step. One, two, three-and-four. Forward, sideways, backwards, swing round–

She finds the banister and uses it to guide herself down the stairs, sliding her hand along the smooth, polished wood.

Her mother's voice: *Alma, whatever are you doing out of bed in the middle of the night?*

Duncan: *Hurry up! Get the tennis racquets out. We've got time for a set before supper.*

You must remember to eat well, my dear – her father's calm voice of reason. *It seems to me there needs to be more research into diet. The rationing will have a long-term effect on the health of our children…*

Alma slips into the common room, closes the door and switches on the light. She's a long way from the bedrooms. No one will know she's here. She looks at the piano for a few seconds. It would be good to sit down and crash through some Chopin, the Preludes, especially the hard ones, blasting them out, using the pedal to disguise mistakes, letting the notes run into each other, not caring about details.

But it would be too loud. Someone would hear and come down to investigate. If other people can manage to sleep, she should let them.

She looks longingly at the gramophone, wondering how low she could set the volume. It must be possible to turn it down so that she can hear it without disturbing anyone else. She needs some music if she's going to dance.

The moment the bomb fell on the hospital: did her parents know what had happened? Was her father burrowing away inside someone's chest, picking out fragments of glass, stopping the bleeding and tying up blood vessels, peering through his glasses at the damage? Was her mother setting a broken bone, talking reassuringly in that bright, cheerful way she had, alert despite the lateness of the hour, steely in her determination to help? Was there any clue that the bomb was plunging silently through the night sky, delicately balanced as it sliced through air currents, unaffected by low pressure, high pressure, wind or rain, heading downwards with streamlined perfection? Did it hit while they were both poised, mid-action, doing what they did best? Was there time to know that they were going to die or had everything simply exploded into nothingness in a second? When does the mind stop thinking? At the precise moment it ceases to be or a few seconds after? Was there time for them to prepare, to think of their children, perhaps, just before the end?

Alma goes over to the gramophone and tentatively winds it up. The handle moves easily to start with but becomes stiffer as she keeps winding. She finds the record she wants: Glenn Miller's 'In The Mood'. She slides it out of the paper cover, but before placing it carefully on the turntable, she adjusts the volume to its lowest. It would be best to increase it gradually, rather than have it blast out suddenly and wake everyone up. She's never operated the gramophone before on her own, but she's watched the others doing it and she understands how it works. She lifts the arm, pushes it backwards until it clicks and the record starts turning. Very carefully, she lowers the needle on to the first outside groove. Nothing happens except the swish of the needle on the record. She remembers the volume and turns the knob carefully.

The beat comes first, then the tune – saxophones, trumpets, trombones – vast numbers of them, coming in gradually, expanding and blending. Alma loves this music, the bigness of the sound. She starts to click her fingers and bounces gently from her knees. It's not fast enough for the frenzied dancing they've been developing together as a group, but the mood is right for this time of night. Strong, syncopated, soulful. She starts to move across the floor, winding herself up, unwinding, becoming part of the music. The moves are instinctive now, but all the time she is planning, calculating, improvising new patterns. She turns to the side, bending and straightening her knees, starts to move her feet faster, letting the beat penetrate and pound through her body. She turns, twists, jumps, clicks, swivels – and stops.

Mr Gunner is standing by the door in a tartan dressing-gown and leather slippers, staring at her.

She sways slightly, struggling to keep her balance.

'Oh,' she says, her voice coming out in an odd croak.

He clears his throat. 'I heard the music,' he says.

'I'm sorry,' she says. 'I did turn it down.'

'I see,' he says. He is clearly finding it difficult to know how to react.

They stand for a few seconds without speaking. Alma is still breathing deeply, her chest rising and falling as she struggles to regain her breath. This is exactly what she didn't want to happen. She keeps her eyes on the floor just in front of his feet, unable to face him directly.

'I wonder,' he says, 'if this is the most appropriate time...' He waves a vague arm at the empty room. The music now sounds out of place, too soft to hear properly.

'Sorry,' says Alma and goes to lift the arm up. It rests in the air above the record, as if annoyed that it has been thwarted. 'I was just–'

'Dancing?' he says.

She nods, aware that it appears strange. 'I couldn't sleep,' she says.

'Most of us read a book if we can't sleep,' he says.

She glances up and sees that he's smiling. He's rather nice, really. Why hasn't she noticed before?

She recognises the moment when he comes to a decision – a small, neat nod. 'Perhaps you'd care to join me in the kitchen,' he says. 'A mug of Horlicks would seem to be in order. I'm reasonably confident that Mrs Anderson wouldn't mind if we raided her stocks.'

'Thank you,' she says, aware of a warm flush creeping through her. 'That would be nice.'

He goes over to the gramophone and lowers the arm to the side, removes the record and replaces the lid over the turntable. 'We'll leave the record on the side,' he says. 'You can put it back in the right place in the morning.'

She follows him to the door. 'What time is it?' she asks.

'About two thirty.'

He opens the door and switches on the hall light. Then he stands back to let her through, turning off the light behind them.

In the kitchen, they wait for the milk to boil, Alma sitting at the large table, self-conscious in her nightie, Mr Gunner standing by the stove. When the milk rises, he switches off the gas and lifts the saucepan away before it overflows. She watches him pour the milk, slowly and carefully, into the mugs, not spilling a drop, stirring in the Horlicks and a small amount of sugar at the same time. The teaspoon clatters against the side of the mugs, busy and competent. He is meticulous in his efforts to ensure the powder dissolves properly.

He hands her one mug and comes to sit down next to her. The Horlicks is too hot to drink at first. Alma is relieved that they don't have to look each other in the eye.

There's something restful about Mr Gunner. He manages to be reassuring without saying very much. His dark eyes are slightly sad, as if he is carrying a perpetual disappointment around with him, a weary resignation, as if the world has let him down in some way and he knows there's no way to put it right.

'It must be very difficult for you at the moment,' he says. 'We all want to help as much as possible.' His voice comes from deep in his chest, low and growly as if he needs to cough.

Alma is shocked to feel tears in her eyes and blinks rapidly, hoping to hide them.

But he pats her arm, an awkward movement that involves him turning sideways and leaning forward at the same time. He almost knocks over her mug of Horlicks, but saves it with his other hand just before it falls. 'You must let us know if there's anything we can do to help,' he says. 'There are a lot of practical matters to deal with, of course, but Miss Cunningham-Smith assures me that she will make further enquiries about your brother.'

Alma touches her cheek with her fingertips, not sure if the tears have actually fallen. Her hand comes away wet.

Mr Gunner sips his Horlicks thoughtfully. 'We've probably sabotaged Mrs Anderson's plans to make tapioca tomorrow,' he says. 'I'll leave her a note to apologise in case she suspects that our students have been raiding the stores and selling milk on the black market.' His hands are large and adult, the nails cut back as short as possible, white and scrubbed. Black hair drifts across the back of his hands and curls up into the sleeves of his dressing-gown. A man's hands, strong and capable.

When Alma goes back to bed, she sleeps deeply and dreamlessly.

The walk to school takes about twenty minutes, easier now that more roads have been opened. Everywhere they go, men and boys are digging, cranes towering above them as they shift damaged masonry. Trucks stand at the side of roads waiting to be filled, driving away with the suspension settling low under the weight of their burden and returning empty, ready for the next load. Everyone with a van is out there. Some people ignore the official demolition squads and dig away at their own little patch, the place that was once their shop or their home, hopeful that they can salvage something of value. The sound of the shovels and the shifting of masonry echoes through the air at all times of the day from first light until it's too dark to see what they're doing.

'Where do you think they take it all?' asks Curls, as they watch a lorry, packed to capacity, pull away in front of them.

It's a good question. 'Perhaps they store it somewhere so they can use the bricks again,' says Giraffe.

'My dad says they dump it out in the country, where no one can see it,' says Natalie.

'Or maybe in the river.'

The workers stop when they bring out a body, pausing to bow their heads briefly, to pay their respects, to deal with the rush of gratitude that runs through them at the reminder that they have been lucky and survived. The bodies have lain undiscovered for weeks, their presence marked only by the smell. The missing, the unidentifiable and the unknown.

Street names have not been replaced – most of them had already been removed anyway, in case of invasion – but the girls are becoming familiar with the new landscape. It's dominated by the twin towers of the cathedral, its windows protected by lagging, now visible from new angles and, with the exception of the south-choir wall, still defiantly intact. Walking along the cleared pathways is like finding your way across the model of a full-sized map, where streets are laid out at right angles, like a grid, much neater than was previously apparent when they were lined with buildings. The wasteland between the roads is bare and empty, its previous existence lost for ever, too devastated even to support weeds.

Curls walks in front with Natalie, and Alma follows with Giraffe.

'Did you get any sleep?' asks Giraffe, after they've walked for some time in silence.

'No, not really,' says Alma. She feels she should say something else, but she doesn't want to talk. She's going over last night's conversation with Mr Gunner. His kindness has surprised her.

'Nor me,' says Giraffe.

They pass the station. **'Is Your Journey Really Necessary?'** says a poster at the entrance. And **'No Smoking in Air-raid Shelters. TIGHTEN YOUR GRIP.'**

'Remember the grip, girls,' calls Curls, as they pass the poster. Her face is pale and tense, as if being cheerful requires an enormous effort but she's going to do it anyway. 'Hang on to your satchels. You never know who's out there.'

It's a standard response, repeated by one of them every time they pass the station. There have been several suggestions of what requires a tightened grip. Boyfriends; maths homework; the only piece of date pudding with a date in it. They have considered the possibility of an earthquake or a tidal wave sweeping up the river Exe and submerging Exeter (unlikely, but it gave rise to several days of good headlines: 'Identify High Ground Now'; 'Do Not Enter Air-raid Shelter if Under Water'; 'Take Swimming Lessons'; 'Don't Panic!'). They can't walk past without a comment, but it's increasingly difficult to be original.

Alma gives Curls a weak smile. She wants her to know that she appreciates her effort even if she can't manage the jokes today.

They pass a large van parked in a quiet side street not far from the school. **'NATIONAL EMERGENCY WASHING SERVICE'**, it says on the side. Volunteer women stand outside, sorting through piles of clean clothes on temporary tables. They smile at the girls as they pass.

'It's a brilliant idea,' says Giraffe. 'For all those people who've been bombed out.'

'As long as they've got some spare clothes,' says Curls. 'Not much use if everything's gone up in smoke.'

'People donate new stuff,' says Natalie. 'Mummy says there's plenty to go round.'

They reach the school gates and Curls turns. 'By the way, I'm doing a concert next week,' she says. 'I'm missing afternoon lessons so I can practise.'

'Lucky you,' says Giraffe. 'Wish it was me.'

'No, you don't,' says Natalie. 'You wouldn't want to play in a concert. You'd just be panicking by now.'

Alma stares at Curls. 'I didn't know about the concert.'

'It's only just been arranged. I'll be expecting you all to come. Miss Cunningham-Smith has loads of tickets for Goldwyn's girls. You'll have to go and ask her, though. Enter the dragon's den. Offer her bribes. Two maths preps for one ticket.'

'That's OK,' says Alma. 'I can do that.'

'Come on,' says Natalie. 'The bell's going to go in a minute.'

Curls starts climbing the steps, faster than normal. Alma wants to keep up with her, be together if they're late, but Natalie and Giraffe are between them now and she finds herself swamped by a group of very vocal lower-fourths. Heat rises in her cheeks and her stomach churns. They're deserting her, forgetting her.

She can hear Curls ahead. 'I don't want to miss hockey. They'll leave me out of the team.'

'Don't be daft,' says Giraffe. 'You never make the team anyway.'

The sound of her voice is fading. Alma is jostled by another excited group of girls, younger than her, twittering like sparrows in high-pitched voices, none of them listening to the others. Everyone's talking except her.

One, two, swivel, swivel. Five, six, triple-step. Forward, back, three-and-four, turn, swing, seven, eight.

ii

Later in the day Robert Gunner, usually the last member of staff to leave, walks through the empty corridors of the Washington Singer building, switching off lights behind him. He likes to remain longer than the other lecturers, enjoying the silence that settles in when everyone has gone, breathing in the smell of ink and wood and dust that has permeated the walls in the past eleven years. The atmosphere is calm and restful, conducive to learning, to academic investigation. It has grown and filled the space, cultivated by the attitudes of the people who work and study there.

There are cleaners somewhere in the building – he can hear them banging around in the distance, but they don't undermine his pleasure. They provide background music to his thoughts.

He steps out of the front door into the warm summer's evening. Part of the legacy of the Streatham Estate, donated to the university with eleven acres of landscaped gardens, was an arboretum of rare trees from around the world. They've flourished in the fresh Devonshire air and matured overtime, witnesses to history, miraculous survivors of the bombing.

It has occurred to Robert, despite his loyalty to the university and his students, that many lives would have been saved if the bombs had fallen on the Streatham campus rather than the densely populated centre of the city. He can't avoid thinking in mathematical terms, calculating probability.

He has in his briefcase tickets for a concert on Saturday. *Jane Curley will be performing Bach and Beethoven in Goldwyn's school hall. 7.30. All proceeds to be donated to the Spitfire Fund.* Miss Cunningham-Smith had phoned him about it. 'I wonder if you and your students would consider joining me and a selection of our girls on a small expedition during the day of the concert, maybe a walk on Woodbury Common and a picnic – a small token of our gratitude for the way you have helped our boarders.'

Robert sat down abruptly as his legs went weak. How could he possibly accept? He needed to keep away from the girls and from Curls in particular. An entire day in her presence would be – unwise.

'In more favourable circumstances, I would have suggested lunch at Deller's café, but such indulgence has become a thing of the past now that Hitler has seen fit to bomb it.'

Deller's café. Robert had taken his mother for tea there after he was offered the job at the University College of the Southwest. They sat at a table on the first gallery, looking down on the people below, overawed by the Greek columns, the oak panelling, the brightly coloured rococo cherubs. They listened carefully to the string quartet on the ground floor, determined to hear the end of the music before ordering, while light flooded in through the glass ceiling at the top of the full-length atrium. Neither was accustomed to such luxury, but they wanted to mark the significance of the occasion.

'I've heard they're going to demolish the remains of the café,' said Robert to Miss Cunningham-Smith. He cannot attend the concert. He considers various excuses. 'Not a high enough priority, I understand.'

'Such nonsense. It was only fire damage, not a direct hit. The structure's intact. We all suffer at the hands of imbeciles who have no appreciation of history or culture.'

'I'm inclined to agree,' said Robert, although not sure if it was wise to be so openly critical of local government. Walls might have ears, but Miss Cunningham-Smith did not appear to consider herself at risk of being overheard, not even lowering her voice.

'The BBC has requested to be at the concert. They will be broadcasting live on the Home Service, so we'll invite as many local dignitaries as possible – notwithstanding their lack of appreciation for culture – and our timing will have to be precise. Quite a coup for Goldwyn's to welcome the BBC. We're having a Steinway piano brought in for the occasion. I thought perhaps we should make it a day of celebration, since your students will soon be going down and we'll have our own boarding facilities back in operation at Goldwyn's by next term. We could think of it as a leaving party. Give everyone the chance to say goodbye properly. Then we can attend the concert afterwards.'

'It's very kind of you to invite us,' said Robert.

'Good,' said Miss Cunningham-Smith. 'I shall

look forward to the pleasure of your company. It's not often we have the opportunity to relax.' She put the phone down.

He wasn't expected to refuse. If Miss Cunningham-Smith decided something was going to happen, it happened. He sat for a while, contemplating the situation. There was very little he could do. He could hardly turn down the invitation on behalf of his students, and if they attended, he had no reasonable excuse for not joining them.

As he walks back to Mortimer Hall, he imagines Curls playing in a formal setting. His heartbeat quickens. It might be his last opportunity to hear her play, to appreciate her remarkable talent.

He is still shocked by his response to her, the intense heat that sweeps through him if he allows himself to think about her. She's only fifteen years old. How can he have such an extreme reaction? He has no recollection of feeling like this before. There's no other flush of excitement in his memory, except a few moments when he was a teenager. Moments he prefers not to think about. He's admired certain women in the past, considered the possibility of courtship before discarding it in favour of his academic career, but the sensations he's experiencing now are quite new to him.

It will be the last weekend before the summer vacation, a final chance for his students to relax before receiving their exam results and making decisions about their future. Many will enlist and may not survive the war. To refuse the invitation would be outrageously ill-mannered.

Robert's hands start to perspire. The evening is grey with a dull drizzle, which is developing into a steadier downpour. He should stop and put on his raincoat, but he is absurdly grateful for the coolness of the shower.

He is a university lecturer, the warden of a hall, a man of integrity. His profession is the life-raft that will save him.

When he arrives home, he can hear everyone in the dining room, the clink of knives and forks against china, voices rising and falling in conversation. It sounds oddly subdued and he assumes the girls have already eaten and left, but when he puts down his briefcase and steps into the dining room, he sees that they're all there and he's miscalculated the time. The room is designed to accommodate twenty students, but the war has whittled down their numbers to ten so, even with the four girls, there are plenty of empty seats.

'Ah, Mr Gunner,' says Mrs Anderson, rising from her position at the head of the girls' table. 'I wasn't sure if you would be able to join us but I have laid a place for you.' She indicates a seat next to hers.

He smiles at her. 'Too much work, I'm afraid,' he says, moving the knife and fork and table mat to a space between Jack Hitchens and Dennis Thwaite. 'I'll sit with my students, if you don't mind. We have some mathematics to discuss.'

'Not at all,' she says, going to fetch his soup.

'Good evening, Mr Thwaite, Mr Hitchens,' says Robert, sitting down and accepting a bowl of tomato soup. He takes a sip. It's very hot, straight from the saucepan, but lacking taste, almost as if

Mrs Anderson has boiled up some water, added some orange colouring and pretended it's soup. It's not likely to improve. The tomato plants in the back garden are struggling. The leaves have turned yellow and the stems are dusted with a grey fungus. There's a slight background flavour of parsley, presumably also from the garden and useful to disguise the lack of more substantial ingredients.

'Do you have the tickets for the concert next Saturday?' asks Jack.

'I do indeed. They're in my briefcase.'

'Who's invited?'

'Everyone. All our students and Mrs Anderson. The girls will be included in Miss Cunningham-Smith's allocation of tickets.'

'They're going to b-broadcast it?' asks Geoffrey Harris.

Dennis pours him a glass of water from the jug.

'So I've been told,' says Robert.

'Which one of the girls is playing again?' asks Tristan Watson. He hardly ever speaks and appears not to take part in the dancing or the singing during the evenings.

'Curls,' says Jack.

Robert can see her without turning his head. She's sitting next to Mrs Anderson, talking passionately about something. She's not particularly pretty, and yet... There's an intensity about her, an animation that goes beyond girlish enthusiasm, an unusual ability to shut out everything around her and concentrate.

'But which one is Curls?' asks Tristan, after staring at them for a few moments.

Can he not see it? Doesn't she stand out to everyone?

'The one with short hair,' says Jack. 'And no curls.'

Tristan watches her intently, apparently unfamiliar with the code of conduct that says you shouldn't stare. 'She doesn't look any different from the others,' he says, and goes back to his sausages.

Jack raises his eyebrows very slightly at Dennis and they exchange grins. They eat politely but fast, and there's never enough to satisfy them. Robert has observed their eating habits before, marvelling at their ability to clear their plates so quickly. He's unable to eat with such speed, maybe because there was never enough food available in his childhood and he wanted to make it last, but more because his mother instilled in him the necessity to hold back, to display good manners at all times. These young men give the impression that they would never stop, even if the supplies were endless.

'They've got hollow legs,' says Mrs Anderson, every now and again.

'She's famous,' says Jack to Tristan, after a while. 'She's made records, you know. My parents have one.'

Robert sips some water, wipes his lips with his napkin and chews slowly on a piece of gristle. He's rarely hungry, these days. He can manage on a bare minimum. He prefers intellectual food: the need to explain in a way that even the less able of his students can follow; his research; his marking.

Dennis turns to him. 'Would you consider joining us after supper?' he says.

'What are you planning?'

'We're trying to get everyone to take part in the dancing tonight. Even Mrs Anderson has said she'll come.'

'Really?' Robert is surprised. Mrs Anderson rarely joins in with the students' activities. He doubts she'll even come to the concert. She's happy in her role as provider and nurturer. Bafflingly, her excitement comes from getting more wear out of sheets by turning sides to middle, or acquiring an unusually large piece of meat from the butcher. 'What about her knees? Her arthritis?'

'She says she'll do it if it kills her,' says Jack. 'We're not sure how seriously we should take that.'

'It's camaraderie,' says Geoffrey. 'The strongest reason why we'll win the war.'

'I'm going,' announces Tristan.

This is even more surprising. 'In that case, Mr Watson, I feel obliged to accompany you,' says Robert, with a sinking sense of inevitability. 'No greater sacrifice can there be than to give up your spare time in the interests of friendship.'

There's a polite murmur of appreciation for this comment from Dennis and Jack.

Jack takes charge in the common room, organising the removal of the tables and chairs to the sides of the room and overseeing the selection of records. Robert stands near the doorway with Mrs Anderson and watches. He's uncomfortably aware of Curls's presence. He wishes he hadn't come.

'Get into pairs,' calls Jack. 'Especially anyone who hasn't tried this before. It's easier if you have someone to hold on to.'

The more experienced ones go round the room and find someone they can help. Colin Streetly pulls Mrs Anderson on to the floor and she giggles with pleasure, her face pink and perspiring before they even start.

'Come on, Mr Gunner,' says a voice from his side. 'Let's have a go.'

It's Curls. Robert can feel terror paralysing him.

She grabs his hand and he nearly snatches it back as a shock more powerful than electricity shoots up his arm. 'It's all right,' she says. 'We'll go slowly.'

She pulls him into the middle of the floor. Mrs Anderson stands next to him, smiling with exhilaration, as if she's fulfilling some long-held ambition. Robert feels enormous and clumsy, convinced that he must be swelling up like a balloon. He's unable to move easily with his crippled leg and knows he will fall over in seconds.

He tries to back out. 'Miss Curley, I really don't think this is a good–'

'You'll be fine,' says Curls, with a grin. 'You can do it.'

He doesn't want to do it, but he's finding it difficult to produce a coherent argument that would excuse him.

Geoffrey puts the needle on a record and the

music begins. Robert recognises it from the time in the middle of the night when he found Alma alone, dancing with a desperate kind of concentration. He'd felt so sorry for her when she sat with him in the kitchen, sipping Horlicks, pretending she was fine. She'd seemed so young and vulnerable, her narrow shoulders hunched over the mug, tears hovering in her eyes. He'd worried about how to deal with the situation, eventually deciding that it might be appropriate to offer a comforting pat. He hoped she would understand his concern, appreciate his presence and accept his clumsy sympathy.

He meets her eye on the other side of the room and smiles encouragingly. A deep flush spreads up her face as she smiles back, her self-consciousness oddly touching. He looks away quickly, not wanting to embarrass her.

Jack and Natalie are demonstrating the basic steps. 'Forward, two, three-and-four.'

'Come on,' says Curls, guiding him.

He lurches forward, unable to move his right leg fast enough. He's never been this close to a woman except his mother.

She's not a woman, he reminds himself.

She puts her head down and studies his feet, pushing her left leg against his right to get him into the correct position.

It's like seeing an express train coming towards you and not having the means to get out of the way.

He can see the top of her bent head, the parting in her brown hair, straight and sharp, revealing the white of her scalp. Each strand of hair bends slightly on the edge of the parting as if it wants to spring up and go its own way, as if it resents being forced to the side. 'No,' she says. 'It's the left foot, then the right.'

She shows no awareness of the effect she has on him. She's interested in the dance, the steps, the fun of it all.

He stumbles and nearly falls over. She grabs him and holds him upright, starting to giggle. 'You can do it,' she says. 'Go on. Left, right, three-and-four.'

Robert doesn't know what has happened to everyone else. He seems to be enclosed in a small bubble, just him and Curls, who is still concentrating on his feet. She's shaking with laughter, her aliveness and determination snaking from her to him, like lightning heading for the most obvious conductor.

He tries. He wants to do it, show that he can be the same as everyone else, but when he glances up, he discovers that the others have moved on without them, bypassing them and leaving them space to work out their own version of the steps. Even Mrs Anderson, who is clearly delighted at being swept along by Geoffrey, is doing remarkably well, despite the arthritis. She's keeping up with the others, moving round the room, vaguely in rhythm. Women find it easier than men, he decides. It comes naturally to them.

His leg is the problem. He can't shift it fast enough, so every time he tries to follow the beat, he has to stop and drag it along behind him.

'That's it,' says Curls. 'We're getting rather good, aren't we?'

For a few minutes he believes her. He finds he can breathe, after all. He concentrates on the movement of his feet.

His right leg catches on the left. He stumbles, makes a grab for support and encounters Curls's shoulder. He refuses to hold on, lets his hand slip past, loses his balance, feels himself falling–

'Steady now.' Jack is beside him, catching him just in time, with Geoffrey on the other side. They place him back on the floor upright.

Robert takes a deep breath, pulls himself up straight, determined to regain his dignity. 'I think, if you don't mind, I'll sit and watch. I'm not entirely suited to this kind of activity.'

'Oh,' says Curls. 'You were doing so well.'

'Nevertheless,' he says, 'I would prefer to sit down for a while.'

He can't leave straight away. It would imply that he hasn't enjoyed the occasion. He'll have to wait for a while and watch. Then, after a suitable period of time, he should be able to get back to his work.

From the other side of the room he can see Alma watching him. He smiles at her again. He avoids looking at Curls.

iii

Dr Guest's wife has helped Alma to find a new dress for the concert. There's a suitable one at home, in Alma's wardrobe, but the thought of home is like an enormous chasm that she doesn't want to jump into, or even to negotiate her way around. She doesn't want to be reminded of the occasion when she and her mother went shopping in April to buy the dress. Mrs Guest (call me Aunt Isobel) came over to Mortimer Hall on Wednesday evening with an armful of her own dresses for Alma to try on. Alma had selected a green pleated one in cotton lawn and Mrs Guest tucked in the extra material with pins, so that she could take it away and alter it. She'd brought it back yesterday evening.

Natalie and Giraffe have had dresses sent by their parents. Curls has two that she wears for concerts and decides on the long red silk for Saturday.

'It's comfortable,' she says, swirling round in the bedroom on the morning before the concert, trying to see as much as possible in the small mirror, which has only ever been intended for the use of young men. She's grown-up and sophisticated in the dress, an adult version of the concert pianist that she has been for so much of her life. Her parents have sent her a string of real pearls, a family heirloom. They sit on the pale skin of her collarbone, warm, glowing and expensive. She has a fresh, clean look about her, as if she's just come out of the bath.

Alma lies on her bed, in a cotton dress, ready for the picnic. She watches Curls, half in fascination, half in dread. Are they nearly there, grown-up, ready to head off into the world? It's frightening. She's not sure she wants to become an adult. Once she does, there'll no longer be any need for her parents and she wants to keep them fresh in her mind where she can consult them, where they're still available, prepared to help. If she grows up, will they fade out of her memory? Will Duncan even recognise her if he comes home?

Natalie and Giraffe burst in. They're wearing slacks and walking shoes. 'You're not dressed!' says Natalie. 'We've got to be at the bus stop in twenty minutes.'

'It's fine,' says Curls. 'It only takes me five minutes.'

It's true. Once she knows what she's meant to be wearing, she can throw it on in no time, even in the dark. Alma gets up from her bed. 'We're nearly ready,' she says.

'I don't know how we'll manage when the men leave,' says Natalie, sitting on the side of Alma's bed.

'I know,' agrees Giraffe. 'It's been heavenly, hasn't it?'

Heavenly? thinks Alma. Have they forgotten Duncan already?

'We'll manage,' says Curls. She seems quieter than usual, more subdued.

The Lindy Hop won't be the same without partners, but Giraffe and Natalie have been losing interest, and the dancing would probably have come to an end anyway.

It's still the only thing that can make Alma excited.

Curls slips off the evening dress and throws on a summer dress. 'Ready,' she announces.

Alma wonders if Mr Gunner will go on this expedition. She hopes so. She wishes he hadn't tried to dance. When she saw him, the agony on his face, she'd longed to go over and rescue him. She would have taken his hand and led him to a chair where he could sit quietly and recover his dignity. What was Curls thinking of, encouraging him to take part when he clearly finds it exhausting even to walk? Alma was partnered with Tristan Watson, who was extremely difficult. He didn't appear to have any sense of rhythm and she spent most of her time dodging his wayward hands and feet, ducking to avoid being whacked by a swinging arm, jumping out of the way just in time before he stepped on her. Every now and again she glanced over to Mr Gunner as he circled with Curls.

She was watching when he lost his balance and saw Jack and Geoffrey dash to the rescue. She willed him to remain upright and only breathed easily when he was sitting down safely.

Tristan's heel ground heavily into her toes.

'Aargh!' she cried.

She imagined how she would feel if Mr Gunner stepped over to her, eased Tristan out of the way, and took over, astonishing everyone with his new ability to master the steps once Alma was helping.

Everyone from Mortimer Hall assembles at the bus stop. Ten students, four girls, and Mr Gunner. Alma smiles at him shyly when she walks up with Curls. He smiles back. When he first came to fetch them from Goldwyn's he had seemed so remote, the representative of distant authority, but now, standing in the middle of his students in his beige loose-weave jacket, sandals and panama hat, the gap between them seems to have diminished.

'I hope the bus won't be too full,' says Mr Gunner, worriedly. 'We'll almost fill the top deck.'

'Nonsense,' says Mrs Anderson, who has come to see them off. She's not going to join them for the walk on Woodbury Common, although she looks as if she is. Her ample shape is squeezed into a white dress covered with tiny daisies and her hair's tied back under a bright blue headscarf, which she has knotted under her chin. She says she is too old for long walks, her hips and knees too creaky. 'There should be plenty of room at this time of day, and if there isn't, some of the gentlemen can wait for the next bus.'

'They'd miss the picnic, though,' says Jack. 'And that wouldn't do at all, would it?'

'Indeed it wouldn't.' She's here to ensure that the food is transported correctly, and that nothing is left behind. It's been packed into six parcels, which have been placed carefully into bags and allocated to some of the students, while plates, cups, flasks, cutlery and blankets have been divided between the rest of them. The extra bags don't appear to inconvenience the men, who carry them on their shoulders alongside their gas masks, as if they're weightless. They move round as freely as if they were empty-handed.

'I wanted to go to the beach,' says Giraffe, in a low voice. 'We hardly ever get the chance now.'

'Just be grateful that we're having a day out at all,' says Curls. 'I can't imagine whose idea it was – Miss Cunningham-Smith or Mr Gunner. Neither of them gives the impression that they would consider recreation to be an important element of our lives.'

'That's a bit unfair,' says Alma.

The bus is approaching too fast and screeches to a halt several yards further down the road. Everyone walks towards it in an orderly fashion, supervised by Mr Gunner.

'Move along there,' calls the conductor, an elderly man whose braces are visible under his jacket. 'We're behind schedule.'

Alma is near the end of the queue and only just manages to get on, behind Mr Gunner who has difficulty pulling up his lame leg, before the bus starts to move away. Geoffrey takes her arm to help and she smiles at him gratefully. She's begun to notice that the students have treated her with extra concern since Duncan went missing.

Jack and Colin are forced to run along behind the bus, leaping on as it gathers momentum, grabbing the handrail to stop themselves falling back off the platform.

'Tally-ho!' shouts Jack, waving out of the rear of the bus at Mrs Anderson. 'Chocks away!'

'That was a bit dicey,' says Colin to the conductor. 'Not much point in having a bus if you don't let people on.'

The conductor shrugs. 'It's the driver,' he says. 'Never been the same since he was bombed out. Says he can't sleep in a different bed. Where to?'

'Woodbury.'

The conductor turns the dials on his machine and cranks out a ticket.

The four girls clamber up the stairs and throw themselves into two double seats. The bus goes round a sharp corner and they roll over on top of each other, giggling. Mr Gunner has remained downstairs so there's a sense of freedom up there. Eric goes along the top, snapping open the windows, and a fierce crosswind whips through, sending their hair flying. Curls tries to close them again, but they're difficult to manage and in the end Jack gets up and does it for her, leaving two open for ventilation.

'Aren't your parents coming down today?' Giraffe asks Curls, from the seat behind.

'I'm not sure what time they're arriving – it depends on whether they make all the train connections and there aren't too many delays. In time for the concert, hopefully, but they might be earlier.'

'Shouldn't you be there to welcome them?'

'Oh, they won't mind. They know loads of people in Exeter. They're expecting me to be busy, anyway – shut away with the Steinway in the school hall, practising.'

Curls's relationship with her parents is strangely distant. Her mother always tries to come down from London if she's taking part in anything, returning late at night if the trains are running on time or the next morning if not. Her father works in the Home Office and finds it harder to get away, but he attends several of the weekend events. They both managed to get to Exeter for the extraordinary occasion when Curls was selected for the netball team (there was an outbreak of chicken-pox at the time and the usual members of the team were falling like flies) in a match against a local team from St Theresa's. Goldwyn's lost for the first time in living memory – by seven goals to thirty, but Curls's parents didn't mind.

'How lovely that they let you take part,' said her mother.

'You'll be able to put that on your Oxford application,' said her father.

'Honestly, Daddy,' said Curls, rolling her eyes. 'Must you reduce everything to success or failure?'

When they turn up, there are no hugs, no kisses, just a smile of welcome. They treat Curls as an adult, an equal, giving her opinions serious consideration and often allowing her to make her own decisions. They're generous, taking her and her friends out for a meal whenever they come, so Alma has met them several times. But she finds them difficult. It's as if they invite the other girls so they won't be left alone with Curls and have nothing to say to each other. They listen to the conversation, rarely joining in, remaining remote and unknowable.

Curls should take more care of them, thinks

Alma now. You can't predict when people are just going to disappear and never come back.

'Do you think they're right – that you should be practising?' she asks Curls.

'There'll be plenty of time when we get back,' says Curls. 'I did almost exactly the same programme at the Wigmore two months ago. It wasn't broadcast then, but it comes to the same thing. And I've already tried the Steinway. It's a good one.'

She's so certain about everything. Does she never have doubts?

They stop suddenly at a junction and jolt forwards, grabbing the seat in front.

'Ow!' yells Giraffe, as her head bounces back into the handrail behind her.

'The driver's completely mad,' says Natalie, rubbing Giraffe's head.

'He should join up,' says Eric. 'He'd be our secret weapon. Driving like that, he could be let loose among the Jerries and run most of them over before they knew he'd arrived.'

'He tried to enlist,' say the bus conductor, who's now upstairs and moving along the aisle, collecting their fares, 'but half of his right hand is missing. Lost three fingers on the Somme in 1916.'

'That explains everything,' says Dennis.

'Is he safe,' asks Natalie, 'driving with only seven fingers?'

'Oh, yes,' says the conductor. 'A few fingers here or there don't make much difference.'

They sit back again as the bus accelerates, the engine loud and throaty, leaving the outskirts of

Exeter behind. There should be fewer unexpected halts now.

Alma studies Curls's profile as she stares out of the window. 'Did you really kiss Duncan?' she asks. She wants her to deny it instantly, to make everything less complicated.

But Curls doesn't reply straight away, and Alma goes over all the possibilities again: they kissed more than once; they had some kind of understanding, which they'd kept hidden from her; he asked her to kiss him, but she wasn't interested in him; she asked him to kiss her but he wasn't interested in her. There's no right answer. Every scenario would be unsatisfactory.

Duncan's probably dead anyway. What does it matter if he liked Curls?

Maybe Curls hasn't heard the question. Maybe her mind is elsewhere, playing through the Beethoven sonata note by note, testing her memory.

Alma tries to work out her motive in asking. Why does it cause her so much unease? Is she afraid that, if he's dead, his last thought was not of her, not of her parents, but of Curls? She wishes she could have been there with him in the transport plane, the last of his family, the only person who mattered to him. She knows she's being unreasonable. He might well have had a sweetheart elsewhere, a girl she knows nothing about, who had some claim on him. But what if the girl was Curls? It's strangely upsetting to think that her best friend could have been the one who had replaced Alma in Duncan's mind, his last recollection before he plunged into the sea.

'I made it up,' says Curls at last, in a low voice that is almost lost in the sound of the bus's engine.

Alma stares at her. 'But – why?'

Curls shrugs, clearly uneasy. 'I don't know. I suppose I just thought he was gorgeous and I was dreaming about kissing him – I haven't really felt like that about anyone before.'

'Yes, you have. You fancied Jack. And that boy at Sherrard's – Derek, wasn't it? You had a real crush on him.'

Curls sighs, as if she's been released from something. 'Duncan was different. He was so... Well, you know what he was like.'

Alma hesitates and tries to be generous. 'I wouldn't exactly see him the same way as you, though, would I?'

Curls smiles a little. 'Maybe not. Anyway, it was just wishful thinking on my part.'

It's as if the wind from the open windows has sucked something out of her. She hasn't been her usual cheerful self since Duncan crashed, none of them has, but now she looks drained. Is she telling the truth, or simply offering an explanation that will satisfy Alma? Is she just saying this to be reassuring, or kind?

Alma takes a deep breath. 'It's OK,' she says. 'I wouldn't have minded if it had really happened.'

Curls gives her a sharp, penetrating glance, seems to hesitate for a second, as if she wants to say more but changes her mind, then settles back in her seat. '*Pax*, then,' she says, with a half smile.

'*Pax*,' agrees Alma. It feels better, even if she knows it's more complicated than Curls is admitting. They needed to say something, bring it out into the open and neutralise the threat to their friendship.

Imprinted in Alma's memory is an image of Curls flying through the air, of Duncan catching her. She examines it again. She sees a silent exchange between them, a shared understanding. She hadn't understood its significance then. Now she does.

She leans to the side, touching Curls's shoulder with her own, letting her warmth flow towards her friend, an electric current that oscillates between them.

iv

Robert lies back, props himself on his elbows, supported by the springy grass beneath the rug, and watches the young people playing rounders. The climb was hard for him, and he arrived well behind the others, determined to get there, but conscious of his limitations. The sky is pale and perfect, and the heat of the sun encloses him in a generous, comfortable embrace. Heather, mauve and deep pink, stretches over the landscape as far as he can see, stirring and rustling in the occasional breeze, interspersed with dazzling yellow patches of gorse. The air has a sharp clarity up here, a freshness that reminds him of his grandfather's lighthouse and the long, still days he spent looking out to sea.

'Another cup of tea, Mr Gunner?' Miss Cunningham-Smith, who's sitting on her deckchair next to the blanket, is hunting in her large hamper for the flask. She's driven here in her spacious Wolseley, doing two journeys to bring all the boarders and the necessary equipment. How does a headmistress convince the authorities that she requires a petrol ration?

'Thank you. Providing you have enough, of course.'

'Oh, I think we can manage another cup each before the young people come back for more. They'll have to settle for lemonade, but I'm sure they'll manage. Your students strike me as polite young men.'

He will miss this year's finals students when they leave in a few days. He always does, but since the war started it's been harder. He wonders what the numbers will be like for the next academic year. He's offered places to several promising students, but it's impossible to know how many will take them up. The war and lack of money are powerfully persuasive weapons against education. Some of his younger students will probably leave too, before they finish their degrees, enlisting, going off to do their bit. He would do the same in their place if he could, but he worries about all that brainpower going to waste, the expertise that should be channelled into research disappearing for ever. Presumably the war will end one day. What will happen then? Will the young men come back and want to finish their education? Will there be room for them all, or will there be so few left that half of the university will have to close? And will the returning soldiers be so damaged that education will seem as irrelevant to them as it had to Robert's father, who had never been able to see any purpose in Robert's studies?

A roar of approval breaks into his thoughts as one of the girls is caught out.

Robert tries to decide if he envies them. Their energy, their exuberance. He was never like that, never able to join in games, never able to race around with absolute belief in his own strength. But he enjoys his present life. He considers himself lucky to have been offered the job as a lecturer and he's happy in his own company, studying, reading, writing. He was born to be an academic, he thinks, someone who prefers the life of the mind to the real thing.

'Come on, Curls!' shouts Eric Westland. 'Your turn!'

Curls has been standing back from the game of rounders, chattering with a group of older girls. 'Coming!' she calls, and bounds across to the game, flashing her skinny legs, amid cries of encouragement from her friends.

'We're depending on you, Curls!'

'Show these men what Goldwyn's girls are made of!'

Next to Giraffe, she appears small and neat, but she moves awkwardly, self-consciously and there's nothing about her physical movements that indicates her enormous talent. Her appearance is not exceptional, yet she still stirs something powerful inside Robert. A surge of embarrassment sweeps through him.

He pulls himself up to a sitting position and watches Miss Cunningham-Smith pour the tea from a flask into two china cups that are balanced side by side on the edge of the blanket, slightly insecure but upright enough to cope with being half full.

Has she seen him watching Curls? Can she see his reaction to her?

'Have you plans for the summer?' she asks.

'I have to stay in Exeter. There'll be an even greater need for fire-watchers once the university closes for the vacation. And I'm working on a research project, so I need the extra time.' He doesn't mention his interest in lighthouses. It's unlikely Miss Cunningham-Smith would be impressed.

'I'll be supervising the refurbishment of Goldwyn's so we can accommodate the boarders next term,' she says. 'It'll only be temporary until we can rebuild, but I'm afraid that's not likely to happen for some time yet. We have a war to win first.'

He sips his tea, grateful for the diversion, but his eyes are drawn back to Curls. She's been caught out at the second post, so she and Alma are watching the rest of the game from the sidelines.

Miss Cunningham-Smith follows his gaze. 'Alma Braithwaite is looking a little better,' she says. 'I'm not at all sure how. She's had a great deal to cope with.'

He nods. 'She's managing.'

Miss Cunningham-Smith sighs. 'That's all anyone can do nowadays. Manage.'

The game of rounders ends as the second team is caught out. They flop down on the ground, exhausted.

'It's so hot,' says a Goldwyn's girl. 'I can't bear it.'

Miss Cunningham-Smith, in a dark dress, hat, gloves, stockings and lace-up shoes, raises her eyes. 'Sit in the shade, Alice,' she calls.

A group of hawthorns have offered them some relief from the sun. The bushes are a curious shape, leaning to one side, moulded by the wind, but they're substantial and give good shade. There's a small stream nearby and the sound of running water is soothing.

'Can we paddle, Miss Cunningham-Smith?' calls Curls.

'As long as you're sensible,' she replies.

'Have you ever known me not to be sensible?'

Miss Cunningham-Smith fixes her with a penetrating stare. 'I think you already know the answer to that question, Jane.'

Robert relaxes during this conversation. It reminds him that the girls are schoolgirls, in the care of Miss Cunningham-Smith, in need of tactful correction. It makes things normal, helps him see the nonsense of thinking of Curls in any other way.

Several girls take off their shoes and socks and step gingerly into the water.

'It's freezing!' shrieks one.

Two of them jump straight back out again, but Curls and Alma stay, rolling their skirts up even though the water is shallow and fast-moving, stepping cautiously over the pebbles. They bend over to look for fish, their heads almost touching and they are children again, united in their fascination.

The heat induces a sense of exhaustion. In the distance, a haze blurs the higher ground. Most of the young people are lying in the shade of the trees, some drifting off to sleep. A welcome breeze stirs now and then and rustles their clothes.

The gentle drone of an aeroplane putters high above them, like a bumble bee circling in the blue of the sky, searching for flowers, hungry for nectar. Most of the men and some of the girls shade their eyes and peer up.

'It's a fighter,' says Eric. 'Can't tell if it's a Spitfire or a Hurricane.'

'It's too far away,' says Geoffrey. The sound is familiar, like the pipes chuntering along in the background at Mortimer Hall, a lone pilot finding his way home.

'Difficult to see,' says Dennis. He's stretched out on his back, long and wiry, staring at the sky. 'He's got the sun behind him.'

One or two young men are draining the bottles of lemonade, tipping them up to their mouths, leaning back and licking up every last drop. Robert watches them, aware that he should encourage them to remember their manners. But it feels inappropriate to fuss over details in such idyllic surroundings. There's a heaviness in his body, as if he's at home in bed, held in by blankets, on the cusp of sleep.

Only Curls and Alma are still upright. Everyone else is lying down, mostly in small groups, picking at the grass beneath them, digging out small fragments of flint, murmuring to each other lazily. There's an occasional laugh, alien in the relaxed atmosphere, hastily subdued.

Robert can feel his eyelids drooping. Even Miss Cunningham has abandoned her usual rigid posture and is leaning back in her deckchair with her eyes closed.

The noise of the plane gets louder, a gradual increase in volume as it descends more rapidly.

It's the girls, thinks Robert, irritated. The pilot wants to observe the girls.

There's a strange rattle, hard and violent.

Robert sits up.

Another rattle. A line of holes appears in the blanket below his feet. He stares at them in disbelief.

A scream pierces the thin, clear air.

'Take cover!' shouts Miss Cunningham-Smith. 'Under the trees!' It's the only possible protection. Everywhere else is visible for miles around.

They scramble between the branches of the hawthorns. The plane makes a tight turn and comes back towards them.

V

Alma and Curls have moved upstream. They're constructing a dam with pebbles, watching the water build up behind it and burst over the top. They don't immediately hear what's happening as the sound of the descending plane is disguised by the rush of the water, the clink of the stones against one another, their debates on how to make the dam work better.

'This is the weak point,' says Curls, piling on more stones.

Alma hadn't wanted to go into the stream. She would have liked to lie down with the others and do nothing. But Curls was insistent.

When they hear the first screams, they turn, puzzled and confused, not immediately aware of the danger.

Alma sees it first, the plane heading directly towards them. 'Get down!' she shrieks. She throws herself at Curls and pulls her down with her, headfirst into the icy water. There's a slight overhang at the side of the stream. 'Under there!' she screams, pushing Curls in front of her.

As the plane passes over them, she buries her head in her arms, trying to hide under the shallow water.

She can hear the clatter of machine guns and struggles to take in what's happening. Why is the pilot flying over Woodbury Common? Why would he attack a picnic? It's private, nothing to do with the war. He has no right to be there.

As the plane roars past them, preparing to turn and come back for its next run, she raises her head to look around. The scene is one of chaos. Bags and blankets lie abandoned on the grass. Some of the men have taken charge, dragging everyone into the centre of the trees, ignoring the cries of protest as they scrape bare arms and legs on the thorns.

'The further in you can get, the less likely you are to be hit!' shouts Eric Westland.

A voice is screaming constantly, breaking only to draw breath, then crying out in pain again.

Someone's been hit.

'Try to remain completely still!' calls Miss Cunningham-Smith. 'He'll find it harder to see you.'

'Bandages!' shouts one of the men. 'We have to stop the bleeding.'

Jack Hitchens is removing his shirt, pulling at it violently with his teeth and tearing off strips.

Alma tries to see who's been hurt, but they've become a mass of unidentifiable people, clinging to each other, many frozen with fear, herded by the men into the bushes. From her viewpoint the hawthorns seem to give only patchy protection, but there's nowhere else to go. Woodbury Common is wide open, high up and exposed. There are no bomb shelters up here.

One of the students – it's Colin – is lying on the ground some distance from the trees, close to the stream, wailing horribly, stopping every few seconds as he tries to catch his breath, then starting again.

'Colin!' shouts Alma. 'Over here!'

He sees them, but seems unable to move. Why doesn't he crawl towards them?

She turns to ask Curls her opinion, but Curls isn't there any more.

She's climbing out of the stream. 'What are you doing?' yells Alma, grabbing her legs and trying to pull her back down.

Curls pushes her off as she scrambles to the top of the bank.

She's panicking, thinks Alma. 'Curls! It's all right. I'm coming with you.' They could grab Colin and lift him together, then get under cover with the others. They can just make it if they hurry, if they do a quick dash over the open ground to the trees. It's worth the risk. But Alma keeps slipping on the mud as she tries to climb out of the ditch and losing her balance. She hauls herself up with immense difficulty, just as the plane returns.

The plane dives towards them, the engine shrieking.

'Curls!' screams Alma, throwing herself to the ground. 'Get down! He'll see you. You're a sitting target!'

Curls reaches Colin, who has fallen silent. She squats and examines his still body, then stares back up at the plane. Her pale yellow dress, dripping with mud and water, stands out against the green of the grass. Her face is silhouetted against the sky. She's screamingly, uncontrollably furious. 'Murderer!' she yells. 'Nazi butcher!'

'Take cover!' Miss Cunningham-Smith's and Mr Gunner's voices unite in urgency as they realise that Curls is not responding. A combination of authority and terror. They expect to be obeyed and don't know what to do when they're not.

Why doesn't Curls hear them? What's the matter with her?

The roar of the engine increases.

Mr Gunner emerges from the bushes, running towards them, lurching from side to side in a curious crablike gait. He's shouting, his mouth moving up and down almost comically, but it's impossible to hear him.

He's come to save us, thinks Alma, with a surge

of gratitude.

Curls gets to her feet and shakes her fists at the sky now, as if she's possessed. 'Who do you think you are?' she yells. 'Destroying our lives!'

It's Duncan, thinks Alma in a split second. It's something to do with Duncan.

There's a confusion of sound: the rattle and crack of bullets firing without a break, a wind that springs up from nowhere, buffeting against their ears, swirling Curls's skirt so that she seems to be dancing, twirling, preparing to leap up and fly through the air – one, two, three-and-four – as if she's expecting someone to catch her, and the ear-splitting roar of the engine as the plane passes just above them, so close that his wheels almost scrape their heads.

Alma scrambles back to the ditch and throws herself into the water, burying her head in her arms again. The ground shakes, the water boils. She pushes herself down, crying with fear, waiting for the moment when the bullets strike.

After one more pass, the plane leaves. Alma waits, huddled in the mud, trembling uncontrollably, expecting him to come back to finish them off. But somewhere in the distance a radio has crackled, a voice has spoken and he has been recalled to his squadron. Who was he? What was he doing up here, so far from anywhere? Are there military manoeuvres on Woodbury Common that they're not supposed to know anything about? How would the pilot know?

A great stillness settles over the whole area. Even the wind seems to have died away. Alma doesn't want to move, doesn't want to check if she's alive or not.

Slowly, slowly, she can hear movement. The sound of sobbing, whimpering, crying that won't stop. A cracking of limbs as people ease themselves out of their positions, a confusion of voices.

Miss Cunningham-Smith's voice echoes out, matter-of-fact, reassuringly in control. 'We need a roll-call. Who's missing? Who's been hurt?'

Alma raises her head and carefully crawls out of the stream, dripping mud and water behind her. She can't find the strength in her legs to stand up. It takes a few seconds for her eyes to clear. People are creeping out from under the trees, hardly speaking but huddling in groups, clinging to each other for comfort and reassurance.

Miss Cunningham-Smith again: 'Bandages, tourniquets...'

In front of her, Curls is lying on the ground motionless.

'We can use my car as an ambulance.'

Mr Gunner is squatting beside Curls, looking down, as if he has only just discovered her.

Alma creeps closer on her hands and knees. Curls's body doesn't seem right. It's bent over unnaturally, like a broken doll, the parts not connecting in the right way, and her head has been almost severed. Everything is red, shiny, gleaming in the sunshine. There's so much blood that there's nowhere for it to go and it settles in pools in the grass.

Mr Gunner has frozen. He doesn't even notice Alma. His face is white and stricken as he gazes down at Curls.

Alma pulls herself to her feet, balances herself carefully and sees his expression. Tears are pouring down his cheeks.

Part Ten

i

22 November 1963

There's a stunned silence in the hall as everyone digests the news about the shooting of President Kennedy. It's followed by an outbreak of talking, which starts softly – exchanges between people sitting next to each other – but expands and increases in volume until the hall is filled with the sound of civilised shock. There's a general sense of not knowing what to do.

Miss Yates takes deep breaths and concentrates on appearing calm. She is trying very hard to expel from her mind the image of President Kennedy lying on the ground with blood pouring from his body. Behind her, she can hear the members of the orchestra and choir reacting with less restraint. She's reluctant to turn round, weary at the prospect of dealing with emotional teenage girls, but accepts that it will shortly be necessary. She can see Mr Gunner in the front row, next to her empty seat, running his hands through his hair over and over again. His reaction doesn't seem quite real, as if he has observed a similar response in a film and thinks that this is the correct way to behave.

Eventually Miss Yates turns to deal with the girls on the platform, but finds Alma Braithwaite standing immediately behind her, motionless, her hands on her cheeks, another response that must surely have come from the cinema.

'Miss Braithwaite,' says Miss Yates, 'I'm not sure we're going to be able to continue. It might be wise to postpone the concert until a later date.'

Alma drops her hands and stares at her. 'Are you serious?' she asks. Red stains have appeared on her cheeks, as bright as if they've been painted on. She's going to be difficult.

'Perfectly serious. It's unlikely that your hard work will be appreciated in the present circumstances. Look at them all.' She waves a hand at the audience and the performers. 'No one would be able to give it their full attention.'

Alma's face is settling into an expression of disbelief. 'We've spent hours rehearsing. We're ready to perform.'

'Are you?' says Miss Yates. Most of the girls have abandoned their instruments on their chairs or the floor and they're huddled together in groups. Several have given in to apparently inconsolable grief, their mouths open and ugly, tears pouring out of puffy, reddened eyes. She feels resentful. What do they know about President Kennedy? How many of them have any idea of the complexity of world politics? They can't possibly have followed his career as ardently as she has. 'It's clear to me that they are not ready to perform.'

'Of course they are,' says Alma. 'They need a distraction. Something to calm them down, take their minds off the situation.'

This could be true, but there's an equal possibility that they'd fail to perform well enough. Miss

Yates makes a decision. 'I don't think that is likely to happen, Alma. Too many of them are hysterical.' She steps forward to the front of the stage again and raises her voice.

'Ladies and gentlemen.' She pats the air in front of her with her palms, slowing the motion to emphasise the need for everyone to calm down. The talking in the hall dies away gradually until there's near-silence, punctuated by dramatic sobs from behind her. She half turns and the sound is hastily stifled. She stands for a few seconds longer, balancing herself with her feet slightly apart, knowing she can hold everyone's attention, while she formulates the correct words. In the midst of her own distress, she savours the sense of power, her ability to capture an audience.

'I have decided that, in the light of present circumstances, we must postpone tonight's concert. I apologise for the inconvenience, but the girls are in no fit state to continue, as you can see, and it would be unfair on them to let all their hard work go to waste. I suspect that most of our audience would also prefer to go home and assimilate the details of this truly shocking event.'

They need her to take charge. They need leadership.

ii

Alma can remember a previous time, twenty-one years ago, when a different headmistress climbed up the steps to the stage in the same school hall and announced the cancellation of a concert. Every seat was filled, apart from the row of chairs left free for the girls and students who had not yet returned from Woodbury Common, two places on the front row reserved for Miss Cunningham-Smith and Mr Gunner and two more for Curls's parents, who had been contacted at their hotel and summoned to the hospital long before the audience gathered for the concert. The BBC were there, with complicated sound equipment. A microphone hung down over the platform, suspended from wires that had been attached to the ceiling. It was after half past seven and the piano stood alone on the platform, a solitary stool in front of it, waiting for a performer who was not going to come.

Miss Cunningham-Smith had taken the most severely injured in her car to the hospital. Ambulances were sent for the others who had been hurt, so there were only seven girls and five students left with Mr Gunner. They made their way back to the road in silence, struggling under the weight of the remaining equipment, unable to speak to each other, and sat waiting on the grass for a long time.

Why hadn't Curls at least attempted to take cover? If she'd stayed in the stream with Alma, she'd probably have been safe. If she'd run to the bushes, or even just flattened herself on the ground, made herself less obvious, she might have been with them now. It was as if she'd lost her reason, sacrificed herself to her own fury. Why was she so angry? The conversation on the bus kept replaying in Alma's mind. But Curls had only known Duncan for a short time. How could she feel so strongly about him? Or were there other reasons? Was there an idealistic side of Curls that Alma had never glimpsed before? Had she grown up and decided to sacrifice herself for a principle? Or had she simply acted impetuously, like a child, without thinking of her own safety?

Alma wonders if she should have run out and stood with her when the plane returned. Two friends against the Nazis. Good versus evil.

At last the Wolseley reappeared and drew up at the side of the road. Miss Cunningham-Smith stepped out. 'I'll take the rest of the girls back to Goldwyn's,' she said to Mr Gunner. 'I've tried to ring from the hospital, but the lines are down. They don't even know that the concert will have to be cancelled. Will you be all right to take the bus back?'

'Of course,' he said.

'Shouldn't we go back to Mortimer Hall?' asked Natalie.

'No,' said Miss Cunningham-Smith, as she loaded deckchairs and bags into the boot. 'You must come with me to Goldwyn's. I'll drive you back later.' She arranged the seven girls in the Wolseley, two in the front, five in the back. Alma found herself squashed up against the door with a lower-fourth, who was gulping back hysterical tears, sitting on her lap. Natalie and Giraffe were separated from her by Sylvia, a sixth-former.

'This is extremely difficult for all of us,' said Miss Cunningham-Smith, as they pulled away. 'But I'm going to have to ask you to be brave for everyone's sake. All the injured are being well cared for at the hospital.'

'But who's...' Natalie was struggling with the words. 'Who's...'

'Two students have been injured – Dennis and Tristan, I think they were – and three of our girls. Rosemary, Felicity and Mary.'

Alma, Natalie and Giraffe looked at each other. They knew who hadn't walked with them back to the road. If they weren't injured, they must be–

'Colin,' mouthed Giraffe.

'Maisie and Rosalind didn't make it,' said Miss Cunningham-Smith. 'And another student. Colin Streethy, I think his name was.'

The lower-fourth on Alma's lap shrieked at the mention of Maisie, then started to cry, snuffling noisily and wiping her nose on her sleeve. Sylvia, the sixth-former sitting in the middle of the back seat, who was friends with Rosalind, breathed in sharply and looked straight ahead, saying nothing.

'What about Curls?' asked Giraffe.

Miss Cunningham-Smith hesitated as she manoeuvred the car through a narrow stretch of road with potholes on either side. 'I'm afraid Jane has also passed away,' she said.

It couldn't be true. Curls couldn't have died. There was too much of her just to vanish. It was impossible.

Alma stared into space, seeing Curls dancing through the air, flying towards Duncan, bullet holes appearing slowly across her body, silent and in slow motion, like a film sequence. 'Why did she do it?' she said, choking back tears.

'She thought she was immortal,' said Giraffe in a low voice. 'She always acted as if nothing could touch her.'

'Well, she was wrong,' wailed Natalie. 'How could she be so stupid?'

Miss Cunningham-Smith drove with her head down, peering ahead from beneath lowered brows, and her mouth set in a grim line. She took the corners too fast. The girls were thrown around in the back and struggled to keep their balance. They clung to anything that remained fixed, although they were wedged in so tightly that no one could fall anywhere. The car swung into the drive at Goldwyn's, roared up to the front of the school and skidded to a halt in the gravel.

'As quickly as possible, please, girls,' said Miss Cunningham-Smith, her voice tense and low as she checked her watch. 'We're very late.'

Late for what? thought Alma. Why does it matter? She felt drained, dried out.

They emerged from the car, dishevelled and distraught, wiping their faces with grubby hands. Alma edged over to Natalie and Giraffe and they clung to each other for comfort. Miss Cunningham-Smith herded them towards the front door.

'Follow me,' she said, striding along the corridor to the hall. The girls had to run to keep up with her, their footsteps loud on the tiled floor. As they approached, they could hear voices, people talking to each other, conversations that were impossible to distinguish, even laughter. Who were these people? What were they doing there?

Alma finally remembered the concert. She looked round the hall in astonishment, unable to believe that they were still expecting a performance. How could they not know? The grand piano stood in the centre of the stage, huge and solitary.

A man in glasses came towards Miss Cunningham-Smith. 'Thank goodness you're here,' he said. 'We're running very late...'

She put out a hand and swept him aside. She marched along the centre aisle, climbed the steps and turned to face the audience. The conversations slowed, hesitated and drifted into nothing. Alma, watching from the back, could feel shock spreading through the room. Miss Cunningham-Smith did not look like the headmistress everyone knew. Wisps had escaped from her hairpins and were hanging down at the sides of her face, her stockings were torn and there was dried blood on her hands, where she would normally have worn gloves.

'Ladies and gentlemen,' she said, her voice as clear and distinct as always. 'I regret to announce that there will be no concert tonight.'

In the silence that followed, a single, horrified cry emerged from Miss Rupin on the back row, immediately stifled by her hand over her mouth.

No one else seemed to know how to react. Alma could see the BBC man step forward, his face alive with panic. But even he didn't speak.

'I am the bearer of very bad news,' said Miss Cunningham-Smith. 'There has been a tragic incident in which several young people lost their lives. While we were enjoying a picnic on Woodbury Common, in the company of colleagues from the university, a German aircraft appeared out of nowhere and targeted us. He fired repeatedly...' she hesitated for several seconds before continuing, slowly and deliberately '...even though he must have realised we were civilians, carrying on our lives in the most normal way possible, even though there were clearly women and children among us. Three of our girls and a student from the university have died and five more have been taken to the hospital with serious injuries. Jane Curley, the brilliant, talented pianist whose performance you have been expecting tonight, is among the dead.' She stopped again and looked round the room, fixing random individuals with a clear, penetrating gaze. 'This is why we are fighting Hitler. This is why we are prepared to go through all kinds of deprivation. So that we can eradicate this kind of evil from the world.'

She waited, as if she was daring anyone to contradict her, challenging them to suggest she was misguided. The silence was denser than before, and Alma thought she could hear them thinking.

Miss Cunningham-Smith looked around the hall one more time, defying anyone to make a sound. 'Many of you will be anxious to know who has been hurt so I will be available in my office to discuss the details,' she said. 'Messengers have been sent from the hospital and all parents informed, so no parent here need be concerned that their daughter is among the casualties.'

She left the stage abruptly, stalking up the aisle between the chairs and out through the swing doors.

iii

'Miss Yates–'

Miss Yates ignores Alma and continues addressing the audience. 'We shall be sending out new invitations once we've consulted the school calendar and found a new date for the concert.'

Many people in the audience, including the staff, are already pulling on their coats, picking up bags and searching for their daughters among the chaos on the platform.

Alma Braithwaite is at her side now, grasping her arm with urgency.

Miss Yates takes several deep breaths before turning to confront Alma. She doesn't want to reveal any emotion and struggles to compose her features, constructing a blank expression that will reveal nothing of her shock and grief. When she finally turns, she has to release herself by prising Alma's fingers from her sleeve. 'Alma,' she says, in a low voice. 'This is inappropriate.'

'What is inappropriate,' says Alma, 'is the cancellation of the concert. We have all worked so hard–'

'I don't doubt it, but it's not practical to continue. We can reschedule.'

'You won't do it, though, will you? The concert will be cancelled, not postponed. I know how your mind works.'

Miss Yates is taken aback by her hostility. 'I really must point out that this is not a personal vendetta against you. It's the only reasonable decision that can be made. We have been overtaken by world events and I regret that I have no means of controlling matters of such importance. Many people here today will be deeply disturbed by the news and anxious to go home. We must allow them to react to it privately.'

'If Bridget hadn't come in,' says Alma, 'no one would have known until after the concert.'

'Nevertheless, Bridget did come in. None of us can change events in retrospect.'

Alma is studying her with an odd expression on her face. 'No,' she says slowly. 'You can't unknow something, can you?'

Miss Yates experiences a sudden lurch of alarm. To what is Alma alluding? Her tone suggests something else, some other event that has no connection with today. What can she know that should not be known? Could she have found out...? No, it's impossible. No one here knows anything about Miss Yates's past. How could they? They have no access to her history. Her previous life is a private story that no one would be able to identify, hidden within a library of books.

And yet there's something unsettling about the

way Alma is standing there, her eyes intense, as if she knows something she shouldn't.

'Perhaps you would care to supervise the girls on the platform,' says Miss Yates, 'make sure they're being picked up by a parent.'

Alma continues to stare at her for two more seconds, before turning away. 'Louise,' she calls sharply. 'Please come and take your cello before it gets knocked over.'

Miss Yates beckons Miss Davies over. 'Cressida,' she says, 'do you think you could supervise an orderly exit? I don't want a riot on the way out.'

'It's already been attended to,' says Cressida. 'Roy's outside organising the cars and Adelinde is on the front door saying goodbye to everyone.'

'It would seem that Adelinde has her uses, after all,' says Miss Yates. 'As always, I am very grateful for your organisational skills.'

Cressida smiles. 'All part of the service.' She's about to step off the platform, but Miss Yates touches her arm.

'Can I have a quick word?' she says.

Cressida stops and raises her eyebrows in query. They are thick and white, a powerful means of expression and a useful outlet for her good-natured cynicism.

Miss Yates leans towards her and lowers her voice. 'Do you think I did the right thing? Cancelling the concert?'

Cressida hesitates for a few seconds, as if she's considering the question, as if she hasn't already thought about it. 'Probably,' she says.

'That sounds as if you don't think so,' says Miss Yates.

Cressida smiles again, her leathery skin creasing into familiar lines. 'Then I'm giving the wrong impression,' she says. 'On balance, there seems to have been little choice. I doubt very much that we could have kept all this teenage emotion under control. I think we know which girls would have taken the lead in a display of hysteria.'

Miss Yates is relieved. 'Not all of the staff are in agreement, but I knew I could count on you. The news is shocking.'

Cressida sighs. 'It's not reassuring, is it, if the most powerful nation on earth can't protect its leader?'

But Miss Yates cannot bring her mind to the political situation. She's thinking about Jack Kennedy. She's so familiar with the details of his face that she feels as if a personal friend has been wrenched away from her. He was only three years older than her, more or less a contemporary. Her thoughts turn to Jackie Kennedy, one of the youngest first ladies to move into the White House. How will she and her two young children cope with the shock? 'We will all struggle to come to terms with it,' she says.

'No doubt we'll survive,' says Cressida, before climbing down from the platform.

The hall is not emptying as rapidly as Miss Yates was expecting. She can hear panicky muttered words being tossed into the air: 'Soviets ... assassination ... anarchy ... the Bomb...'

They're afraid, she thinks. Suddenly it feels like the Cuba crisis all over again, but worse because this threat has become reality.

Cuba was a turning point, not just for the world

but for Miss Yates in a more personal way. While everyone held their breath, convinced they had only a few days left before the world exploded in a nuclear conflagration, Miss Yates had made a decision. If disaster was averted and everything carried on in the same way, she would leave her present position as headmistress of the Thomas Cromwell School in East Anglia and apply for a post elsewhere. But before she went, she would face up to her blackmailer.

Marlene Uppingham was the school secretary, a self-important, constantly busy woman who had been at the school for so long that she genuinely believed she was running it. She was the one who discovered the truth. Whether by chance or out of a desire to pry, she had opened a letter that was addressed to Miss Yates, although it was clearly marked PRIVATE in the top left-hand corner. It was a letter from Miss Yates's first employer, Miss Jenkins, the headmistress of a small private school in Northumberland. Miss Jenkins had appreciated Miss Yates's skill as a teacher and approved of her ambition. She'd advised her not to mention that she didn't have a degree when applying for her first headship and offered to write her references without referring to the problem.

'My dear,' she had said, in her quiet, persuasive manner, 'the absence of truth can be as valuable as the real thing. Allow people to draw their own conclusions about your time in Oxford.'

Miss Jenkins had been a welcome motherly presence in Miss Yates's life. It was with great sadness that she had heard of her death a few years after she'd moved away. The letter, written shortly before Miss Jenkins died, had been long and rambling, as if her mind was disintegrating and fragments were breaking off, floating backwards and forwards through time, unable to distinguish the present from the past. Her collusion in the deception about Miss Yates's qualifications drifted in and out, like a leitmotif, like a death-bed confession.

Marlene had asked for favours: a rise; a holiday that extended over the beginning of term; a place in staff meetings; the right to overrule other members of staff in important decisions.

It couldn't continue.

By the time of the Cuban missile crisis, Miss Yates was trying to juggle everything around Marlene's growing desire for power. When President Kennedy announced to the world that an agreement had been reached – how had he done it? What astonishing negotiating skills had he employed? – Miss Yates experienced a clearing of the mind, a sharpening of the senses, along with the collective sigh of relief from everyone around her. The entire episode had been a reminder of the shortness of life and the need to set matters straight. I'll confess to the governors, she thought, throw myself on their mercy. The school has thrived since I've been here. They might be prepared to overlook my lack of honesty. I'll approach them before Marlene does it for me.

But, as it happened, she didn't need to. Unbelievably, fortuitously, Marlene had had a stroke on the day they heard that Russia would be withdrawing all missiles from Cuba. It was as if she couldn't cope with the relief or the concept that everyone could agree.

Miss Yates went to see her in hospital. Marlene lay motionless in her bed, surrounded by tubes, her eyes blank and unrecognising. Her jaw moved up and down without making any recognisable sound and dribble oozed constantly from her half-open mouth.

'Will she recover?' Miss Yates asked a nurse, as she left.

The nurse, glancing behind her at the almost motionless body in the bed, gave a little shake of her head. 'They rarely do. Not when it's been that severe.'

Marlene died two days later.

Miss Yates breathed the fresh air with gratitude. Two narrow escapes. One for the world and one for her. She was meant to live, to be doing what she did so well. But now that everything was all right, she found she didn't want to stay in the school. She could move on with a clear pathway ahead of her.

Her future was secure. She had the original references from Miss Jenkins and from her present school. She would declare the degree in her application form and no one would be any the wiser.

Miss Yates knows, as her mother did, that she was born to be a headmistress. She is good at her job. She can turn a school round, introduce innovation without disruption. She can take on the role of a ship's captain with instinctive expertise, her hand steady and safe at the helm.

She arranged a memorial service for Marlene.

It was on a Thursday at four thirty, but no one came. No relatives, no family friends, no staff from school. She was unloved and unmissed. The poignancy of being the only mourner distressed Miss Yates. It made her all the more determined that this would not happen to her. She intended to leave a mark on the world that could not be ignored.

The platform has been cleared. Most girls have left by the side door and Miss Rupin is outside, arranging lifts for the girls whose parents couldn't attend for one reason or another and were expecting to fetch them later in the evening. In their haste to leave, they've pushed chairs to one side, overturned music stands and scattered sheets of music over the floor. It will have to be cleared before tomorrow morning's assembly.

Miss Yates longs to get home for the nine o'clock news. She needs to be on her own for a while – to take in the enormity of the situation.

'A word, Miss Yates?' Alma is once more at her side.

She sighs inwardly. 'Of course, Alma.'

Most of the staff have remained behind to stack the chairs along the walls, ready for Roy to take them back into storage before school tomorrow morning. 'Not here,' says Alma. 'In your office.'

Miss Yates swallows her anxiety. 'Of course,' she says. 'But could you help me set up the stage for tomorrow's assembly?'

iv

Alma has sorted out the girls, sent them off in the right direction – 'No, Catherine, all that practice will not be wasted... I don't know how it happened... I'm sure it doesn't mean that America will bomb Russia... Please stop crying, Patricia. You can't change anything...'

But an all-consuming anger is growing steadily inside her. It's defying any attempt at control, preparing to blast out with the force of an erupting volcano. Miss Yates should not have stopped the concert. It was the wrong thing to do. The choir and the orchestra have been rehearsing all day and it will be impossible to produce the same enthusiasm a second time. How dare Miss Yates override her opinion?

Alma's hands are clenching and unclenching, as if they're preparing to hit someone. She has to grit her teeth, force herself to exercise control until she can speak to Miss Yates.

She doesn't want to, but she must. The time has come to challenge her. She's seen Miss Yates on the platform, watching while the hall clears, somehow asserting her power by remaining there and allowing her staff to do the work. She's enjoying this, thinks Alma. She can rule other people's lives by making whatever arbitrary decision she wants, then reinforce it by overseeing the operation, using her presence to ensure that her intentions are carried out fully. Miss Yates the dictator, whose every whim must be indulged.

Alma longs to undermine her dignity, knock her over, send her tumbling over the side of the stage. She restrains herself and grabs three music stands instead, lifting them through the exit roughly as if they are responsible for her fury.

She knocks firmly on the headmistress's office door.

'Come in.'

Alma enters and shuts the door behind her. Miss Yates is standing with her back to her, staring out of the window, as if it's possible to see the school garden in the darkness.

'Miss Yates...' begins Alma.

She waits for a response. Nothing happens.

'Miss Yates?' Alma speaks a little louder.

This is ridiculous. She's deliberately ignoring her, making a point.

Miss Yates turns. 'I'm sorry, Alma,' she says. 'I was – distracted.' She puts up a hand and wipes her cheek, almost as if there were tears to brush away. 'It's an emotional time for all of us. I was a great admirer of Mr Kennedy – as we all were – such a tragedy, a man in the prime of life–' She stops, apparently aware that she is becoming incoherent. 'Now,' she says, as if all those words were just a formality, an introduction to the real business, 'how can I help you?'

Alma is confused by the unexpected display of emotion and the abrupt change of tone, so she takes a few seconds to collect her thoughts. While she waits, Miss Yates examines her face seriously, pretending she's interested.

Alma breathes in, then says, 'I would like to register an official protest about the cancellation of the concert–'

'I'm fully aware of your concerns,' Miss Yates interrupts. 'I realised that you wouldn't be happy with my decision, but it was my duty to consider the girls, their parents and the rest of the audience. I know that a great deal of work went into the preparation for the concert, but nobody would have been able to concentrate, and all your efforts would have been wasted. Surely it's better to wait for a time when people can give it their full attention.'

Alma doesn't want to hear Miss Yates's excuses. 'I should have been the one to decide. What gives you the right to overrule me, to make a major decision that affects my department without my consent? Those girls have been practising for weeks, and parents have made time in their busy lives to come and watch their daughters perform. You can't just wave it all away with a few words.'

'I have no intention of waving it away. On the contrary, I would like it to be appreciated.'

Alma hasn't come for a reasonable conversation. She's seething with indignation. 'You should have consulted me. I'm the only one who would know if we could do it or not.'

'I understand that, of course. But I also suspected you would not be prepared to cancel.'

'How could you possibly make that assumption?'

'Because I know you, Alma.'

Alma is outraged by this. 'No, you don't. You

know nothing about me. You can't possibly predict how I would behave in certain circumstances.'

'You make your feelings very clear. It's not difficult to anticipate your reaction.'

'Are you suggesting you can read my thoughts?' asks Alma. 'Since you rarely take the time or trouble to ask my opinion and refuse to listen to it when you do, anything you might think you can expect from me is little more than guesswork.'

Miss Yates's voice rises to match Alma's. 'You have made your position absolutely clear over the last few months. You do not like me and you will do everything in your power to prevent my headship from being a success.'

Alma stares at her. Has she really given that impression? 'I've never said anything of the sort.'

'You don't need to. It's written all over your face, demonstrated by your behaviour in staff meetings.'

'Whatever do you mean? Are you suggesting I deliberately stir up revolution because I don't like you? I cannot believe you would even think such a thing. When have I ever given you cause for complaint?'

'All the time. You challenge everything I say–'

'That's because your edicts are dictatorial–'

'You undermine me on every possible occasion–'

'Nonsense. I'm perfectly willing to work with you. What would I gain from trying to undermine you?'

'Alma, you have resented my presence from the moment we first met because I am not Miss Cunningham-Smith. You will always dislike me for that precise reason. I don't know why you stay here, clinging to the past. Why don't you move, go somewhere new, find a place where you're not weighed down by it?'

'How dare you imply that I can't move with the times? What you mean is, you don't want me here. Why would I allow you to push me out? I've known Goldwyn's since I was a child. I know everything about the school. It's in my blood.'

'Exactly. That is your problem. You cannot stand back and view anything objectively.' Miss Yates's voice is harsher than usual.

In the silence that follows, Alma becomes aware how loud their voices have become. Any staff remaining in the building, parents who have not yet gone home or governors who might have come up to the office to have a quiet word with Miss Yates would have been able to hear the argument. Alma listens intently, but all she can hear is a thumping in her head, blood pounding through her veins, the drumming of her pulse in her ears.

She experiences an unexpected sense of satisfaction, of relief. She's managed to prick Miss Yates, penetrate the smooth, controlled exterior that makes challenging her so unfulfilling. Now they are facing each other as equals.

'Look, Alma,' says Miss Yates, in a more conciliatory voice. 'I'm not trying to push you out, but have you ever considered that you would be happier if you found a post elsewhere? You were clearly fond of Miss Cunningham-Smith, and I appreciate your loyalty. But we're never going to agree and it might be better for both of us if we parted company.'

Alma flinches, as if Miss Yates has suggested physical violence. 'Are you threatening me with the sack? Is that what this is about? You've planned this whole thing so that you can get rid of me.'

'I hardly think that's likely, do you? I didn't hire the assassin who killed President Kennedy.'

'You're twisting my words. That wasn't what I meant.'

'I'm not trying to dismiss you, Alma, although, goodness knows, an outburst like this would give me the ideal excuse. I just want you to consider other options. Branch out, change your life in some way. You've become too tied to the school and you can no longer see anything clearly. You need to stand back from yourself. Find something new that will satisfy you.'

Alma's vision blurs for a couple of seconds while she struggles to digest Miss Yates's words. A hot rage is surging through her in uncontrollable waves. It's an accumulation of all her anger from the past, from times when she hasn't been able to find the means to express herself. Her hatred for Miss Yates has become overwhelming. It's so enormous that she can imagine herself hitting the woman, pounding her with fists, kicking her when she falls to the floor. She forces herself to wait until she's capable of speaking calmly.

'You're the one who should be thinking of leaving,' she says in a low voice. 'I know about your lies.'

'Lies? Whatever are you talking about, Alma?'

'I have evidence that you do not have a degree from Oxford.'

A chill creeps into the room. Neither of them speaks for a few seconds. I'm right, thinks Alma. It's not necessary for Miss Yates to say anything. Her guilt is proved by her reaction. Alma is elated by her sense of power, but also shocked by her ability to make the accusation and her descent into a murky, manipulative world.

Miss Yates turns towards her desk and sits down heavily without taking her eyes off Alma. She doesn't say anything, presumably waiting for more information.

But Alma doesn't think she needs to say more. She's aware of a sense of exultation. She's set in motion something that will not go away and she can dangle it in front of Miss Yates for as long as she wants to, both fascinated and repulsed by her ability to do this.

'So,' says Miss Yates at last. 'How did you find out?'

'Guesswork,' says Alma. 'I just couldn't believe you were as perfect as you would have us believe. So I did some investigating. And guess what I found out?'

Miss Yates stares at her for some time without speaking, as if she can read her thoughts. Her gaze is so penetrating that Alma starts to feel uncomfortable. 'Have you never done anything you regret, Alma?' she asks softly.

'Never,' says Alma. This is about Miss Yates, not her.

'Remarkable,' says Miss Yates. 'So, what do you want from me?'

Alma sinks down into the chair opposite the desk, her legs shaking with the release of tension.

What does she want? 'I don't know,' she says at last.

Miss Yates raises an eyebrow. 'I find that difficult to believe.'

But Alma's first reaction was correct. She can't think of any useful way to use the information.

'So why have you brought it up now?'

Why indeed? She's losing control of the situation. 'Because I don't like the threatening way you've been talking,' she says.

'Threatening? In what way?'

'Asking me to leave.'

'I didn't ask you to leave, Alma. Have you not been listening? I was suggesting that it might be good for you to make the choice to move on.'

'Don't patronise me,' says Alma. She's still struggling to work out how she can use the information about Miss Yates. 'I could tell the governors, who would presumably dismiss you, unless you stop obstructing me in everything I want to do in the school. I'm good at my job.' Is this true? She's suddenly not so sure. 'I know Goldwyn's better than anyone. Why should I have to sit back and watch you turn everything upside-down, destroying the ethos that has been nurtured so carefully over the years?'

'So you do want something from me.'

I want you to leave, thinks Alma, but she can't quite bring herself to say so. Not after Miss Yates's suggestion that she moves away. It would sound as if she was retaliating with spite. It would make her petty, childish.

'I'm afraid,' says Miss Yates in a firm, smooth voice, 'that I'm not prepared to be blackmailed this time.'

This time? Alma is not the first to discover her secret. 'What do you mean?' she says. 'Why would I blackmail you? It's against the law. I don't need money.'

'It's not money you want, though, is it?' says Miss Yates. 'It's power.'

Alma studies her with surprise. Is this true? Is she so determined to have power for herself that she cannot tolerate it in someone else? How had this happened? When had she turned into someone who could do this?

'I'm afraid I'm not going to give in to you,' says Miss Yates, calmly. 'I shall write to the governors myself, explaining the situation and offering to resign if they wish it.'

'That's entirely up to you,' says Alma. Maybe she won't have to do anything. Maybe she simply has to wait and let circumstances take their course. The truth will emerge, regardless of her part in it.

Miss Yates sits back in her chair and breathes deeply, as if all the tension has left her and she is free to say what she wants. 'I would have had a degree if it wasn't for the war,' she says. 'I was offered a scholarship to St Anne's at Oxford, which you presumably know. But in 1940, not long after I started, the Germans began their carpet bombing of Coventry, my home town. The destruction was dreadful – you must have heard about it – and I had to go back to my family. But they'd all died. When I returned to Oxford, I found I could no longer concentrate and it was hard to see the relevance of my studies. I took a job as a librarian in the end. At another college. I've obviously regretted it since then, but grief can make you act irrationally.'

I don't want to hear this, thinks Alma. Now that her anger has come out into the open, she's finding it hard to maintain. She's shocked by the crumbling of her resolve.

'I know you don't agree with me on this,' says Miss Yates, fiercely, 'but I've always felt it was a worthwhile deception. My references have been slightly exaggerated and the school has the benefit of a good, forward-looking headmistress. It seemed a fair deal.'

Suddenly Alma can't cope. Tears are forming inside her, and guilt, huge and tight in her chest. She's not a blackmailer, a woman without a moral code who can destroy careers with pleasure. How could she have allowed herself to fall into such behaviour? She doesn't know what to do. She rises from the chair, stumbles to the door and escapes into the corridor.

The tears are now splashing on to her cheeks, hot and desperate. She's never cried like this before. She can't understand where it's coming from.

She races out of the building and into the school grounds. She needs to be somewhere on her own where she can calm down. The Vaughan Williams Building rises out of the darkness ahead.

iv

Robert hasn't gone home. After Miss Yates's announcement, while everyone was milling around in a state of panic, he hovered uncertainly, wanting to be of use but somehow not managing to participate in the communal distress. Even now, as they start to clear the hall, he feels redundant.

Pippa dashes up to him in her coat, clarinet in hand. 'Isn't it absolutely dreadful?' she says.

'Are we referring to the missed concert or the death of President Kennedy?'

'The assassination, of course.'

'It's shocking. I think Miss Yates made the right decision. A concert can always be rearranged, but it's not every day a president dies.'

'Susan says I can stay the night with her. Is that all right?'

'Well,' he says, uncertain, 'won't you need a nightie, toothbrush, hairbrush...'

'It's all right. Susan says she's got everything I need. They've got loads of money, so they would do, wouldn't they?'

'Pippa!' says Robert.

She grins. 'But it's true. You know it is. And they don't mind at all.'

'Are you sure it's Susan you're interested in?' asked Robert.

Pippa's eyes grow wide. 'Daddy! Whatever are you thinking of? Susan's my best friend. I wouldn't want to go otherwise.'

He's not convinced. 'I was under the impression that Susan's brother, Steven, was "gorgeous".'

Pippa rolls her eyes. 'Please don't, Daddy. You sound ridiculous.'

But she's been talking non-stop about Steven, who is also a friend of Godfrey's, for the last few weeks. Even Miss Dodds has noticed and mentioned it to Robert.

'It's just a crush,' he had said to her. 'It'll be someone else next week.'

'Nevertheless, you should keep an eye on her. Girls today do not behave in the way they did when we were young.'

An image of Curls had flashed into Robert's thoughts, her hand on his shoulder, her eyes on his feet.

'So can I go, Daddy?' asks Pippa.

'All right,' he says. 'But please be sensible and try not to be a nuisance. Should I speak to Susan's mother?' He glances round the hall, but he can't see her.

'No, Daddy, honestly, it's fine. She says it's all right with her if it's all right with you.'

She leaves a few minutes later, arm in arm with Susan, off into the night. Robert finds himself wishing he hadn't agreed. He's beginning to worry that the children are abandoning him too soon and wonders if, in the end, the concept of the warmth of human connection will fade from his memory.

When Grace died, there was so much to do that he didn't have time to think about the loss of her hand on his shoulder, her lips on his cheek as he set off for work every morning, the whistle of her breath in his ear in the middle of the night. The silence from her absence in the house seemed to nurture his own silence. Somehow he felt that she was still with him, if not in presence at least in spirit. His life continued and he coped with it, only really missing her when he went to bed and slipped between cold, unwelcoming sheets.

But he's starting to suspect that he might have neglected something in his relationship with his children. And now it's probably too late to rectify it.

He waits at the back, watching the last parents leave. Now the hall is emptier, the atmosphere's calmer and snatches of conversations become more audible. They're subdued and overawed, as if everyone has become aware that this is yet another historic occasion. It reminds him of the outbreak of the Second World War.

'I can't believe...'

'Who would...'

'It makes you want to go home and gather all your family together.'

'Well, it is America. They don't do things like we do.'

Curls is hovering in the background, still fifteen, still at the onset of a brilliant career, not yet destroyed.

This is where Miss Cunningham-Smith would have returned after the attack on Woodbury Common, striding over the same parquet floor in her strong, idiosyncratic way. The audience would have been waiting for Bach – and Jane Curley.

The BBC presenter would have been prepared

with opening announcements, expecting to introduce the concert for the Home Service. He would have had to ad-lib, desperately searching his fund of knowledge for topics of conversation that might interest the listeners while they waited.

When Robert had arrived back at Mortimer Hall with his students, he had withdrawn to his room, sat at his desk and sunk into the welcome silence, allowing it to wrap round him and slowly untangle his thoughts. He found himself trying to pinpoint some elusive detail in his memory, some unknown factor that could have changed everything and saved them all, if only he had seen it. But the details remained just out of his grasp. It was a situation that couldn't be represented by a formula, a problem with no solution.

One of his students had died too, but he could think only of Curls playing Bach. The non-stop semiquavers pounded through him with the relentless force of typewriter keys or the drumming of rain on the roof. Fast, insistent, unstoppable.

He can remember the shock of glancing up and discovering Mrs Anderson standing in front of him with a cup of tea. He hadn't seen her come into his room.

'Are you all right, Mr Gunner?'

He was picking out the third strand of a four-part fugue as it wended its way through the thicket of notes on either side, transferring from treble to bass, bass to treble. Curls's fingers – long, unbelievably agile – were in front of his eyes, blocking his view of Mrs Anderson, making that middle strand sing, refusing to allow it to be choked by the surrounding chords.

Mrs Anderson had walked closer and bent her knees (not an easy task with her arthritis) so that she could look directly into his eyes. As if he was a child and needed careful attention. 'Mr Gunner?' she said.

'Yes, yes,' said Robert, shaking his head, not wanting to lose that third part before it became too entangled. 'I'm fine, thank you.'

'You're covered in blood,' she said.

'It's all right,' said Robert. 'It's not my blood.' He wondered at that point if he should cry. But crying seemed so pointless, almost presumptuous, as if he had the right to mourn Curls or any of the others who had died on that picnic.

The image of her crumpled, wrecked body in the yellow dress was imprinted on the forefront of his mind, refusing to budge.

Why did she do it? Why did she leap up, make herself so obvious? It was as if she couldn't see the danger, as if she didn't believe she could die.

There were several profiles of Curls in the national press, but the picnic was hardly mentioned. People were dying all over the place, so a small group of schoolgirls and students at a picnic was not of great significance. The big story was that the Americans were coming – some had already arrived. Nobody wanted to dwell on the injustice of a local raid.

The parents of Colin Streetly, the student who had died, travelled down from Taunton to supervise the return of his body. They shook hands with Robert, their faces pale and set, thanked him for all the help he'd given their son ('He always spoke so highly of you, Mr Gunner'), then walked back down the hill to the station carrying Colin's possessions in a large leather suitcase. At no point did they allow their faces to crumple or tears to fall.

Curls's parents would have had a similar conversation with Miss Cunningham-Smith, who had already driven to Mortimer Hall and collected Curls's belongings. There would have been no reason for them to meet Robert.

He helps the staff to move the chairs in the school hall, ready for tomorrow's assembly, following directions from Cressida Davies, head of maths, who is now thin and elderly.

'It's Mr Gunner, isn't it?' she says.

'Yes,' he says. 'I'm impressed that you recognise me.' He remembers her sweeping up the bomb damage, that time he went to pick up the four schoolgirls, but she must encounter so many new faces, parents she meets only fleetingly.

'Never forget a face,' she says, before turning away to arbitrate between two teachers whose piles of chairs have collided.

Robert doesn't know any of the remaining staff. He caught a glimpse of Miss Rupin earlier, looking exactly the same as he remembers her, if smaller, more shrivelled, but she is no longer in the hall. Miss Yates and Alma have already gone, so he eventually says goodbye to Miss Davies and walks outside. He hesitates, restless, oddly reluctant to go home. The house will be empty. Godfrey's staying the night at a friend's house, working on a physics project.

Everyone on the train will be talking about the assassination. Television, radio, tomorrow's newspapers will be dominated by it. Mass reactions make him weary. It's so much effort to join in. During the war, everyone kept their emotions in check, knowing that it would be unpatriotic to allow personal grief. But he still remembers the hysteria of Armistice Day and the personal difficulty he had when he was requested to join in the celebrations. Sentimentality reminds him of the barley sugar his mother kept in the canister on the top shelf in the kitchen for moments of crisis. He hated it, but she wouldn't believe him and insisted that he share it with her when necessary. It was sharply, cloyingly over-sweet. The same sentimentality was evident in the aftermath of Cuba. Everyone wanted to talk about it, to tell others where they had been at the time, how they had felt during the three days of the crisis. They had been in imminent danger of world destruction, of course, but once it was resolved, there should have been nothing more to say.

Robert is aware that he doesn't react in the same way as other people. He can see that they find comfort in talking, analysing, offering reassurance, but he prefers to draw his own conclusions.

Instead of heading down the drive with the last remaining parents, he turns in the opposite direction, wondering how well the school has been rebuilt. He takes his time, allowing his eyes to become accustomed to the darkness, and wanders between the buildings, finding little passageways that lead him to new areas – netball courts, tennis courts, a wide stretch of grass with a goal-post at each end, presumably the hockey pitch. He identifies the laboratories after putting his face to a window and shielding his eyes from the outside reflections with his hands. He can see benches, stools, Bunsen burners.

Complete darkness is a thing of the past. During the war years, in the absence of streetlights, you couldn't see anything unless there was a moon. Everyone preferred the sky to be overcast, so that they could have a good night's sleep, safe in the knowledge that they couldn't be targeted. Now there are several lights around the school.

A tall ivy-coloured building, with the name Merrivale carved into the large stone above the entrance, stands several yards to his left. It must be the replacement boarding house. He thinks this was where he first met Miss Cunningham-Smith, so he stands for some time, remembering his first visit. The ivy gives an impression of age, as if it has been there for longer than twenty years. Lights are blazing from almost every window and a group of girls are gathered in a lower room, their heads bent over a chessboard. He becomes aware that he shouldn't be there.

Vast piles of blackened bricks, the smoke of smouldering fires, twisted metal girders. Teachers everywhere, crunching over broken glass, overshadowed by the hollow shell of the destroyed boarding house as they attempted to clear up, undaunted by the enormous task ahead of them.

Miss Cunningham-Smith, refusing to take orders from an ARP warden.

How dedicated those women had been. How inadequate he had felt in their presence.

Standing there now, it's hard to reconcile the two scenes. Only twenty-one years later, the reconstructed buildings and the courtyards seem solid, permanent and untouchable. It's impossible to conceive of them collapsing with such ease.

He can hear music.

He shakes his head and listens more carefully. For a few absurd seconds, he believes he can hear Curls again. He follows the sound. It's coming from a new, modern construction, surrounded on three sides by grassy banks. A large sign outside says, 'The Vaughan Williams Building, Music Department'.

Who would be playing the piano at this late hour?

He recognises the F minor Prelude, the gentle, resonant ending, and waits for the leap into the following fugue. It's the one that Curls was playing all those years ago when he discovered her in the common room.

He pushes the front door but it's locked, so he walks round the side, looking for another entrance. There are no lights on. Someone's in there alone, playing in the darkness. He finds a door, pushes it, and it opens. He steps into a darkened hallway.

It takes his eyes a while to adjust, but there's a glass ceiling and a faint glow from the moon and the outside lights, which makes it possible to see where he's going.

He walks towards the sound of the music, pushing open doors on the way, progressing along the corridor towards a door at the end. He pauses outside, listening. The F minor fugue has just finished and the player has moved on to the next prelude. Up a semitone. F sharp major. He pushes against the door and it creaks open.

The music stops abruptly.

There's a long silence.

'Who's there?' calls a vaguely familiar female voice.

Robert slides his hand along the wall by the door, trying to locate the light switch. He catches it with the side of his hand, fumbles for a moment, then flicks it down. The room is flooded with instant light.

Alma is sitting at the piano, staring at him, her face unusually pale and her eyes wide.

For a moment, Robert is paralysed by an intense disappointment. He had somehow persuaded himself that it must be Curls. As if he's circled round and gone backwards, found himself watching her again from the darkness, outside the circle of light that surrounded her as she played, longing to be drawn in.

But it's not Curls. Something inside him pops like a balloon. He can almost hear the whoosh of air as it fizzles away.

'Miss Braithwaite,' he says eventually, embarrassed to have interrupted her. Why should it be any of his business if she chooses to play the piano with the lights out? 'I'm so sorry. I didn't mean to interrupt you. I was just ... curious.'

'No, no,' says Alma, rising awkwardly. 'It doesn't matter at all. How nice to see you.'

'I'll leave you to your playing,' says Robert, wondering how to back away with dignity. He doesn't want to talk to anyone.

'It's not a problem,' says Alma, too eagerly. 'You're welcome to stay.'

He can hear the longing – or loneliness – in her voice and can't bring himself to refuse, so he steps forward and slips on to one of the chairs. The room is large and bare with a wooden floor and big windows. The sound of the piano would be magnified by the openness of the space, which explains why he'd heard the music from outside.

'Do carry on,' he says. Music would be easier to deal with than talking. He should be able to listen for a while, then make a tactful retreat.

But she gets up from the piano stool and walks over to him. She sits down, leaving two empty chairs between them, and clears her throat. A flush has crept across her face and down her neck. 'I'm afraid you wouldn't really enjoy my playing,' she says.

'On the contrary, the music was very inspiring.' He's not sure this is an accurate assessment, but can't think of a more suitable compliment.

She smiles, almost to herself. 'No,' she says. 'It's not necessary to be so polite. I've never been in the same league as Curls.'

Robert is shocked that she's mentioned Curls. He's not heard her name spoken aloud for more than twenty years. Alma can't possibly have known what he was thinking. He should contradict her, be polite about her playing again but it's difficult to find the right words.

Alma doesn't seem to have noticed his reaction. 'She wasn't quite as perfect as everyone thought she was, though. She did make mistakes. I mean, obviously she was heaps better than I could ever be, but she might not have been an actual genius. She was just so young and exuberant, and everyone had such high expectations–'

'She *was* a genius,' says Robert. 'She only had to play a handful of notes and they came to life, altered in some way, more profound together than separately.' Robert sees Curls's long back before the piano, bending like a tree in the wind, a sapling, its strength protected by its willingness to be flexible. Had she been as innocent as she appeared? How could she have been? The music had come from somewhere inside her, a cache of emotion available to be exploited, a fund of understanding that she could draw on and convey to the listener. She must have known that she could do it. Or was it the other way round? Had the music taught her a maturity that she would not otherwise have known? Whatever the reason, there was something inside her that was clearly much older than her years.

'I've thought a lot about why she did it,' says Alma, 'why she didn't take cover. And I've decided she was just so angry – about Duncan, about the disruption of the picnic – that she stopped thinking. She wasn't rational.'

Robert stares at her in horror. He couldn't possibly discuss that day. But she's waiting for him to speak. 'I see no merit in revisiting the past,' he says eventually.

'I used to wonder why the German aircraft was there, but I've heard it's something that happened. German pilots flying over, shooting into crowds, killing anyone around. It was just a bit of fun to them, destroying an innocent picnic – a children's day out. That was all we were, really, children…'

'I'm not sure that's quite true,' he says. 'The war made everyone grow up too fast. In a way, we lost our children.'

She studies the floor. 'Yesterday I watched the young people next door to me having a party. They dance in a different way now – have you heard of the Beatles? They were dancing to their music. It's not like the Lindy Hop – there are no real steps – but their commitment is the same. They seemed younger than we were, although they were older in age.'

'Young people don't have to take responsibility in the same way as they did during the war,' says Robert. His students had been adults. High-spirited, it's true, but adults nevertheless. Sober most of the time, dignified, with a sense of duty. 'They don't expect to die at any moment.'

Alma looks at him directly. 'I saw something in your face when Curls died. I've never forgotten it.'

Robert starts to sweat. Had he been so transparent?

'It was only for a second,' she says. 'But I'm right, aren't I?'

'I think you're probably imagining something that wasn't there,' says Robert. 'It was a very long time ago.'

'It doesn't feel so long ago,' says Alma. 'You cared about her, didn't you?'

'Of course I did,' says Robert. 'She was a brilliant musician. How could we not care?'

'That wasn't what I meant. You *cared* for her. More specifically.'

Robert doesn't know how to respond. Should he deny it? Ignore the implications of what she's saying? Pretend he doesn't know what she's talking about and insist on the rational explanation for his reaction?

'It wasn't even as if she was particularly attractive, was it? Natalie was the pretty one – all that glorious red hair...'

Robert can't think clearly. 'Curls had an extraordinary ability,' he says. 'Everyone must have seen it – it shone out of her.'

'But not everyone was in love with her.' She continues to stare at him.

He wants to look away but finds he can't. In the absence of a reasonable response, he says nothing.

'The silly thing is,' says Alma, 'and you'll laugh at this, all the time you were fancying Curls, she was after my brother – Duncan, do you remember him? – and I fancied you.'

Robert is startled by this. 'But, my dear, you were only fifteen. I was nearly twice your age.' He remembers her as a young girl with little awareness of the world. Why was she so different from Curls, also only fifteen but on the cusp of adulthood? Why had he perceived them in such a different way?

She sighs. 'It didn't stop you wanting Curls, though, did it?'

Robert flushes. 'It wasn't like that.' He regrets coming here, allowing himself to be seduced by the music, and now he's trapped by Alma. 'It was her talent I admired,' he says at last, with excruciating embarrassment. 'I had never heard anyone play like her before.' Even after all this time, it's almost impossible to put into words. It has become a part of him, a significant landmark in his history, but it's private.

She seems surprised by his explanation. 'How ridiculous we must all have appeared,' she says. 'Curls chasing Duncan, you chasing Curls, and me chasing you. A chain of people. I was dangling at the bottom, of course, with no hope, rejected by every single one of you. We could have survived the loss of the other links in the chain if we'd been able to connect, but that was never going to happen, was it?'

Robert wants to get up and leave, but he can't find a way of doing so. He feels very sorry for Alma. She seems unable to move away from the trauma of her wartime childhood. Pippa has told him she's too strict, sometimes unfair, but he can understand that it's not her fault. She has lost too much. 'I'm sorry,' he says. No other words seem suitable.

Alma looks at him carefully. 'Do you know?' she says. 'When I first found out that Pippa was your daughter and you were a widower, that we were going to meet again after all this time, I had this crazy idea that we would make a new connection because we shared a common past. Maybe we might even like each other, go out. Goodness knows, there weren't enough men left after the war, and the decent ones who survived are married. One's chances diminish dramatically as one gets older – there are too many other unmarried women like me in the country, who lost fiancés or husbands in the war, or who never even had a boyfriend. The competition is too fierce and the men are only interested in the next generation. One can't blame them – younger girls are so much prettier. So I thought, since I already knew you, there might be a possibility...' She shakes her head.

He wants to look away but keeps watching her. He has an overwhelming desire to be kind, but can't find a way to express it.

'I thought your secret desire for Curls could be redirected towards me instead. Just a half-turn of the screw, maybe, so you could see me in a new light. But the thing is – the thing is...' she pauses, and her voice goes thin and weak '...I must have misread you. I thought you were in love with Curls, but now you're telling me it was the music – only the music – that drew you to her. I don't know if I can believe you.'

This is the reasoning that he's worked at all these years, but can he excuse himself in this way? It's tempting – but dishonest. It was more than that. He can't bring himself to voice the fear that's been lurking in the back of his mind for so long, the secret that he was never able to share, even with Grace. That he had once experienced a passion for a girl who was not old enough for marriage. He allows silence to answer Alma. He can't explain himself to himself, let alone to her.

'When the war ended, I thought you'd left Exeter. Otherwise, I might possibly, if I'd had the nerve – once I was an adult – have come to find you.' She sits up straighter, as if she has grown, gained something from this conversation. 'You shouldn't reduce Curls to her music,' she says. 'She may have been brilliant, but she was much more than that. She was the best friend I've ever had, and when she was gone, it was as if I'd been thrown out of a ship in the middle of the ocean and left to drown. You wouldn't understand that. It was easy for you. You just sat back and enjoyed the music, fancied the pianist, at least for a while, and then when she stopped, you picked up and carried on as normal.'

Robert stares at her with rising indignation. 'Do you really imagine it was easy for any of us?' he says. 'Curls wasn't the only talented young person to die or incur such serious injuries that recovery was impossible. We were all affected in ways you cannot even imagine. My students had become my friends. They weren't much younger than me and they were among the best brains of their generation. Many of them lost everything.'

He stops, astonished at the anger that's flushing through him. He regulates his breathing. 'I'm sorry,' he says. 'I don't know what came over me.' His legs are trembling. He takes his glasses off and wipes them with a handkerchief. He puts them back on, and continues. 'I cannot and will not enlighten you further on my feelings for Curls, but I can tell you that I resisted every unsuitable thought and never, absolutely never, considered taking any action. I have always attempted to act with honour and dignity and I'm only sorry that you cannot agree that I did.'

Alma doesn't reply for some time. 'I'm sorry too,' she says, in a low voice. 'I don't know what made me say that.' Her face fills with colour and she starts to breathe heavily. 'I'm– I'm– How foolish I have been. So ridiculous, so thoughtless...'

It's all been too much, thinks Robert. He puts a hand gently on her arm. 'Alma,' he says. 'It's all right.' He tries to make his voice firm but friendly. They can't part like this.

'He didn't come back, you know,' she says.

He's confused, not sure what she's talking about.

'Duncan. My brother. He didn't come home at the end of the war.'

'Ah,' he says. 'I did feel it was too much to hope.'

'But – I know this is crazy – I still imagine he's alive somewhere, that one day he'll just turn up. I'll go home and he'll be there, the same as he used to be – do you remember him? – so dashing in his uniform.'

'I'm sorry,' he says again.

She takes some deep, even breaths, and gains control of her voice. 'You must forgive me for talking such nonsense. I haven't been thinking clearly recently. It's been a shock to meet you, to go back.'

He thinks for a few moments then selects his words with great care. 'We probably needed to have this conversation, but I've been married, don't forget, to a woman I still love in my own way, even though she, too, has died. I have a son and a daughter, who fulfil my need for – affection. I appreciate your interest, but I have no desire to marry again. I've been lucky enough to have had a happy and fulfilling life. It's quite different for you.

You're still young and there's so much you could do. You must move on from the past. The war destroyed so much for all of us, but there's nothing you can do about it except move on and find other ways to enjoy yourself. Remember how you used to love dancing? Could you not find a way of...?'

'You think I'm still young?' says Alma, with disbelief. 'I'm thirty-six years old, never married, never even been desired. Nobody has ever looked at me and thought, You are the most important person in my life. The idea of getting older, remaining alone, terrifies me.'

A fog of exhaustion is overtaking Robert. He's tried to reduce the conversation to the rational, but she reverts so quickly to the emotional. He would like very much to go back to his own world, where everything is predictable. Even Grace never demanded this kind of conversation from him. But he clearly can't leave yet. 'Have you ever thought about moving away from Exeter, selling your house with all its memories and finding a job elsewhere? Maybe you should consider changing your career, free yourself from Goldwyn's altogether and try something completely different.'

Alma doesn't reply.

'Or at least take a sabbatical, a prolonged holiday,' he continues. 'Give yourself time to reappraise your life. Meet new people who might challenge your expectations of yourself.'

She's nodding. 'Maybe. Miss Yates said the same thing.'

Ah, Miss Yates. A sensible woman in the mould of Miss Cunningham-Smith. 'Then perhaps you should listen to her advice.'

Alma doesn't reply, but she seems calmer. Logical thought is always the strongest cure for hysteria. 'I know it makes no sense,' she says, after a while, 'but I think, if I leave Exeter, what if Duncan comes back and can't find me?'

'That's easily solved,' says Robert. 'Leave your contact details with someone who remembers you both. He wouldn't give up without a search.' After a decent pause, he stands up. 'I'm afraid I'll have to leave you. I have a train to catch.'

She stands up too. Then, unbelievably, she throws herself against his chest. 'Robert!' she cries.

He briefly considers responding, putting his arms round her, imagining she's Curls, but he can't pretend. He carefully unclasps her hands from around his neck and removes her arms. 'No,' he says firmly. 'This is not the way to go.'

She pulls back almost immediately. Then she summons a dignity he doesn't expect. 'I wouldn't like you to think I always behave like this,' she says. 'I think the cancellation of the concert has upset me more than I realised. Miss Yates would not consider allowing it to continue, despite my appeal to her better nature.'

What if Curls had behaved like this, come over to him when they were in the common room alone, embraced him? What would he have done? What could he possibly have done that would have been right? He edges away from her, slowly and carefully.

She turns as he opens the door. 'Thank you,' she says. 'For your understanding.'

He still hesitates, uncertain if he should leave her. She doesn't call him back. In the end, he leaves the door open and walks as quietly as possible back along the corridor.

Outside, he pauses to work out precisely where he is and which way he should go. His legs are unsteady.

'Mr Gunner?'

The voice of Miss Yates cuts through the darkness and shocks him. Please, not another draining conversation. 'Good evening,' he says, walking hastily past. 'I'm afraid I really must dash. I don't want to miss my train.'

He limps along the drive as fast as he can, hoping desperately that she doesn't follow him. Halfway down, he glances back over his shoulder, but there's no sign of either woman. At the bottom, he sighs with relief and looks up the road. There's a telephone box a few yards away on the right. This would be a good time for a taxi. He takes out his wallet to check if he has enough money on him and pulls some coins out of his pocket for the phone.

He knows there's a small stone post on either side of the entrance to the drive, but he thinks he's passed them. As he turns towards the phone box, examining the coins in his hand, he cuts the corner and catches his foot against the left post. He stumbles, hovers in mid-air for a few seconds, fighting to regain his balance, then tips awkwardly forward. He falls heavily on his bad leg. The wallet flies out of his hand and into the nearby laurels.

V

Miss Yates watches Robert Gunner walking down the drive. Why is he still here without Pippa? The concert was abandoned ages ago and all the girls have left.

It seems an age since she sat next to him, waiting for the concert to start, aware of the warmth of his arm against hers. She was shocked to experience a frisson of excitement, a ridiculous desire to whisper to him, to put her hand up to his cheek and feel the contours of his bones under the skin. 'Stop it,' she'd said sharply to herself. 'This won't do at all.' The only word she can think of to describe her reaction is 'girlish'.

I haven't been a girl for a long, long time.

From where she is standing, at the top of the drive, she can see much of Exeter, the neon letters of the ABC Cinema on the high street, the dark, strangely empty roads. In the rows and crescents of residential streets, everyone's eyes will be fixed on the fluttering grey images on their television screens, as they all struggle to absorb the shock of the assassination.

She hasn't been a girl since she travelled from Oxford at the news of the bombing of Coventry, hurtling into the nightmare of the ruined city. Her train dropped her on the outskirts – most of the centre had been destroyed, including the cathedral – so she'd had to walk for several miles.

She's never been able to forget what she saw on that first day. The raids hadn't finished until six fifteen in the morning and Coventry went on burning until nightfall, when the bombers came again, their path lit by the fires of their previous raid. She didn't know at that point that all of her family were dead – it took nearly a week to sort through the confusion – but she soon discovered her life could never be the same again.

The way Mr Gunner was hurrying, limping, managing his lame leg, moves her. The limp is an integral part of him – he's clearly lived with it for many years – and it gives him an air of stoicism; heroism with a touch of vulnerability.

Call him back, she thinks. But she doesn't, because she knows she's being ridiculous.

She starts to shiver. It's very cold.

I am the headmistress. I am powerful, influential, in control.

Until she writes to the governors and throws herself on their mercy. What then? What if they accept her resignation?

She should be angry with Alma but, surprisingly, she isn't. Somebody else will come along later, even if Alma doesn't carry out her threat, someone who stumbles upon the truth and recognises its value. And even if no one comes, she will always have the nagging fear of an unexpected knock on her door, a request for a confidential talk, a whisper in her ear.

A sense of calm is seeping through her, icy as the night air but refreshing. This is a crucial moment in her career, in her life. The governors can decide her fate.

Merrivale is shutting up for the night. Downstairs, the curtains have been drawn and lights turned off as the girls go to bed. But there's a light on in another of the school buildings – it looks like the Vaughan Williams Building. Who would still be here? Miss Yates is always the last to go home, believing that her position as captain of the ship means she has an obligation to remain until everyone else has left.

Could there have been a break-in?

She hesitates for two seconds, then marches towards the music block with determination. She will not allow fear to prevent her doing her duty.

vi

Alma is playing Chopin – imperfectly. She plays Romantic works rarely nowadays because the act of performing them is too personal. She left expressive music behind a long time ago.

The opening right-hand melody sings out over repeated chords in the bass, sweetly innocent, offering no suggestion of the turmoil to follow. Alma is back in the wartime years. She learned the piece shortly before the bombing and the destruction of Merrivale, and Curls helped her improve it on the piano in the common room at Mortimer Hall. They delighted in the drama of the crescendos, the sudden drop back to stillness before preparing for another crashing climax.

It feels as if the emotion of a lifetime was compressed into those few short months during the war and she will never again capture that immediacy. Every significant moment of her life was lived at that time. Everything was used up too early and lost before she had time to grasp it properly.

Curls. Her parents. And Duncan, who didn't come home, whose body was never found. She'd waited for him at the end of the war, not knowing how long before she could be sure. A year? Two? Five? There was never a time when she could know for certain that he was dead, never a precise moment when she could mourn. She wrote letters, made all the enquiries she could, but no one had any further information. He was just one more casualty among millions.

She has a severe headache. It started just after the concert was cancelled and now it's building ominously. She can feel it thudding in time with her pulse, which is not the same as the beat of the music.

Could Mr Gunner and Miss Yates both be right? Should she leave Goldwyn's and pursue a different way of life? It's hard to imagine that this is a sensible option. When she went to London to do her teacher training, she became tight and insecure, longing for the familiarity of Exeter. The enormous relief she experienced every time she returned to her empty home for the holidays made her see how tied she was to the area. Would it be any different now she is older? Is she ready for change?

The music is building, becoming exciting–

'Alma!'

She jumps violently. Her left hand slips on to a cluster of unrelated keys. The sound jars and echoes harshly through the room. She turns and finds Miss Yates behind her. How long has she been standing there? Embarrassed, she jumps to her feet.

'Whatever are you doing?' says Miss Yates. 'It's well after nine o'clock. Everyone's gone home.'

'I wasn't aware that it mattered,' says Alma. She doesn't want to sound apologetic or give the impression that she believes she's at fault. 'I always lock up when I leave.'

Miss Yates appears to have shrunk since their last meeting and seems uncomfortable. She's not radiating her usual power or energy, as if part of her has broken off and drifted away, leaving her incomplete. Is this what happens when secrets are brought out into the open?

'Do you often stay this late at night?' asks Miss Yates.

'Occasionally.'

Miss Yates narrows her eyes. 'On your own?'

Alma nods.

'In future, I should like to be informed. It's my job to know exactly what's going on in the school.'

'Roy knows when I'm here. He just leaves me to it.'

They stare at each other. Alma can feel heat charging through her, sweat breaking out on her forehead.

A door closes – or opens – somewhere else in the building. Miss Yates swings sharply round. 'Who's that?'

Alma is equally surprised. 'I don't know. Did you leave the outside door open? Maybe the wind blew it shut.'

'No,' says Miss Yates. 'I did not leave the door open.'

There's someone else in the building.

They hear footsteps, shuffling, hesitant, alarming. Someone with sinister intent? A burglar? Alma moves a little closer to Miss Yates, who moves a little closer to her.

The door into the music room opens. Alma can hear Miss Yates breathing with her mouth open. A foot appears, a leg, an arm–

It's Robert Gunner, curiously dishevelled, his jacket undone and his tie pulled to one side. A drop of blood is trickling down from a cut on the side of his forehead, which he is dabbing with a large white handkerchief.

'Whatever's happened?' asks Miss Yates.

'Come and sit down,' says Alma, taking his arm.

Miss Yates stands back. 'Have you been attacked?'

'No, no, nothing so dramatic.' He allows them to guide him to the chair, sits down, and attempts to wave them away. 'I simply tripped at the bottom of the drive – one of the posts by the entrance, they're not very noticeable in the dark – then lost my balance and fell. Unfortunately I was holding my wallet at the time and it flew into the bushes. I've just spent the last few minutes trying to find it in the dark – without success, I'm afraid. And now I find myself at a disadvantage. I can't get home without my season ticket or any money so I've come to throw myself on your mercy and ask for a loan until tomorrow morning when I can hopefully find the wallet.'

'But you're hurt,' says Miss Yates.

'I'm merely inconvenienced,' he says. 'Once I'm home, everything will be fine.'

'Would it help if we go back down to the entrance with you to try to find your wallet?' asks Miss Yates.

'No,' he says, in a tone that does not allow for contradiction. 'It really is impossible to see at this time of night. I would prefer to come back in daylight and search properly.'

Alma can feel heat radiating off her cheeks. She doesn't feel well. I could dash back home for some money, she thinks. There's a ten shilling note underneath the cushion of the red sofa. It's there for emergencies and this is an emergency.

But she doesn't want to leave Robert with Miss Yates.

'Is there any petty cash here in the music block, Alma?' asks Miss Yates.

'No, I'm afraid not. But there should be some in Bridget's office. She keeps some loose change in one of her drawers. For odds and ends, emergencies–' She stops, suddenly conscious that Miss Yates might not be aware that the money stays there overnight. 'It'll be locked, of course, but presumably you have a key.'

'I have a key to every lock in the school,' says Miss Yates. 'Do you intend to continue playing the piano?'

Is Miss Yates trying to get rid of her?

'No, I'll come with you,' says Alma, 'since I

know where to find the money. We can lock up on our way out.' She refuses to look at Miss Yates.

I'm just as capable as you are, she thinks.

They step outside into the darkness.

Alma is very aware of her proximity to Robert as they make their way to the main block. Miss Yates is walking on his other side.

'I feel as if we've stepped out of a *Famous Five* book,' he says, with a laugh that sounds cumbersome and contrived.

'In which case, we'd be the Tremendous Trio,' says Miss Yates.

'I don't think I've heard–' says Robert, then chuckles gently as he realises that this is a joke.

'Or the Thrilling Three,' says Alma.

The buildings around them are crackling in the lowering temperature, creating rhythms like voices in a Bach fugue, weaving together into an unexpected harmony.

Alma is finding the situation oddly disturbing. She feels as if she has just leaped backwards through time without the opportunity to draw breath or the ability to work out what's going on. Sweat from her forehead is dripping down on to her cheeks like tears. Why is she so hot when the temperature out here is below freezing? She has an irrational desire to laugh. She glances round, expecting to see Curls, Giraffe and Natalie clustered behind her, waiting for the bell to go, the damaged shadow of the bombed Merrivale teetering behind them.

Her eyes are aching and she's finding it difficult to see properly. She thinks of the Thrilling Three and convulsions of laughter rise inside her. She has to concentrate to keep everything under control. She can hear voices, Mr Gunner and Miss Yates, but she can't make sense of what they're saying. She sways helplessly, struggling to pull herself back into the present.

A melody pops into her head, out of the blue. It's perfect for the Lindy Hop.

'One, two, three-and-four,' she says. She moves her feet. She can still do it.

She bumps into someone. 'Turn around, seven-and-eight. Jump.' She doesn't think she can jump. Not enough energy. And she's not quite sure if Jack or Dennis will be there to catch her.

She can feel hands on her. 'My head hurts,' she says. The violent thud of the headache consumes her attention.

'Everything's all right, Alma,' says a voice from far away.

'I know,' she says, although she doesn't think it's true.

There's music in her ears. They're in the hall, and Curls is playing Bach, after all. The concert that never took place. But if Curls is all right, that means Duncan's all right and her parents are all right.

The music isn't Bach or Beethoven. It's Chopin. No, it's the Lindy Hop.

Her feet are moving under her, feeling the rhythm. It was always the rhythm she loved most. More than the tunes. The beat pounds through her with such urgency, the beat that's the only way to ground herself–

She's laughing, furiously and uncontrollably at

some joke she can't quite remember.

But her cheeks are wet. Why is she crying? She never cries.

An unfamiliar voice, like a clap of thunder, interrupts her giggles. Who's this? A man? Another man? So there are men left over. They didn't all die.

'I think you need to come in and sit down for a few minutes, Alma,' says the voice.

Miss Yates. Not a man after all. Why did she think the voice was unfamiliar?

The taste of disappointment in her mouth is so strong that she thinks she might be sick. 'Give me a minute,' she says, in a low voice, suddenly aware of where she is. 'I'm not feeling very well.'

'Do you think she's been drinking?' says Miss Yates's voice, cold as the air around her.

'No,' says another voice.

Robert Gunner? Is he still here?

'I'm sure she's fine. It's been a long evening.'

The voice of reason. A man who always knows the right thing to say.

She can suddenly see more clearly. The clouds that previously overshadowed the moon have cleared and a silvery light illuminates their position outside the school. The sky is black and star-studded. The chill that surrounds them is sharp and crisp.

Part Eleven

i

23 November 1963

It's late by the time Wilhelmina Yates finally returns home. She and Mr Gunner didn't manage to search for the cash until they'd taken Alma back to her neglected mausoleum of a house and made sure she was comfortable and safe. They then went to the secretary's office, found some money and phoned for a taxi for Mr Gunner. Now, back at home, Miss Yates turns on the gas fires in every room and draws the curtains. She runs a hot bath, almost too hot to tolerate, climbs in and lies motionless under the weight of the water, letting the heat soak into her bones, attempting to clear her mind.

So much has happened, it's hard to know where to focus: Alma's threats, her subsequent unravelling, her inability to see anything except through her own perceptions; the assassination and all its appalling implications; the pleasing sense of calm security generated by the presence of Robert Gunner.

The problem of Alma's knowledge hangs in the air, as tangible as the steam from the bath. She could threaten to inform the governors about Alma's outrageous behaviour tonight, suggest she was drunk, use it as a bargaining tool, tell her that Mr Gunner was a witness. But even if they manage to come to an understanding, Alma's too unstable. She would be more interested in Miss Yates's downfall than her own survival. It would be like sitting in a bomb shelter during a Luftwaffe raid, waiting for the inevitable hit.

Miss Yates almost feels sorry for Alma, having seen her distress this evening, but that is not a basis for assuming she can trust her. Her hostility has a subversive effect – Adelinde Bauer has been reporting on her conversations with other members of staff – and her desire to keep everything exactly the same is obsessive. Why did she take such an instant dislike to Miss Yates right from the beginning? Was it simply a manifestation of her grief after the death of Miss Cunningham-Smith?

A disturbing image bursts into her mind: President Kennedy at the moment when the first bullet hit, his blood bursting out, spattering his wife. Miss Yates is filled with a sense of desolation, grief for someone she never knew, a sense of powerlessness about the future and her own part in it. She pictures the president as he's always appeared in public: calm, controlled, his voice measured and thoughtful. But the face she's seeing is not that of Jack Kennedy.

It's Robert Gunner: the strong black hair, which displays no sign of thinning or greying at the temples; the long, expansive forehead; thoughtful dark eyes behind his glasses; his fine mind. And his manners, the old-fashioned courtesy that makes her ache for her father, even after all this time. Mr Gunner has let her glimpse the pre-war world of her family life, when the outward veneer of good manners was not seen as superficial but as a manifestation of civilisation.

Should she resign? She wouldn't have to reveal everything. She could simply offer her resignation, mention personal reasons and move away.

Later, in her darkened sitting room, wrapped cosily in her thick woollen dressing-gown and fur-lined slippers, Miss Yates turns on the television. Scheduled programmes have been cancelled by the BBC and there's a special tribute to President Kennedy for the last half-hour of broadcasting. She watches every detail. There are no pictures of the actual assassination. Television cameras had not been set up for that stretch of the parade – it was thought to be insignificant – so they missed the crucial moment of history.

The film that's available shows the motorcade with the Kennedys in the open-top car. They're smiling broadly, waving to the Texan crowds, surrounded by motorbikes and security people. They look so healthy, cheerful, alive. The golden couple, undimmed by the black-and-white footage.

She watches until the close of transmission, and follows the final dot with her eyes as it shrinks to nothing. She continues to stare at the screen for a long time afterwards, finding it difficult to accept the enormity of events.

Mr Gunner coming into the music room, a strand of hair straying over his forehead, disconcerted by his accident but not diminished.

'Let me help you to a chair.' She was tempted to put an arm round his shoulders and wipe the blood from his face, but she was aware of the need to allow him dignity.

Her eyes stray to the boxes of plates, cups and saucers, milk jugs, teapots, new acquisitions still in brown-paper parcels and some older ones she hadn't had time to deal with when she originally unpacked. They're lined up in front of her cabinets, awaiting her attention. She hadn't planned to sort them out until the holidays, but December seems such a long way off. She stands up, stretches her legs and makes a sudden decision. She will unwrap them tonight, at this moment, while the world is mourning.

A phantom knock on the front door. 'Why, Mr Gunner. How pleasant to see you. Do come in. You will see that I'm sorting out my china. The obsessive behaviour of a collector, I'm afraid.' Could he be a collector as well? Could this explain the strong affinity she feels she has with him?

Under the shadow of the photo of her fiancé, Raymond, who was not really her fiancé but Betty's, she tackles one parcel at a time, worrying away with her fingers at the knots in the string, then winding the long strands into a ball. If they're tied too tightly, she snips the string, as close to the knot as possible, with sharp scissors. Once it's been rescued and preserved, she carefully opens the brown paper, removes the box and folds the paper into tidy squares, ready to put away in the drawer in the kitchen. Old habits of saving and reusing, learned with urgent necessity during the war, cannot be simply pushed aside, however generous her salary. It's impossible to throw anything away. Everything has a use, even if you can't immediately identify it.

Most of the Royal Worcester comes in presentation boxes. Miss Yates lifts the lids and spends time admiring the china, each piece nestled in blue satin, made more precious by its surroundings. Then she takes out one at a time, handles it, delights in the luminosity of the glaze, runs her finger round the smooth, perfectly finished edges. She opens the glass doors of her cabinets, breathes in the aroma of the wood, alters the grouping of the china already displayed and places each new piece in its rightful position. There's plenty of space. The cabinets have been waiting.

'You have a collection too, Mr Gunner? What a coincidence. I would be delighted to see it. I understand how valuable it must be to you.' What would he collect? He's like a Victorian with his immaculate manners, his carefully polished exterior. So his collection would reflect Victorian interests – butterflies, perhaps, birds' eggs or animal skeletons. He probably has a display room at his university hall, where he keeps his specimens in glass jars, meticulously labelled. A white card placed in front of each one, black ink, strong, idiosyncratic handwriting, set methodically on long polished shelves.

After each piece of china has been put into its place, Miss Yates stops and sits back on the sofa, taking time to check that she has pinpointed the exact spot.

She's aware of the portrait of John Kennedy that's hanging on the wall next to the door.

He stares out of his official portrait, his jaw

strong, his face youthful. There's kindness in his eyes, almost a smile, as if the necessity to pose with such earnestness is alien to his good nature. He's a man at his peak, with vast reserves of energy, who gives the impression that he can't wait to dispense with formalities and get on with his job, a man with both charisma and intellect.

Some things simply don't seem reasonable. How can someone with so much energy, so much fire, someone with a beautiful wife and young children who need him, simply expire? How can a bullet enter a body with such ease and extinguish life?

Her brothers and sisters are congregated around her. Avril, George, Herbert, Barbara, Thelma. Their parents bestowed such distinguished names on them because their expectations were high.

When she's finished, when the paper's folded, the string rolled into a large ball, the boxes stored in the cupboard under the stairs, all ready to fulfil their duty should it be necessary to pack away the china again, Miss Yates makes herself a cup of cocoa and contemplates the result. She is quietly satisfied.

At half past four in the morning, when the night gives the impression that it will never relinquish its iron grip, when the cold and dark are at their most severe, it seems certain that Alma will inform the board of governors as soon as possible. Until this point, Miss Yates has assumed that the governors would be prepared to consult her, consider the circumstances, bear in mind her successful record at the school so far, before making a decision. Now she considers the possibility that they'll dismiss her without argument or discussion. What if she doesn't have the option of resigning?

Miss Yates considers her future without the status of her headship. She will have to find work – her financial position isn't secure – and she'll need somewhere to live. Lectures for adults, perhaps, educational foreign tours, tutoring individual children. They're all possibilities, although none would be as rewarding as managing a school. But her great strength is that she can make a success of whatever she does.

Perhaps she should consider marriage seriously, start looking for a suitable husband.

Miss Yates compares the photographs of Betty's Raymond, the young RAF pilot, and the one of President Kennedy. She moves Raymond's picture closer to President Kennedy and decides that there would be room for another photograph. She tries to imagine Robert Gunner alongside the other two. All three with vigorous, springy hair and serious eyes, which have a way of looking past the viewer, past the photographer, into the future, as if they can see so much more than the life immediately in front of them. Mr Gunner's glasses give him a slightly more earnest appearance, but maybe Mr Kennedy wears them in private, for reading, and who's to say that Betty's Raymond might not have needed glasses if he had lived?

Two are dead now, of course. But they were men with vision.

At six thirty, the newspaper boy pushes the morning copy of *The Times* through the letterbox.

Miss Yates doesn't move. She knows very well that the pages will be full of the assassination. She will read it all – every word – when she's ready.

I'm not lonely, she thinks, not a desperate spinster. In many ways I'm very happy to live on my own with my china. I make my own decisions. There is much to recommend this. Marriage would only complicate things.

At seven o'clock, the post drops on to the hall floor, envelopes scattering over the mat.

Still Miss Yates doesn't move. It's Saturday. There's no rush. At a quarter past seven, she gets up, walks into the kitchen and puts on the kettle, then goes upstairs, washes and dresses, and comes down again to make herself some breakfast.

She picks up the newspaper and the post, placing them on the hall table, still not prepared to take the time to read them. Normally by now, even on a Saturday, she would be on her way to school, marching through the grounds in the dark before dawn, checking that all is well before going to the front entrance, unlocking the double doors, locking them behind her, and striding along empty corridors towards her office, her authoritative footsteps ringing out. Ready to settle at her desk and start wading through the paperwork.

It is not until a quarter to eight, as the early-morning sun finally announces its presence through the cracks in the curtains, that she picks up a piece of headed notepaper and sits down at the Chesterfield desk in the corner of her sitting room.

She could achieve so much at Goldwyn's. But Alma – Alma erodes her power. Alma is the virus that Miss Yates cannot eliminate, the weakness that demonstrates her failure. She starts to write, but pauses after only a few words, lifting her pen from the paper.

She stares unseeingly in front of her and sighs. Miss Jackson, the only woman governor, has always been sympathetic. Maybe she should try to talk to her first.

ii

Robert catches the eight o'clock train to Exeter. He would have liked to leave home earlier, but there was little point since he needs daylight to search for his wallet. The thought that he was compelled to borrow money – actually to ask two women for help – appals him. He's picked up some cash from home, which he can post through Miss Yates's front door with a note of thanks. Meanwhile, he's optimistic that he will retrieve the wallet.

He slept only sporadically last night, but woke with a surprising burst of energy. He's grateful to Alma for forcing him to analyse his feelings for Curls. That time has been a permanent shadow in the back of his mind, a dark place that he's always avoided. It's been refreshing to re-examine the events and find no reason for reproach. When he shaved in front of the bathroom mirror, he confronted himself in a new way, saw the man he has always believed himself to be, but more clearly defined, outlined with a sharper pencil.

The train is deserted. Robert sits by a window and attempts to look out at the estuary, but a dense fog has settled over the water and it's not possible to see far. He takes out a notebook from his briefcase and reads through the latest instalment of his lighthouse research. It's taken more than twenty years to visit every lighthouse round the coast of Britain, and he now has a personal record of original photographs, drawings and observations. The project has engaged him for so long that the thought of the end approaching makes him nervous. Bishop Rock, four miles to the west of the Isles of Scilly, was the last one. He took Godfrey and Pippa there last summer.

'It's the eastern end of the North Atlantic shipping route used by the ocean liners,' he had said.

'Thank goodness you've told me,' said Pippa, who was huddling into her waterproof anorak, holding the drawstring round the hood as tightly as possible so the wind couldn't penetrate. 'I've always wanted to know that.'

'Where was the western end?' asked Godfrey.

'New York. The entrance to Lower New York Bay.'

'We can go and see that end, if you like,' said Pippa. 'I wouldn't mind going to New York.'

'Oh, yes, of course,' said Godfrey. 'They're the measuring points for any liner wanting to beat the transatlantic speed race.'

Robert worries about Godfrey. He seems to be becoming more like him every day. Robert has become accustomed to giving out information that his children don't listen to, but he goes on doing it because he likes saying it out loud. It's comforting to continue a ritual that started when they were very small, even though he's been aware for years that he's talking to himself. When had Godfrey become interested in lighthouses?

He studies his drawings, sketched hurriedly on the deck of the tourist boat when it had proved difficult to take photographs. There'd been a surprisingly strong swell from the Atlantic, despite the calmness of the weather, and although they'd managed to get close, Robert had struggled to keep the camera still. But the isolation of the lighthouse is clear, even from the photographs.

'It's the smallest island in the world with a building on it, according to *The Guinness Book of Records*,' he'd told Pippa. 'The most western lighthouse of Britain.'

'Another vital nugget of information,' she'd said, hunting in the picnic bag for a mint.

'They built the first lighthouse on cast-iron legs sunk into the granite, with the accommodation and the light on top. They thought the waves would roll freely between the legs, and cause less damage than they would against solid concrete. Only just after they'd finished it a storm washed away the entire tower and they never actually lit the light.'

Robert gazes out of the train window again. The fog is clearing a little so he can see the birds, busy digging, searching for worms in the chilled mud flats. He finds himself thinking of Alma. When she had confessed her frustration about her single state, he had found her emotional outburst embarrassing, even annoying. But now he keeps thinking about her words.

'Nobody has ever seen me as the most important person in the world.'

He is curiously affected by this. It's not something he's worried about for a long time, but he hasn't needed to. He was important to Grace. He is important to Godfrey and Pippa. But there was a time after his mother died when he had been alone in the world. And he can remember the sense of isolation that descended on him, which he should have welcomed yet somehow did not. As if he could only appreciate isolation when he chose it, but he didn't care to have it thrust upon him.

He remembers now – how can he have forgotten? – a recurring dream that troubled him regularly until he married. Wandering through endless streets lined with houses, searching for a particular house, a particular person, yet knowing he would never find them because they no longer existed.

'After the first lighthouse was washed away,' said Robert, to Pippa and Godfrey, 'they didn't give up. The engineer started straight away on a second design. This time he decided to build it on the actual rock. It was a few feet under water, and they had to build a dam and pump out all the water so they had a dry area to work in. Then they cut the granite blocks on the mainland and numbered each one precisely so they could be shipped across and dovetailed in. Like a giant jigsaw.'

'Two years later, the bell was torn away in another storm,' said Godfrey. 'All five hundred and fifty pounds of it. You can resist the sea, but you can't win.'

Robert looked at him with surprise.

'You've just read that in the brochure,' said Pippa. 'Cheat.'

Alma in the music block. 'I am thirty-six years old. The idea of growing old on my own terrifies me.'

Is he being unreasonable? Should he consider the idea of a second marriage? Build a foundation out of the small parts and make them fit together?

A few years after Bishop Rock was completed, they found evidence of damage and weakness, so they decided to enlarge the foundations and build a second tower around the first, completely encasing it.

A lighthouse within a lighthouse. You see the outer shell, but there's an inner heart, a separate entity that hides inside the outer version, the reality camouflaged by its slightly larger twin. Would you be able to see beyond the obvious? You would have to take a boat, land on the treacherous rocks, climb the rungs on the outer shell, reach the doorway, go up the steps to the lamp room. And even then you might not see the evidence. Are there two front doors? Can you climb between the layers, or are they sealed together like two skins?

Has Robert been blinded by his obsession with Curls and never seen the inner layer of Alma? He has an uncomfortable feeling that he's been selfish and it worries him. The thought of yesterday's fiasco is exhausting, but he wonders if he could have handled everything better.

Is he too much like his grandfather? So fond of

silence that he can't hear what people really want to say?

Robert feels that he has never fully understood the women in his life. His mother fussed around him, but her experience with his father had blunted her somehow, distracted her, so that even after he died, she no longer had much talent for warmth. Grace brought Robert a brief period of satisfaction, but she died so soon that it now seems too fleeting. How would they be today if she had still lived? Would they be going in separate directions, finding their own interests, separating again and only coming together for important events?

What will he do now that he's completed his study of lighthouses? There's an uneasy gap in his mind. Should he wait for the children to leave home so that he can start all over again, travelling around the coast on his own, documenting the lighthouses for a second time, wandering in silence, avoiding people completely?

But Godfrey and Pippa will always be there in the background, claiming his attention.

He is miles from land, alone in the sea, battered by the waves, at the mercy of the elements. But built on solid rock.

He's not like Alma, he realises. He doesn't need to be afraid of growing old alone.

As the train glides into Exeter Central, Robert rises, pulls down the window and leans out, ready to open the door. The train stops and he yanks the handle, stepping on to the almost deserted platform. He checks his watch before heading for the steps, moving fast in the cold. The train has arrived precisely on schedule. There should be plenty of time to find the wallet, return the money to Miss Yates and catch the train home. He has to pick up Godfrey by half past eleven, then take Pippa to her dance class at twelve o'clock.

iii

Alma sleeps badly throughout the night, waking at regular intervals, her face burning and her head thumping. At four o'clock, she sits up abruptly. 'I'm ill,' she says aloud. 'I have a temperature.'

She goes downstairs, shivering in the cold night air, and searches through a kitchen drawer filled with sticky old medicine bottles until she finds some aspirins. She takes out two, swallows them with water and stands for some time holding on to the edge of the sink, gazing into the invisible garden, unable to pick out anything in the darkness. She sighs and goes back upstairs to bed.

She wakes with a jump at ten o'clock. She leans over to pull back a curtain and examines the sky, waiting for her heart to stop beating so fast, trying to work out why it's so late. The house is still. She has a curiously expectant sensation, as if it's earlier and there is much to do. The blue of the sky is hazy, soaked and scrubbed, but waiting for the detergent to be rinsed away.

Miss Yates. Robert Gunner. Curls. They are all on the edges of her consciousness.

Her head is a little heavy, but clear. She stares round and sees with new eyes, still delicate after her high temperature, what she has seen every morning for most of her adult life. Why is the room so untidy? Why are her clothes lying around in piles when they could be folded and put into drawers? Why are there so many empty mugs on the window sill, such a huge pile of dirty washing by the door instead of hidden away in the linen basket? The floor is covered with books, magazines, musical scores that she's considered for the choir and orchestra, some of which have been there for years, embedded in long-term dust. Their collapsed piles drift across the unswept floor like trails of foam through the murky waters of a stagnant pond.

She knows the state of the house, but she's always been reluctant to change anything. A hoover sucks away the dust of the past, the traces of the old life, so she's only ever cleaned the essential spaces. Now, suddenly, her lack of effort seems strange. Why has she never seen the squalor?

She hasn't even opened her mother's wardrobe, let alone emptied it. Every day she walks past her father's cricket gear, still leaning against the side wall of the porch, her parents' macs hanging from the hooks in the hall, Duncan's old university books lining the walls of the upstairs landing...

The list goes on and on.

The curious thing is, she's always been aware of the existence of this accumulation but until now it has never mattered.

What day is it? Friday, Sunday, Tuesday?

She sits up suddenly. The concert. The events of the previous evening are slightly uncertain in her mind, but she knows there's cause for concern. Robert Gunner was there, Miss Yates, Curls – no, Curls wasn't there. There have been two concerts that never took place – twenty-one years apart...

There are ridges of ice inside the window frames, and when she breathes, she can see her breath, a cloud that hovers in the air before dissipating and making room for the next one.

It's 23 November 1963. Yesterday President Kennedy was assassinated and the world is in shock.

But Alma is not in shock. She feels as if she's the only person in the world who can see everything clearly – for the first time.

She scrambles out of bed and throws on her dressing-gown, her hands dithering with the buttons and her feet icy as she searches for her slippers on the lino under her bed. She walks briskly to the bedroom door, along the landing and down the stairs. A weak sun is filtering through the glass panels of the front door and along the side of the house. Alma pauses for a moment and admires the rays as they cross the hall floorboards, threading their way through the vast piles of unopened post.

'Goodness,' a pupil's mother once said to her, as she followed her into the living room. 'What a lot of letters.'

'Oh, there's nothing important,' said Alma. 'I get far too much unnecessary post.'

'Don't you worry that you've missed something vital?'

'It's easy enough to recognise the bills. The others don't matter.'

Goldwyn's has been the only part of her life that has mattered, and everything she's done for the school has been well thought-out, planned with precision. But at home the part of her that needs to be tidy seems to stop functioning.

She moves from room to room and the cloud of her breath is like a poisonous gas, released from inside her and floating away, mixing with the cold oxygen of the room and neutralising itself.

What's different about today? Why do I feel like another person?

Where have I been all this time?

The clock in the hall strikes the hour and Alma counts the chimes. Eleven. Time to start doing some work.

She needs to have breakfast, get dressed. There's so much to do.

She starts in her parents' room, opening the wardrobe and drawers. Her father's suits; ties; old gardening jumpers; socks, neatly folded, two pairs each of grey, black and navy; his underpants. How interesting. Alma has never really studied men's underpants before, yet here they are, off-white, cotton, unattractive. Long johns for the icy mornings when he had to start the car with a crank shaft; long-sleeved vests for the night shifts, for the cycle ride to the hospital in the blackout. Six shirts hanging in the wardrobe, still white and starched, ironed by the lady who used to come in twice a week to help. What was her name? Nora? Norma? How strange that Alma can't remember her face. What happened to her after the bombing? Did she come round on the next Wednesday as usual and do the ironing, go away, come back on Friday and find no sign of habitation, no new shirts to iron? Did she have to apply for another job urgently, needing the money to pay her rent, buy her groceries? Or did she die in the bombing? Or lose her home and never come back, spending the rest of her life with guilt, having nightmares about her employer going to the hospital in increasingly grubby shirts, his wife having to do the laundry herself after a heavy day in the delivery wards?

Alma is halfway through her mother's wardrobe, throwing outdated silk dresses on to the bed in a careless heap, when she remembers Goldwyn's.

She stops. What is she doing? She should have been in school hours ago. Why has nobody phoned to see where she is?

She sits on the side of the bed and breathes deeply, aware of the cold, and catches sight of her pink, flushed face in the mirror. How ill am I? she wonders. Should I be in bed?

She has never missed a day of school in her entire life. Even with a heavy cold, she has dragged herself in, dosed up on the Panadol prescribed by her doctor, believing that she's needed, knowing that no one else is capable of standing in for her. She's intolerant of teachers who are unreliable. 'I'm a professional,' she says to herself, when her nose starts to drip or her throat tickles. 'Professionals carry on regardless. Goldwyn's needs me.'

But something has changed. It's not just the illness that has affected her. Something seems to have cut the tie between her and Goldwyn's and she doesn't want to think about her form congregating in Room Eleven this morning without knowing where she is. She can't seem to summon a sense of urgency.

I don't care, she thinks.

The thought is shocking but extraordinarily liberating and she sits back for a few seconds to savour it. She becomes aware that the block in her chest, the knot that has always been there, has dissolved. Her breathing has altered – air fills her lungs easily and when she swallows, the sensation is comfortable.

But she has not been entirely liberated. After waiting for a few seconds to gather her strength, she pulls herself to her feet, stumbles down the stairs, grabs her coat from the peg and drapes it over her shoulders to keep warm before picking up the phone on the hall table.

'Bridget,' she says. 'It's Alma here. I can't come in. I'm ill.'

'It's Saturday,' says Bridget. 'You don't need to come in.'

Alma pauses, surprised that she hasn't worked this out for herself, inclined to disbelieve Bridget. 'Then why are you there?'

'Miss Yates asked me to come in especially to help her sort out some details for the last weeks of term. But she hasn't turned up.'

'That's not like her,' says Alma.

'And,' says Bridget, lowering her voice, 'there's something funny going on. Someone's been in here since yesterday, tampering with things, moving them around.'

Alma doesn't want to remember heading for the office with Miss Yates and Robert Gunner.

She puts the phone down.

She's shivering again, so she goes into the kitchen and takes some more aspirin. She makes a cup of coffee and carries it into the drawing room. The curtains are still drawn – they often remain closed between piano lessons – so she sweeps them back, switches on the small electric fire by the piano and sits down on a sofa. She slips her arms into the sleeves of her coat and tucks her feet up on the chair where they can warm up.

Robert Gunner. She has an uncomfortable memory of saying things to him last night that she shouldn't have said, but she's unsure about the details. She was angry with him, she thinks. What did she actually say?

The letter from Oxford University about Miss Yates catches her eye on the corner of the coffee-table and she hesitates for a few moments, diverted by a startling vision of herself plotting to undermine Miss Yates.

Why did she go to so much trouble? Why had it mattered so much?

I don't have to go back to Goldwyn's if I don't want to. I don't have to face Robert Gunner again.

She shivers. Glancing up at the window, she can see the top of Merrivale in the distance, shimmering in the bright sunlight. She bends down, moves the waste-paper basket so that it's just below her knees, picks up the Oxford letter, and starts to tear it into small pieces, dropping the fragments into the bin.

Underneath, she discovers Lillian's letter about her trip to America and picks it up. A leaflet about the liner, the *Queen Elizabeth*, slips out of the envelope. There's a photograph on the front, some facts and figures, and a drawing of a man and woman dancing in the old way, formal and sophisticated. Alma studies the leaflet with new interest. Robert Gunner is not the only man of a suitable age. There are others.

Is she too old for dancing? Are you ever too old?

She has spent most of her life believing she's a teacher, someone who must dedicate her life to her pupils. But is that really true? She needs to be honest about this. The arrival of Robert Gunner has made her think again, and she suddenly wants more.

I'm only thirty-six. It's not too late.

The swirl of yesterday is beginning to settle in her mind. The fragments of disasters that seem to have been only narrowly averted, that no longer seem to carry as much weight, swirl in the air, then flutter down to the ground and gather into inconsequential piles that need to be hoovered away.

The clock in the hall strikes one.

She's a good piano teacher. She likes her individual pupils and they like her. It's the class teaching that depresses her, her inability to exercise control. Maybe she should travel for a while, meet new people, do some dancing, then move to a different part of the world and teach from home. Maybe Robert Gunner and Miss Yates were right.

She goes out into the hall, picks up the telephone receiver and dials.

'Directory Enquiries. What name, please?'

'Smith and Smith, the house-clearance people in Exeter.'

Afterwards she returns to the drawing room and looks out of the window at the bindweed, the nettles, the brambles. Frost glitters in areas where the sun hasn't penetrated, some of it as thick as snow. The garden is very still. There's no breeze, not the flutter of a leaf or the sigh of air moving. It's all held and contained by the intensity of the cold. Branches of trees are encased in thick layers of white. The sky is deep and blue, leading the eye up and beyond to an invisible space.

A dark cloud appears in the distance, rapidly heading towards the garden, a shadow that gradually fills the sky overhead as it draws nearer and blocks out the sunlight. But there's no roar of engines, no whirr of propellers, no deadly load waiting to be unleashed.

It's a vast flock of starlings, imposing a brief darkness as thousands and thousands of birds wheel and swoop, wing-tip to wing-tip, on their way to find a roost before nightfall. Why don't they collide? Why don't some of them crash down to the ground? What extraordinary method of navigation and collision avoidance do they operate?

They continue on their journey, not interested in Exeter. The shadow passes and the sun's rays fight with a benign strength to loosen the clenched hand of the frost.

Acknowledgements

I would like to thank the following:

Maeve Clarke, Chris Morgan, Pauline Morgan, Jeff Phelps and Gina Standring, for their willingness to read large sections of this novel in advance of our meetings and then discuss it with such commitment.

Carole Welch, who reads with such discernment, Hazel Orme, whose fearless attention to detail puts me to shame (her personal memories of 1963 did not always coincide with mine, but she was probably more right than me), and Lucy Foster who organises things with such good humour.

The many people who have contributed their personal memories to the website, *Exeter Memories*. Their wartime experiences introduced a sharp sense of reality to my second-hand knowledge.

Exeter News Photographs by Todd Gray, published by Mint Press and *One Man's War in Exeter, the images of Ken Jackson*: by Peter D Thomas, published by Thomas Castle. The vivid photographs in both of these collections graphically depict the appalling devastation faced by Exeter after the bombing.

The publishers hope that this book has given you enjoyable reading. Large Print Books are especially designed to be as easy to see and hold as possible. If you wish a complete list of our books please ask at your local library or write directly to:

Magna Large Print Books
Magna House, Long Preston,
Skipton, North Yorkshire.
BD23 4ND